GUESTS OF WAR

ROBIN JENKINS

B&W PUBLISHING

First published 1956
This edition published 1997
by B&W Publishing Ltd
Edinburgh
ISBN 1 873631 70 7

British Library Cataloguing in Publication Data:
A catalogue record for this book is available
from the British Library.

Cover Photograph © George Rodger/Magnum Photos
Reproduced by kind permission
of Magnum Photos

To Bill Russell

Printed by Werner Söderström

GUESTS OF WAR

ROBIN JENKINS was born in Cambuslang in 1912 and educated at Hamilton Academy and Glasgow University. He taught English in Scotland, Spain, Afghanistan and Northern Borneo, and has written twenty-three novels.

As well as novels set in Scotland, including *The Cone-Gatherers*, *Guests of War* and *A Love of Innocence*, his extensive travels have provided the backdrop for other highly-acclaimed work, such as *Dust on the Paw*, based on his experience of Afghanistan.

Robin Jenkins lives in Argyll.

PART ONE

I

AT the mouth of her close, dreaming of buttercupped meadows and green hills, Mrs. McShelvie watched the thin black terrier as it limped hungrily down Wallace Street, sniffing at every likely garbage on pavement or gutter. It yelped and squirmed into the wall of the high tenement when a lorry rattled by; perhaps its lameness had been caused by one. As it prowled on again, suddenly it was bombarded with stones. Some boys, playing at hunters, had transformed it into a wolf. One stone struck it and off it scampered, yapping feebly in protest. It was not, she felt sure, whining for mercy.

Smiling in grim sympathy, she murmured to herself: "Never, wee black dog, whine for mercy." Neither of her sons was among the boys. Tom's absence was no doubt accidental, but Sammy would never be one of the world's stone-throwers. Some said he was too soft in the head to be, and sniggered at his bespectacled simplicity; but most admitted the softness, and greenness, were in his heart. As a substitute for those meadows and hills, Sammy all his twelve years had sufficed.

As she dreamed thus, and reflected, she was also listening to the chatter of her neighbour, that had the skite of the stones on the pavement in it, and also the careless ferocity that had hurled them. Meg Aitchison accepted her lot as a slum dweller; somehow that acceptance had given her a confidence and a faith in her own worth that neither poverty nor disease nor dirt nor the sneers of respectability nor the deaths of two children had ever weakened. Many who lived beside her in Wallace Street refused to call their homes slums; they pointed

1

to other streets more squalid, with more frequent fights and drunken squabbles. She would throw back her skinny yellow neck, open her mouth with so many teeth missing, and cackle with malignity; but, her amusement expressed, she delivered arguments, each one like a scart from venomous claws: the tenements were so decrepit keeping them clean was a useless travail; a child, she said, could be put out in the morning scrubbed, scented, kissed, with a white ribbon in its hair; an hour later it was filthy, stinking, bruised by some playmate, with the ribbon either torn off or wilting—this was her favourite phrase—like a flower flung out on a midden. She knew, she shrieked: she had tried all those experiments herself when she had got married at sweet eighteen; but she had never pretended to herself they had not failed or were worth persevering with. A flower on a midden, she cried; and under the noses of those whose eyes hinted that a weed would be more truthful, her fingers became castanets of defiance, disdain, threat, and merriment.

Now at the close-mouth, on this sunny afternoon towards the end of August, 1939, she was cursing Hitler the madman, not because he was about to turn all Europe into a slaughter-house but because he might force her to leave Wallace Street and go to Langrigg, in the south, where the big hills and the mooing of cows would, she swore, with an emphatic scratch of her head, drive her melancholy. Hills, she asserted, were huge scunnersome things, fit only for sheep to guzzle; and though there was a rumour that cows gave milk, well, her weans had always preferred lemonade.

Mrs. McShelvie treated this preference of Meg's for the grime and racket of the city seriously. To her it seemed dreadful that human beings, with only one life to live, should have to live it in such dreary places as Wallace Street and its sur-roundings: especially when Scotland was one of the most beautiful countries in the world. Nevertheless she could not despise those who had out of necessity turned these gloomy streets into home, to be yearned for as nostalgically as any Highland glen, and to be fought for in war just as heroically. She respected them always, and envied them often. They seemed to be adding a strength to their living, to be in an important way loyal to their children born here; whereas she, with her longings for fields and hills and kye coming hame, was growing weaker with the loss of all that heart's ambition, and with the abiding sense of disloyalty.

People, she believed, transcended the dreary ugliness of the places in which they lived. For instance, she knew that Meg was lousy, but she did not, as many did, withdraw a little or wince or sneer: she preferred to remember that Meg was also indomitable, generous, light-hearted, and candid.

It would not have been fair there at the close-mouth to compare her own appearance with Meg's. She was groomed and dressed to the best of her resources; except that her head was bare she would have been ready for kirk, if ever she went there. Her hair was no longer the strong gleaming black of her girlhood; now it was lack-lustre, well mixed with grey. The skin of her face and hands was, as Meg had once told her in sharp compassion, the skin of a woman of seventy, which meant a greying and withering twenty years in advance. Her coat had been bought before Sammy was born, and like him it bore many marks of injury, tenderly healed. She had spent ten minutes in polishing her shoes, and luckily these did not dishonour her feet, which were, as she often boasted, her best feature. They were strong and shapely, and to them she owed many pleasant walks on the outskirts of the city.

She looked therefore as well as she could. In front of the mirror she had for a daft minute hesitated with her daughter Flora's lipstick in her hand; but she had ruefully decided that Mr. Grahamstone, the headmaster, whom she was going to interview that afternoon, would only be confirmed in his opinion that she was a typical trollop if she crimsoned her lips. He did not like her or approve of her: he blamed her for the wildness of her Tom, the recurrent illnesses of Effie, and the scholastic backwardness of Sammy, but he never seemed to congratulate her on the cleverness of Jean, who was always first in her class, or for that matter on her keeping them all clean and tidy. The headmaster, in spite of his position and university degree, was a simple-minded man: if a woman

3

applied to him for a position as helper with the evacuees, she must have signs of success about her, as visible as golden earrings or jewelled rings or new clothes. Mrs. McShelvie had none; yet this chance to escape to Langrigg for a week even, or longer if she was lucky, was so important to her that she could not face the thought of losing it. For twenty years she had been shut up in the city, without a holiday by the sea or in the country; if Mr. Grahamstone said yes, he would be giving her a glimpse and a breath to sustain her for the next twenty. But it was far more likely he would just repeat his previous grunted "I don't think so."

Meg was cheerfully pessimistic.

"What you need's a fur coat, Bell," she said. "What aboot cadging wee Fish-face's?"

Mrs. McShelvie knew "Fish-face" was their neighbour Mrs. Aldersyde, whose unbrawness gave Meg constant delight in inventing new nicknames.

"But you've got as much chance o' cadging that one, Bell, as you'd hae of stealing it off the back of a polar bear."

Meg spat to show what she thought of a neighbour so disobliging: she herself would lend even her comb if anybody wanted it.

"It'd be too wee for you onyway, Bell," she said; "and Christ kens what kind of itch it'd gie you. My Roger says some night her man'll bring hame one o' his razors and slash her throat. He's studied psychology, Bell, and he says it's bound to happen."

Mrs. Aldersyde's husband was a barber, a small meek quiet tormented man. They had two children, twins twelve years old, called Hazel and Gordon. By a freak or jest of nature these were as handsome as she was ugly. God had given them to her, she said, to keep and cherish for Him; therefore in their defence she was a tigress, to clothe them in blazers and kilts a miser, and to keep them uncontaminated by other children a bitter little misanthrope. That they were turning out rather unpleasant, being impertinent to their father, and in the boy's case ungrateful to her, was their neighbours' revenge. Mrs. McShelvie did not share it: every mother with children to bring up to face the world had to find her own way of doing it, and Mrs. Aldersyde's was more self-sacrificing than most. That it was not successful was matter for pity and kinship, never for rejoicing.

"But I'll tell you again, Bell," said Meg boldly, "in case you've forgotten it."

"I've not forgotten it, Meg."

"I'll say it all the same. You're running away, Bell. Gie it what fancy names you like, and there's only one body wi' fancier names for things than you, and that's my Roger; ca' it what you like, Bell, it's still running away."

Mrs. McShelvie smiled and trembled.

"Your place is here at hame wi' Isaac and Flora. Now that Isaac's managed to get started work again he'll need to get special attention, or else, Christ forgie me for saying it, you'll be haeing him to bury before his time. And Flora's sixteen, which is a bad age for going wrang. I've a right to say that, for I went wrang myself. Roger's got fancy names a' right, but when he got me he got nae clean potato. That of course is a woman's secret, Bell, as you'll understand."

"Isaac says I should go, Meg."

"Isaac would loup frae the suspension bridge if he thought it would please you, Bell. You're baith wife and mither to him."

"Flora will gang her ain road whether I'm there to see or not. She says she's earning the right."

Flora worked as a weaver in a local carpet factory.

"I'd gie her a dunt on the lug if she spoke to me like that, Bell."

Mrs. McShelvie smiled: she had heard Gary, Meg's youngest, aged two, swear viciously at her, only to be laughed at and admired as a prodigy.

"I've got other weans, Meg. There'll be nobody to look after them yonder."

Meg, guardian of truth, would not let even that subterfuge by.

"All the teachers are going, Bell," she said, "as weel as these helpers. You're running away."

5

The truth, thought Mrs. McShelvie, bit even more sorely in the mouth of such a toothless outrageous liar as Meg. Then her sense of humour failed, and for a moment she felt a desire to strike that mouth which, with its oaths, its thoughtless blasphemies, and its vulgar joy, was not fit to pass judgment upon her in her predicament. But a moment after, when Meg poked a skinny finger of sympathy into her side, she turned away in shame.

"You're right, Meg," she said. "That's all I'm doing, running away."

Here indeed was her battlefield: the enemy she had to fight was despair at the ugliness shutting her in, at the inevitable coarseness and pitiable savagery of many of the people shut in with her, and above all at her inability to keep her own family healthy, sweet, and intact. She was weary of fighting. Even soldiers in war were given relief. But Isaac was not well, though he had started work; he might soon die, and all the sooner if she forsook him. Flora, with her lipstick, dancing, tawdriness of mind, and resentment at having to work to help to bring up her brothers and sisters, might grow up to be little better than a prostitute; she needed, as Meg said, more control now rather than less. The battle was at its height, therefore, and she had made up her mind to desert.

"I'm just a coward," she murmured.

Meg guffawed. "Whit aboot the time I got these oot?" she cried, pointing to the gaps in her teeth. "I caught the man's hand and kissed it and begged him no' to hurt me. There's not a bigger feartie in the country. But look wha's coming. Napoleon's wife herself. If it's brave ye want to be, just gie yourself a rub against her."

Mrs. McShelvie frowned at that vindictive sarcasm. She liked and admired the young woman who was approaching. Mrs. Raeburn also lived at 14 Wallace Street, but often went the rounds of the factors looking for a house in a better district at a rent which would not make it impossible for her to feed and clothe her two children as well as she wished. Her husband Dick, whom Meg called Napoleon, was a labourer in a ropeworks, with a small wage. His pretensions were enormous.

Everybody but his wife laughed at his pugnacious conceit. He knew everything, even how to deal with the upstart Germans; and in his impetuosity to have his methods of warfare adopted he had bounced into the Territorial Army, where he was still a private finding his puny rifle, as well as the bureaucracy, handicapping him. If war broke out he would be called up immediately. His wife, normally given to shy understatements or to even humbler reticence, proclaimed him a hero to anybody who hinted, or in Meg's case shrieked, that he was a wee mug rushing away before his turn.

She was a small pink-faced woman just under thirty, with a meek but thrawn mouth. Her person, and those of her two children, seven-year-old Jess and baby Richard, were so splendidly clean that there was no doubt she was still winning the campaign against dirt and resignation. Hence Meg's animosity: she saw Mrs. Raeburn as a flower that miraculously did not droop on the midden, that stayed fresh and sweet. Her children too bloomed, although Jess was prematurely solemn, and now and again, to Meg's delight, would come away in her grave Sunday school manner with a good old-fashioned Wallace Street profanity.

Mrs. Raeburn lingered for a minute with her neighbours. Have nothing to do with them, her Dick ordered; don't even talk to them. But she knew Dick was wrong: to be more ambitious than her neighbours was not to be better; and once she had sent him into a towering huff by saying she'd never be as good a woman as Mrs. McShelvie. To him the latter was an ordinary Gowburgh slut, with enough sense to keep her mouth shut and so not advertise her sluttishness; whereas his Bessie was an angel, preserved from the depravities of her neighbours by her own goodness and by his protection.

"This is me on my way to see auld Grahamstone, Bessie," said Mrs. McShelvie.

"I hope he lets you come wi' us, Mrs. McShelvie," she replied, "if we have to go, which God forbid."

Meg leant towards her. "You and me, Bessie," she cried, "are of the same mind there. We want peace. Bell here wants a war."

Mrs. McShelvie shook her head. "Don't be daft, Meg." But in a way it was true.

"Nobody wants a war," whispered Mrs. Raeburn. "I don't think even the Germans want it, certainly not the German mothers."

"There's women, Bessie," said Meg, "like fine to be the mithers and wives of heroes."

"Heroes are sometimes dead."

"Aye, and if they're not, they're worse; they're lying on their backs paralysed, or they're withoot airms and legs, or they're blin'."

Mrs. Raeburn knew such fates were being arrayed for her Dick's benefit; but in loyalty to him she would not show her forebodings.

"Medals hae nae sicht in them," added Meg, shutting her own eyes with significant tightness.

"They hae honour," murmured Mrs. Raeburn, and then with a smile at Mrs. McShelvie she went off up the close to have her man's dinner ready when he came home from work.

Meg Aitchison looked after her with eyes that, as wide as could be with dislike, were still blind.

"I'll get away myself," said Mrs. McShelvie.

"Bell, you're my freen', but I canna wish you luck."

Mrs. McShelvie began to walk slowly up the street, stooped a little, breathing heavily, greeting acquaintances quietly, and noticing, calmly but with a terrifying finality, the irremediable drabness of this place where she had spent most of her life. The street was dirty with all kinds of litter. The buildings in which people lived were dirty too, sour-smelling, dilapidated, and chalked with amorous taunts or religious obscenities. There were various works and factories, with tall chimney-stacks filling the air with smoke and soot and stench. Even the shops were dowdy in this part of the wilderness, with dead bluebottles in the windows. At her steady pace it would take a quarter of an hour's walking to reach the main streets which were wider and cleaner, but no more refreshing or beautiful.

The school was in a cul-de-sac called Gordon Street. The building was ancient, insanitary, and condemned. From the classrooms the views were of the backs of tenements with the red-bricked spines containing the outside lavatories, of a cardboard factory now derelict, and of a scrap-merchant's yard. It was not likely that the teachers, while their pupils were working at sums, would stand by the windows and gaze out: they would more likely try to seek relief in working at the sums themselves. The playground was spacious enough to allow of one game of headers and one of peaver to go on simultaneously, without the respective players coming into collision; but with a dozen or more of these games determinedly proceeding, accidents, fights, and usurpations were rife, even with a teacher on patrol.

Mrs. McShelvie had been educated at Gordon Street school. When she was six her family had flitted from a small village about ten miles out of Gowburgh. The contrast between the school she had been attending, with its green fields and spaciousness, and this grim stony noisy prison, had given her a shock from which all her schooldays she had never recovered. Her teachers had thought her a dour, unhappy, introspective, unresponsive child: with as many as fifty or sixty in her class, they had not the leisure to probe deeper into the cause of her unhappiness, even if they had had the desire or the skill.

Now as she took her time going up the worn stairs to the headmaster's room she remembered how about two years after coming to Gowburgh she had been hustled up these very stairs by a teacher called Miss Cordiner, a tall woman with a yellow tormented face and a black velvet collar. Ink had been spilt on the classroom floor under Bell's desk. No one had owned up. Miss Cordiner, requiring a culprit to maintain discipline and also to appease her own thwarted soul, had accused Bell, and had striven to shake, cuff, and drag a confession out of her. Failing, she had taken her to the headmaster, Mr. Durward, the small fat amiable possessor of a black Lochgelly, a tawse able to bring the toughest boys to their knees in tears. With a wink at Miss Cordiner, he had drawn Bell on to his knee—she had been rather a striking child with her glossy black hair, smooth skin, and meditative eyes—and had tried to wheedle her into confessing. When she refused he had opened his drawer

9

and taken out the thick black belt with its three fingers. She had still refused, and he had seized her hand and was whacking it angrily when a knock had come to the door. There had stood Alice Pringle, weeping, ill even then, terrified of pain, but even more of anger. She had confessed that it was she who had by accident spilt the ink. They had not punished her. Three years later, still a pupil, Alice had died; but for Mrs. McShelvie she was resurrected there among the dusty sunbeams on the landing outside the headmaster's door; and with Alice rose too out of the dead past her own girlhood, with all its hopes and dreams.

If she had dreamed for a home, she had one, at 14 Wallace Street; if for a husband, Isaac, though weak and unable to earn much, loved her well; if for children, there were Flora, Effie, Jean, Sammy, and Tom. Yet with an inevitable heart-breaking disloyalty, she admitted, as she stood waiting for her knock to be acknowledged, that the home of her dreams had been otherwise and far away; that the husband wished for had been tall, sunburnt, strong, smelling of hay and clover; and that the children of her imagination's womb had been without spectacles, without the pimples of poor nourishment and impure air, and without the twists of character enforced by the necessity to conform to a twisted society. Young lonely girls dreamed of perfection; it was up to the women they became to cherish the disappointments.

Young Mr. Roy, Sammy's teacher, opened the door. Though he greeted her with a pleasant grin, she felt embarrassed and ashamed. In so many ways he resembled her lost ideal of manhood that she could not forgive or even like him: somehow he seemed the embodiment of her betrayal of Isaac and her sons who, however lucky, would never grow up to be so tall, well-built, clever, self-confident, and able to shape the world to their needs. Life so far for him was an adventure or experiment; the war would be an opportunity for his courage and recklessness. Sometimes he drove up to school in an old red sports car. Apparently he had a degree which entitled him to teach in a high school, but he had asked to be transferred here in the slums where humanity was more important in a teacher than scholarship: his salary had dropped as a result. She could readily believe that story: his face, too rough-hewn to deserve the smooth word handsome, was always frank, frequently humorous, not seldom compassionate, and on occasion formidable. She knew he was not married, but did not know if he had a sweetheart; likely he had had several. Sammy idolised him.

He came out on to the landing beside her and closed the door.

"Mr. Grahamstone's interviewing somebody," he said. "A Mrs. Brora. Do you know her?"

She nodded, with sinking heart. Mrs. Brora was a big loud-voiced widow who wore black hats with coloured feathers. She would not take no from so white-haired a ditherer as Mr. Grahamstone. Any decent woman coming after her must appear feeble and incapable.

"A sergeant-major," she said, with irresistible envy.

He was amused.

"Was she impressing him?" she asked.

"Enormously."

It was a joke to him, she thought: hundreds of mothers and children might be torn from their homes, and all he would do would be to chuckle and puff at his cigarette.

"I lack the grandeur," she said, bitterly.

"Grandeur's hardly what's wanted."

"It's what counts."

He felt sorry for her: he knew her name was already scored off on the probably unfair ground that she was too much of a slattern herself to have any influence among the others. Roy himself felt neutral. He expected to be called up by the Air Force shortly, and thought Langrigg might be a more congenial place to wait than Gowburgh.

The door opened, and out strode Mrs. Brora, booming her thanks. She wore a tight red costume that emphasised the massiveness, and the jubilation, of her bottom.

"You can depend upon me in any emergency, Mr. Grahamstone," she cried. "I never lose my head." Then with skirling laughter, that had room for a little disdain as she glanced at Mrs. McShelvie, she strutted off on her high heels, swinging like a piper playing a victory march.

11

Mr. Grahamstone gazed after her in awe; then he gave Mrs. McShelvie a glance, with the awe by visible degrees sliding down into peevishness.

"I'll see you in a minute," he muttered, and went back into the room where his second-in-command Archie Campbelton sat wiping his high ample bald brow with a white silken handkerchief covered with red dots.

"She'll be a valuable acquisition," muttered the headmaster.

For a moment Campbelton said nothing exquisitely, so full, eloquent, and fastidious were his lips.

"A loud-mouthed harridan," he said, "more suited to herd bulldogs than to soothe frightened children."

Grahamstone laughed: he was never sure when his assistant was being ironical.

"She's down anyway," he said.

Campbelton took off his rimless spectacles, blew on each lens, and then elegantly wiped them with his handkerchief.

"This one that's waiting," muttered the headmaster, "needn't waste our time."

"Mrs. McShelvie?"

"Aye. You once said she reminded you of a witch."

"I was referring to her uncanny eyes, which seemed to me to have clairvoyant qualities."

Grahamstone grunted. "Her kids are as thick-skulled as any in the school."

"It seems to me," murmured Campbelton, with suave impertinence, "that we could be doing with an attendant witch, able to look into the future. Remember war is about to be waged, not between Great Britain and Germany, but between ourselves and the inhabitants of Langrigg's cottages, villas, mansions, and miniature castles."

"That's not my fault. You know I warned them it was a damned stupid place to send us. But surely you're joking about taking this woman with us?"

Campbelton was joking, but the joke would only be successful if he managed to get Mrs. McShelvie enrolled.

He leant forward and tapped on the desk with his long manicured finger.

12

"When some of the younger women were up here the other day enrolling," he said, "they spoke of her highly; they recommended her; they urged she should be allowed to come."

Grahamstone looked incredulous. "They must have been her pals," he muttered.

"On the contrary. One"—she happened to be the only one—"was Mrs. Raeburn, who is as tidy and decent a young woman as there is in the district."

"Raeburn? I don't remember her." Yet it was a good sign he didn't; the termagants, the pullers of teachers' hair, the mothers of truants, he remembered vividly.

"You can take my word for it. Mrs. Raeburn is a credit to the school."

"Of course, Archie, I'll take your word for it." But the tone in which that assurance was spoken was thick with scepticism.

"Besides," said Campbelton, "you are short of helpers."

"I could always make sure she comes back next day."

Campbelton shrugged his shoulders: one day, or a month, the joke succeeded. He and Edgar would have some chuckling whiskies in a Langrigg hotel lounge over this.

"Shall I ask her to come in?" he asked.

Grahamstone nodded, whereupon Campbelton ushered Mrs. McShelvie in as courteously as if she was a councillor's wife at promotion time.

Roy came in with her. It was he who asked her to sit. The chair was no doubt the one in which Mrs. Brora had presided. She tried not to squirm and drop her eyes.

To her surprise Campbelton continued to give her the benefit of his celebrated gentlemanliness. He smiled with charm, and wished her good afternoon; so much so she almost preferred the older man's scowling.

Campbelton moved his chair back so that his chief would not be able to hold a consultation in his ear. He abhorred the habit, particularly because it was humiliating to himself.

"What qualities do you consider an evacuees' helper should possess, Mrs. McShelvie?" he asked, as if it was extremely important.

13

She wasn't sure whether the question was sincere or whether he was merely trying to score off his superior.

"Patience, I suppose," she said, "and toleration."

"Oh, excellent." He clapped his hands.

"What about hard work?" asked the headmaster.

"I have worked hard all my life," she replied quietly.

He grimaced impatiently to show he didn't mean by hard work the scrubbing of stairs or the cleaning of kitchen ranges. He meant—but, indeed, he didn't quite know what he meant. This evacuation would be carried out without rehearsal; not only the menials' duties were vague, so were the commanders'.

"You'll be on your feet all day, and all night too, maybe," he muttered.

"I understand that."

"Add endurance then to patience and toleration," said Campbelton, "and I should say we have the complete equipment. What do you say, Edgar?"

Roy, standing in a corner, laughed.

Grahamstone put his hand on top of a pile of official forms. Were endurance, patience, and toleration really enough?

"Obedience," he said. "What about obedience?"

"I can take orders," she replied.

"You're lucky," he grunted, with a scowl at those forms, "if you get orders you can make head or tail of. The whole thing's ahead of us, and we're not sure how it's going to turn out. Improvisation. That'll be needed too. By God, it will."

"Mrs. McShelvie seems to be a woman with ideas," murmured Campbelton, with the urbanest wink possible.

She smiled.

"What d'you want to go for, anyway?" demanded the headmaster.

"There's money to earn."

"Is it that, though? Are you sure you're not wanting to go so that you can look after your own children? We've had others up, you know, with that in mind. One brazenly admitted it. She went out of that door shrieking she'd write to the Prime Minister."

Mrs. McShelvie wondered if that tormented woman had

14

been Mrs. Aldersyde. Certainly she had applied and been rejected.

"My children can look after themselves," she said. "I thought I would be looking after women with babies and toddlers."

"So you would," he said. "All right. I'll put you down as a day helper."

"Does that mean I come back next day?"

"That's right. Other helpers will be needed to stay for a week or two till everybody's settled in. They might even have to wait there for months. It's a new situation. We'll just have to see how things work out."

"If it's possible, I'd like to stay, and help."

"It's not possible. Is it, Mr. Campbelton?"

Campbelton smiled, with mellowest regret.

Grahamstone relaxed, and became almost affable.

"It's largely a matter of expense," he explained. "Though the Government's not being stingy, we're asked to be as economical as possible."

"I understand," she said, rising. The glimpse she was going to get of Langrigg would be too brief to have any sustenance in it; she would come home more starved than ever.

Roy showed her out. On an impulse he followed her on to the landing.

"Tell me," she asked, "is Mrs. Brora to stay?"

He nodded. "You're disappointed," he said, sympathetically.

"I didn't say I was."

"No, but I can see it. Is it really the money you're after, Mrs. McShelvie?"

She stood at the top of the stairs, and suddenly shuddered. She did not look at him as she made her confession.

"I came to Gowburgh when I was six," she said, "and I've been here ever since. Before then I lived in the country, and went to a school that had a great field of buttercups outside it. There were peewits. We used to find their eggs. There was a big pond with hundreds of seagulls. I hae never forgotten. I thought Langrigg might be a bit like that. Is it?"

"I believe it is."

She said no more on that subject. As she began to go down

the stairs she remarked: "When I was a lassie here, they had an auld piano that played 'Come o'er the stream, Chairlie' as we marched up and doon. Does it still play it?"

"It does. Mrs. McShelvie?"

"Aye?" She turned, far enough down, she hoped, for her stupid tears not to be seen.

"If I were you, I'd come prepared for a longer stay than a night."

"You heard him say it was just for a night."

"Yes, but didn't he also say we'd have to wait till we see how things work out? I can promise nothing certain, of course, but I'll tell you this: if it can be worked at all, you'll stay."

"And wha's going to work it, Mr. Roy?"

"Me."

Instead of gratitude it was, strangely, resentment she felt. She hid it. "Thanks. Don't get yourself into trouble for me."

"It'll be no trouble," he said, "but for Sammy's mother I'd risk a lot. Goodbye."

"Goodbye," she said, and continued downstairs out into the playground and the street.

By a coincidence on her way home she met the little hungry limping terrier.

"Am I going to be luckier than you?" she asked.

When she stopped, and tried to coax it over to her, it stared at her suspiciously, raised its head and gave a heart-rending yelp of denial, and ran away.

Looking after it, she remembered that the price of her luckiness might be the betrayal of her husband and the destruction of millions of innocent people.

II

Germany marched on Poland, and the exodus from Gowburgh was ordered. The night before it took place the school was thronged with last-minute enrollers, who hurried through the dark quiet streets expecting every minute to hear the drone of

16

hostile aeroplanes in the sky, where the barrage balloons hung like unlit lamps.

In the school itself darkness and anxiety reigned, with the headmaster their first minister. Nobody could tell him to his satisfaction whether the black-out was in force yet. Those oracles, the newspapers, differed. Even the local police-station, when asked by telephone, was non-committal. Consequently, since there was a choice between light and darkness, he chose the latter: though inconvenient, it was less risky. His whole career had been based on this calculation of inconvenience minus risk; and he had risen to be a headmaster, whereas Campbelton and Roy, who objected, pointing out that sepulchral shadowiness would hardly reassure distraught parents, were still subordinates. Therefore he suddenly banged his fist upon his desk and declared for darkness.

His own room, however, had to be lit; it was, as it were, the brain centre. Blinds were found for the windows, but they were too short and had to be supplemented by two maps of the world, which accidentally were hung upside-down. He wished this remedied, for a reason he would not divulge; really he thought it a bad omen, war would come, would be lost, and that earliest of exploits in it, his expedition to embattled and inhospitable Langrigg, would be a fiasco. Depressed by these superstitions, he was peevish with Campbelton, who wanted to know where he and the other teachers on duty were to interview inquirers. Heaving himself up from his desk, like a general having to stoop from loftiest strategy to demonstrate the firing of a rifle, he showed how by leaving the door ajar a beam of light would reach the landing. Unfortunately, in doing this he became uncertain how far ajar the door ought to be. If too wide, too, much light would escape, visible to hypothetical bombers through the landing windows; and in addition the interviews in his room, the most important ones, would not be private enough. If too narrow, too little light would issue, giving to the people on the landing the privacy of complete darkness. Therefore he experimented with various distances, holding on to the handle, like one, whispered Campbelton, reluctant to be born.

17

Roy, sorry for his chief's senility, decided that this must be counterbalanced by swift, daring, generous decisions on the dim landing, and by still swifter, still more daring and generous rescindings of decisions taken in the lighted room.

For example, a young woman of about twenty came out, carrying an infant in a shawl. She looked bewildered, miserable, and desperate. A boy of ten, apparently her brother, was with her, imitating her misery. Roy took her into the shadows and asked what was the matter. It seemed she had been born and brought up a Catholic, but a year or so ago had forsworn her religion, and perhaps condemned her soul to everlasting pain, in order to marry a Protestant. She was going to Langrigg with Gordon Street School. She wanted her brother, who lived with her, to go too so that she could look after him; the snag was, he was still a Catholic.

Mr. Grahamstone had refused, in horror. He had nothing against Catholics, except that he thought they were bigoted, sinister, powerful behind the scenes, and revengeful. To defy them might mean persecution till the end of his career: priests would whisper to councillors, councillors would bellow at council meetings, the director of education would be sharply instructed, and official reproof would be shot in Mr. Grahamstone's direction like a torpedo. He was too old now to fight religious wars. Far safer to tell the young woman that her brother must go with his Catholic school. In war-time separations were inevitable.

With Roy listening to her account stood Harold Scoullar, the other male teacher on the staff. He kept nodding in understanding and pity, but could not see what other advice the headmaster could have given: individuals who confronted vast movements, he thought, were trampled underfoot. It was with fascinated disapprobation therefore that he heard Roy stifle an oath, and saw him proceed to fill in the requisite forms for the boy's enrolment, using the wall as a desk. To add to the irregularity, he told her not to say anything to anybody till she got to Langrigg; surely there would be a Catholic school there, to which her brother could go.

She hurried off, clutching the papers as if they were visas

18

for heaven. But Scoullar, though his pity had not diminished, could not wish her godspeed.

"Perhaps that was foolish, Edgar," he murmured.

"Perhaps," agreed Roy, and walked off towards a woman who had just come out of the room weeping.

Following him, Scoullar thrilled to think that in the coming war he would make a better officer than Roy, who despised regulations and never understood that departure from them could mean only inefficiency and failure, as well as reprimand and loss of status.

A minute later this confidence of pips for him and ignominy for his colleague was strengthened. The weeping woman was being comforted by Miss Oldswan, the senior mistress, who soothingly was explaining that Mr. Grahamstone, in refusing to allow her son to accompany her and her other children tomorrow, was only obeying his written instructions, which stated that anyone with a skin complaint must have a clearance line from the school clinic. Her boy had a rash on his arm; he had no clearance line from the clinic; therefore he was ineligible. It was bitter, but simple. She should have enrolled earlier. By leaving it so late she was herself at fault. The clinic of course was closed that night.

The woman was neither convinced nor soothed; indeed, she showed symptoms of hysteria. Accordingly, Miss Oldswan, who was very busy, was relieved when Roy whispered to her that he knew Mrs. Brodie and would talk to her privately.

The talk was not altogether private. Scoullar insisted on overhearing, as a duty towards his chief. Roy, however, ignored him.

"Let's see this rash," he said, and struck a match to examine it. "It looks harmless to me," he said.

"It *is* harmless, Mr. Roy," she sobbed. "I've got a certificate from his ain doctor proving it."

"Good God," cried Roy. "Let me see it."

Scoullar whispered into his ear. "Often the department won't accept a private doctor's certificate. It's customary for them to demand one from their own clinic."

Roy paid no heed. "Mrs. Brodie," he said. "On the strength

19

of this I'm going to make out an enrolment form for your boy."

Her gratitude was almost hysterical. He had to ask her to moderate it.

"If there's an epidemic, Edgar," whispered Scoullar, "you'll have it on your conscience."

Roy's comment on that was so rude he could not utter it in Mrs. Brodie's presence.

"Just to be fair, Mrs. Brodie," he said, "when you get to Langrigg, see a doctor."

"I'll do that, Mr. Roy. God bless you, sir."

She too went off very happy.

Roy, grinning, took out a fag and began to smoke.

Scoullar was about to remind him that the head had said there must be no smoking in the public places of the school; he refrained, on the ground that it was silly warning a man against a peccadillo who had already committed enormities. Edgar, he reflected, intended to enter the Air Force. Surely they would never entrust to his care an aeroplane costing many thousands of pounds?

About half an hour later Scoullar was given an opportunity of putting to the test his own theory of regulations adhered to with tact, consideration, and uprightness. A bantam of a man, no more than five feet, fidgeted at the end of a small queue waiting to consult Roy. He carried a book under his arm, but his face in every way lacked the refinement, patience, and humility of a student. Under his canopy of large flat cap, his glances kept darting about with the rapidity, craftiness, and belligerence of a tiptop flyweight boxer. When Scoullar accosted him, he at first indicated by a series of quick scrutinies that the tall, thin, gaunt-faced teacher with the melancholy brown eyes might not suit his immense purpose; but a second later he relented, forgave, made allowances, was willing to try, shook hands, and led the mesmerised Scoullar aside.

"My name's Raeburn," he said, "Dick Raeburn, of the Black Watch. Report on Monday. My wife's going with your crowd tomorrow, with my two kids, Jess who's seven and Richard who's just five months. Now I'm going to be frank with you, man to man. I'm not the chap to shirk a boast if I think it's justified. Here it is then straight from the shoulder. My Bessie's not to be classed with the scruff you'll be handling in bulk. She's my wife, and she's a lady; and her children, and my children, are as clean as any teacher's children, and as good. That's understood."

Scoullar was quick at mental arithmetic, but slow at the quirks of mind. Moreover, unlike Roy, he was married, with a little girl of three. He frowned, seeking the exact nature and scope of this insult. At the same time, diplomatically, like one whose official role was comforter, he murmured interim approval.

Dick resumed.

"I want your word of honour," he said, more grim than solemn, "that you'll see to it personally that my Bessie is not taken advantage of because of her shyness and decency. You'll have women with you all snarl and grab, like she-wolves. My Bessie's more like a deer, if you see what I mean. If you were to offer to put her into a cowshed, she'd go with her heart crying out for the kids' sakes, but she wouldn't complain."

Scoullar's voice was cold with dignity.

"No one will be billeted in cowsheds, Mr. Raeburn," he said.

"No. It was an example just. I thought you would see that. You'll be billeting them in houses?"

"Naturally."

"There are houses muckier than cowsheds."

"Here in Gowburgh, yes, unfortunately; but in Langrigg, no. They are people of substance yonder. Indeed, some of us here are of the opinion that it was a mistake to send us there."

"If they were all palaces, they wouldn't be too good for my Bessie," said Dick fiercely.

Mr. Scoullar was finding this uxorious braggadocio distasteful, especially in such a shrimp of a man. He too loved his Agnes, but he did not make of that love a stick to rattle along railings or cudgel passers-by.

"If I understand you correctly, Mr. Raeburn," he said, "you are demanding preferential treatment for your family."

21

"You understand me correctly, sir."

"Then let me tell you that I most strongly disapprove."

Like a boxer smitten by his opponent's knee with the referee applauding, Dick staggered back.

"I suppose nervousness has warped your judgment," said Scoullar.

It was the other knee this time.

"Are you serious?" gasped Dick.

"Extremely so. Your wife and children, Mr. Raeburn, like the rest of the people in our care, will be treated with the utmost humanity, both by us and, I am sure, by our Langrigg hosts. Good night, sir."

Then Mr. Scoullar walked away, as dignity required. Unhappily there was nowhere to walk to save along the dark corridor, where dignity groped and stumbled, but also brooded on this diabolical paradox: in Britain's army would be many as selfish and corrupt as Raeburn, and many worse. Right had to be served by wickedness as well as by virtue. That could be God's colossal irony of course, and as such deserved a sad smile of reverence; but it could also be the consequence of man's own hellish entanglement, which deserved the headshake and shiver of aversion.

When he was sure his tempter would be gone he returned to the landing, to see Raeburn not only as rampant as ever but obviously enjoying success in his soliciting of Roy, who was listening to him with vulgar good humour and shameful compliance.

Screened by others, Scoullar watched. He saw Raeburn take the book from under his arm and offer it to Roy. The latter laughingly refused, but when pressed took it and opened it. At once Raeburn snatched it back, eagerly found a page, and was reading from it with the intensity of a spy when Scoullar walked past. It was a quotation from Burns, expressing sentiments trite, shallow, and unhelpful. "The rank is but the guinea stamp, the man's the gowd for a' that." Roy laughed as at some new-minted happy innocent joke. Yet, in plain terms, was he not at that moment a traitor, a receiver of bribes, and an accomplice of corruption? That he did not after all accept the book was no extenuation; he had accepted the commission of favouritism. Once in Langrigg he would forget to honour his ignoble promise; thus dishonour spread.

Scoullar did not speak to him again that night.

One of those waiting to consult Roy had been Mrs. McShelvie. Their conversation lasted less than a minute. She had come to ask if he had managed to fix anything definite about her staying in Langrigg for a while. Her excuse for troubling him, she said, was that she would have arrangements to make at home. He was pleasant, encouraging, but not positive. "You remember improvisation?" he had asked. "Well, it'll depend on that." She had smiled back, had resisted the temptation to beg him to reassure her, and had quietly gone away, sickened by her own lack of pride and by her persistence in what she knew was wrong. Isaac, so easily dominated by her, and so anxious to make amends for being the cause of her discontent, had urged her to come and inquire. Flora, anticipating freedom to stay out at nights as late as she liked, had thought it a good idea. The other four children, keen to have their mother with them in the strange town, had clapped their hands.

There were several unusual cases to be dealt with. Perhaps the most puzzling was a woman, nine months pregnant, who came gallantly up the school stairs, cleeked by two neighbours, to ask in cheerful faith if it would be all right for her to travel tomorrow. When Grahamstone in consternation cried that she might give birth in the train, she agreed and mentioned one or two other cases of unlikely birthplaces she had heard of: a lift, a taxi, and a telephone kiosk. She was not in the least timid or contrite about her predicament. Those like Miss Oldswan and Scoullar, who thought her drunk, could smell no spirits off her breath; whereas those like Campbelton and Roy, who thought her valiant and fey, saw sparkles in her eyes. If she got to Langrigg all in the one piece, she cried, she would find out the Provost's name and call her child after him, even if it was Paddy. If it happened on the train, she'd call him after the engine-driver, or after Mr. Grahamstone if he liked. She did not seem to think the child might be female; perhaps the presence of the three lady teachers banished the thought.

23

The headmaster did not enjoy her ebullience. A woman in her condition ought to be humble, cowed, and, damn it all, ashamed for having arranged things with the obvious intention of snagging his plans. If he set out with 885 as his official count, it would be awkward if he arrived with 886; he'd be made a laughing-stock. She laughed so much when he muttered this that she suddenly seemed to feel a twinge and grabbed her middle. But it was a deliberately false alarm, to terrify him at the prospect of the birth taking place in his room under the world upside down. When at last they got her away, he sat and dabbed at his face like a doctor after a difficult delivery.

Campbelton, for all his sybaritism, was as resolute a celibate as any Tibetan monk. Yet it was he who ushered the indomitable woman to the door, and told her it was spunk like hers which would win the war.

They discussed her.

"I think," said Miss Oldswan, "her levity was disgusting."

Misses Carnwath and Calder concurred, the latter with contradictory giggles.

Scoullar stood with his arms folded. No need to give his opinion. His own wife's pregnancy had always been spoken about only in strictest privacy, and then holily; her parturition not at all. One would as soon spit in a church.

Roy laughed; he sat on the head's desk on top of important papers, smoked a cigarette, and laughed. He seemed at ease, as if the multitudinous problems of humanity bothered him no more than the smoke rising in front of his eyes. He never went to church, he smoked, he drank, he laughed at lewd stories, he had visited a brothel in Nice, but worst of all he loved to find authority foolish so that he could deride and flaunt it. How in Christ's name, thought Scoullar, could such a man be called upon to preserve Christianity and civilisation from barbarism? Surely with such a champion the cause must fail. Yet envy sharpened his anguish: Roy, he knew, might walk through the murks of depravity, but he would also soar into the clear sky, in his silver aeroplane, and grapple with the dragons of the enemy.

The good quiet peaceable man's obscurity in war-time,

thought Scoullar, would be honoured by God, if not by the shouting multitudes.

III

That night in many kitchens all over Gowburgh, the big zinc baths were dragged out from under beds, emptied of toys or rags or clothes-pegs or kittens, filled with warm water from kettles on the hob, and then occupied by skinny-bottomed, ribby children who laughed and cried through the soap-suds. Those were thorough ablutions: ears especially were delved into as if to dislodge stubborn earwigs. Towels were then applied vigorously, combs ruthlessly, needles patiently, and flat-irons wearily. Fathers, ousted from their privilege of brooding over the newspaper or wireless, were made to help by harassed mothers. Thus at the intimate kitchen hearth, the sanctuary of the family, were the preparations made to thwart the far-off enemy.

The stipulated equipment was gathered together, as much as could be: in some cases pyjamas were lacking or toothbrushes or changes of underwear. The small bundle was wrapped in paper, mostly brown, but sometimes newsprint was all there was; and one family in Wallace Street used some spare wall-paper, cream with red roses. The owner's name was printed plainly in ink, as the leaflet advised. Then finally excitement had to be quelled, lamentation soothed, courage inspired, and sleep enforced. In many cases prayers were ordered: a compulsion that astonished but in no way offended. They knelt in joy and confidence, and more or less reminded God of His duty to take care of them and their parents, from whom they were to be parted. Then they lay down, two, three, four, and at least in one case five in the bed, and after a period of noisy adjustment at last fell asleep, while their fathers sat by the low midnight fires comforting their quietly weeping mothers.

Of course in some households preparations were not so painstakingly or conscientiously carried out. As Meg Aitchison

25

remarked with scurrilous emphasis to her consenting husband Roger, it was a war they were about to embark on, not a Sunday school trip. No army had time for all that palaver of baths and combings and ironings. Winking, she asked him what would happen if their own weans, for instance, turned up without the necessary campaigning kit. Rubbing his bristly chin with that look of consummate fat obuteness that was his favourite camouflage, he reflected for a long minute and then gave it as his opinion that they would just have to do without or else steal someone else's. She nodded so hard it seemed she was trying to loosen her remaining teeth; but a minute later she uttered the contradiction he was keenly and joyfully waiting for. They would not do without, she shrieked, nor need they steal, unless it was to supplement their equipment. The authorities, she howled, must provide. They were giving the marching orders, let them supply the gear. This conversation took place in the malodorous uproar of their kitchen. Nowhere in the city was there a husband who, over the heads of their offspring locked in civil war, cast at his wife a glance so calm and satisfied in its admiration. She had, he said, the spirit that caused revolutions. They were, of course, shaped and completed by profound thinking like his own. He and she were, he thought, a revolutionary pair.

As for the scrubbing, combing, and darning, cried Meg, who knew where they would all lie tomorrow night? It might be in places no grander than her own kitchen, in which case all that cleanliness would be wasted. Downstairs, she knew, Mrs. McShelvie, helped by Isaac the teenie, in an apron, was rubbing the skin off her weans, or, what was even crueller, was making them do it themselves.

Socratic in his dirty shirt, Roger expatiated on this treachery of Mrs. McShelvie's. The Raeburns and Aldersydes were reactionaries: he would not waste an analysis on them. But Bell McShelvie, apart from her bourgeois gift of reading tea-cups, was a true proletarian, shrewd and staunch. If she had been living at the time of the French Revolution she'd have sat and knitted as the guillotine chopped off the heads; she'd have used red wool, too. She was not reconciled to poverty. She did

26

not look on it as a blessing, a kind of hunger imposed so that after death the so-called succulences of paradise would be all the more relished. No, she had the intelligence to see it as an injustice, perpetrated and perpetuated by Christian capitalists, who conveniently forgot that their own God's son had gone hungry as a boy. In short, she had the ability to make herself the leader of a movement within the evacuation, to turn this into a subtle kind of authorised hunger march, inevitably effective because of the hordes of women and children weeping genuine tears. Such tears to revolutionaries were, he implied, scarcer than they should be. Under her instruction they could make it clear that they were not going to occupy such places as Langrigg temporarily; they were moving in to the citadels of wealth and privilege to stay, and they were going to throw out the present occupants and give these a taste of destitution.

In this disquisition he forgot Hitler's bombers, which would spill the blood of rich and poor alike; but in fairness it should be added that he forgot also the internecine pandemonium around him, proving his concentration to be truly philosophical.

IV

It was a splendid, an argonauts' morning. Sunshine glittered on the silver balloons serene in the sky, and on the sparrows' beaks as they breakfasted in the early dung of the streets. Mothers, hurrying to school with their children, were like so many Ceres, with so many recovered Proserpinas, whom they were resolved never to lose again, even to the King of Hell himself. If they had wept as their husbands, before leaving for work, kissed them goodbye, they had pretended to their unusually attentive children that the tears were in fun, for poor daddy would have to make his own breakfast in future, come home to cook his own dinner, and sleep alone. To the children, shivering in the early light, that desertion of father seemed funny enough, especially when he pulled long faces and grumbled about the fine holiday they were going to have

27

in the country. They promised to write him letters, and he promised to visit them as soon as he could. After he had left for work, the house already, with the rest of them still in it, seemed silent, and abandoned.

As for those mothers like Mrs. Aldersyde, who, not having any children under school age, were not to be allowed to accompany the exodus, they were to come back to those forsaken houses, and begin all the usual work of the day, the emptying of ashpans, the kindling of fires, the washing of dishes, and the sweeping of floors, as if everything was the same as yesterday morning, and at any minute in the children would run, dirtying the floor with their muddy feet and clamouring for something to eat. They would remember then, in an agony of love, how they had scolded and perhaps refused.

The school was the gathering point. Mr. Grahamstone had fixed the hour for muster much too early. His teachers and some of the parents had protested, but he had been adamant. Only to Campbelton had he justified himself by declaring, with messianic zeal, that it was better eight hundred should wait than that one should be left behind. The illogicality of such an attitude was manifest, but so too was its gorgeous ludicrousness, and Campbelton metaphorically tiptoed away from it in case he should waken it up into dreich common sense.

The eight hundred, packed into classrooms according to their initials, waited on the hard forms with patience and fortitude. Babies, some only weeks old, were not aware of the historic occasion and, waking up, sensed insecurity in their mothers' arms; they complained loudly. They had to be taken out into corridors and walked up and down like bagpipes. Nothing could silence some: all the traditional methods were tried, dummy-teats, loving croons, dandlings, pats on the back, exasperated slaps, and even red-faced recriminations. Mothers who had reached that last stage were avoided by the headmaster on his regular rounds. During these he gazed into each classroom, saw pretty much what he had seen last time, cautioned the same boys to sit still, and then moved on. He did not show it, but he was possessed by an enormous ache to be the saviour of them all, like another Moses; and it was the physical impossibility only that kept him from picking them up, stuffing them into pockets and suitcase, and delivering them, safe as bank-notes, into the Langrigg vaults. It was not the first time that this incompressibility of human material had vexed and baffled him, and it wasn't to be the last.

Without meaning to, or wishing to, or even being aware of doing it, Campbelton helped to preserve calm and confidence. Immaculately and fragrantly shaved, resplendent in green tweeds and discreet tartan tie, he strolled from one room to another like a benevolent laird visiting his dispossessed crofters. Felici-tations on the weather flowed from his suave lips. Disgruntled mothers whose backs ached were assuaged, and in at least two cases he succeeded where dummy-teats dipped in jam had failed. He had a true catholic condescension: to everybody he spoke with beaming courtesy and exquisite articulation. If a baby smelled, or a mother's coat was dirty or a child's nose needed wiping, he raised his fragrant palm in benediction, as if they were all pilgrims and he the abbot in charge of the shrine. Not even to Mrs. McShelvie, whom he suspected of seeing through him, or to Meg Aitchison, to him the symbol of depraved motherhood, would he permit himself a single jujube of disdain. As he told Roy, this forbearance was all the more praiseworthy in that, as was well known, he had a pathological hatred of dirt on human carcases, and moreover was in command of an invective the equal of any Gowburgh tram driver's.

Roy sought out Mrs. McShelvie to ask her to point out to him Mrs. Raeburn. He found her trying to pacify a young mother who, with her baby asleep in her arms, was sobbing uncontrollably. It had been the infant's crying, as if in pain, which had set hers off: now it was peacefully asleep, and her own weeping might waken it into another bout of sore fretting.

"She bides in a single-end," said Mrs. McShelvie, as she accompanied him to the room where the R's were, "in Living-stone Street, wi' an unrestricted view of the gasworks. Did you no' smell the gas off her?"

"I can't say I did," he replied, not sure whether the question was ironical.

She smiled. "What's she breaking her hert for, then?" she asked. "Wherever she lands up in this place Langrigg, surely she'll be better off?"

"I would think so."

"She's just twenty, of course. Can romances flourish within the sicht and stink of the gasworks, in a single room that a scalded cat wad cross in one loup?"

"It seems they can."

"If they sicken sooner than they would in a hoose wi' a bathroom and a garden full of trees, where's the wonder?"

"Where indeed?"

They came to the room of R's. She indicated Mrs. Raeburn in a seat at the back.

"Do you want to meet her?" she asked.

"Do you think I should?"

"Are you thinking the rest might be jealous? But aren't you committed already? In ony case, here's Bessie herself to speak to you."

Blushing, but tight-mouthed, Mrs. Raeburn came down the passage, carrying the baby. Little Jess stayed behind, nursing her negro doll.

Roy was relieved to find his protégée so presentable. Dick had bragged in a good cause. He could not help grinning as he recollected the small man's huge praises of his wife.

She spoke with an effort. "I want to apologise, Mr. Roy," she said, "for my husband. He had no right to ask you to put me in front of the others. If there's anybody deserves special consideration, it's poor Mrs. Ross there. She's got six weans, and she never utters a word of complaint. Thank you all the same."

With a pale smile to mitigate the ungratefulness of her words, she hurried back to her obscure seat.

Roy grinned. "Well," he said, "that's my gas in a peep."

"Bessie's no' the first wife having to go behind her man to tidy up his mess, whether it's spoken or acted. That's Mrs. Ross in the black coat, though to maist of us she's mair

30

recognisable through her weans. I never see her withoot some
o' them clinging to her. Her man's a labourer in Lloyd's
ironworks. Many folk would say she cannae afford six weans,
and should hae kent better. But if you're thinking of rebuking
Nan Ross, whaever you are, make sure your ain hert's pure.
Not that she'd dream of answering you back in anger. It's just
that if it's a penance to hae that number o' gifts frae God, she
suffers it—like an angel."

Those last three words were added, after a pause, with grim
warm humour; so much so that Roy, as he gazed over at Mrs.
Ross, realised afresh that these women were much more than
the populators of the surrounding dreary buildings and the
supplicrs of the very raw material for his craft of teaching. No
doubt Mrs. McShelvie was exceptional, just as her son Sammy
was; but in some vital way each and every one was exceptional.
Mrs. Ross, for instance, would at other times have struck him
as a fat soft lump of placid stupidity, for whom the necessary
checking and chastising of her brood was too much disturbance;
now, through Mrs. Raeburn's and Mrs. McShelvie's eyes, he
saw her dedicated to a task beside which the flying of a Spitfire
was childish play.

"I hae never heard her complain," said Mrs. McShelvie,
"though I hae seen her in tears. She has twa weans deid.

"I hear you had a visit last night frae Mrs. Barclay," she
added.

"Mrs. Barclay?"

"Aye, she was expectant."

He remembered. "Was?"

"Your heidmaister will be relieved to ken it happened last
night. She's in the maternity now, wi' a girl."

"We admired her spirit."

"Weel you micht."

Then they were interrupted by Sammy McShelvie, who came
along the corridor looking for his mother. Roy, as he always
did, involuntarily smiled on seeing the thin gawky bespectacled
unperturbed boy, who seemed to him to live in some hollow
oak in a perpetually sunlit wood haunted by benevolent elves.

Mrs. McShelvie noticed his smile.

31

"He's been like that," she said, "since the day he was born; except for the specs of course. He was fully three when he got them."

Roy was astonished and indignant.

"There's no need to be bitter, Mrs. McShelvie," he said. "There's not a boy in the school I like better than Sammy."

"And him such a numbskull?"

It was true that at all the subjects for which prizes were awarded, such as arithmetic, grammar, poetry reciting, and religious knowledge, Sammy was a dunce. For good-heartedness, comic, original, and endearing, there could be no official prize; but every teacher, in his or her own heart, always presented it to Sammy.

"Numbskull's a hard word," said Roy. "Nobody who knows him would ever call him that."

"Mr. Grahamstone has called him worse," she said, "and wi' reason enough. He brings hame report cards that are a disgrace."

"We can't all be scholars, Mrs. McShelvie."

"No, but some of us wha weren't given brains were given brawn or cheek for compensation. Boys a heid shorter can bully him."

"I can readily believe Sammy'd never lift a hand against anybody smaller than himself."

"It's no' just that."

She turned to her son, who had been standing politely aside. "I thought I warned you you weren't to come pestering me? I'm here working."

"It's Jeanie, mither," he said. "She says she's got a sore stomach."

"Why come to me? Is there a helper in your room? Are there teachers aboot? I hae my ain folk to look after; you're not among them."

Roy was annoyed by this sarcastic scrupulousness.

"I don't think anybody would object if you went to see your girl," he said.

"I ken one wha would object," she answered grimly, "and he's got the say." She turned to Sammy. "Go back and tell Effie to take her doon to the lavatory."

32

"Effie's reading. Will I take her?"

"It'll be the lassie's lavatory she'll go to. How can you take her?"

"I'll play in the playground till she's finished."

"What will you play at? Peaver?"

Peaver being a girls' game, the query was satiric. Sammy was invulnerable. He nodded. "Or I'll stot my ba'," he said, and produced a tiny ball from his pocket.

Roy patted the boy's shoulder. "You go and do that, Sammy," he said. "Look after your sisters."

"Tell Effie from me," said Mrs. McShelvie, as her son moved away, "that I'll be alang to warm her ear for her."

"She says," remarked Sammy, "she's got a sore stomach too."

"You see, they've got him for a proper sumph," said his mother.

"I expect they have sore stomachs, with excitement."

"Weel, if it was the world coming to an end," she said, "it wouldn't excite him."

"But not because he's a numbskull, Mrs. McShelvie."

"Why then?"

"I think," murmured Roy, smiling, as he made to take his leave, "your Sammy's one of the elect."

She watched the tall handsome, clever young man stride away.

"One of the elect?" she repeated. "What does that mean? Aye, so he is then; and it's me kens it better than you, Mr. Roy. Do *you* ken though it means he'll be taken early?"

And though she rebuked herself as a typical numbskull's mother, with her foolish superstitious forebodings, she could not smother the fear which had lurked in her since his birth and which had been fed by many signs significant to her as spae-wife, that he would die young.

V

If Sam McShelvie was one of the elect, Willie Baxter was one of the damned. He was the school villain, and he played the role with grinning red-headed gusto. He swore, he stole, he smoked, he bullied, he plunked, he seldom washed, and he was insolent to his teachers. No effective punishment had been devised: sarcasm, even as polished as Campbelton's with waspish stings, was blunted against his soul so calloused; and similarly his palms were proof against the tawse. Indeed, most of the ladies had long since given up strapping him. They maintained it was a snare by which he brought them down to his brutal level, or even below it: he, so cool, unwincing, and unapologetic, seemed heroic; they, flustered, dishevelled, sobbing, appeared villainesses. Now they sent him along to Mr. Grahamstone, who gave him six of the best on each hand, not because there was any redemptive virtue in that procedure, but because when there is nothing else to do it is wise to fall back upon orthodoxy. The boy seemed to understand, and to bear no unusual malice: once certainly he had hidden the janitor's bell, thus disrupting the school, and once he had poured ink over a form that the headmaster had piously filled up to be returned next day to 129 Tubb Street, where the demigods of officialdom lived.

The police were patient with Willie, and his younger brother Tom. They knew that sooner or later the probation certificates would be torn up, and the reformatory gates opened.

Their mother was dead, and their father was a morose drunkard. Often they came to school hungry; usually in rags; and more than once cramped from sleeping in coal cellar or washing house, their father having locked himself in the house in a stupor. Neighbours pitied them, but feared them more: their own children were sheep to these wolves. Even Roger Aitchison, who saw them as victims of capitalist corruption, had seen fit to threaten to shatter their backsides if they ever again anointed his Gary with tar, or tied his Bella to the clothes-pole with her own ropes.

Roy had consulted nobody when making up his mind that

this flitting to Langrigg might be a turning-point for the Baxters. In any case, Gowburgh itself under the dark licensed conditions of war, would certainly mean final ruin for them. Soon they would be at the difficult stage of turning from boys to men: regeneration or lifelong depravity was ahead of them. Perhaps it was sentimental to hope that the fields and hills of Langrigg would purify what the streets and backcourts of Gowburgh had helped to pollute; but it was just as sentimental surely to believe that out of the brutality and bloodshed of war would emerge kindness and brotherhood.

Roy, therefore, had made up parcels of equipment for the two boys. He had seen to it their father signed the form authorising them to go. Now, this morning, when they had failed to appear, he was determined to fetch them.

Slipping downstairs, he met the headmaster, who was alarmed to learn he intended to leave the premises, and apoplectically horrified to hear it was for the purpose of fetching the Baxter brothers.

"Those young buggers!" he wailed, with a burst of irresistible sincerity.

Roy grinned, yet was displeased.

"They are down on your official list," he said solemnly.

His chief grasped him by the arm and came close.

"I've been praying they wouldn't show up, Edgar," he whispered hoarsely. "You know fine what they are: born saboteurs."

"They're just boys, one twelve, the other ten."

"They're demons. There will be a hundred, a thousand opportunities on this trip for mischief-making. They will seize every one. You know it, but I know it better. I have seen it all happen in nightmares. In any case," he added, "they won't have any pyjamas or toothbrushes or clean underwear. We can't take them and expect Langrigg folk to equip them."

"I've done that."

"Done what?"

"I've bought those things for them."

"With your own money?"

"Yes."

35

The headmaster's astonishment, having reached its climax, slowly turned to gloomy resentment.

"Scoullar's right," he muttered. "You'll go to any lengths to obstruct authority. I was in uniform once. Wars are won, Mr. Roy, by obedience to orders, not by hare-brained whims and recklessness."

"I'm sorry," said Roy. "I've no time to waste."

As he gazed after his subordinate, Grahamstone took out his watch and looked at it: in another three quarters of an hour the march would begin. Time was a madman, with a starter's pistol. Soon out of the rooms would rush the stampeding horde. He, representing order and sanity, would be trampled on. All the way turmoil would be in command. Children would get lost, some would fall out of the train, babies would die in convulsions, mothers in hysterics, and the entire mass, so tidily arranged on his sheets, would be as unmanageable as a herd of buffalo. He, perhaps the one blameless person involved, would be blamed: at the end of his career the bitter grapes of contumely would be given him to suck, instead of the sweets of honourable retirement. He would go to his grave a persecuted embittered man, and the forces which had brought about his downfall were symbolised surely by this sinisterly humanitarian action of young Roy's, this going out of the quiet and innocent school to bring back into it disruptive evil.

Then the headmaster, feeling much older and afraid of wasting any more time, hurried upstairs to his room, where he sat at his desk lifting and dropping forms completed to the last comma.

It was, thought Roy as he strode in a temper through the streets, a bloody disgrace that people should have to live amidst such squalor, especially in a country proud of its spacious liberating beauty. No wonder Mrs. McShelvie would even disown her kids to seize the chance of escape for a while. How could anybody expect the Baxters to be other than rascals? If the shells were rotten, could the kernels be wholesome? Surely it was obvious: remove the children from these filthy buildings,

36

give them space and sunshine and flowers, and they themselves would bloom.

As this angry optimism spurted in his mind, he began to hear Archie Campbelton's cool contradiction.

"You are a young man, Edgar: belief in the perfectibility of your species becomes you; it is the Red Cross on your shield. Alas, swords plunged into the blatant beast of human nature break off in fragments until only the hilts are left. If not thrown away these turn into jewels, with which the crusaders' souls are bought. Throw away that hilt in time, Edgar: face the world empty-handed; you still then may prevail. I omitted to throw mine away. Therefore I am become a portion of the blatant beast upon which the young crusaders' swords shatter. I have wooed councillors to gain promotion; I have danced the saraband of the knees. Beneath these well-tailored clothes, dear boy, and under this pampered and talcumed fat, there is, secreted like ambergris, a tiny germ of self-loathing. It is only that which keeps me comparatively sweet. Slums exist, Edgar, because our ambitions are slums."

Archie, thought Roy angrily, made of his cynicism a haven in which to lie back and enjoy the luxuries produced by his small-souled shallow-hearted fellow-men: it was an attitude not even wit could make condonable. Just as infuriating of course were Scoullar's stale metaphors out of the church hymnary about the stormy seas of life, God the pilot, and faith the anchor. To Roy it seemed that principles, once formulated, became like money in the bank, which need never be withdrawn and spent. The parson preached of humility, and applied every week for a church with a better manse, bigger stipend, and pleasanter parishioners. The teacher as student read books and wrote essays on the noble aims of education, but as practitioner judged the job by the pay and length of holidays. The politician vowed to spend his life in attacking abuses like these slums, but later in the House of Commons won popularity by those very attacks. Far better, thought Roy, to go by instinct and leave principle to effete old age: far better to laugh at absurdity, help when one could, and pity in silence when one couldn't; to enjoy food, drink, bawdry, and good singing;

to prefer one's own country but give second place to any other country one happened to be visiting; to be improvident, prejudiced, and unrepentant; to relish the vast variety of human experience; and above all to see no man, whatever his position, as a demigod. But the important thing was to stay clear of principle.

He arrived at the tenement in which the Baxters lived. In that dreich street, it was the dreichest; and their close was the meanest in it. Obscenities, feeble in their huge irrelevance, were scrawled over it. Dogs' filth defiled the stone floor. The walls sweated a shame that itself stank. It looked like a tunnel leading to some kind of Neanderthal existence. Yet Roy acknowledged, as he entered, breathing shallowly, that in some of the houses some effort would have been made to salute civilisation: a carpet on a floor perhaps, a vase with flowers, polished candlesticks, a photograph of ancestors, or a baby's cot decorated with pictures illustrating a nursery rhyme.

He had to knock on a door to ask which of the nine houses up those stairs was the Baxters'. The one he chose had a brass plate bearing in Gothic characters the fine Scots name of Douglas. The inhabitants, he thought, would be at least articulate.

He had to knock three times. At last the key turned with a long creaking. An old woman with white hair over her shoulders gazed out at him with eyes that he saw were blind. From her and the house behind her came a smell of decay.

"Wha is it?" she asked, in a timid querulous voice.

He wished he had chosen another door.

"I'm sorry for disturbing you, Mrs. Douglas," he said.

"That's no' my name," she whispered.

"I'm a teacher from the school," he went on. "I'm looking for the Baxters' house. I know it's up this close somewhere."

Before she could answer the door opposite on the landing opened. Out thrust a fat sleepy vacuous female face without teeth, and with curlered hair.

"This evacuation of yours," she said, in a tired voice, "it's a fraud. That one's blin', as you'll likely hae noticed; and she's"—here she tapped her brow—"forby. The landing above, middle door, God curse them." That second last word might have been "bless" so amiably was it spoken.

The old woman was shaking her head. "He will grant mercy," she muttered, "to the worst of sinners."

Her neighbour again tapped her brow. "First thing in the morning," she said, "and last at night. Sure He will," she added indulgently, "the same mercy they showed to Mrs. Sneddon's cat when they flung a lighted rug on its back. Hell was invented for their kind."

"Puir mitherless lads."

"Murderers hae mithers: that proves naething."

"When I was their age I could see," said the old woman. "It's them, puir lads, wha are blin'."

"They can see weel enough to steal; aye, and to catch a boy smaller than themselves and spit all over his face. We talk aboot the Nazis, but we've got as bad amongst us here at hame."

There seemed no especial animosity in her voice, which was the reason why her accusations had chilled Roy's blood.

"Are you talking about the Baxter boys?" he asked.

"Wha else, mister? If it wasnae that I've got my bare feet, I'd gie you a complete recital o' their villainics. Your evacuation's a fraud, but if it gies us a rest frae them for a while it'll hae done some guid."

"They've got een," whispered the old blind woman, "but they hae never seen God's licht. It cam to me when I was a lass o' twelve."

Her neighbour rubbed her cheek against the edge of the door. "And it went when you were twenty-three," she said, yawning. "Locks herself in like the Bank o' Scotland, day and night."

"Thank you both very much," said Roy, in a hurry, and hastened upstairs to the next landing. Behind him both doors closed.

As he rapped on the Baxters' door he was astonished to feel exhilaration rising in him. Surely despair at such heinous cruelties as he had just heard of would be more appropriate. Yet nothing could stop that exhilaration. Knock on any door, he cried inwardly, and there confronting you were the mystery, excitement, sadness, and fun of humanity. Slums, war, cruelty, injustice, were real and must always be boldly faced; but one's allies were potent and multitudinous. Archie's symbol of the sword with the shattered blade was false.

The door cautiously opened, and a face peeped out at him lower than he'd expected. "Oh Jesus," he heard, and then, "Wullie, it's big Roy!" A scuffle, and he caught sight of a shirt-tailed behind.

Grinning, he wondered what the etiquette now was. Obviously the two boys were in alone, and just as obviously he wasn't welcome. Ought he to respect their right as present house-holders to shut the door on him if they wished? In the meantime his foot prevented that. Or should he regard himself as *in loco parentis*, enter, see them dressed, and drag them off to the school? He went in.

Willie, just out of the heap of rags that was his bed, was scrambling into his shorts. Tom stood snarling sleepily over at the sink. On the table stood half a dozen empty beer bottles. In the fug in the little kitchen the stench of beer and beery urine was the strongest. This was the only room in the house. Roy did not sit down. The nearest chair had a puddle on it. One by the fireside had its stuffing protruding like a growth.

"Good morning, boys," he said pleasantly. "I thought you must have slept in, so I came along to waken you up."

Willie stuffed his shirt into his trousers, dragged on his jersey, and crammed his feet into his sandshoes, with such speed he seemed to be penitent for having overslept. But it was really self-respect in presence of the teacher. When his nakedness was covered, he grinned insolently.

"We're no' gaun," he said, clawing at his red tousled hair. "We're no' weans."

Tom's hair too was red, and it could shake with great determination.

"You cannae make us go," he said.

"Your father signed the forms," said Roy.

"Ach, he was drunk." Willie grinned. "He thought he wad get money for signing. Money for booze."

40

"All the same," said Roy, "I think you're going."

"You cannae make us," snarled Tom.

But Willie was winking. "Was it Mr. Grahamstone sent ye for us, Mr. Roy?" he asked.

In one so young, it was devilish humour.

"No," replied Roy, taking out a cigarette and lighting it. "I want you to come."

"Whit for, Mr. Roy? Naebody else wants us to go. I mean, at the school; everybody in the close wants us to."

"I want you to," said Roy. "Get on your clothes, Tom."

Tom made no effort to obey. Suddenly his brother yelled at him.

"Get your claithes on, you fool."

Startled, Tom obeyed. His trousers had a large hole in the seat.

"Are those the only pair you've got?" asked Roy.

They both jeered at that absurdity of owning superfluities.

"They'll do," said Roy. "Have you had any breakfast?"

"There's naething to eat," said Willie. "We're going to wait till the pubs open, and then we'll get a tanner on thae bottles."

"I'll get you something on our way to the school," said Roy. "There's one thing I'd like to ask. Is it true you threw a lighted rug on a cat and burnt it?"

It was Tom who answered, in a passionate yell. "It killed my pigeon."

Willie nodded. "It killed his pigeon, Fantail," he said reasonably. "We kept it in the coal-cellar, and auld Sneddon's cat killed it."

"That was unfortunate, but it certainly doesn't excuse your appalling cruelty. You two are human beings, you're supposed to know what's right and what's wrong. A cat's an animal, it just obeys instinct, it didn't know to kill your pigeon was wrong, it didn't even know it was your pigeon."

"Aye, it did," yelled Tom. "It slunk away. It had bits o' Fantail in its mooth like whiskers. Its een were squinting, just like auld Sneddon's."

Again Willie calmly confirmed. "She once said she'd like to shove us into the washhoose fire, Mr. Roy," he said. "She's a bad auld bastard." He paused, his eyes widening as he considered his enormous gaffe. Then he grinned. "So's her cat," he added.

"That's enough of such language," said Roy angrily. "Let me tell you this, I can forgive most things, but never cruelty."

Tom turned away, to hide tears. "Fantail was my pet," he muttered.

"That's right," agreed Willie. "It wad sit on his heid for 'oors."

Roy had noticed a portrait on the wall. "Was that your mother?" he asked.

Willie glanced at it indifferently. Tom continued to mourn his pigeon. Willie nodded.

She looked very young. Perhaps it had been taken when the disease which had ultimately killed her had already established its hold: she seemed tired and defeated. If she had lived she might merely have lamented the degradation of her husband and sons without being able to prevent it; indeed, she might have shared it.

Roy shuddered. "In this place Langrigg where we're going," he said, "there are hundreds of pigeons."

Tom would not be consoled. In the world were millions; the one which had sat on his head in trust and love had been killed.

"Right," muttered Roy, "let's go."

VI

The signal to march had to be given. It was not possible to padlock the iron gates, sharpen the spikes on the railings, lock all doors, mesmerise every woman and child within the building like the sleeping beauty, and so keep them all there until the Last Trump sounded or the bells announcing armistice, whichever was the sooner. The land of fairytale, thought Mr. Grahamstone, in many ways had advantages over reality: he'd seen children in rags and scabs with magic in their eyes. But there was no magic in his, as he gave Roy permission to start the trek to the station: put mothers with babies at the front, he muttered, to keep the pace seemly.

Suitcase at feet, gasmask slung over shoulder, hat in hand, head bowed, like a statesman superintending surrender and retreat, he stood in the playground and watched them stream past. Their cheerfulness shocked him; nor was he calmed by Campbelton who, burdened only by his gasmask which he wore like a camera, jaunted up and complimented him on being, after all, a superb psychologist: it had been a master-stroke having them sit so long in the school, with their irritation tightening like a spring; now in the relief and pleasure of its unwinding, they had forgotten or overcome the anguish of leaving their homes and loved ones. Grahamstone, who always faced up to his lieutenant's praise as he would have a snake with its fangs unextracted, merely wanted to know where the other's case was. When informed it was being lugged by two boys for a shilling apiece, he felt envious but at the same time disgusted: children in school might be asked or bribed to do favours for teachers; but these were sorrowing refugees, or ought to be. Grunting, he picked up his own case and had humped it as far as the gate when the husband of one of the women in the procession approached him and politely insisted on carrying it. The headmaster was grudgingly grateful: was he being honoured as leader or pitied as decrepit?

He walked as if at a funeral, and could not understand why everybody else did not do likewise: thus had he foreseen it. But not only was the procession cheerful, it even went fey. A small man, who looked like a professional backcourt entertainer, appeared at the front with a set of aged bagpipes and led the way with defiant skirling tunes. It was clear he was playing for love; he would not pass his cap round for pennies. Boys whooped like Redskins; three of them dashed ahead into a shop that sold penny whistles, and fell in behind the piper. Girls lifted their heads. Babies howled lustily. Mothers, wishing to scold and weep and grieve sorely enough to satisfy even Mr. Grahamstone, were surprised into laughter. Few in that march were immune. Even the two policemen who had been sent to ensure safe passage across busy streets turned jolly; one of them, with four children of his own, took a little girl by the hand. Fathers, such as Isaac McShelvie, who had got permission to come out of the adjacent works to wave their families farewell, walked along the pavements for a minute or two longer than they should, shouting cheerily, and even running among the marchers to pick up their children for a last hug. Roger Aitchison every ten seconds gave his own peculiar salute, like a walrus's flip. He wore no waistcoat, for the man who had given him the suit had once spewed on it. Guardian of the proletariats' dignity, Roger could not like the others round him shout hoarse foolish encouragements to his wife and children; but he kept flipping, and once, when Gary escaped from his mother's clutches by biting her finger, he dragged his other hand out of his pocket with the abandon of one daring all for love, and tickled the infant's sticky chin.

Despite the piping, the hilarity, and the boomeranging of family jokes, Mr. Grahamstone persisted in walking as if behind a hearse: it was not perversity, but duty. Jollification was light in head as well as in heart. Unless someone lent the ballast of solemnity, panic might at any moment scatter the whole expedition like autumn leaves, or sink it like a top-heavy ship. He was gratified to see that one or two of the profounder spirits agreed with him. Miss Oldswan, reverent in black coat and white hair, chided gently but unremittingly. Miss Cairncross, terror of diminutive delinquents, towered there among them like an Amazon paying stern penance for the many warriors she had slain. Mr. Scoullar wore an expression that caused even Mr. Grahamstone who approved of it to look unguardedly for the Bible under his oxter: it was an authentic going-to-Communion expression. One or two mothers assisted, particularly Mrs. Aldersyde, whose alliance he did not alto-gether welcome, seeing she had once, by a kind of magic he could never appreciate, produced from behind his door a genuine sergeant of police, and proceeded in the presence of that notebooked potentate to charge him with assault. All he had done was to strap her six-year-old son, Gordon, for deliberately jabbing a sharp pencil into Miss Calder's thigh.

The matter had not been easy to smooth over: the sergeant had been officious and unhelpful, Mrs. Aldersyde had shrieked, and Miss Calder had refused to show the wound. Such crises of course were common in a headmaster's life, and that one had by no means been the worst; but still, he had afterwards been unable to regard Mrs. Aldersyde as one of his favourite parents, although it was indisputable that, from the point of view of cleanliness and dress, her children were a credit to the school. Now he saw her in the procession, clasping her twins' hands, and weeping in a melancholy that was, if anything, a shade too desperate. She was, besides, not a bonny-faced woman, so that laughter perhaps would have become her more than these heart-broken grimaces. Her hat had been knocked askew in the crush, so that, as he heard one of her neighbours remark, in sardonic pity, she looked either drunk or saved.

Mrs. McShelvie did not walk beside her own children. Effie and Jean had wanted to, in tears, but she had put them in Sammy's charge; Tom, as usual, had stravaiged with his pals. She carried Mrs. Ross's Billy, while Mrs. Ross herself carried Moira, aged six weeks. Billy was a lively armful. With his little fists punching at her face and pulling at her hair, she still had leisure to notice Isaac's thinness, and to remember how that very morning, when everybody might have been expected to show kindness even to enemies, Flo had been impudent to him, and he, impelled by love to rebuke her, had only advertised his weakness and his proper role of resignation. Alone in the house they would quarrel thus every night and morning. Flo, aware she was breaking a commandment, learned in Sunday school but written on her heart in the womb, would grow still bitterer in her unacknowledged penitence; and Isaac, who would not strike her if she were to claw his eyes out of his head, would in this era of universal retaliation find himself more and more despised. If she stayed at home she might prevent this degradation in her home. No soldier in war, running from death, would be a greater coward than she. That he would be seeking to save his life, and she to revive her belief in life's loveliness, would be unacceptable as excuses or extenuations. She would be punished; but if the fields and

45

hills of Langrigg resurrected her as she hoped, she might be able to endure that punishment, whatever it might be, and still have faith enough left to return home, sustain Isaac, reclaim Flo, and so win the war for her own family.

A mascot attached itself to the procession. Down a side street came limping a thin black terrier to gaze in astonishment at this noisy but benevolent multitude. Finding no stones flung, no jugfuls of water, no pans of ashes, no curses, it ran into the street, was trampled on accidentally, yelped its appreciation of the apologies and pats, and trotted along behind the piper, now and then raising its eyes to the silvery balloons and uttering an ululation that, better than the music, expressed the true feelings of many in that long procession.

There were many onlookers, and none was neutral. Shop-keepers, who saw customers with bills unpaid thus candidly absconding, nevertheless waved bon voyage. Bus and tram drivers, forced to halt, neither hooted nor clanged: they did not care that minutes were lost, schedules disarranged, and inspectors displeased; they waited in a fabulous patience, and smiled. Inside one tram a man on the way to an appointment for which he was already late forgave those delayers. Everybody waved: known curmudgeons who had reported many of the boys for football in street or squibs in keyholes; mourners with the bills still to pay; misers who at Hallowe'en gave to the guisers fists for apples and knuckles for nuts; a daftie often baited by the callousness of children; a street bookie chased yesterday by the police over midden cans, through railings, and under washings; a street cleaner who knew that that many-headed serpent would leave behind it an excrement of apple stumps, sweetie papers, orange peel, paper pokes, and likely a dummy-teat or two: all those found their right arms raised in cordial salute, although there were some whose faces still wore their customary misanthropic scowls.

The marchers waved back, with interest. Boys bore no ill-will to old wives who last Christmas had salted their slides; mothers forgave shopkeepers to whom they were in debt. Meg Aitchison towards Cheesy Jamieson the grocer made a friendly fingers-at-the-nose gesture. At least ten times in the past year had she sent to him for food on tick, with notes as desperate as any carried by wounded siege-breaker from a starving garrison; ten times had the answer come back with a huge SORRY that lacked all compunction. He had condemned her family to hunger. Yet that bright morning she forgave him, and even found herself loving his inhospitable shop: the red paint below the window scuffed by the girls' feet as they played at guesses, the name above in faded blue, the tins in the window, the coloured packets, the big artificial cheese that had given him his nickname, and even the dead bluebottles; she loved them all, for they were familiar, she had seen them every day, they were home.

VII

Since it was a district station with a small narrow platform, only those travelling in the special train were allowed through the gate. These were recognised by their gasmasks and the labels round their necks. Most endured the exclusion bravely, but Mrs. Aldersyde almost went mad. Her children's hands had to be wrested out of hers, for she was causing an obstruction. She screamed she would write to the king about this refusal to allow her on to the platform to see her children off. Most filing past her were sympathetic, although they did not like her. Meg Aitchison was one; nor did Meg's sympathy turn to rage when it was furiously flung back at her like, so Meg remarked to the woman next to her, with a grim cackle, "fishes' heids". Naturally the woman did not quite understand, since it was a private Aitchison allusion.

The platform was crammed. It was even worse, muttered a porter, than on a Cup Final day, with the Rangers one of the finalists. The football crowd had bottles at mouths; this went one better: at least one woman gave her baby the breast. Others gathered round to conceal her, but he saw, and remembered, and told his wife that night once, twice, three times, and was snubbed at the fourth. A woman giving her baby the breast, his wife cried, was a common enough sight, it wasn't a freak, for God's sake. In a way he saw that, but in another way, which he couldn't explain, the sight was rare and marvellous. Indeed, that porter, before the war was won, was to visit Africa, Italy, and Germany, and was to look on death, mutilation, and ruin; but always, astonishing him, and strangely reassuring him, would recur that vision of the Gowburgh woman, screened by other Gowburgh women, suckling her baby on his platform.

At one end the platform grew narrower and disappeared into a dim tunnel. Mr. Grahamstone had proved on paper that it should not be necessary for any of his contingent to wait in that section inside the tunnel, where it would be a heaven-sent opportunity for some scoundrel of a boy to fall on to the line and be mangled by a train. But people were greedy and ambitious: it was not only in Germany that *Lebensraum* was demanded; here on this humble platform they insisted on having room to breathe and move their arms and avoid trampling on their toddlers. Hence it became necessary for some to be pushed into the tunnel. Among these were the Baxter brothers.

They had been behaving themselves, despite the scope for enterprise. They had promised Roy, and besides each was wearing a new pair of trousers and carried under his arm a parcel containing (through holes in the paper they had investi-gated) pyjamas, a shirt, underwear, a comb, a toothbrush, and a tin of toothpaste. These acquisitions subdued them: fortune's happy blows can be as stunning as its bitter ones. Therefore they stood, suffering themselves to be pushed and squeezed without punch or kick of protest. Their hands indeed were prisoners in their pockets, so that when Willie's nose grew itchy and he wished to scratch it, he had to free his left hand. Force was needed, and perhaps a little temper. It came loose at last, but before his nails reached his nose his elbow had banged against Bella Crail's parcel, skiting it out of her grasp down on to the track, where it fell across a rail.

Simultaneously with Bella's scream of dudgeon, and the yells of women who had seen that deliberate rascality with their own eyes, came the whistle and rumble of an engine approaching through the tunnel. Along rushed the headmaster,

48

like a sheepdog irascible with fidelity, to chase them all back from the brink, to bite if need be. He was in time to see what he could not believe, for nowhere, certainly not among the hundred regulations in his briefcase, was permission ever granted for such a deed. Willie Baxter, still with his own parcel tucked under his arm, jumped down on to the track, lifted Bella's, threw it up, and helped by his brother clambered back up. All the time the roaring in the tunnel increased; the platform shook; babies and infants shrieked; women shouted; girls sobbed; boys cheered; and Mr. Grahamstone's incredulity rushed through his head, as if it too was a tunnel for thundering locomotives.

Then the engine's arrival obliterated all other sounds. The headmaster shut his eyes and saw dozens of children being devoured by the smoky ogre as it passed; one, though, it rejected as too indigestible even for its iron belly. Yet when it was gone and the smoke cleared, he could not see Willie Baxter, although no other child seemed to be missing. Bella Crail hugged her parcel and wept. Babies still howled. Mothers, distracted, blamed this too on Willie Baxter. He ought not to be allowed to go with harmless people. Mr. Grahamstone agreed, but the boy had had an official form filled up and signed on his behalf, he wore an official label round his neck, and his name appeared on the official list. To leave him behind might satisfy God's justice, but not authority's. Roy of course was chiefly to blame. His place might be in a tank or an aeroplane, it certainly wasn't at a teacher's desk; he lacked the discretion for that.

When all eyes were shut as the engine rushed past, Willie had escaped, whispering to Tom that it would be better for them to separate for a while. He noticed Roy, but avoided him. He also noticed Mrs. Aldersyde; she interested him. She was clutching the iron bars of the gate as if, like Tarzan, she was going to pull them apart. Her cries too were reminiscent of Tarzan's summoning of his apes. Willie nodded in approval; he did not know what she was yowling for, but she was shocking the ordinary folk around her, and that was good enough for him.

49

He slipped into the gents'. This was a small green iron box attached to the waiting-room. It was not empty, as he wished. Each of its three places was being legitimately used by a boy. Under the water tap in a smelly corner hung another boy's head, with the tongue out; another boy waited by for a drink. There were also three waiting with their buttons already loosened. Still another was banging in a peculiar agitation at the lock of the W.C.; it seemed he had put in a penny, but the door was jammed. Finally, Gordon Aldersyde stood in the midst, wearing his kilt and chewing. He did not seem to be in any queue; his purpose, indeed, was simply to keep out of his mother's sight.

Willie wished to smoke a fragment of a fag he had found, and also to ponder for the last time whether he ought to go with this rabble of women and weans and jessies. Quiet meditative smoking, especially with a cigarette an inch long, required solitude and space.

"Get to hell oot o' it," he announced, and grabbing the biggest by the neck of his jacket, threw him out.

The rest objected. One, who danced from one foot to the other, pleaded. The banger on the jammed door seemed not to hear the order, being under the stress of a greater tyranny. Gordon remarked coolly that the place wasn't private. The boy waiting for a drink snatched one so quickly he rattled his teeth against the tap.

Inside a minute Willie was alone. He knew those ejected would warn anybody else intending to enter. Carefully choosing a dry spot on the wall he struck his only match and lit his fagend. Three puffs later he was interrupted.

Roy entered. Instinctively Willie moved aside to allow the teacher to do what he supposed even teachers did; but his left ear was seized, twisted, and so sadistically pinched that he had to open his mouth wide, with the result that his fag dropped out. His ear was then released.

"Is this the way you keep a promise?" asked Roy. "First you throw Bella Crail's parcel on to the track, and then you kick half a dozen boys out of here, where, I may say, they've a better right to be than you."

Meekness was best when one was at least half innocent.

"It was an accident aboot Bella's parcel," said Willie. "She got it back," he added, meekly contemptuous.

Roy stopped a grin. "I understand, like a damn fool you nearly got yourself killed."

Willie glanced down at his crushed and sodden fag-end, and obviously grieved more over its loss than repented of his foolhardiness.

"If I may say so," said Roy, "to risk your life for a toothbrush and a spare pair of drawers was a bloody stupid thing to do."

Willie frowned, indicating in his opinion a teacher ought not to use such language, unless of course he allowed others to use it.

"For God's sake, let's get out of here," said Roy. "It's not the sweetest place for a chat."

"It's quiet, sir."

"Only because you've got a 'No Trespassers' notice outside. Come on."

As Willie went out, he couldn't help looking for that notice; he grinned when he couldn't see it, for of course it was there all right. Several boys waited to get in; one or two had fetched their mothers. Seeing Willie, the latter flyted him: one accused him of being a Hitler; another demanded if he wished to give her son bladder trouble.

"Apologise," ordered Roy.

"Sorry," he muttered.

"You'll be hanged," said a woman, "and that's our only consolation." Roy marched him off to look for Tom.

"Tom and you are going to travel in the same compartment as me," he said.

"That'll be nice, sir."

Roy smiled. "We'll sit and look out at the nice green fields."

"Yes, sir."

"With the nice cows in them."

"Yes, sir."

"And horses. And trees."

"Yes, sir."

51

"And maybe some bunny rabbits."

"Yes, sir. Please, sir?"

"Well?"

"Can we sing?"

Roy had to turn away to hide his smile. "All right, Willie, we can sing."

"Good."

Roy could not withhold his admiration.

"Not only can we sing, Willie," he said, "but I think we've got something to sing for."

Willie nodded, as if never for a moment had he doubted it.

PART TWO

I

IT was not the first time the people of Langrigg had made
ready to receive invaders. Almost two thousand years ago
they had skulked in their hills and woods to watch the Roman
legionaries burn down their huts of clay and wattle. No doubt
when darkness fell they had sneaked down for a rash and impudent blow at the masters of the world. Later came the English
on their revengeful incursions: in a fit of imperial pique during
their retreat from Bannockburn they had destroyed the Abbey.
The Abbot, a Langrigg man, had ordered the bells to be rung
in rejoicing at the rout and departure of the would-be con-
querors; some of the latter had heard. The ruin ever afterwards
was more venerated than the later cosy churches with their roofs
intact: it symbolised Langrigg's noblest defiance and starkest
faith. The town's motto, indeed, was: "Gang wi' God's Grace."

On this fine day at the beginning of September, 1939, as the
leading men of Langrigg waited in the little railway station to
deal with this latest invasion, their task was more difficult
because more complicated, than any their predecessors had
faced. If an invader was foreign and came with weapons, driving him back might be bloody and dangerous; but to do it was
a clear duty, sanctioned by God, applauded in churches, and
practised universally, even among the aborigines of Australia,
those most backward of men. On the other hand, if the invaders were native, and came with uncouth but recognisable
tongues, possible dirt, probable vermin, indisputable noise, and
government permits, the problem of reception could not be so
instinctively solved.

There was no precedent, as Councillor Michaelson had so cautiously whispered at least a dozen times during the special meetings to devise a campaign. Never in the history of the country, despite its innumerable wars, had hospitality towards victims or refugees been made a duty. It was, he humbly suggested, a disruption of nature thus to enforce what ought to be allowed to rise up spontaneously out of the heart, like a spring of purest water on Brack Fell, that part of Langrigg territory nearest to heaven.

Mr. Mair-Wilson, though not a councillor, had been co-opted during those meetings for several reasons. He was rich, his house was as large as a castle, he was irresponsibly generous, and though he could not be expected to billet the whole eight hundred, every one he did take in would be one delivered from some unco-operative ratepayer, upon whom otherwise the dreadful and unnatural power of compulsion might have to be used. In appearance Mr. Mair-Wilson was more like a jockey gone to fat than a plutocrat; and indeed he had rushed to contradict Michaelson, as if on a white charger. "Did patriotism," he cried, in his squeaky voice, "in a country that had produced a Wallace, require a precedent? The children who were coming for shelter to Langrigg had fathers who pretty soon might be dying to save the homes of Langrigg. Was it not as simple as tit-for-tat?"

Of course it was not just so simple, and several, each with his or her own peculiar kind of tact, best suited for reasoning with a man worth half a million, had tried to explain it to him. Softly, humorously, twittingly, twinklingly, regretfully, they had given the following, and other reasons. Not everybody, they pointed out, had a house so large that a dozen riotous boys could be accommodated without their host ever hearing or seeing them. Also, it was likely enough that many of those children had fathers who earned three or four pounds per week, and who would indignantly repudiate this bargain of tit-for-tat with the director of an oil company. Furthermore, Langrigg had only one school, and as it would have to be shared with the incomers, this would mean that the local children would have to go on part-time instruction, which particularly disquieted those councillors whose hobby was education. Besides, many housewives in the town and landward area were too frail-fingered and silver-haired to become foster mothers overnight: what servants they had would soon migrate to munition work as less harassing and more profitable. In addition, the question of compensation for damage done to private property by these public protégés was still obscure. The treasure of the nation would be poured out on aeroplanes, guns, tanks, and battleships; a broken window, an uprooted rosebush, a kicked dog, an escaped canary, or a soiled carpet, would be considered, on a national scale, trivial; whereas, on the domestic, they would be of enormous consequence.

Mr. Mair Wilson's retort had been brief, rude, and, for a Croesus, logical enough. "Damned tommy-rot," he had cried. "Where there's a will there's a way."

But on that sunny afternoon, after weeks of anxious reconnaissance, the way was still not clearly seen. Nobody was traitor enough to say so. Everybody as he walked up and down the platform admiring its roses still beautiful so late in the season, agreed with each colleague he passed that it was a blessing the day was dry, that rain would have been calamitous, that the town was looking its best with the touch of autumn in the leaves, that the rest was up to them, and that surely their organisation was foolproof. In the town hall several ladies under the guidance of the Provost's wife were ready to serve tea and biscuits. In the school other citizens, responsible, representative, and capable, not likely to let Alden the town clerk's dubious leadership affect them, were waiting with the list of volunteered accommodation and the billeting forms. The way therefore should have been as clear and as exalting as the passage of those curlews across the adjacent wine-red moors, or as familiar and heart-warming as that of the bumble-bees buzzing from one rose to another. The foundation of intelligent planning, on the bedrock of goodwill, should withstand any human shock. There might be a breach here and there, for of all materials young humanity was the least inert and the most explosive; but there seemed no mortal reason why by nightfall every child should not be as snug in his allotted bed as bird in

55

heather or bee in grass. Fate, though, on which they were mounted, was not a steed to be wholly trusted: it would not be the first time a brave and honourable man, sword in hand, had been galloped off the battlefield against his will. Had it not happened to Bloody Clavers himself at Shrike Stone, two miles away, during a skirmish against some Covenanters? Therefore behind every rosy face on the platform, with one exception, lurked this private canker of apprehension.

The exception was not Provost Reik, despite his mild white beard and his aura of genteel judicial uncommittedness. Now retired from his profession as lawyer, he still kept on his post as factor to the Earl of Rollo, who owned much of Langrigg and the surrounding countryside, including Brack Fell and other mountains. Like the rest of his colleagues, the Provost had been warned by his wife, in the secrecy of their bedroom, to pick out two small, amenable, clean, and if possible well-favoured little girls as his quota. Once or twice it occurred to him, not hostilely, but rather as a bee visits a flower or a curlew an upland field, that as Provost he ought perhaps to show an example of self-denial and humanitarianism by choosing the dirtiest, rowdiest, and least lovable of these guests whom war was thrusting into his chaste childless home.

Nor was Major Orinshaw the man free of doubt. Worry, he believed, was necessary; but it must be controlled. Tall, thin, lame, with a bushy grey moustache and a perpetually conscientious yet homeless expression, he felt then, as he had felt all along, that the whole manoeuvre under the generalship of Alden, the town clerk, must fail. Alden had never had shrapnel in his leg; he had never heaved men over in the mud to hide their grins of death; he had a moustache womanly in its delicacy and fragrance; and above all he had been given the post as commander simply because he was town clerk, not because of his proved valour and skill in organisation. To lead these children into bliss and safety in a town shrinking from their approach would need as much finesse and gallantry as to lead exhausted soldiers across no-man's-land to seize trenches savagely held by the Hun. With no experience of the one, how could Alden succeed in the other?

The Reverend John Galway Mackdoe, though a full inch short of five feet, was at all times, in pyjamas or in robes of office, a monument of self-reliance. Unlike his colleague the Reverend Henry Maybright Sandeman of the newer, handsomer, and much more lucrative West Kirk, Mr. Mackdoe always in public wore clerical clothes; and as his chunky chin was dark with untameable hirsuteness his very smiles were of ministerial sobriety. Firm in everything and especially in impartiality, he resolutely considered himself a better Christian and a more convincing preacher than the young soft-voiced intellectual tall Sandeman, whom everybody knew had been promoted far beyond his merits in the councils of church and town, because of his wife's family's wealth. Envy and covetousness being impermissible, Mr. Mackdoe always greeted his colleague and spoke of him with punctilious cordiality. To his own wife Sarah, however, who had brought him piety only, two doting ears, and recently a son, he frequently and fairly recounted his rival's failings and fortunateness. Now this sunny afternoon from the platform of the station he could see the spire of the West Kirk soaring above the trees; and though it was truly magnificent, fashioned after that of St. Giles in Edinburgh, the sight paradoxically saddened him and subtracted substantially from his faith that these poor children, refugees from the pagan city, would be welcomed here in a dynamically Christian spirit. Would Mrs. Sandeman, for instance, in her opulent manse, suffer any to go unto her?

Not the Provost then, nor the Major, nor the Minister, was the man without misgivings. This blithe soul was Bailie Rouster. In light-grey linen suit with a yellow rose in his buttonhole, and with a Panama hat hiding his peaked baldness, he stalked up and down laughing confidently at the confidence within him. Having spent many years in accumulating his massive unawareness, he could hardly notice then that his laughter was frowned on as inane and even ominous. With his own small ones glaucous with conceit, he peered into colleagues' eyes, as if seeking the mote of misgiving, and shouted in his jolly fatuous voice that he hoped nobody would forget he had been elected to lead the procession from the station to the town hall, and thence to the school. Thus he would be, he pointed out joyously, foster-father to them all. All agreed, for none had wished the honour, and all wanted to ask him if his being foster-father meant that his wife would be foster-mother. No one dared, however: conversation with the Bailie could so soon become a maelstrom of furious inconsequentialities; and besides, his wife, for all her lavender, her white and lilac feathers, her golden adornments, and her smile, was a Medusa, potent even in absence. Therefore everyone nodded, and urged the Bailie on to his next victim; he went as willingly as small boy to ice-cream barrow.

These four then, and some others, each wearing the white armband of authority, waited on the platform. Outside the white fence were gathered a few housewives anxious to see what conundrums they were to take into their homes, and also many Langrigg children who, though never consulted and now relegated to such obscure positions as the branches of tall elm trees, would nevertheless be the true hosts of the incomers. It was, for instance, a boy in a tree who first caught sight of the train as it sneaked round Harlaw Wood and crept across Martyrs' Moss, like a long caterpillar caricatured by its own white steam above it. He announced it, in a trumpet shout, and all those on the ground rose on their toes and stretched their necks to see. They heard at least; for the engine-driver, loyal to his peculiar freight, blew his whistle once, twice, three challenging times, as though to cry: Look out, Langrigg, here we come, bewildered by your hills and green spaces and silences, terrified by your remoteness from our homes, weeping many of us, pale-faced most, hungry, thirsty, homesick already, but with our celebrated Gowburgh indomitableness, by some miscalled impudence and vulgarity, sustaining us now and forever!

Over the river rattled the train, and before the potentates on the platform could perform the secular equivalent of crossing themselves, into the station it rushed, impetuously, as if it had changed its mind and was not going to stop. Alas, it jested. One minute those small intense Gowburgh faces were glowering out of the windows, next they were on the platform, as numerous as the wild hyacinths in Harlaw Wood in May, but not so sweet or beautiful or so contented to stand still. Major Orinshaw was instantly vindicated. Alden's organisation collapsed at the first onset. These children, so easy to manage as symbols on paper, became as bawling complainants quite unmanageable. No one had commanded them to sit quietly in their compartments and disembark in orderly instalments. Out they spewed, with fierce shouts of relief at the freshness of the air and its spaciousness. The latter, though, lasted only for seconds; then the platform became insufferably crowded. That there was still, upwards to the blue sky, illimitable room, merely exacerbated the situation.

The Langrigg officials were submerged. Provost Reik had placed himself in the centre, intending to meet Mr. Grahamstone the headmaster there, shake hands with him and bid him welcome, with an absence of palaver characteristic of Scotsmen, and perhaps reminiscent a little of Livingstone and Stanley in equatorial Africa. Indeed, as the train stopped, he had his hand ready for the shaking and the quiet sincere words on his lips. Within a minute more hands than there were hairs in his beard seemed to be clutching at him: fat shiny wedding-ringed hands, babies' hands like crumpled butterflies, boys' tight and sticky with truculence, girls' pink and flaccid; some hands even bearing flags. He could never have shaken them all physically; nor, when he saw at such close quarters the faces accompanying them, could he do so spiritually. The coarseness of the Gowburgh poor, as proverbial as the thriftiness of Aberdonians, was then no legend. So violent a concentration of it there, on the threshold of his refined Langrigg, overwhelmed him. Though he kept smiling, as leaders must though doom is imminent, inwardly was a wail of disillusionment and foreboding. The council's protests ought to have been more insistent. In a stunning apocalypse he remembered all the stories whispered in the past weeks about the Gowburgh tenements, where the privies were shared by all and so kept clean by none; about the profanity used by mothers to their babies, and that returned; about razor-slashing thievery, bottle-throwing debauchery, football rioting, violence and filth. Was his town, renowned for its sobriety, cleanliness, and tone, to be flooded by such abominations diluted, so slightly it seemed, by age and sex?

Major Orinshaw at first kept roaring for order; but even as he did so he saw that those still within the train were struggling to get out, were indeed frantic at not being able to join in the general suffocation. It was the authentic hysteria of war, and for a moment, with pain intense in his leg, he thought he heard German bombers roar from the direction of Brack Fell. The moment after he gave in, and devoted what little energy he had to protect his wounded leg. He was a done man all right, he confessed bitterly in that yelling throng: the War Office, in rejecting his services, had after all been moved by wisdom rather than ingratitude. He ought to go home and look to the stakes supporting his chrysanthemums.

The Major, though done, was tall; Mr. Mackdoe, far from done, was tiny. Later that bombastic diminutiveness, so typical of Gowburgh's poorer streets as well as of its famous regiment, was to endear him to those Gowburgh women, some of whose husbands were no bigger and no more diffident; but then nothing of him was noticed, neither his stature, his collar, his armband, nor the struggle between his Christian forbearance and his human indignation at being so ruthlessly jostled and trampled on.

In the midst floated Bailie Rouster's Panama hat. Under it he was panic-stricken, for in such confusion the trek might start without him. In his anxiety to break out and see what was happening he was less chivalrous than he ought, with the result he got buffets in return from at least two outraged mothers carrying squashed babies.

Thus for nearly five minutes the platform was jammed from railings to train with howling, shoving, weeping, cursing, cheering, laughing, women and children. Some were scratched with the thorns of rosebushes, others were pushed headlong into the tiny waiting-room, and three women with infant girls in their arms found themselves, to their everlasting indignation, in the gents' lavatory.

Outside the station the Langrigg children kept cheering. They knew everything had been arranged by their elders, and saw no reason to believe this furious congestion and pandemonium were not according to the programme; indeed, it was such an arrival as they themselves would have planned, with noise, excitement, comedy, temper, and passion. The Langrigg housewives, on the other hand, after the first shock, began to murmur among themselves that surely there were more people on the platform than there ought to be: some of the babies might be hurt; it was, they said, a shame.

The Provost found himself given space by a vigorous young man whose very tie seemed angry. However, he felt grateful at being rescued. "Thank you," he tried to murmur.

"For God's sake," roared his rescuer, "what fool's in charge here?"

Before the Provost could reply, if indeed reply was possible to such blasphemous rudeness, Roy again bellowed: "Aren't there any gates out of this place?"

The Provost lost his temper. "Of course," he shouted back, "but they are being kept locked."

"Why? For God's sake, why?"

"I'll tell you. Because no one is being allowed off this platform until he or she has been properly medically examined and given a clean bill of health." The Provost's voice grew shriller as it asserted a position the council was unanimously pledged to maintain. "That is why, young man. We feel we have a duty to our own people."

"But didn't somebody tell you these people have already been medically examined?"

"By your own authorities in Gowburgh, yes. We in Langrigg like to satisfy ourselves. You must allow us that privilege. My nephew who is a final-year medical student, and his friend, are waiting. The sooner we begin the better. You should not have let them come out of their compartments in the way they did. You are not Mr. Grahamstone?"

In the circumstances it could not have been a satisfactory conversation. For one thing, many people wished to take part in it. One of these, Meg Aitchison, went so far as to advise Roy, in a termagant shriek, to "tak' him by his billy-goat beard and throw him ower the engine." She was exasperated at the time by having her tenderest corns trodden on, and by having

61

her hair tugged by Gary who, in addition, had wet himself in the squeeze.

There was only one thing to do, decided Roy: get the people back into the train, and then allow these pettifoggers of Langrigg to demonstrate their inefficiency properly. He calculated that even the most perfunctory medical examination of every woman and child would last till the moon was full. But the command to return into the train might be interpreted as retreat; those with spirit would object; those wishing to comply might be prevented by those objecting; and homesick children, thinking they were being sent home again, would suffer a damaging disappointment. Others more enterprising, like the Baxter brothers, might at any moment decide to escape by the other side of the train.

War, thought Roy, was simpler when it was just a matter of killing enemies.

Then he saw the red but curiously contented face of Grahamstone approaching. At the same time he noticed that a woman—he recognised her as Mrs. McShelvie—had begun to shovel boys and girls back into the train. Leaving the headmaster and the Provost to introduce themselves he hurried to help her.

Ten minutes later the platform was again clear, except for the Langrigg officials and the Gowburgh teachers. Out of every window in the train hung three heads, most of them silently inquisitive, but some loud with scurrilous and pertinent complaint.

Mr. Grahamstone felt so much at home in that atmosphere of uncertainty and precariousness that he even offered advice with a dash of daring in it. Was it, he asked, worth sickening the whole contingent just for a handful of nits or a few scabs? When the Provost, supported by Mr. Mackdoe, obstinately demurred, the headmaster was so pleased he wanted passionately to congratulate them on their want of initiative: all his life he had been bedevilled by it, now he was comforted to find the dignitaries of this handsome town fellow-sufferers. Theirs too was the present responsibility. His job was well done; he had brought his people without one having fallen from the train or fainted on the cushions. His calm smugness disgusted Campbelton, himself calm with the iciness of contempt; it surprised Scoullar, who looked for one or two righteous expostulations; and it amused Roy.

Mrs. McShelvie earlier had reproved him.

"You're no' enjoying this collieshangie, are you, Mr. Roy?" she had asked.

"I always enjoy the antics of my superiors, Mrs. McShelvie. I can't help it."

"What if they're in uniform?"

He just grinned.

"Will you laugh then?"

He had gone off, grinning, but inwardly damning her shrewd impertinence.

It was he, all the same, who got the inspection started. He showed them all his wrist-watch. They frowned at it as if it was the first critical scab.

"I'll time the examinations," he said.

Langrigg rallied together to combat such alien insolence.

"I hardly think that's necessary," said the Provost.

"By no means," cried Mr. Mackdoe, rising on his toes.

"If it must be done," muttered Major Orinshaw, "time doesn't matter." As he spoke he was remembering occasions of war when time had been very precious: a good friend of his had been killed because of a few lost seconds.

Bailie Rouster was relieved. If the visitors were to be allowed out in twos, it was impossible that a procession could form and set off without his noticing it.

Campbelton stepped forward.

"I do not wish to be offensive, gentlemen," he said, using his loftiest and most patrician tone, "but I must in honesty give it my opinion, as Mr. Grahamstone's second master, that this medical examination is unauthorised, supererogatory, inhuman, reactionary, and idiotic."

He paused, evidently not pleased with his choice of epithets.

Two or three of the women teachers murmured qualified approval.

"Surely," said Miss Oldswan, "now that we are here, we must proceed?"

63

"Suppose," said Grahamstone, as one baffled commander to another, "you do find a dirty head, what will you do?"

"Exclude, I'm afraid," answered the Provost promptly.

"Do you mean," pressed Grahamstone, "that head will be sent back?"

"Unfortunately, yes."

"But," cried Grahamstone, in triumph, "there's no provision for that. I doubt if it's legal."

"I am a lawyer, sir. But legality aside, it is certainly not ethical to demand that a decent housewife, with children of her own, should take into her home a child with lice."

Grahamstone shook his head. "Pardon my saying so, Provost," he chuckled, "but really, you know, you're in a cleft stick."

"We shall see," said the Provost. He knew there was no law on earth, in war or peace, for the toleration of lice.

"Let us begin," he cried.

"Yes," said Mr. Mackdoe, "it may be we are discussing difficulties which will not arise."

Scoullar shook his own head at that, for he had seen several children scratching theirs.

The two students in their long white coats were nervous, willing, and affable. One sat by the small gate, the other by the large. Sheepish policemen stood on guard.

Meg Aitchison offered herself first. From the train cronies yelled bawdy facetious advice. She carried Gary, and her two other children Bella and Maggie clung to her coat. Mr. Mackdoe, ignoring witticisms about his size and imputations about his intentions, escorted her gallantly over to the examiners.

"Am I to strip to the buff?" she demanded.

All were disconcerted.

She glanced all round. "Nae X-rays? Nae soonding-tube? Nae bottles for urine? Whit is this? A fraud? I micht hae cancer."

This, realised the Provost, must be the famous Gowburgh humour. He tried to smile.

"Young woman," he said, "we are anxious to help you. Please understand that."

"Whit I understaun'," she retorted, "is that this past month's been naething but medical inspections. Whit's it a' in aid of? Has somebody made the discovery we're valuable? Or is it juist a new game to please the weans? All right, I'll play. Bella, let the man look at your heid if he wants to." She dumped Gary down upon the table, where he howled and damped the documents. "Here you are. Finding's keepings."

Demoralised by her sudden laughter, the student poked a finger into Gary's hair as if into a wasp's byke, while his colleague likewise searched Bella's. Meg watched, as if to detect cheating. The Provost plucked at his beard. Sarcasms volleyed from the train. Grahamstone, with sandboy's relish, watched these other people's muddle rear higher and higher, with downfall inevitable. Campbelton, far along the platform, was sniffing at roses. Roy kept his eyes on his watch. Scoullar thought of his own wife and child far away.

Gary's student whistled in relief, but Bella's groaned in dismay. He beckoned the Provost, who went to him accompanied by Mr. Mackdoe.

Meg waited, obviously withholding her fire till she could see the lies upon their lips.

"We're deeply sorry, madam," said the Provost, "but your little girl cannot be admitted."

"Juist tell me why."

"She has nits," he whispered, softly, so as not to shame her in public.

"Then I don't ken whaur the hell she got them," she shrieked. "She had nane when she left Gowburgh this morning. Look at them again. Are you sure they havenae got the Langrigg trademark on them? Christ kens, we've been here only a wheen o' minutes, and we've already caught the black scunner. Why no' nits?"

Major Orinshaw the soldier approached the lawyer and the minister.

"This won't do," he whispered. "We cannot admit the mother and reject the child."

"No, we must reject the entire family," said the Provost.

Mr. Mackdoe shivered: was such justice really Christian?

"If Gowburgh's bombed tonight," went on the Major, "as it well might be, on whose heads would be their deaths?"

"I fail to see the usefulness of such a speculation, Major," murmured the Provost.

"Wherever we are we are in God's care," said Mr. Mackdoe, but somehow it sounded even to him cold counsel.

"I may say, Major," said the Provost, lowering his voice, "there are lice as well."

"I have seen a colonel burn out the lice from the seams of his shirt," said the Major.

Orinshaw's military reminiscences, whether false or merely exaggerated, were without doubt tedious and repetitive. Usually the Provost was a sturdy listener. Here, however, he fluttered his beard at such imbecile irrelevance.

"We cannot do it," said the Major. "We must open those gates and let them all through. It is our duty. Why not give them a chance here in Langrigg to get rid of such things as nits? I mean, if we can save them from bombs, why not from nits?"

Mr. Mackdoe, whose wife was forty-three, had been presented with a son a year or so ago. Paternity so unexpected had extended his vision. Now he saw that the simple Major's proposal was revolutionary in the Christian sense of that suspected word.

"Oh, I agree," he cried. "We must admit them all."

To the Provost this was treachery. The decision to exclude for lice had been taken by the council, and ought to be honoured. As he hesitated, Roy stepped forward with the flamboyance of a herald.

"It has now taken seven and a half minutes," he announced, "to handle this first case, and it is not yet cleared. For the sake of quick arithmetic, let us say there are eight hundred persons to be examined. Seven and a half multiplied by eight hundred comes to, I believe, six thousand minutes, or one hundred hours, or four days four hours. This is 1.30 p.m. Saturday. The last person should be through the gate by 5.30 p.m. on Wednesday, if we keep to schedule."

One man was impressed by that fantastic calculation. Chortling at his own foolishness, Bailie Rouster imagined under the trees outside the station tents like giant mushrooms. Would it be in order for him to go home, and return after tea on Wednesday, to do what he had covenanted to do, what certainly ought to be done in hospitality's name, and what others thought beneath their dignity, which was, to act as official host and lead the procession up the main street of the town?

The Provost rebuked Roy for unhelpful levity. Mr. Mackdoe, more charitable, appreciated the young man's mathematical quickwittedness, commendable in a schoolmaster; it might also come in useful for navigating an aeroplane.

Meg Aitchison too looked at Roy, her protector. She gave him a fond gap-toothed ogle, and compared him with her far-off Roger, who was shorter, fatter, scruffier, cannier, dirtier, but for all that, she discovered with a yelp of astonishment, dearer.

In a compartment Mrs. McShelvie was attending a young woman who had fainted. When Roy's clowning with the watch was reported to her she did not smile.

"To Mr. Roy," she murmured, "everything's just a lark: Meg's wean's dirty heid, Mrs. Baird here feeling faint. He's no' properly grown up yet; maybe he never will. I don't ken where or how he was brought up, but I'd be surprised if he'd ever had to do withoot onything he wanted. This war, if there is one, will be an entertainment, put on for his benefit.

"Yet it'll be his kind wha'll win it," she added.

The Provost was consulting his colleagues; they advised him to yield. Mr. Grahamstone's sanction was sought but not granted; neither was it denied; he merely said the matter was out of his hands. The students slunk off like stoats; the policemen stayed to help. Superintended by the teachers the evacuees began to file from the train in order and pass through the gates. Outside they were marshalled into line principally by Bailie Rouster, who was impressed by their tractability; this, however, was not caused by his air of authority, but rather by his breathtaking temerity in thinking that he, so Langriggish with his white hat and well-fed purplish face, had any jurisdiction over them so fresh from Gowburgh.

William Bruce Alden, commander-in-chief, sat in the school, at a table placed strategically near the top of the stairs, holding, by the lightest of reins, his own jovial lack of confidence. With grasshopper nonchalance his wits leapt from one aspect to another of his formidable duties. What to others was a mountain range bristling with danger seemed to him a delicious field of sunny grass. Admonitions hissed into his ears by his assistants, the billeting officers, were as puffs of scented breeze. The news of the contretemps at the station had genuinely amused him, and he had applauded the abandonment of a scheme of which he had been chief engineer. Further news of the collapse of the commissariat in the town hall had made him sigh and pout; that department had nothing to do with him, but he was sorry to hear that the visitors had not got enough to eat. The best was still to come, he implied with every dashing humorously-glum twirling of his sweet sharp moustache. Before him on the table lay the lists of accommodation volunteered. When the census of the town had been taken, it had somehow been overlooked that mothers with babies would also have to be accommodated; hence no one had offered to welcome these, and perhaps no one would. Without doubt some of the blame for this negligence was his; but blame was dull, unkind, and fruitless. Had not Authority erred in appointing him chief billeting-officer? And had it not even more splendidly blundered in choosing to send people from the slums of Gowburgh to fastidious Langrigg? He bore no one ill-will: laugh rather, he suggested with every twinkle of his small blue eyes; toast good luck in the best whisky available; become drunk slowly and humanely; forgive traducers; and afterwards sleep like a child that has said its prayers.

Beside him at the top of the stairs sat his secretary, dark-haired Miss Elsie Cheam. The whole town knew she loved him, and schemed to save him from disgrace, dismissal, and debauchery by marrying him. Almost as if she were already his wife, she saw all his blunders before he did; some she prevented, others she covered up, and others again she pretended were her own. This present one, there being no accommodation bespoken for the mothers and babies, she could do nothing about, except perhaps to hate those mothers and babies for being the cause of it. Under the table their knees kept touching. It was her way of showing sympathy. He thought his own clumsiness was responsible, and every time he apologised.

"They're coming," shouted someone.

There was a rush to the windows from which a view of the main street could be had. Alden went too, in glee. The approaching host, headed by the Bailie, reminded him of the Redskins of his boyhood being driven from their native hunting grounds by the rapacious white man. There seemed a vast disproportion between it and the skimpy lists lying on his table. It was going to be gallons in pint bottles all right, or the loaves and fishes over again. They were hungry and angry too, for the food in the town hall had been eaten before all had fed; and the lucky ones had complained that the cookies and sandwiches were stale, and the tea weak. Still, the sun was shining brightly, yonder against the blue sky soared Brack Fell, and the houses of Langrigg, peeping amongst the trees, were all capacious. Why should not human hearts too soar, be bright and big? That those hearts had more than once proved small and dark at his expense never occurred to him. He had a faith in humanity that, unlike his liqueur glass, never needed replenishing.

Beside him Michaelson, the stationer, small, bald, and secretive, pressed an insect against the pane with his thumbnail neatly, and smiled at the speck of blood.

"I shall take a boy," he murmured, "to support me in my struggle against the monstrous regiment of women."

Mr. Sandeman the minister heard, but did not smile; the quotation was borrowed from him, not from John Knox. He had once used it good-naturedly to this sinister little man who seemed to forget nothing, and never to improve what he remembered. Now it was used against him, for in his own manse matriarchy ruled. Michaelson too was married, with a wife to whom he was sacred, and two small daughters prim as priestesses.

But Mr. Sandeman had his own problems that afternoon.

69

"I intended," he murmured, "to take two—" he held up two long fingers, to give reality to his claim—"either a brother and sister, or two sisters. I was rather looking forward to having them." That was sincere; he really liked children, though he was not good at showing that liking. "So was Margaret, of course." That was not quite sincere; she looked forward not even to children of her own; why, was a bitter mystery. "Unfortunately she got a message today saying her mother was coming through from Edinburgh. She's been ill for years, you know: silence is essential."

Michaelson snickered. "What is it the good book says?" he asked. "In my manse there are many corners." He smiled as if his impertinent paraphrase was quite innocent.

Outside the Bailie, swinging his arms like a drum-major, led his army into the playground. He had long since reached the conclusion they did not deserve such leadership, what with their cat-calls and aimed cookies, but he was not the man to desert till his job was done.

"To your posts, gentlemen," cried Alden. "Remember, the procedure is simple. I find accommodation for each party. You make out the billeting slips. A runner will conduct the people to the address stated. Patience and goodwill will win us the day."

"Are you sure, William," asked Councillor Henderson, rather fretfully, "that it wouldn't speed things up a bit if you shared out those lists?"

This was the sixth time the Councillor had made that suggestion that afternoon. He was well known to have a fidgety, worrying, not too astute mind; but the town clerk knew him to be kind-hearted, and his name was down as being willing to take in to his home an entire family, as many as four, including the mother. Alden liked him, and often at council meetings tried to retrieve him from silly positions; if sometimes he implicated him deeper, afterwards they shook hands. It was a pity Henderson was a teetotaller; in the Curly Lamb they could have had many a laugh and many a weep at the big comic blundering conceited world.

"I'm afraid not, George," replied Alden gently. "It would only make for confusion."

"I'm damned if I see that," muttered Henderson; but then he knew he had been saying for months he was damned if he could see how there could be a war. It now looked as if he *was* damned.

"You go downstairs, Naismith," said Alden, "and see that nobody comes up till I give the word."

"Very good, Mr. Alden," said Naismith, though really he thought it atrocious. He was a fat public-spirited ratepayer, who had volunteered to help this afternoon. The duty of acting sentinel at the foot of the stairs had been assigned him earlier. Being an old soldier, he wouldn't question an order; but he was privately of the opinion that the swarming mob of women and kids couldn't be contained in the classrooms downstairs, and would mutiny if asked to sit outside on the concrete playground, especially when they found out that upstairs the school was empty.

"I'll do my best," he said, and went down to do what turned out to be a task harder than that of Horatius.

Downstairs the babel was terrific.

"You'd think," remarked Alden to his secretary, "old Girnie McIntyre had brought his cattle in and was whacking them with a stick, under the impression they were members of the council."

He laughed merrily at his own witty reference to the irascible farmer's funny feud with the council, but Miss Cheam's answering smile was faint. Downstairs surely were maddened bulls, judging from the squeals and tramplings. Her William, whatever his other virtues, was no toreador.

"They may," he conceded, "be a bit cramped for room. I wonder if we could risk letting some of them up here? I wanted it quiet though, to let us concentrate. What do you say?"

Before she could say anything, up the stairs rushed one of the bulls that Miss Cheam had been visualising. He was young, big, tawny-haired, rude, and red-faced; his nostrils blew wide with rage, and his fists were lifted to pound her William into unresentful sweet-smelling pulp.

Indeed, Alden rose to shake hands with this representative of the folk from Gowburgh.

"My name's Alden," he said, "the town clerk. I'm in charge here."

Roy had intended to be pugnacious and nasty; he still was, though from the first glance he liked the little town clerk.

Alden was always sorry for people in a temper.

"Sit down, and have a cigarette," he invited. "I suppose there's plenty of time. I hear there was a bit of a hold up at the station. And the buns ran out, eh?"

Roy's liking for this amiable ditherer increased, but still he roared: "Does this town specialise in stupidity?"

Alden laughed. "No more than any other town, really," he said. "All flesh is grass. But we do our best."

"Are you aware there's downstairs a riot of infuriated women and children?"

Alden plucked at his moustache. "Are there many women?" he asked, with a glance at his lists.

"Listen to them."

Alden listened. Certainly there seemed to be many. But he smiled, as he remembered somebody's mother-in-law. "Silence is not essential you know."

Roy gave the table a great angry thump that loosened Miss Cheam's teeth for the rest of the day; or so she imagined.

"You couldn't," cried Roy, "organise the giving away of bottles of whisky to thirsty Highlandmen."

Alden was almost nettled; not that he suspected a dig at his own whisky-drinking; it was simply that the happiness and friendship he found among his Curly Lamb cronies was being sneered at.

"Please remember, young man," he said, with dignity, "that this is the first time in history such an operation has ever been attempted. First times are always awkward." Here he recalled a joke told in the pub a night or two ago about honeymooners, and he just had to laugh, not for bawdiness' sake but out of gratitude for human companionship. After the bunglings and the anger and the regret came always the quiet room, with the glasses clinking and friends chuckling. "The first man to drink whisky," he said, "coughed it up again."

Upstairs then panted Naismith, pursued by Grahamstone and Campbelton.

"We'll have to let them up, Mr. Alden," gasped Naismith.

"Then why are we waiting, Robert?" cried Alden. "Let them come up."

As Naismith peched down to carry out this other dangerous mission, Grahamstone introduced himself tartly. He was no longer the calm observer of other men's folly. Several of the women had accused him of standing by and letting them be unfairly treated; they had threatened to write to the authorities in Gowburgh. In addition nobody so far had told him where his own head would lie that night. The ladies of his staff, it seemed, had gone off to scour the town for lodgings. They had been told most of the hotels and boarding-houses were full.

"Funkers," snorted the headmaster. The one word wasn't enough; he had to explain.

Alden agreed. "You will appreciate, gentlemen," he said eagerly, "that such an unofficial influx hasn't made our task here"—he patted those lists—"any easier."

Then conversation became impossible as up the stairs gushed the furious surplus. Children wailed and wept, mothers bawled, babies slept.

Alden stood up and kept bowing, not heeding the barrage of criticism, some of which was personal.

"I can appreciate their feelings," he said. "They're bound to be tired. Once they're settled down in the classrooms, they'll be fine."

"That depends," said Roy, "on how long they've got to stay settled down. I take it, they've not to sleep here?"

"Good heavens, no. Everything's fixed; well, almost everything." He laughed. "You know as well as I do, gentlemen, we are a nation that likes to leave room for strokes of genius. Rigidity's like cement; there's no poetry of motion in it." He glanced at his watch. "It's now 3.35. I think I can safely promise that every child in this building will be billeted by six."

He did not notice Miss Cheam shaking her head in warning against his fatal optimism, on which so often he whizzed along merrily as on skates, until inevitably he crashed.

In this case, however, even that mad optimism was not enough.

"Six o'clock!" howled Grahamstone. "Are you aware that these people have been on the move since before eight this morning?"

Alden nodded sadly. "But, sir," he said, "this may well be war. The whole of Europe may soon be on the move, homeless and sleepless. We must at times take the broader vision."

Campbelton had at the station taken a vow of silence in this town of lunatics. Now he broke it.

"I have heard rumours," he said, "that you were not expecting mothers with the children. However incredible that may seem, is it true?"

"True and not true," replied Alden. "Two months ago we did not expect them; two weeks ago we did. Unfortunately, it was two months ago we compiled our census of accommodation. The mistake, I believe, originated in Edinburgh. But, gentlemen, why hold post-mortems when we are all alive and kicking? The difficulty is not insurmountable. Suppose a housewife has agreed to take in four children; surely if we change her order, so to speak, to three children and their mother, she will raise no objection?"

"Are you married?" asked Grahamstone rudely.

Miss Cheam blushed; but Alden tittered, and shook his head.

"I thought not," said the headmaster, "or you wouldn't talk like that. A woman likes to be queen of her own kitchen."

"Well put, sir," chuckled the town clerk. "Oh, I appreciate that. We bachelors, you know, have our reasons. But I suggest that we commence. Here is what I propose. Fetch your people along to me in units, and I'll see where it'll be best to put them."

"Are you," asked Roy, choked with awe, "going to deal with every case yourself?"

"Ah yes. Otherwise there will be no end of confusion and duplication."

Campbelton's vow had been renewed; again he broke it.

"I thought," he said, "that Langrigg had no industries. Surely there is a flourishing trade here in bottlenecks?"

"Touché," cried Alden, delighted with such good-humour

74

in so anxious a situation. He lifted up his pen as if it was a sceptre. "Who's going to bring me my first customers?"

"Leave that to me," said Roy promptly, and hurried away.

Alden beamed at such energetic co-operation, but Grahamstone scowled: he was afraid that Roy for spite would fetch the most disreputable, least billetable specimens in the company, such as the Baxter brothers or some bristling trollop like Mrs. Aitchison.

He was wrong. When Roy returned he had with him Mrs. Raeburn. Not only was she neatly and cleanly dressed, she was also long-suffering: she would not swear though swearing was justified. Her children too were models of infantile decorum. Mr. Grahamstone felt grateful towards her.

Not so Mr. Alden. He liked her appearance, appreciated her patience and humility, noticed how bonny and free from smells her children were, and altogether recognised in her the qualities of devoted motherhood: in short, she was a credit to the human race. But, alas, were not mothers here *de trop*? He was reminded of Bethlehem, two thousand years ago.

"Here is a test case," said Roy, rather aggressively. "If you cannot billet Mrs. Raeburn, you can billet nobody. I may say that her husband is already in uniform."

Alden acknowledged that additional credential with a military salute. All the same it did not much reduce her ineligibility. He put his finger accusingly on the lists; they were to blame.

Then Miss Cheam whispered into his ear; he brightened; his forefinger, from a severe judge, turned into a gay dancer.

"Of course," he cried, "the very place. Sir Robert insisted it was all the same to him whom we sent. Not out of indifference; oh no, out of sheer kind-heartedness."

"Sir Robert?" asked Roy, in glee.

"Yes, indeed," replied Alden. "Although he's been with us only two or three years, Sir Robert has endeared himself to us all. It's a pity, poor man, he doesn't enjoy better health. Sir Robert Cargill. He was an important civil servant in London. He retired to Langrigg for health reasons. Our climate, you know, is invigorating and salubrious. His wife is gone, poor woman; but his daughter keeps house for him: a charming girl. It's a large house. Plenty of room and a most hospitable welcome for our young friend here and her children. What did you say her name was?"

"Raeburn," said Roy, still gleeful that he was honouring his promise to Dick so grandly that even that bantam would have been impressed. "The little girl is Jess. What's the baby's name, Mrs. Raeburn?"

She could hardly speak. They had to wait until she struggled out what ought to have been the pleasantest sound on her lips. "Richard," she murmured.

"I don't need names," said Alden. "That's the billeting officer's job. Just take this note along to any one of them, and he'll fill in the appropriate slips. He'll also provide a runner, who'll take the little lady along to Lammermuir, which is the name of the house."

Again Miss Cheam whispered into his ear.

"Quite right," he cried. "It's just the kind of gesture one would expect from so fine a gentleman. My secretary reminds me, gentlemen, that Sir Robert said he would send his car along for his guests. The house, you know, is on the outskirts, quite a walk carrying a baby. Elsie, would you mind telephoning from the headmaster's room? Thank you. Ah, gentlemen, you are now seeing another side to Langrigg, eh? Find your way through the maze to the heart of corn at the centre."

He laughed so blithely and confidently that the rest joined in, even Campbelton.

Mrs. Raeburn did not laugh. Two or three times she had tried to speak, but timidity had parched her mouth too much. Now she managed.

"If you please," she whispered, "I'm sorry to be a bother, but please, if you don't mind, send me to some other place."

They were all astonished.

"Don't be daft," grumbled Grahamstone. "This is a chance in a thousand. I wish it was me that was getting it. God knows where I'll be sleeping today; under a hedge likely."

"Go in my place," she offered.

"It's out of the question," he said, after a flicker of con-sideration.

"Madam," said Alden, "you'll want for nothing at Lammermuir. There's an enormous garden for the children."

"That's just it," she burst out. "The hoose is big and the gairden's enormous and he's called Sir Robert. I'm no' used to that kind of thing. I could never be comfortable there. God forgie me for saying it, but I think I wad be happier in a hovel than in sich grandeur. At ony rate, I could clean the hovel."

"I said it was large," said Alden, "but it's not a castle, you know."

"It will be to me."

Campbelton stood with his arms folded and his lips firmly closed. No one, he thought, could offer poor Mrs. Raeburn any helpful advice. In this clash of class she was the first casualty. There would be many others.

"Forby," she added, "if the gentleman's ill, it's not right to put weans into his hoose."

"We're holding everything up," muttered Grahamstone.

"I'm sorry," she said.

"You'd be in clover there," repeated Alden.

Her hand tightened on her purse. "I want to pay for everything I get."

Roy intervened; he had decided her scruples ought not to be respected. "What would your husband advise you to do?" he asked.

"I've got a mind of my ain, Mr. Roy."

"I see that, Mrs. Raeburn. But I think Dick would advise you to try this place at least. I'll give you this guarantee: if after a week you still don't like it, I'll get you a shift. How will that do? Please remember, this is an emergency."

As she swithered unhappily, looking even at her sleeping baby for counsel, Campbelton leaned forward and whispered into Roy's ear: "Is this chivalry, Edgar? Or are you using this poor body to demonstrate your own dash and initiative, contrasted with Langrigg's muddle and sloth?"

"You go to hell, Archie," Roy whispered back, but when he turned to Mrs. Raeburn for her answer he felt in him a stound of shame.

"All right," she whispered, "I'll gie it a trial. I've nae right to be keeping everybody back. There's poor Mrs. Ross; she's got five weans. Could she no' be sent to this place instead of me?"

"Mrs. Ross will be looked after too," said Roy.

Miss Cheam had returned. "The car will be in the playground in a few minutes," she said.

"Good," cried Roy. "Come on, Mrs. Raeburn. I'll carry your luggage downstairs. You'll be out of here and having a nice meal before Jess can give Sambo six kisses."

Alden looked after them in admiration.

"A handsome young fellow," he said, "with bags of go. I like go. Now, gentlemen, my next customer, please; a child for a change."

Grahamstone glanced at Campbelton.

"Will you do it, Archie?" he asked. "I'm wabbit."

"Do I look electric with vitality?"

"You're a younger man than I am."

"It is my soul and dignity that are fatigued," said Campbelton.

"It's my feet."

"Where the hell is Scoullar?"

"Downstairs somewhere."

Campbelton savagely unlinked his arms and swooped on Alden.

"Do you really expect me, sir, after my travail from dawn, to act as Charon, ferrying these unlucky children from the Charybdis of those rooms to the Scylla of this table?"

Alden laughed. "You have the advantage of me, sir," he said. "It is many years since I attended school."

Campbelton stalked away, growling like Cerberus.

III

As Roy escorted his victims along the corridor he met Mrs. McShelvie standing at one of the windows. It was a surprise to see her there alone, because every other time he had seen her

78

that day she had been in the midst of her charges, carrying out her duties of assisting and comforting them with a steadfast, effective, yet somehow satiric conscientiousness; there had been in her smiles something he couldn't just understand. Now as she gazed out of the window she seemed, despite her tiredness, transfigured; so much so, he realised with a shock, that in her youth, before and perhaps immediately after her voluntary incarceration in the prison-house of poverty-stricken marriage, she must have been not just bonny and sensible like Mrs. Raeburn, but even beautiful and exciting, with her refined almost austere features and her profound awareness of what was happening to her, in the slum, and to her children. He had seen her husband, a small, nervous, self-effacing man, outwardly, at least, not her match. Now as he passed her, with a smile and a nod, he glanced out of the window to see what it was she had been gazing at, with such disciplined rapture. He saw, across fields, woods, and upland moors, the green peak of Brack Fell against blue sky and white cloud. Remembering what she had told him about her country birth, he felt more than understood that all those years in the grimy suffocation of Gowburgh's slums she had kept a part of her mind dedicated, private, and pure. The thought humbled him, and he hurried on to arrange about Mrs. Raeburn's billeting slips.

Mrs. Raeburn paused, in tears, to confide in her sympathetic neighbour.

"Do you ken who they're billeting me wi', Mrs. McShelvie?" she asked. "Somebody called Sir Robert."

Mrs. McShelvie smiled rather remotely. "Well, Bessie," she said, "he'll no' hae horns."

"For me he will hae. He's sending his car for us." That was said as if in accusation.

"That's obliging o' him. You seem to hae landed lucky, Bessie."

Mrs. Raeburn was not so much convinced as rebuked by that dry congratulation. "Do you think so?" she asked.

"Surely. I never doubted that folk can be kind though they are weel-off."

"I mean to pay for everything I get," said Mrs. Raeburn sharply, as she went off to join Roy.

Mrs. McShelvie gave a last glance out of the window before returning to her duties.

"That's a high price, Bessie," she murmured, and wasn't quite sure herself what she meant.

Mr. Michaelson was the billeting officer. When Roy entered, he was seated in a corner behind the teacher's desk, pressing with exaggerated anxiety into the radiator at his back. It was as if he was pretending that in front of him, instead of a roomful of weary women and children, were contagious baboons. With his hunched shoulders, bare wrinkled brown scalp, slightly pointed ears, and especially his grin of atavistic balefulness, he seemed to be trying to look simian himself. Yet he filled up the forms quickly and capably.

"This should be a good billet," he said. "Space in a house, or a country, always promotes good feeling. They say that's why the Germans are marching. Lammermuir, now, will have ten rooms at least. Tell me," he went on unexpectedly, "what's the name of that boy in the row second from the door, one, two, three from the front?"

Roy looked. The boy was Gordon Aldersyde, almost unrecognisable in his smiling fortitude. He mentioned his name.

"Quite aristocratic," murmured Michaelson.

That was a staff-room jest. "Yes," said Roy, "isn't it? He's a twin. That's his sister beside him."

But poor Hazel's eyes were so red, and her whole face so woebegone, she hardly resembled her resolutely composed brother.

Michaelson had no interest in the girl.

"A very handsome boy," he said.

"Very."

"Extremely well-dressed too, in comparison with the rest."

"A doting mother."

"Not an affluent father?"

"He's a barber, I think."

"Oh." Michaelson, with a gesture that lacked all humour, stroked his own baldness. "I'm looking for a boy myself," he said. "He would do. I must have one that's quiet and mannerly. I have two small daughters."

Roy knew about Gordon's puncturing of Miss Calder's thigh; and also about his attack on his sister in the playground, because she had not given him a big enough share of her bar of toffee: he had split her lip. He was, the lady teachers maintained, vicious, selfish, calculating: a young monster. The men were more charitable: Roy and Campbelton thought he might be an example of maternal spoiling; Scoullar, for whom the boy gave out the Bibles every morning, declared him misjudged. Whatever the truth was, Roy saw no reason to malign him to this stranger.

"I don't think their mother would want them separated," he said.

"I suppose not. I take it he comes from the same kind of home as the others?"

Roy nodded.

"Slum?" asked Mr. Michaelson.

Roy didn't like his tone, nor his smile.

"Some of these women," he retorted, "have homes that would be a credit even to Langrigg."

"I don't doubt it, young man, I don't doubt it at all. In the stone-age tribes the firemaker was always a woman; and of course home was built round the hearth, the sacred hearth."

As Roy went away he heard Michaelson laughing, and the sound irritated him far more than it should.

After the crowded turbulent school, the playground was pleasantly quiet and empty. The open gates suggested to Roy that somewhere in the town was an hotel with a room and a bar, both for him. It would be recuperation, not desertion. Later he might return for the night-shift.

The baby had wakened and was fretting. In Mrs. Raeburn's harassed efforts to soothe him were incipient shrillnesses of hysteria.

"Give him to me," said Roy.

She even smiled.

"I'll not let him fall," he promised, and taking the burden

81

from her strode up and down, vigorously dandling and truculently crooning.

Little Jess, seated on her suitcase, watched him gravely. Her own black doll, called Topsy, was held in expert fashion; it slept.

To other watchers the scene was comic. From a window in one of the upstairs rooms hung out the red heads of the Baxters. Their laughter was raucous and derisive.

"Where did you get the wean, sir?" This was Willie, with a touch of good-natured banter.

"Ye're a rotten nurse." This was Tom, matter-of-fact and contemptuous.

"Say poetry to it, sir"; and Willie began to bawl what Roy had taught him, Wordsworth's "Daffodils".

"Bang its heid on the pavement," snarled Tom, obviously interested in the hanging that would follow.

It was impossible for Roy to check them effectually, without giving the morsel in his arms a shock. He shouted up, more or less amiably: "Get in, and get that window shut."

"Wad you like an aeroplane to please the wean wi', Mr. Roy?" shouted Willie.

"It's mine," howled Tom, making to prevent its launching.

There began a struggle, during which it seemed that both boys would accompany the paper aeroplane in its descent to the playground.

"Who the hell's in charge up there?" wondered Roy audibly.

Then the car arrived.

Since they had a better view than Roy, who stood with his back to it, the brothers saw that the car was driven by a woman, a young well-groomed woman, deserving the description "smasher" and the wolf-calls of homage which they proceeded to let loose.

"Impertinent young beasts," thought Roy, again audibly, at least to the baby, which nevertheless smiled. "Your arses will feel the toe of my boot first chance I get."

He turned in a temper to face whoever was driving the car.

Meanwhile Mrs. Raeburn had been looking at the car as it swept into the playground and turned. Only at her wedding had she ever travelled in so smart a car. Thus it reminded her unexpectedly of her husband, now a soldier, willing to die in defence of his country. To cower because a car was large and glittered was to betray Dick; to wish it had been an old tin-can, rattling and rusty, was to dishonour Dick's children; but to hold her head up and speak with dignity and politeness to the young woman driving it was to act as Dick's wife. To give her courage so to act she needed the baby in her arms. Therefore she went over to take it from Roy, and perhaps was just in time, for he, stricken, might either have squashed or dropped it.

She was not the most beautiful woman he had ever seen, but she was easily the most entrancing. Her mouth was too large for film-star perfection, and the twinkling humour of her wide greenish-grey eyes in itself would have barred her from such a fate. So unlikely did she look as heroine of any scenes of passionate love in jungle or on ice-floe, that it was not possible for him to refrain from wondering how so cool, so intelligent, so wide-eyed and sparkling a personality would develop in any scene of genuine love. As she swung her legs out of the car, they were seen to be shapely and long, so that when she stood up she was tall enough for her head to reach above his shoulder. Her hair was less fair than his, and this superiority in what was not important made him realise his inferiority in what was. Here was a woman worth knowing— no, a woman whom he *must* get to know—and at this first meeting he was grubby, dishevelled, with the trademarks of his profession on him as revolting as a butcher's, with his arms still damp and crooked from holding a baby, and with two of the scrufffiest of his minions hooting from above. No wonder there was for him quizzicality in her smile; and for Mrs. Raeburn, Richard, Jess, and even Topsy, warmest and most charming welcome.

A demon from hell could not at that moment have deceived Mrs. Raeburn: false affability, dutiful hospitality, and conscientious kindness she would have detected at once; just as swiftly and instinctively did she recognise true friendliness.

She had a way of raising her eyebrows which he found

tremendously fetching. Even at rest she gave the impression that in walking she would take long jaunty debonair steps. To climb Brack Fell with her, he thought, would be like realising a life's ambition; and for an instant he remembered Mrs. McShelvie at the window.

Her voice was quiet, bright, and utterly without patronage; her accent not too English.

"My name's Elizabeth Cargill," she said. "I hope I haven't kept you waiting."

As Roy stepped forward as introducer, one of the Baxter brothers, Tom the younger he thought, shouted what was undeniably a lewd expression, for which the punishment in the circumstances ought to be flayed alive or tongue cut out. That Miss Cargill heard, and understood, was evident; but she did not blush, or turn pale, or titter, or gawk in horror. She raised her brows a saucy fraction, inserted infinitesimal delicious pauses in her still-cheerful remarks, and said, with ravishing irony, that no doubt all the children, poor things, must be feeling very tired and depressed after so trying a day. She had to be introduced to them all, including Topsy; even the last-named, it seemed to Roy, had to grin in pleasure at that dainty but playful prod in the stomach.

"My own name's Roy," he said, "Edgar Roy."

If it was anti-climax, she did not show it. She shook hands with him too, but more briefly: it was a social gesture, nothing more; he felt ridiculously jealous of slavering Richard and black-faced Topsy.

He helped to install the Raeburns and their luggage in the car.

"I'll be along to see how you're getting on, Mrs. Raeburn," he said.

"Surely, Mr. Roy," she whispered, implying that it wasn't really for her to say.

Miss Cargill responded.

"Any friend of Mrs. Raeburn will be welcome at any time," she said. "She's to look on Lammermuir as her home from now on."

"That's very kind of you, Miss Cargill," he said, rather feebly.

Then she drove away, and he was left in the desolate play-ground, feeling so sorry for himself that even the prospect of a bath and a drink and a change of clothing at a good hotel no longer seemed enticing. Lammermuir was where he wanted to go.

IV

There were the Baxters to chastise. He was about to dash into the school on that half-retributory, half-revengeful purpose, when another car, even larger and more splendid than the Cargills', entered the playground. He waited to see what specimen of Langrigg plutocracy it contained. She was a tall stalwart woman, who gave the impression she ought to bulge before and after, but somehow, in a masochistic way, didn't: her corsets must have been of steel. She had the face of a beleaguered sixty, but the make-up and dress of a thirty at peace with life. Before she alighted from the car, helped by the obsequious chauffeur, her scent of lavender preceded her; that too was the colour of her costume, hat, and even her shoes and stockings.

Roy, at the top of the steps, watched her come up them with a dignity so rigid he expected it to snap before his eyes. He held the door open for her. Before she thanked him and entered, she gave him and his hand a long scornful stare as if considering whether an entrance indebted to such shoddy human material ought to be accepted. He felt his spine crinkling in resentment; what Archie called his Freudian devil stirred in his darkest depths. This woman was a vampire; she must be exorcised.

Certainly, as she stood within the school, her nose began to twitch disgustedly; if according to her nature she must suck the blood of young children, she would do it as medicine rather than food.

He set about his vampire hunt.

"Madam," he said, as smart and deferential as any salesman, "I am a Gowburgh teacher. Is there anything I can do for you?"

"Perhaps there is," she replied, in a deep voice. "My name is Mrs. Rouster. My husband is Bailie Rouster."

Her husband in the end had been adopted. His prancings and his shouts had been silly but for the public good. He had been recompensed with a dozen nicknames, none really offensive; and the few stale cookies shied at him, after the fiasco in the town hall, had come from the hands of such as the Baxters, who knew no gratitude, to man or God. Mrs. Rouster, though, would never, in war or armistice, be adopted by Gowburgh folk.

"I want two little girls," she said, and indicated the height required with her lavender-gloved hand. "They must be clean, obedient, quiet, well-spoken, house and bed trained, and without a criminal pedigree."

Nodding like submissive sharp-for-business shopman, inwardly he ranted: "What you really deserve, you arrogant bitch, are the Baxters; and by God," he added, "you're going to get them." It would be, he saw, like putting the cat among the vultures.

"But I doubt if you have any such," she boomed.

"On the contrary, madam. We have quite a fine selection of such little girls."

She snorted, suspecting mercantile fraud or blarney.

"I prefer to satisfy myself," she said.

"Quite so, madam. Just come and have a look."

"That's why I am here, young man. I know very well I ought not to be. I know the fools got up some idiotic regulation about not allowing people to come and choose their own. My own husband was one of those fools. I happen to believe, however, that in a free country, which thank God ours still is"—here she gave Roy a look which asked more rudely than words why he was not being eviscerated somewhere to preserve that freedom—"though perhaps not for much longer," she went on, "seeing how the fools have as usual blundered into war without being prepared for it—I happen to believe that we are entitled to refuse to harbour scoundrels, actual or potential. Gowburgh has a vile reputation."

"Just take a look into this first room, madam," he urged.

"I have only a minute or two to spare," she said. "I am on my way to afternoon tea with my friend Mrs. Mair-Wilson at Harelaw House."

"With my help, madam, matters can be expedited."

In that first room, on one of the front seats, were two sisters called Morag and Sheila McDonald, one ten, the other eight. They sat on the one seat and held hands. No children in Christendom could have been sweeter-faced; perhaps many could have been dressed more expensively, but none more effectively to enhance their fair-haired long-ringleted clean-skinned prettiness. Their red coats were new, with berets and ribbons to match.

Even Mrs. Rouster approved.

"Long hair?" she murmured. "Will it be clean?"

"I can guarantee it."

"In any case, if it isn't, it can be cut. All right, I'll speak to them."

"Very good. I'll bring them out here; it's more private."

"Yes." Rudely she returned the rude stares of the women in the room. "Ill-bred insolence," she muttered.

Roy brought out the sisters. Their answers to her cross-examination were satisfactory.

"They'll do," she said. "But I don't want them with me."

"Of course not. That can easily be arranged. What is the address, please?"

She laughed. "Everybody in Langrigg knows Ebenholm," she said.

"Very good, madam."

He saw her to the door.

"You've been obliging, young man."

"Thank you," he murmured.

"Mind you," she said, as he held the door open for her, "I don't think this evacuation nonsense was necessary. It smells of panic to me. There will be no bombs. In any case, war is war, you can't run away from it." She sharpened her look then, as if she saw him about to gallop helter-skelter from Armageddon.

"No, madam."

"You'll not be waiting here long yourself?"

"No, madam."

"Wars are for young men," she said, with a last-second mellowing; she even smiled. "Good afternoon."

"Good afternoon, madam."

The moment she was gone, upstairs with the McDonald sisters he rushed, to find Alden's table surrounded by children waiting for billets. Grahamstone and Campbelton were being assisted as ferrymen by Scoullar; or rather each seemed to be in business for himself, with acrimonious rivalry. Councillor Henderson hovered like a hawk, his eyes hungry for Alden's lists. On these rested a hand as chirpy as a sparrow.

"How are we getting on?" asked Roy, of Campbelton.

"Counting your Raeburns, Edgar, we have disposed of twenty-three souls. Five may be returned. This is, of course, utterly hellish. I am contemplating flight and desertion."

"Wait a few minutes, and I'll go with you."

Roy pushed through and addressed Alden, whose whiskers, he thought, had begun to wilt.

"Excuse me," he said. "Have you Mrs. Rouster's name on your list? Her house is called Ebenholm."

Alden's whiskers drooped further. He nodded. "I know Mrs. Rouster," he said mournfully.

"She called downstairs, looking for two little girls."

"She had no right to do so, of course."

"Does she think we're running a slave market?" demanded Grahamstone.

Alden nodded.

"Well, score her name off," said Roy. "She's been attended to."

"Did you give her these two?" cried the headmaster, pointing to the McDonald girls. "Dammit, they're among our very best." It was as if they had been taken out of the shop window.

"No, other two. I thought I'd bring these two up; they should be easy to billet."

"How right you are, Mr. Roy," cried Alden, his optimism revived. "Beauty is always acceptable. Just let me see: two little girls, sisters if possible." His finger danced down the list. "Ah, here we are: Mrs. Stevenson of Beechgrove. If I had children of my own I should be happy to send them there." He laughed at those phantoms, but Miss Cheam looked pale and haunted.

"Thanks," said Roy. "I'll see that Mrs. Stevenson gets these girls."

As he made off he was clutched by Scoullar, who looked reproachful and desperate.

"Edgar," he said, "perhaps you'd like to know I've been waiting for nearly ten minutes trying to get those two Thompson boys fixed up. Does it help to break the queue?"

"Sometimes it does. It's helped these girls, hasn't it?"

"Please don't equivocate to me, Edgar. I am in no humour to stand it. What about that Catholic boy you brought here? Have you given a thought to him? Or to the one with the skin disease? You saw to Mrs. Raeburn all right, didn't you?"

Roy was astonished at so much spleen; he was about to give it back when Councillor Henderson interrupted them.

"We must speed up matters, gentlemen," he said. "And the only way to do it is for Mr. Alden to share out those lists of accommodation."

"That would help," said Scoullar.

"Ask Alden then," said Roy.

Henderson closed his eyes. "He's been asked a dozen times. Your headmaster's asked him. So have I. It's no good. He just won't give them up."

"I suppose he knows what he's doing," said Scoullar. "After all, he *is* the chief billeting officer."

"No, no, that has really nothing to do with it," said Henderson.

"Surely it has."

Henderson, who had been casting pirate's eyes about him, began to suffer a relapse into frustrated respectability. He appealed to Roy.

"Well," said the latter, grinning, "what were you going to suggest?"

Henderson recklessly closed his eyes. "I was going to suggest," he said, "that if somebody would decoy William away from that table for just one minute, I would steal them."

"Steal them?" squealed Scoullar.

"Why not? It would be in the public interest, and in William's too."

Roy patted the small man on the shoulder.

"Just you do that," he said. "Mr. Scoullar here will be glad to co-operate."

"Why not yourself, Edgar?" sneered Scoullar. "Surely this is more in your line?"

"It is," agreed Roy, "but I have other business to attend to. Good luck."

He left them, pirate and moralist, gazing at each other dubiously.

It was a simple matter to get billeting slips for the sisters. When he had seen them off, happy and confident, Roy sought out the Baxters.

He found them prowling predatorily from room to room, followed by a small snivelling boy whose apple they were eating. His tears were as dew upon it, so ecstatically did they munch. Stalking them from behind, Roy seized an ear of each and, not caring who saw to misinterpret, he began to kick their behinds in rotation, not at all jocularly. At first, not knowing who their torturer was, they protested profanely, with the result that he felt justified in making the kicks still brisker. When they saw him, Willie submitted stoically, but Tom threatened to inform the police. One enthralled spectator was the owner of the apple; he thought their punishment was on his account, so that as he ran off to begin a boasting that would last for weeks, revenge, sweeter than any apple, made his mouth water.

Roy dragged them into a quiet corner.

"That's just a sample of what I would like to do to you," he said.

Willie rubbed his bottom, and grinned as if he thought matters were even. Tom glowered, passionate with grievance.

"You've not got a spark of decency in you," said Roy.

"It was just in fun," muttered Willie.

"What this filthy pup shouted wasn't in fun."

"I told him he shouldn't."

90

Tom mouthed something about his pigeon.

Roy had to turn to Willie for a translation.

"Och, that's whit he says every time he's checked, Mr. Roy. He says he's never going to be good, because his pigeon was killed."

"That's a stupid way to behave. It was a cat killed it, wasn't it? You can't blame the whole world for it."

"He does, sir."

Can you have a feud against the world, if you're just ten? wondered Roy. Looking at Tom, he saw you could; especially if nobody ever said a kind word to you, and everybody belittled the death of your pigeon which had sat on your head for hours. At any moment the boy might burst into vicious swearing or, what would be even more disastrous, vicious weeping. Better to leave him alone, even if he had insulted Miss Cargill.

It seemed more profitable to address Willie, who at least smiled like a boy.

"I've found a place for you," he said.

"We're no' going to be separated," replied Willie instantly, with an instinctive clenching of his fist.

"Keep your hair on. This place is for you both."

Willie's incredulity was not so boyish. "They were a' saying," he said, "that naebody would take us in; as if," he added in scorn, "we want to be taken in. We can sleep under a tree."

"There will be no need for that. This place is a mansion. You'll have a room of your own."

"You're kidding."

At that point scruple, with a face like Scoullar's, admonished Roy. After a moment's hesitation he told it to go to hell.

Willie noticed the hesitation; he grinned like one who could take a joke, even if it did contain what he would never admit was a disappointment.

"I knew you were kidding."

"No, Willie, I'm not."

"Well, where is it?"

"I'll tell you who owns it. Do you remember the gentleman who led the procession?"

Even Tom smiled.

"Wi' the white hat," asked Willie, "and the flower in his jaiket? We chipped cookies at him."

"I hit him," said Tom.

"Yes, him. He was all right, wasn't he?"

Willie reflected, and then nodded. "He was daft," he said, "but he was a' right."

"Well, it's his house you're going to. But we'll have to be very careful about this."

"I kent there must be a catch in it."

"No, Willie, there's no catch. You see, we've to go the minister in the room along there to get forms filled up. Now you know very well you must behave yourselves in front of a minister. Will you? That's the question." Roy winked towards Tom, who certainly would give no personal guarantee.

Willie nodded; but he had his own private thoughts on the matter.

"Mr. Roy," he asked, "is it true that you go straight to hell—when you're deid, I mean—if a minister wearing his white collar puts a curse on you?"

"No. Don't be stupid."

"That's whit they say."

"Who?"

"All the boys in oor street."

"It's no' a minister," muttered Tom, "it's a priest."

"They're juist the same," insisted Willie.

"What's this about, anyway?" demanded Roy.

"That one alang there," said Willie, without apparent impertinence, "was trying to put a curse on us."

Roy's heart fell. "What are you havering about?"

"We were in the room, and he put us oot."

"No doubt you deserved it. What were you up to?"

"Nothing. Absolutely nothing." Willie was quite vehement.

"Come off it, Willie. Nobody would throw you out for nothing."

"He was kittling Maggie Ross," said Tom, in disgust. "She's his tart."

Willie aimed a blow at his brother, but it was half-hearted and easily blocked by Roy, who had them both to rebuke.

"Cut it out, Willie," he said. "And as for you, Tom, don't let me hear you saying 'tart' again. If you want a word, say sweetheart."

Willie looked as if, forced to make a choice, he'd prefer tart himself.

"But let's leave Maggie Ross out of it," said Roy. "I want you both to come with me. Say nothing unless you're asked to speak; and if you are, for God's sake, be at least civil."

"Should you say 'for God's sake', sir, when you're going to talk to a minister?" asked Willie. "Miss Oldswan told us once that that was worse than swearing."

With perfect distinctness Tom uttered the swear that was more orthodoxly considered the worst in the language. Roy pretended not to have heard, but he began to feel a little sorry for Mrs. Rouster.

He had not chosen the minister out of anti-clerical prejudice. Rather was his choice of Sandeman a compliment; any layman, unhampered by the decrees of Christ, might refuse to put his signature to any form consigning the Baxters to the Rousters. Wee Michaelson for instance, who looked a connoisseur in the wiles and wickedness of the world, would have smelled trickery sooner than such fragrant goodness emanating from Mrs. Rouster. But no minister's ethereal nose ought to be so suspicious in its sniffing.

That nose, so long, sensitive, and spiritual, had across it a pair of gold-rimmed spectacles which, along with his gold-filled front teeth, recalled by ludicrous contrast the swashbuckling days of the Klondyke or the brutal exploitation of natives on the Rand. He had a high, pale, theological brow, and a mouth that might have been firm if he could only have become convinced of the propriety of firmness in a world ossified by self. That his wife, dark as Leah, and richer than all the tribe of Jacob, was unyielding in ambition, and impervious alike to Christian humility and heathen envy, contributed greatly to his rather desperate and conspicuous yearning for softness, unselfishness, and above all a general movement of the human heart towards Christ. There were those who considered him a gold-plated humbug; these were, however, mostly people who would have regarded Christ Himself as an upstart, too big for the boots whose laces they certainly would never have stooped down to loose. Mr. Sandeman knew of their existence too well: he allowed them, in his wife's opinion, to dictate to him in his conscience as well as in his pulpit, instead of consigning them to the hell of his prosperous indifference. Without her to rescue and guide him he would have stayed stuck in the unsavoury Edinburgh district where she had found him. She it was, or her family rather, who had got him the fine West Kirk of Langrigg, with its manse coveted by ministers' wives from the Shetlands to the Solway Firth.

He was trying to console a six-year-old girl when Roy approached him with the Baxters. Seeing them caused him to reflect that with children he was in every way a failure, being able neither to scold nor comfort them. Perhaps that fatal inability lay behind Lena's refusal to have any; if so, it was perhaps a more honourable reason than the one he had most frequently suspected, the dread of having the privacy of mind and body broken even by her own child. So seldom, and then so shamefully, was he, her husband before God, allowed to intrude.

As he gazed at the two slum-urchins, he felt, physically, the disgust Lena would feel. In his own person he kept smiling and nodding. This confusion caused him to hear, but hardly to understand, what Roy was saying to him with such quick deliberate casualness.

Roy was surprised; he was even contrite. This minister, for all his intellectual look, was as simple-minded and trusting as his collar warranted. He was willing, for the sake of his faith, to take the risk of being called a "mug"; for of course in that sense Christ of Nazareth had been the greatest "mug" in all history. So impressed was he, Roy thought of abandoning the deception.

By picking up his pen, Mr. Sandeman returned to reality.

"Whom did you say the boys were to go to?" he asked, and suddenly was aware that the answer to that question must reveal the name of a better Christian than himself, even if it belonged to one of the workmen from the new council houses, who gambled, drank, and never attended church.

Roy was astonished. He had already named the Rousters at least three times. Was the minister drunk? Bending slightly, he smelled only manly hair cream and aftershave lotion.

"Bailie Rouster," he said, clearly.

Mr. Sandeman dropped the pen as if it was an asp, and whipping off his spectacles began to polish them.

"Bailie Rouster, of Ebenholm," repeated Roy remorselessly.

"Oh, I know where the Bailie lives. He and Mrs. Rouster sit in my congregation. Young man," he added sternly, "you are surely prevaricating."

Roy, who was no more than six or seven years younger, began to bristle.

"Why d'you think that?" he asked. "Are you implying that because they are members of your church it is impossible that they should offer to take these boys into their home?"

The boys, grinning like monkeys, were enjoying the quarrel.

"Of course I am implying nothing of the kind." But truth, as well as logic, accused him of lying. "I merely mean . . ." but, so fertile in subtle theological analogies in the quiet of his study, here in public his mind as usual grew desiccated.

"What do you mean?" demanded Roy, thinking that if there was a divine pen at work above, as his mother used to say, it would certainly mark down his own lie in blackest ink; but for the minister's scepticism capitals and underlining ten times would be necessary.

"I mean, there must be a mistake surely."

"Isn't there enough room for them at Ebenholm?"

"It is one of the best houses in Langrigg. They keep two cars and a chauffeur." It was, again, Lena speaking in him; he sat too ashamed to heed the young man's contempt, though it was by no means delicately expressed.

"I shall go elsewhere for the billeting-slips," bluffed Roy.

It is a lie, thought the minister; this young man is Mephistopheles, sent to ensnare me. If I sign these forms, Lena, the Rousters, the kirk session, will charge me with vindictiveness or what will be worse in their eyes, gullibility. My detractors will find out and snarl their merriment all over the town. I will be mocked and humiliated; and I shall be smugly reprimanded by men and women who would not receive Christ Himself into their houses, if He called barefooted on a night of blizzard.

"There is no need to go elsewhere," he said, picking up his pen. "What are the lads' names?"

Roy grinned as he gave them. He did not understand why the minister had decided to oblige, although obviously still unconvinced.

"I only wish," said Sandeman, as he handed over the forms, "that I could have received them into my own home."

Here Willie and Tom both shrank back, no longer like monkeys; what they feared was beyond the apprehension of monkeys.

"Thanks," said Roy. He looked round the room. "There's any number to choose from."

"Not for me. Not for me. Not for me."

Twice, in that lugubrious tone, might have hinted at tragedy; thrice was melodrama: probably, decided Roy, all he means is that his meditations over his sermons mustn't be desecrated by the pagan hullabaloo of children.

"Will somebody take them along to Ebenholm?" he asked.

"Of course." Mr. Sandeman signalled to one of the three youths standing in a corner of the room. This one, a curly-haired eager lad, stood by the desk at attention to receive his orders; these had the effect on him of an instantaneous and griping medicine.

"Mrs. Rouster won't be at home," said Roy, applying first-aid. "She's out at afternoon tea with Mrs. Mair-Wilson, I think she said."

"Mair-Wilson said he would take at least twelve," murmured the minister.

At first Roy wondered whether the twelve were cups of tea or children; then he realised they must be children. "Twelve?" he repeated.

"Proving there is in the human heart a fount of goodness," said Mr. Sandeman.

Like an apprentice zoo-keeper in charge of bears, the curly-haired youth led off the Baxters. To these Roy gave a last caution; they listened with teeth big and ears small; and then, with their parcels under their arms, they trotted off to find out what sort of cage Ebenholm was likely to be.

Roy went off too in search of Campbelton. It was easy for them both to slip away in the commotion caused by Alden's discovery that a rival clearing-house had been opened in Councillor Henderson's room.

"It is not desertion," said Campbelton, as they sneaked out of the school door, "when front-line troops take advantage of the relief that has been provided for them. It is customary military practice, as well as bloody common sense: a co-incidence you will discover to be rather rare. What were you up to, Edgar, with those Baxter brutes?"

Roy was about to explain when a small bus entered the playground. From it bounced a tubby little man in a tweed cap, white sweater, and shabby flannels. "I'm Mair-Wilson," he cried. "I hope I'm not too late?"

"For what?" asked Campbelton, who disapproved of slovenliness in dress.

"For my quota. I want twenty-four."

"Twenty-four what?"

"Boys! I'd like a mixture, but I'm afraid my accommodation's not up to it; wouldn't pass the censor. Am I in time?"

"You'd be in time, sir, if your quota was two hundred."

"Good. Two hundred? It could be done, with some enthusiasm. Where there's a will there's a way."

He dashed into the school. They noticed he was wearing black sandshoes, with the lace of one of them loose.

Campbelton addressed the bus-driver. "Who was that gentleman?" he asked.

"Mr. Mair-Wilson, of Harelaw House."

"Has he really brought that bus to take twenty-four boys home with him?"

"That's what he hired me for."

Campbelton said nothing, but stood there in the sunshine, with his hat in his hand, visibly shedding cynicism.

"Mind you," whispered the bus-driver, "he can well afford it. He's worth half a million, they say."

97

"They also say," said Campbelton, "that a rich man will find it very difficult to enter the kingdom of heaven."

"That's true enough," agreed the bus-driver, much perplexed.

The two teachers left the playground and strolled down the wide main street in the shadow of the lime trees.

"Tell me, Edgar," asked Campbelton, "what motive could possibly compel a man to take into his house twenty-four of our brats?"

"Philanthropy," suggested Roy.

Campbelton nodded.

They walked on again, and suddenly the trees, the shops, the buildings, the citizens, even the fallen leaves and the stray dogs of Langrigg, were beautiful.

V

The Curly Lamb stood in the cobbled lane to which the grand main street dwindled at its southern end. It was so old-fashioned an inn as to have, scratched on one of its window-panes, reputedly by the poet himself, a couple of lines from "Tam o' Shanter". Its name commemorated the time when the town had thrived on its trade in wool, and the inn's appearance, white-washed and small-windowed, was more suited to those plain couthy roistering days than to the present era of elegance and hygiene as an inland spa. The larger hotels, such as the George, the Cheviot, and the Royal, catered for holidaymakers who wished pleasant motoring jaunts to secluded scenes of historic violence, easy strolls in hill air, uncongested golf, polite company, and perhaps a daily draught from the mineral well which was discreetly advertised as being "beneficial in the relief of most rheumatic ailments". The present guests, at the beginning of this September, suffered rather from fear, whose stiffness they hoped the town's inconspicuousness amongst its green hills, its lack of provoking factories, and its unsuitability as a target for bombers, would in time alleviate. These were evacuees acting on their own initiative and paying their own expenses, which were high; and there seemed to be enough of them to fill all the hotels except the Curly Lamb, where Roy and Campbelton, after a long indignant scrounge elsewhere, finally found a room, food and drink, a bath, and in the case of the latter a nap.

While his colleague snored, Roy prised out of the jolly mountainous maid a few jewels of information about Miss Cargill. He learned that she wasn't engaged and wasn't even courting; that she played golf; that she had good teeth, which were more than likely to be her own; that she went walks frequently with a black dog called Scout; that her legs weren't noticeably bowed or knock-kneed or varicose-veined; that she was often seen going in and coming out of the library carrying books, which she no doubt was able to read; that she attended wee Mr. Mackdoe's kirk rather than Mr. Sandeman's more swanky one; that she was the sole heiress of her father, whom local rumour put down as well-to-do, if not quite in Mr. Mair-Wilson's class; that she painted as a hobby; and that she was a friend of Mr. and Mrs. Kilburn, who wrote books about birds and bees and children exploring islands.

In order to obtain all that gold (some of it intermingled with impurities) Roy had to put up with heaps of dross about Alden the town clerk, who, it seemed, lodged at the Curly Lamb, and was Mirren the maid's ideal man. It was not true, she declared, that he had to be carried up to bed every night; even if he had, she would be proud to do it. He was a good kind-hearted man, at the mercy of schemers like Provost Reik and Bailie Rouster, not to mention his sly bitch of a secretary Miss Cheam. For weeks he had been thinking of nothing else but the welfare of the poor children to be evacuated from the city. Everybody looked for the mistakes he would make, nobody for the kindness he would show even to a mongrel dog. Thus she went on, while half the time Roy was dreaming of golf on the upland course with curlews and Miss Cargill; the other half he dreamt he was leading her up to the cairn on Brack Fell.

Later, when he stood outside the door enjoying a cigarette, he saw Mrs. Ross carrying her baby and, followed by her other

99

five, walking along the other side of the lane in the direction of the school. Shame almost sent him slinking indoors. Besides, he had promised Archie not to break their present neutrality. But in some way, not unconnected with his dreams of Elizabeth Cargill on the links or on the mountain, he found the fat black-coated woman's plodding steadfastness, and her children's coat-clinging dependence on her in the strange town, not only moving but even uplifting. He could not resist going over to speak to her.

He noticed that the children were munching at sandwiches, and one, a little fair-haired girl, carried a few flowers. Maggie, the eldest, Willie Baxter's sweetheart, was burdened with a small brother.

Roy wished he were Mair-Wilson, worth half a million, instead of a thriftless teacher whose sympathy, even, was limited.

"Hello, Mrs. Ross," he said, as cheerfully as he could. "Still on the go?"

She had stopped, and in spite of the heavy restless child in her arms contrived to look as comfortable as the tree in whose shadow she was standing.

"Wherever it is, Mr. Roy," she said, "we'll get there when the time comes."

"But where are you heading for now?"

"Back to the school. It's the second time. I'm getting to ken the toon. I think I'll like it here."

"Were you sent to some place and they wouldn't let you in?"

She smiled, rejecting his noble indignation.

"Wha could blame the woman?" she asked. "Naebody likes to open the door and find the children o' Israel on the door-steps, wi' tickets for admission." She showed the slips in her fist.

"It's a disgrace," he said angrily.

"She said she was sorry, and I believed her. There was nae profit to me in thinking the body a liar. She gie'd the weans pieces, when there was nae need for her to do it; and when she saw May there admiring the flowers in her garden she let her pu' some. What mair could she do?"

"She could have taken you in. I'm sure her house was big enough."

Mrs. Ross nodded. "It was a fine big hoose," she conceded. "But I always judge folk by what I think I wad hae done in their place. She had a braw new carpet doon in the hall yonder, and weans hae dirty shoes. Wad I hae welcomed such a cleckan in to dirty my new carpet? I doot it, Mr. Roy; though I think I wad hae gi'en them pieces and a flower or twa."

"But what now, Mrs. Ross?"

"Back to the school and wait. There's a big bundle of us being shunted back and forward. We're the ones hard to sell. As you can see, we're nae bargains." She smiled. "Meg Aitchison's come back three times." She paused to wipe her infant's nose and mouth with a rag. "Meg's too fierce, though she's cheery company. She looks in ither folk for what's no' in herself. Ye'll hae noticed that nae matter how poor a body is there's always somebody poorer. Beggars come and chap at oor doors in Gowburgh yonder. If one chaps at Meg's door, what does he get? A swearing for waking the wean frae Meg, or a lecture on politics frae her man. Meg doesn't mak allowances. She's no' her lane in that, though. Isn't there going to be anither war?"

The more she spoke, the greater grew his astonished respect, and the bitterer his frustration at not being able to help.

"You say there are many of you still in the school? Women with big families, you mean?"

"Maistly them. They tried splitting us up. I wouldnae hae that. I like to hae my weans aboot me. Are you fixed up yourself, Mr. Roy?"

In almost any other woman that placid inquiry must have been disguised sarcasm, able to be answered with brazen coolness. But Mrs. Ross was sincere.

Roy had never felt meaner in his life.

"Yes," he muttered.

"Ower there?"

He nodded.

She gave the inn a smile of approval. "You should be a' right in there," she said. "I like auld-fashioned buildings. They

101

were saying Mr. Grahamstone and Mr. Scoullar are to stay wi' the minister."

That was news.

"Which minister?" he asked.

"The big sad-looking man, wi' the golden specs. They were saying his manse has fifteen rooms in it." She went on with no criticism in her voice, only genuine curiosity. "Will every one be furnished? That always puzzles me wi' big hooses. But I'd better get back and report."

"Is Mr. Alden still in charge?"

"That's the wee man wi' the whiskers that Meg said were like a pet moose's tail? Weel, he thinks he is, but as far as we're concerned, it's really Bell McShelvie wha's in charge. Do you ken Bell?"

"Yes, I know Mrs. McShelvie. Her son Sammy's in my class."

"They say he's no' very bright at his lessons?"

"Not very."

"There are some weans," she said slowly, "mak you laugh, and some that mak you greet; Sammy McShelvie maks you laugh and greet in the same braith, always has done so since he could creep. But I'm keeping you here in the cauld, Mr. Roy. You never kent, did you, I was so fond o' a blether? Thanks for listening to me."

"It's been an honour to listen to you, Mrs. Ross."

She glanced round at her children. "I'll say this," she claimed, "my weans are weel-mannered."

"Very well-mannered, Mrs. Ross. Cheerio, and the best of luck."

"Luck?" she repeated, pausing. "My man says there's nae such thing. He says, whit's for you will no' go by you; he says it was a' planned oot before the start o' time."

Thus, with absolute humility claiming her present situation to have been the occasion of God's special foresight and wisdom before the evolution of the stars, she set sail along the main street, followed by her flotilla. Gazing after her, Roy had in his vision too the large red-sandstone West Kirk, with its fine steeple; but it was she and her children who brought the awe into his mind. Humanity, he had always known, was

102

many-sided; it was comic, sad, wise, foolish, chaste, lustful, generous, greedy, sincere, hypocritical, and so on to the exhaustion of his vocabulary; but there was another element, not so easily named, there all the time possibly but seen only in glimpses, and when seen, as now in Mrs. Ross, making the vastness of churches intelligible.

He glanced at his watch. It was after seven. Billeting had been going on for four hours. Inefficiency was by no means a rare plant in the human field, but here in Langrigg it seemed to have found a soil and climate particularly congenial, with earnest goodwill its manure. He pictured Alden, Mirren's ideal man, with all those women and children to dispose of, and nowhere to put them. If he and Campbelton hurried to the school, all they would be able to do would be to join the town clerk in contemplation of this indisposability: they might do it more intelligently, but not any more effectively. Better perhaps to skulk in the inn, and attain the philosophical stage of drunkenness.

VI

Campbelton refused even to consider returning to the front line until he had had his dinner: calmness, he said, before attack. All through the meal, which was substantial and leisurely, with flowers on the table, he expatiated on this prudence of returning into battle with soothed nerves and pampered digestion. It was inevitable, he pointed out, that the leaders of the garrison, being hungry, tired, irritable, and discouraged, besides being demoralised by shrieks of mutiny, must be finding ideas absent or costive. If he and Roy must go there, let them go as liberators, able to rouse things out of their soul-numbing inertia. When Roy asked how they were to do that, his friend just smiled, like a man who has sipped good sherry and intends in another minute to sip it again. He let his long civilised fingers run like a spider across the white cloth to touch Roy's sleeve.

"We are about to enter a slavering, snottery, gnashing, bloody, excremental, universal madness, dear boy," he said gently. "I refer of course to war. It will not do to gird on your sword, like Sir Galahad, and rush off to slay the ogre responsible for it all. You will achieve your ambition, Edgar, and become the pilot of an aeroplane. You will cross to Germany with a load of bombs and drop them to the best of your ability upon some munition work, but really they will fall on tenements filled with women and children similar to those at present detained in the school. I need not elaborate the consequences. You will fight the good fight, in the twentieth-century style. You may become a hero, with medals. But, bless you, you will never be Sir Galahad, who slew only ogres and on whose soul consequently there was not to be found one blemish."

"And what," asked Roy, rather peevishly, "am I to make of all that?"

"You are simply to enjoy your dinner, Edgar, and let me enjoy mine. Thereafter we shall stroll along under the first stars and proffer our assistance, which, for all the largeness of our hearts, may well be meagre."

Meagre indeed their assistance turned out to be. They could use their recuperated strength to give inertia some heaves and kicks, but it did not budge. They could not waft the mothers and children out of the cold dark classrooms into warm bright homes. Nor ought they, in fairness, to have blamed the officials, who also lacked the necessary magic wand. All day those officials, to their own amazement, had been given that wand to wield; that its efficacy might wither before the end had always been anticipated: it was not in the nature of things to achieve perfection. As Alden hoarsely but proudly whispered, billets had been found for nearly eight hundred souls. Those still homeless, he implied, would have confounded Utopians in their own land: women with at least three of a family; several with at least five; and one with eight.

They stood in the dusk, communing silently with nothing. Roy was the first to mention compulsion. It was an evil word.

"Never," said the Provost, who was there because he had been sent for.

"You've got the power," insisted Roy.

They united in chiding him, especially as they had all heard about his callous and motiveless deception on Mrs. Rouster.

Mr. Sandeman was there, saying little; he had been home to get permission to invite the headmaster and a teacher as his guests; and he had also been speaking to Mrs. Rouster over the telephone.

Mr. Mackdoe also was there. "Compulsion," he said, "is the embrace that breaks the angel's wings."

The Provost applauded, but in Sandeman's sigh of tribute was surely a theological qualification. He did not, he had once confessed, believe literally in angels; but then, he did not believe in the Immaculate Conception; and his belief in the miracles was tepid.

"When volunteers are not forthcoming," said Campbelton, "and conscripts are not allowed, who fights the battle?"

"We can't stay here much longer," grumbled Grahamstone. "We can't see one another's faces."

"Of course," said Alden, "the conclusive objection to the use of compulsory powers is simply that the women themselves have declared they will not go where they are not wanted."

Roy scowled, for it was true: he had asked them, and with one exception they had said they would sleep in the school first or on the pavements. The exception had been Meg Aitchison: she had seen, she cried, police throw poor folk out, for not paying rent; it would be only justice then to give them a chance to throw some in. Once in, she wouldn't be the one to run out again: it would be more like a ferret in a rabbit burrow.

Alden it was who produced the solution.

"Why not," he asked, "put them in Cairnban?"

He himself laughed, emphasising the silence of the others.

"We have Captain Wotherspoon's permission," he said, "and it's commodious enough."

Their silence began to break up into little groans, nervous

105

sclaffings of feet, and anxious breathings. Mr. Mackdoe, damming a spate of eloquence, alone preserved silence. Michaelson had long ago gone home with Gordon Aldersyde; otherwise his malevolent cachinnation must then have had good practice.

"What's going on?" demanded Grahamstone. "What's this place Cairnban? Is it an institution, a poor-house or something?"

"Oh no," replied Alden. "It's a private mansion, an excellent one. Captain Wotherspoon, who owns it, wrote to me, in my capacity as chief billeting officer, offering it for hospitality purposes, if it ever was needed."

"Well, by Jupiter, it's needed now, isn't it?"

"I think so."

"Then what's all this humming and hawing for?"

"I shall tell you frankly, Mr. Grahamstone," said the Provost, "why I personally am, as you put it, humming and hawing. Cairnban is a very fine house, recently renovated at considerable expense; it has extensive grounds."

"All the better, I should say."

"Now really, Mr. Grahamstone, would these people respect such a property? I am sure they would not. Within a month, perhaps less, would they not have it grievously damaged? I think they would. And who would compensate the Captain? The Government? Perhaps. Most likely it would have to be the town council, acting for the ratepayers. I do not think I have authority to sanction this."

"I agree," murmured Sandeman. "Besides, there is the question of the houses adjacent to Cairnban. Will the occupants, who are amongst our foremost citizens, not consider themselves most unjustly treated if we allow to be set up in their midst what will become, in a short time, a slum?"

It was then time for Mr. Mackdoe to remove that dam. He, too, had been home for a meal and a rest. He had confided to his wife how the gibes about his corporal smallness had stung, and he had been consoled by her common sense and sympathy; that she was six inches taller in no way invalidated her consolation. Moreover, while he was at tea, taking great delight in feeding his son with a rusk soaked in milk, a mother with a child of two had come apprehensively to his door. With his

106

wife's blessing, he had taken them in and made them welcome. Misgivings about future domestic arrangements smote him, specially when the two-year-old stranger appropriated his own child's teddy-bear, so that both howled, the one when it was taken and the other when it was restored. But smiting him still harder was the knowledge that he had done what Sandeman refused to do, and what their Master had bade.

His tone was modest. "I am surprised, and a little disappointed," he said, "to hear your opinion, Provost, and yours, Mr. Sandeman. I can only conclude you have both lost sight of what is of the chief consequence here: neither the safeguarding of glass chandeliers or azalea bushes, nor the protection from disturbance of worthy people. No, it is surely the rescuing from the cold and dark and unfriendliness, of these mothers and their little ones, who are at our mercy. The vessel of civilisation, gentlemen, on its voyage through the waters of eternity, dare not ever ignore that sacred rule: women and children first."

Peering pacifically at his tiny rival, Sandeman was thinking: as a prizewinner in the theology class at the University, and as a voluntary student of that subject ever after, I could, in any debate, reveal you in two minutes to be the shallow homunculus you are; and some day, soon, I must do it, for the good of both our souls.

Outwardly he murmured, "I was speaking in my capacity as councillor."

Mackdoe was not a councillor, although he had tried to be. "I was speaking as a minister of the gospel," he said, unaware of the theological dynamite being heaped under him. "As such, I say then, with cool sad deliberation, that in this matter even hesitation is unchristian."

Along in the rooms where the women were, this speech was reported by their spies. All were grateful, but few were surprised: the very nearness of his jaunty bottom to the good earth had been a guarantee that either he, or his immediate ancestors, were from Gowburgh; where of course, as well as indomitable diminutiveness, justice, decency, and honour, were indigenous.

"Unchristian!" repeated Sandeman, shuddering at the confident use of this vastly dangerous word: it was as if a child should handle a bomb.

"Yes, sir, unchristian."

Mr. Sandeman had decided that very afternoon to become an army chaplain, whether Lena approved or not. Yet he could not resist murmuring: "If there is war, Mr. Mackdoe, will it be unchristian to thrust bayonets, drop bombs, fire shells, sink ships?"

"Are you trying to insinuate an attack on my patriotism, Mr. Sandeman?"

"Not at all. The problem concerns me."

"Though considerably interested," interposed Campbelton, "I should like to suggest this is neither the time nor the place for such a discussion. Would not the next meeting of your presbytery be more appropriate? This is the school; the time is a quarter to ten; there are eighteen women, and their numerous progeny, to accommodate."

"I agree," cried Grahamstone.

The Langrigg men withdrew a few paces to confer.

Grahamstone used the opportunity to grumble about his having had to accept the minister's invitation. As in the opposite camp, whispers were used.

"If there's one time in the week I like to relax," he lamented, "it's Sunday morning. How in God's name am I to do it in a strange manse? They say too his wife's a Jezebel."

"Why didn't you refuse?" asked Campbelton scornfully.

"Good God, Archie, wasn't I thinking up some form of refusal when Scoullar here butted in and accepted for us both?"

"I beg your pardon," said Scoullar bitterly. "I thought your hesitation was due to shyness."

"Shyness? What the devil do you think I am? I've seen the world, you know. This'll be my third war. Why should I feel shy? In the first place, my salary's as good as his."

"I thought you might unwittingly be exaggerating the awkwardness of living in a manse," said Scoullar. "I happen to have had some experience. My wife's uncle is a minister. We have spent several holidays with him. But I apologise."

108

"Don't worry," chuckled Campbelton. "He'll bring you up your breakfast in bed, and the *News of the World* to read."

Grahamstone scowled. "All right for you to laugh," he muttered. "Sneaking off to get yourselves into a hotel."

Campbelton let out a breath rich with sherry and roast chicken.

No more could be said, for the Provost led his colleagues back.

It was capitulation.

"But I wish to address the women and children on the subject of wilful damage," he said.

"Tonight?" asked Campbelton.

"Tonight."

"By the time transport's arranged for them," said Roy, "it'll be nearly midnight."

"True," murmured Alden, who would have the task of arranging that transport.

"Then tomorrow," said the Provost, "at the latest."

"Tomorrow," remarked Campbelton, "war will be declared."

VII

Thus at last, battling even so resourceful a sceptic as Campbelton, Langrigg had opened its doors to every refugee. Although behind some of those doors the hospitality offered might fall short of cordial, nevertheless the gesture by the whole town was admirable, not to say miraculous; and all over the country similar gestures had been made. From the savagery of war women and children must be saved, not merely because their husbands and fathers might otherwise be reluctant to contribute to it, either by making shells or by firing them, but also because Authority, likewise protected from that savagery for other reasons, could not with equanimity anticipate the mutilation, blinding, maiming, and roasting of innocent children under its jurisdiction. Chivalry, compassion, and conscience haunted even chancelleries; and perhaps, when duty compelled that orders be issued encompassing the mutilation, blinding, maiming, and roasting of innocent children under the enemy's jurisdiction, those ghosts have not even then been wholly exorcised, they still linger and receive their tribute of solemn obeisances and heroic salutes. But perhaps Langrigg is too small and unimportant a place to give rise to such mighty issues; here we must be concerned with the women and children, and their impact upon their hosts.

Take Sammy McShelvie, for instance, billeted in the bungalow Elmwood situated on the edge of a small plantation where at least a quarter of the trees were beeches. His foster-parents there were Mr. and Mrs. Kilburn, the silver-haired co-authors of *In the Foxglove Dell* and *Children of Wild Flower Island*, and other similar titles; they were also the friends of Elizabeth Cargill, who was the same age as their own daughter Amaranth. When he arrived, they were for the first hour discreetly but profoundly disappointed. They had ordered a boy about twelve or thirteen, for it had been a persistent point of criticism against their books that though girls were always faithfully and deliciously portrayed, the boys were too effeminate. Here, they had thought, was an honourable opportunity to study a manly type of boy within their own home. But at first, and indeed second, glance Sammy seemed as out of place in the foxglove dell as an ape; his milieu was so demonstrably the grimy tenements and narrow streets of slumdom, where not even grass grew. The children in the Kilburn books, confronted by this freak of humanity, would instantly lose all interest in flowers, birds, bees, and enchanted islets, no matter how desperately their creators wrestled for dominance; they would degenerate horribly, and become like hounds pursuing this long-legged toothy hare.

He was clean enough, but far from bonny; indeed, with his spectacles mended in the leg by fuse wire, his slightly cross eyes, his chaotic freckles, his incongruous dimples, his hedgehog hair, and his Gowburgh dialect, cacophonous and often incomprehensible, he would, as Mr. Kilburn whispered with courageous humour, as soon eat flowers as sniff and admire them. Though courteous enough, his way of doing things was inexhaustibly uncouth. For example, he tackled a boiled egg, not by slicing the top off with his knife, but by gently bashing it all round on the table, and then, with a patience that bird-watchers like the Kilburns had to appreciate, removing the shell particle by particle with pauses to cool his fingertips by licking them, and finally gathering the debris into a neat pile on the tablecloth beside his plate. That done, he proceeded to eat the egg as if it was an apple. Unluckily, it was very softly boiled, so that the yolk spurted out all over his mouth and fingers. For a moment disconcerted, he glanced round, smiled at the sympathetic consternation of his three witnesses, and then began to tidy up and at the same time salvage yolk by using pieces of bread as sops. In spite of this and similar contretemps, he seemed to enjoy his tea, and ate substantially.

The Kilburns wondered in dismay what amiable monster they were to house and nourish; but inside an hour they were completely captivated, by his immunity to ridicule of even the friendliest sort, by his gratitude unadulterated with shyness or calculation, and above all by his innocence which, in some strange way, was creative, not only dissolving their dislike and putting strong affection in its place, but also making them feel happier just by being in his presence. As for their crucial test, he passed it marvellously well: Tabs the orange cat, Tibs the black and white terrier, and Tib-tabs the gorgeous budgerigar, all of them usually jealous even of sparrows in snow-time, took to him at once. Tabs rubbed himself against his leg, Tibs licked his hand, and Tib-tabs alighted on his hair, a compliment paid outside the family to only Elizabeth Cargill, and in her case hours of coaxing had been necessary. Since the Kilburns believed (maintaining there was scriptural authority for such belief), in the instinctive wisdom of the animal creation, so far as trusting and distrusting human beings was concerned, this instantaneous adoption of Sammy was like a sign from heaven to them. In awe and simplicity they thought this boy from the slums must be under the guardianship of a higher power than any government.

Making no claims, Sammy enjoyed his egg (especially as at home he would never have been allowed to eat it in such an

111

interesting fashion), stroked Tabs and Tibs, tolerated Tib-tabs although its tiny claws were scratching his scalp, took the bath prepared for him without mentioning he had been scrubbed last night, said prayers on behalf of the entire universe, and afterwards, when the Kilburns had whispered their awestricken good nights, lay in bed, missing his brother Tom with whom he always slept, smelling the sweetness of the flowers in the garden, remembering the shining roller-skates his hosts had promised he could use, and then, for a long minute, suffering without tear or whimper or grimace in sympathy with his mother who had seemed to him that afternoon very tired, and who was all the time, he knew, worried about his father and sister at home. There was nothing he could do then to help her, for he did not even know where she was, and so he suffered; but when the minute was past he fell sound asleep.

The Michaelsons, too, thought they had found a treasure; nor had they, as it were, to scrape off the dirt to see the gold glittering beneath. From the moment Gordon Aldersyde entered their trim little bungalow his gentlemanliness shone. In the tiny hallway he greeted his hostess with courtesy and gratitude so graceful and yet so boyish that her heart would have melted had not, as usual, the ice in her husband's smile prevented it. Towards the two sad little girls Gordon in his kilt and tweed jacket conducted himself like a gallant young prince, bringing pleasure to their mother, and adding to their father's cold amusement.

Gordon overacted; he had to shake off the disappointment at the smallness of this house compared with so many others he had passed. Even the one that Sammy McShelvie was in, further along the avenue, was bigger, as well as having a grander, more beautiful garden; and he had been told by Mr. Michaelson that Bona Vista, the house to which his sister Hazel had been sent, was a mansion. He faced the possibility therefore that this opportunity, for which he had prayed so long, and which a war had brought to him, might after all be ruined. After Wallace Street in Gowburgh this bungalow in the avenue of trees, with a field on the other side, was splendour and freedom; but he had dreamed of and schemed for something much grander. One compensation was that the Michaelsons were so easily taken in; really rich people, he felt, would not have been. Mrs. Michaelson, for instance, was almost in tears when at the supper table he told how his mother had begged him not to become separated from his twin Hazel, and how, through nobody's fault, he had not been able to prevent it. Mr. Michaelson chuckled over that story, with his eyes closed most of the time; but that was obviously his way of hiding how deeply touched he felt. In Gordon's twelve years of watchful experience he had come to the conclusion that men's pity, though often disguised as gruffness or indifference, was often more positive than women's, who wept, and kissed, and lamented, and so did nothing. These winks that Mr. Michaelson kept giving him, behind his wife's back, were more promising than her cheap exclamations of sympathy. Indeed, it was apparent to Gordon after he had been in the house for an hour that the queer little man with the strips of hair across his scalp despised his wife and daughters for their silly simperings one minute and their sillier earnestness the next. It should not be hard to sneak in ahead of them in his estimation. Had he not already confided that for years he had wanted a son just like Gordon? He was, he had whispered, just a wee bit tired of female company in the house all the time.

Thus as Gordon lay awake in bed, reviewing his position, it seemed to him that if he played the game carefully the prize would be a chance to remain here in Langrigg for the rest of his life, to become the heir to Mr. Michaelson's big shop in the main street, to be left all his money in the bank, and in the end to live in this house alone. Before falling asleep, he conjured up his mother as he had last seen her with her face crushed against the iron bars of the station gate. He listened again to her screams, begging him to come back; then inexorably he shook his head. A few minutes later he was asleep, still smiling; so that when the Michaelsons, on their way to bed, tiptoed in to look at him, that smile so perturbed her in her own private unhappiness that she sobbed herself to sleep, while he, remorseless by her side, was pleased that out of the barrenness of his

113

life had grown this prospect of evil, for which there could be no retribution, and from which might be plucked the flowers and berries of rejuvenescence. As husband, as father, as merchant, as church-goer, as councillor, as worthy respected citizen, he had for years felt himself growing feeble, senile, and contemptible. Hence his secret adulation of Hitler now setting Europe on fire; and hence too his vision of his own home in the coming weeks as a kind of battleground where by methods more subtle than tanks or bombs he, too, on the side of darkness, would win a victory.

In Bona Vista, in a bedroom three times the size of Gordon's, his sister inconsolably grieved for her mother. Mrs. Merrick, the owner of the house, made no effort to restrain the girl; yet her sympathy, though unexpressed, was neither trite nor perfunctory. By the bedside, outside the room, and on the stairs, leaning upon the stick she found necessary nowadays, the tall, white-haired, impassive woman remembered how she, too, many years ago, in a land thousands of miles away, had wept for her mother, whom she was never to see again. Hazel's tears were her own flowing again, and for both their sakes she wished them to flow. "You are very welcome here in my house, Hazel," she had said, "and you will be taken excellent care of; but you must never forget that your first and greatest loyalty is to your mother. Write to her in the morning. Tell her there is no need to worry about you. Tell her, too, that if she wishes to visit you she will be welcome here at any time. I would rather cut off my own hand or pluck out my own eyes than come between a mother and daughter." At that last vow she had smiled, contemptuous not of the sentiment, which was sincere, but rather of the theatrical shoddiness with which inevitably it must be expressed. But Hazel, weeping, would hardly have noticed had the actual threats been carried out in front of her. "She is a very beautiful child," thought Mrs. Merrick in wonder, "and so I shall cherish her; but I shall not allow myself to love her, I shall not take advantage of her unfortunate mother." She had seen how easy it would be to take advantage of poor Mrs. Aldersyde who, in the portrait

114

contained in the locket round Hazel's neck, appeared a plain, plebeian, unintelligent woman. Handsome herself, erect in spite of her lameness, dignified, impregnably aloof, and so intelligent as to have long ago conquered self-deception, Mrs. Merrick was confident few women could defeat her, if she entered the contest in earnest: certainly not Mrs. Aldersyde.

At Lammermuir, where the Cargills lived, Mrs. Raeburn had only one complaint: they were too unrelentingly kind to her. Ingratitude she hated, and was incapable of showing: therefore this feeling of being suffocated, or nullified, by all that assiduous attention and generosity, remained shut up in her, making her so miserable and irritable that once, when Jess looked too smugly at ease amid that alien luxury, she slapped the child and then wept at her own cruelty, unjustness, and unworthiness. As soon as she could, she resolved, she would get Mr. Roy to transfer her to some other house where her money would not be refused and where no servant would be asked to attend to her.

As for the Baxter brothers, they had not been daunted to find themselves in a hostile citadel. Bailie Rouster's frank and guffawing inability to believe his own popping eyes when they were introduced by the already retreating escort, had been easily endured by their iron-hard susceptibilities. Indeed, they had laughed with him, remembering that he was the man in the white hat who had led the procession and at whom they had thrown some stale cookies. But his wife's performance on seeing them was too insulting, even for boys who had been pelted with fish-heads by a chip-shop proprietor whose penny-in-the-slot machine they had jammed with metal washers. She had not laughed, as her husband had; she had not cursed either, like Jack the chipman. She had collapsed into a chair with bouncy springs, and screamed, with her lavender-gloved hands flying on and off her eyes, like butterflies off flowers. They had not known how to react: there was nothing they could do to help her: one woman they knew in Gowburgh, a Mrs. Logan, took fits, but she was a wee thin body who just fell down on to the pavement and lay harmlessly squirming, with froth on her lips. This fat woman with the powdered face and the horrible squeals seemed, on the contrary, dangerous: if she bit them, would they go mad? Even her husband, as he stood blowing out his cheeks and playing soldier-sailor-tinker-tailor-poorman-richman-beggarman-thief with the buttons of his jacket and cardigan, looked all the time ready to bolt.

When she did calm down, it was as sudden as thunder. There was not a speck of drivel on her lips. Under her lavender hat her hair was a little ruffled. Her dog, which had slunk behind a sofa, now peeped out with its ears hanging low. She questioned them, shrewd and inquisitive as a sheriff. Feeling innocent, they had boldly told the truth, Mr. Roy's part in the story she seized on fiercely, like a hungry dog with a bone. But when they described to her, with grinning accuracy, the minister who had signed their billeting slips, she had become suspicious, sniffed all round their description, barked at her husband not to butt in, sniffed some more, and finally, in a series of astonished yaps deepening to bays of fury, had accepted Sandeman as the blunderer. There had then begun a squabble between her and her husband, reminding the boys of a dog worrying a cat: Mr. Rouster, indeed, kept looking round as if for a tree up which to run. The fight was over them. She wanted them flung out immediately, he mumbled that they would have to be kept for decency's sake till the morning. It went on till the Baxter pride was hurt, and the Baxter truculence roused. She used the one word of opprobrium they could not stomach. Inured to every monosyllabic obscenity, tolerant of such terms as riff-raff, scum, rubbish, midden-rakers, hooligans, and dirt, they had from babyhood been taught to resent with teeth and nails, with sticks and stones, and with retaliatory abuse, the appellation guttersnipe. It alone with mystical sharpness could find its way through their tough defences to their tender souls: to suffer it, and not object, whoever the inflictor, was to surrender their birthright as Gowburghians, as Scotsmen, as human beings, as children of God. "For Christ's sake, missus," yelled young Tom, "shut your bluidy mooth." And out of the house he raced, followed

116

by Willie, who, passing the ship's bell that hung in the hall, clanged it as if to signify war was declared.

They climbed a tall tree in the grounds for reconnaissance and meditation. Soon the dog came and yelped below. It was hostile, and they might have broken off branches and bombarded it, if they hadn't remembered how, during its mistress's tirade against them, it had crouched behind the sofa. They debated the plan of running away and stealing a lift on any lorry going in the direction of Gowburgh; Tom was in favour. Willie, however, advised patience; later escape might be attempted, with honour and advantage; now it would be a cowardly and foolish satisfying of the enemy. Better in the meantime to wait till dark, climb up a drain pipe into the attic bedroom that the Bailie had allotted to them in his wife's absence, lock themselves in, sneak down when the house was asleep, raid the food cupboards and then return to bed. In the morning they could decide which one of a thousand enterprises would profit them most.

It was the Bailie who spoiled that plan. Just when they were about to descend the tree, he appeared furtively at its foot and called to them. Since it was obvious he was terrified his wife would hear, they trusted him. He wished them to follow him. This they did, as stealthy as Redskins about to scalp sleeping settlers. Into the house they crept, up the broad carpeted staircase that led to the main bedrooms, and then still higher up the narrow bare stairs leading to the attics. When they were safely in their room, their guide took his finger from his lips to whisper that he would have food sent up as soon as it was convenient; which meant, they saw, when his wife was out of the way. Tom wondered if he was going to murder her, and hoped he would. Outwardly, on the more interesting subject of food, Tom asked if they could have hot chips with tomato sauce. The Bailie laughed rather louder than he evidently thought was prudent, and shook his head. No chips, he said, but cold chicken instead, cold tongue, trifle, and maybe coffee. Though they had not tasted some of these, they were not as mollycoddled children who will eat only what they are accustomed to; they were campaigners who tried whatever came

117

their way, and only declined what, such as fish boiled in milk, was utterly nauseating.

Then the Bailie turned solemn, and addressed them as if they were the town council. They could not, he was sorry to say, live there: his wife wouldn't have it; and if it was necessary she would produce a dozen medical certificates to prove their presence would destroy her nerves. He himself would have been willing to give them a trial: granted they looked as choice a pair of impertinent young ruffians as he had ever seen—this stricture was softened by his chuckles—but wasn't it the case that in the war looming up meekness, respectability, aye, and law-abidingness, would be qualities more likely to hinder than help? Milksops could never be trained to stick a bayonet into Huns' bellies. But his wife, like most women, preferred not to know that wars must be won by bayonets in men's guts. It might be, he said, or it might not be, a good thing if that brutal and bloody truth was brought home to them. It was at this point that Tom Baxter interrupted with the yawned remark, "Mister, I'm bluidy hungry." Regretfully the Bailie had to leave unresolved this absorbing theme of the bayoneting of bellies, in order to slink off and bribe the maid to fetch food for the filling of them. When he was gone his guests discussed him, and agreed that, though he was a "blethering auld eedjit", he would pass. Tom, however, said he was going to ask him if *he* had ever stuck a bayonet in a man's belly.

It was a question which had the Bailie later that night sorrowfully making thrusts with his bedroom poker, and recalling his career in the Pay Corps in the last war.

Tom McShelvie was one of the twenty-four seized at random by Mr. Mair-Wilson, who had dashed into the school pretending he was a pirate chief in search of a crew. Off in the bus they had gone, bellowing choruses of "The Quartermaster's Store", with Mair-Wilson himself singing the comic verses. Up the avenue lined by sixty-year-old beeches, some turning golden already, they had sped until they came suddenly in sight of the house, which was so huge, had so many windows and turrets, was covered with such fiery ivy, had such a tall white flagpole, and was surrounded by so vast a sea of lawn, that many of the boys wondered in trepidation and glee if the small fat man in the white jersey had after all not been kidding, and they really were pirates going to capture this castle as large as an ocean liner.

On the broad steps outside the front door, Mrs. Mair-Wilson was waiting, as resigned as any chatelaine about to hand over to barbarians. Her friend, Mabel Rouster, watched from the lounge window. As they plopped out of the bus with their bundles gripped like weapons, Mrs. Mair-Wilson counted them: after a dozen, she threw up her hands; after twenty, she clapped them to her head. Her husband, leading his buccaneers, rushed up to her and saluted. He introduced them as a company, promising to present each one separately after they had been installed and fed. Her he introduced as his wife, and their hostess. He called for and led a cheer in her honour that roused the rooks from the tops of trees a quarter of a mile away.

Then into the house they streamed, along corridors, upstairs and downstairs, through passages broad and narrow, until they reached the two large rooms fitted out as dormitories with double-tiered beds. Each was allowed to pick his own bed, and in five minutes this was done, after only three squabbles, one fight, and one usurpation. Their washroom was next visited, and used: again their host merely observed, as pleased with the cat-licks of most as with the hippopotamus splashings of the three who stripped to the waist. Then off to the dining-room where a three-course meal was served to them by maids who at the beginning weren't quite sure whether they regarded this extra duty as a joke, an imposition, or a patriotic concession, and at the end were even more uncertain.

After eating came the writing home: this was compulsory. Tom McShelvie didn't know whether he should write to his mother or his father. Being an independent boy, who preferred his own mistakes to the advice of adults, he did not consult Mr. Mair-Wilson, but decided to write to his father, on the ground that his address was known and his mother's wasn't. Tom did not content himself with the official formula: his new address, and the intimation he was safe and well. He also said, in his customary misspelt scribble, which got him the belt twice a week from Miss Cairncross, that he was glad there was going to be a war, as this place he was in was "grate". As censor, Mr. Mair-Wilson passed that addition without comment, but with the resolution that as long as the war lasted this experiment in national co-operation would last too.

The two McShelvie girls, the delicate Effie and the clever Jean, were received by an old couple called Duncan, who were patient and kind, but who also worshipped dimness and silence. Their little house, at the edge of a field, was as quiet and shrouded as if someone lay dying or dead in it. They communicated with each other in signs, so secret that the girls could not detect them; and to the girls themselves they used the gentlest whispers. Even the clocks ticked faintly, and the big fat black cat never miaowed at all. When the old man listened to the wireless he had his ear touching it; and his condemnation of the Germans, though extreme, was expressed in shakes of his fragile head. Used at home to the merry hammering of their father cobbling their shoes, to Sammy and Tom trying to mend an old bike that somebody had thrown on the midden, to Flo screeching the latest songs, and to their mother keeping everybody in order, the McShelvie girls found this hush eerie and intimidating. They could not weep for fear of disturbing it; for the same reason, they dared not giggle. They almost did not enjoy their tea because the cups and spoons and their own careful jaws made too much noise; but the food was so good and plentiful, and their host and hostess so insistent with gestures on their eating well, that it was a grand tea after all. Later, cuddling each other in bed, they covered their heads with the blankets and had a good mixed greet-and-giggle; after which they went quickly to sleep, just too soon to hear the town-hall clock strike nine, with nine resonant outrageous clangs heard all over the town.

The eight Gowburgh women teachers, after a characteristically thorough exploration, discovered a boarding-house, which with a squeeze could put them all up. It turned out to have no fires in some of the bedrooms, and to be so understaffed that they had to fill their own hot-water bottles in the kitchen. Moreover, to some a compensation, to others an additional ordeal, four Polish officers were temporarily stationed there, in uniform so splendid and with manners so ducal, that an encounter with one in the narrow lobby was a long harassing experience of heel-clicks, bows, and knightly smiles. Even those who approved were a little embarrassed; the rest were mortified.

Afterwards, when relating his evacuation reminiscences, Mr. Grahamstone usually began: "I know well enough I'm considered too severe a judge, with the result I've got something of a reputation for grumbling." He could have put it simpler by saying: "I'm not called 'Greetin' Tam', for nothing." However, he felt he had to have such a warning preamble, otherwise nobody would have believed his tale of hardship and humiliation in Langrigg's handsomest manse. As it was, many did refuse to believe it, knowing him to be biassed against the cloth; while others, including his own wife, accepted part and discounted the rest as pardonable hyperbole.

The truth, nevertheless, was strange enough to need no help from bias, spite, conceit, or revenge. In the first place, Mrs. Sandeman, dressed in black and as elegant as the receptionist in a hotel catering for royalty, received them as if, so Grahamstone said in dudgeon to Scoullar, they were plumbers in to mend the W.C. There was no shaking of hands, no smiling, not even much speaking. She addressed what little she had to say to her husband as if he was an interpreter. Their room was prepared, she said; a meal would be served them in it; there was to be as little disturbance as possible, as her mother had arrived from Edinburgh and was resting. Then she departed, leaving her husband to show the guests to their room.

That room, asserted Grahamstone ever after, was the meanest in the house; it was, in his apoplectic opinion, the reverse of the guest room, it was the chamber of discouragement. While the rest of the house, including untrodden corners, was richly carpeted, this cold cell under the roof had an austere strip in the shape of a coffin along the side of the bed. For a man subject to asthma like Scoullar, pointed out the headmaster, walking on chilly linoleum could easily be lethal. Scoullar might have retorted that in that case he ought to be given the side with the carpet; he might have, if his presence of mind hadn't been ravished by horror that he, who at home had twin beds, must sleep with one who though professionally his superior, was fat, clumsy, selfish, querulous, and no doubt an all-night snorer. This aspect of the situation, on the contrary, was a little comfort to the headmaster, who, fingering the bedclothes, found them thin and few: they would even, he said, have to provide their own heat.

For nearly an hour they sat in that cold dismal room, waiting for the meal that had been promised them. Once Grahamstone dashed out and roared down the well of the stairs: "Hello, there!" No one responded, and he had to retreat in fury. It was no balm to him, or to Scoullar either, to reflect that in the profane Curly Lamb, Campbelton and Roy, those dodgers, were living like lords, eating and drinking whatever they liked, reading the day's newspapers or listening to the night's news by a roaring fire, and looking forward to a long sleep on beds with interior springs and down-filled quilts. Indeed, it embittered the headmaster, as he stood at the window gazing down at Langrigg, that the very humblest of his contingent, the grubbiest babe, was in all likelihood in a nest of comfort and benevolence compared with him, the commander-in-chief. Aye, he had brought all those souls safely from Gowburgh, had made sure every one of them was properly billeted, and then, and only then, had yielded to the demands of his own body and soul for sustenance and rest, to be given this! It was so grotesquely unjust, so imbecilely against the established order of things, that he had to laugh, or rather snigger. Where ought he to apply for redress: Langrigg Town Council, Gowburgh Corporation, the Scottish Education Department, the local Presbytery, or the General Assembly?

At long last, after Scoullar though still hungrily awake had gone to bed, a maid arrived with a small folded table. She was skinny and forlorn, and seemed peculiarly astonished at seeing Scoullar in bed; but without comment she erected the table, ignored the headmaster's plea for haste, and then left. About fifteen minutes later she returned with a tray on which were a small silver coffeepot, two tiny cups and saucers, a midget bowl of sugar with a jug of milk to match, a plate with four small thin pieces of buttered toast, and a silver salver with four biscuits. These she set forth on the table. Before she could escape, Grahamstone grabbed her and demanded if that was all. She nodded in glaikit listless fashion. To his roared inquiry as to whose orders she was acting on, she said her mistress's. Thereupon, trying hard not to pull the uniform off her in his rage, he bade her tell her master he wished to speak to him at once; otherwise he would rush down and explode his anger all over the drawing-room, whether one or fifty mothers-in-law from Edinburgh were resting. He would not, he vowed passionately, eat one crumb; that was to say, he added with vigorous scorn, he would not embark upon the feast, until her master did come. Promising to convey that message, but showing no sign of being able to do so intelligently, she went away. Grahamstone exonerated her: anybody could see the poor girl was half-starved; God save her if she was going to be working in that household much longer.

Scoullar succumbed: muttering that he was tired (really he wanted to try to get to sleep before the snoring started), he drank his coffee, and ate his toast and biscuits. Grahamstone was staunch: for nearly half an hour he paced round and round that table, tempted to overturn it with a furious foot, watching the margarine (he was convinced it could not be butter) congeal on the toast, and sensing the coffee grow cold. His reward for his abstinence was paltry. Mr. Sandeman did come, was evasively apologetic, tholed thunderclaps of contumely with meekness, heard without a whimper the news that his guests intended first thing tomorrow morning to flee to a more Christian atmosphere, and in his defence merely murmured, irrelevantly, that he expected soon to be in uniform as a chaplain. Grahamstone's response to that was: God help the troops; but to his credit he expressed it after the minister's departure, to Scoullar feigning sleep.

After a fight with his pride, by no means fairly fought, Mr.

Grahamstone sat down, scunnered himself with the cold coffee, and gnashed at the toast and biscuits. Then, in shirt sleeves and with his braces dangling, as a revengeful stroke, he went off in search of a bathroom and found what, from its opulence of tiles, glass, chromium, and flowered porcelain, must have been the best in the house. He stayed in it much longer than he needed, just for devilment; and kept regretting he hadn't his pipe with him.

Upstairs in the garret again he undressed, belching out grumbles, and then on the carpet side climbed into bed, where he found his troubles were not ended, for Scoullar, stubbornly asleep, proved to be an instinctive blanket-hogger, upon whom an armoury of snores seemed to have a strangely stimulating effect.

PART THREE

I

HAD Mr. Grahamstone known that his tribulations of that night were after all not half so sore as his second master's, his own, by a principle to be found in no mathematical textbook, would have been divided by four. It was the headmaster's belief that suffering became no one, with the exception perhaps of schoolboy truants: even martyrs burning in the flames, he used to think, must look repulsive rather than sanctified as they screamed and scorched. But of all the sufferers on God's earth, he was convinced, Archie Campbelton was the least spartan and the most extravagant. He had seen him, for instance, put on a look of crescent horror, of prodigious incredulity, and of infernal affliction, just because he'd been asked to attend to some absent lady's class for half a day. To believe his hands, dying like doves in his pure-white cuffs, one would have taken Miss Calder's boys and girls to be imps of hell, ready to pierce him with spikes, poison him with serpents, and snip off his flesh with red-hot shears. His attitude, Grahamstone maintained, for all its histrionics was really equivalent to the small boy's ear-shattering howl on being hurt, however slightly: it was intended to frighten off the injurer; and it usually succeeded, as Grahamstone was in an excellent position to know, for often he'd done some clerical chore himself rather than sit through once again Archie's performance of good nature devilishly abused, zeal shamelessly taken advantage of, and capability ridden far too ruthlessly. He had often wondered how Archie would react to some really considerable grievance.

Had he been in the lounge of the Curly Lamb at a quarter past eleven he would have had his curiosity satisfied. It was very peaceful in the lounge; only Campbelton and Roy were there, seated in the most comfortable seats in front of the fire. Roy read the day's newspaper, but Campbelton, who had already devoured it, births, deaths, marriages, and all, professed contempt of such quotidian trivialities, and himself was reading with his eyes shut half the time a batterless copy of *King Lear*, which by accident had found itself among the typical lounge trash. At less than arm's length each had a glass of whisky, to which every so often he resorted for a tranquil revivifying sip. On the mantelpiece the clock, in spite of the gilt eagle on top, coo'd the time away till bed.

Upon this scene stumbled Alden, still wearing his hat, and still with his whiskers wilted. This latter appearance surprised them, for they supposed that he had come from some enclave where, with grace and celerity, he had been imbibing whisker-stiffeners of various delicate hues. Campbelton in particular was compassionate: the small man was not only a connoisseur of whisky, he was also a co-martyr in the agony of the billeting arena. Therefore he welcomed him with warmest eloquence.

Alden dragged a chair along to sit beside them; he crinkled the carpet, but not half so much as his face.

"Gentlemen," he gasped, "I've just come from Cairnban."

They nodded. In the course of his duty he had been to see that the women and children were settled in.

"I got an urgent S O S," he went on. "Bob Gilliespie, passing the place in his car, brought it."

"An S O S?" repeated Roy.

"Yes, Mr. Roy. It seems he met some women out on the road at the house gates. They had their babies and luggage with them. He nearly ran them over. They were acting as if demented. He's a good soul, is Bob, and he persuaded them to return while he went for help."

Campbelton returned, rather ostentatiously, to the agonies of Lear; there, his manner implied, he would find gigantic, ennobling, and universal sorrows; why waste his time in listening to these parochial clishmaclavers?

Roy, however, had flung aside his newspaper. Since his meetings with Miss Cargill and Mrs. Ross, chivalry had been bothering him like a heartache.

"What was the matter with them?" he demanded.

"That's what I went to find out. Really though there was no need; I knew before I went. Mr. Roy and Mr. Campbelton, what I am about to say amounts to self-condemnation."

"Why?" asked Roy. "How is it your fault?"

"Well, you must understand, we never thought Cairnban would be required."

"I gathered that in the school tonight. But everybody praised the place. In fact, weren't they afraid it was too good for the purpose?"

"Structurally."

"What d'you mean?"

Campbelton turned a page.

"The house is empty," murmured Alden.

"Empty!" roared Roy.

Campbelton turned another page.

"Empty," repeated Alden, shaking his head. It was a word he always disliked; here it was at its most sinister and gloomy.

"But surely there are beds?"

A blink of shameful eyes abolished beds.

Campbelton had to turn still another page; he kept finding references pertinent to the conversation going on beside him.

"I have done all I could," said Alden. "Alas, it was not much. I sent for straw and palliasses. Luckily we had some in store." He plucked some wisps of straw off his coat. "At least they will be saved from the hard floor. Tomorrow, gentlemen, I intend to have every minister in the parish make an appeal from his pulpit for furniture of every kind for Cairnban. I am sure the response will be generous. But tomorrow is a long night away."

Campbelton yawned and stretched out his arms. Though Lear sat on his lap, it was Macbeth he quoted:

"'Sleep that knits up the ravell'd sleave of care,
The death of each day's life, sore nature's bath,
Balm of hurt minds, great nature's second course,
Chief nourisher in life's feast.'

I think," he added, "I'll go to bed."

Alden looked at him anxiously. "Have you been following me, Mr. Campbelton?" he asked.

"Yes, he has," said Roy, "very closely. So they've got bags of straw to lie on. What then?"

"This then, Mr. Roy. They say, or at least the woman Mc-Shelvie says, and hers is the only sane voice there tonight, that if they are asked to spend the night in that great dark house by themselves, they will refuse to do so, they will lie down in the main street rather and so perish of exposure on Langrigg's doorstep, as it were."

"Dark?" Roy was crying. "Why the hell is it dark?"

"You might well ask, Mr. Roy. We forgot the Captain had not put in electric light, and the gas of course has been turned off. I've sent for Jack Houston of the Gas Department, but he's not an easy man to find on Saturday nights. I sent some candles along."

"Well, by God," cried Roy, "there's a muddle-up if ever there was one."

"And, of course," added Alden, determined to confess all, "there was no food. In fact, there is no food save what the ladies brought with them from Gowburgh."

Roy clenched his fist. "Do you know what I think?" he cried.

Alden bowed his head. "Yes, Mr. Roy, I know. I have been criminally negligent. I deserve to be jailed."

Roy jumped to his feet.

"Well, we've got to do something about it now," he said.

Alden leapt up too.

"I knew that you and Mr. Campbelton would not let those poor women down," he cried. "You see, what I really came here to tell you was that they have asked specially for you two gentlemen to go and spend the night there with them."

128

If Roy looked taken aback by that proposal, Campbelton's reaction was beyond description: Gloucester with his eyes gouged out, Lear carrying the dead Cordelia, were pictures of rampant joy in comparison.

"In your names," went on Alden, faltering a little because of that colossus of anguish and affront writhing on the chair by the fire, "I promised you would go to them at once. In their turn they undertook to remain there until you came. But, gentlemen, time is short."

"Time," whispered Campbelton hoarsely, "may be as long as the distance from here to the outermost galaxy of the expanding universe, and yet be too short for that journey."

Alden did not understand.

"I have a car waiting," he said helpfully.

Campbelton louped up and began to take fierce tragic strides over the carpet.

"Why us?" he cried. "Are we not unmarried men?"

Again Alden could not see the significance.

Campbelton halted and struck an oratorical pose, extravagant even for a statesman upholding civilisation, with the iconoclasts howling at the gates.

"I shall speak for myself," he said. "Edgar can do as he pleases. I am a bachelor, Mr. Alden, from principle. As you can see, my physical appearance is not such as to repel females: I have the voice to woo them, and the conceits, too, if I was so minded. I possess that unfailing lure, money in the bank. I shall without doubt rise to the top of my profession; such a peak may be no Everest of prodigious adventure and achievement, but from it a fair vista of material prosperity may be seen: dearer to the feminine heart than icy glory. In short, few men are more eligible; few have been ogled by so many mistresses of arts. Yet I remain a bachelor. It may therefore be, Mr. Alden, that my soul—to use the only word appropriate—boaks at the mere thought of the connubial hearth, with lisping sticky-fingered brats to call me da. It may be I have had with pertinacious resource to protect myself from that fate. And yet you come here to propose that I walk voluntarily into that seraglio of—of pelican daughters and unnatural hags, with their

129

foul fiends of offspring, and spend the night there, on a couch of straw! Even Shakespeare himself would lack the words to describe the effrontery and iniquity of such a proposal."

"Come off it, Archie," said Roy, grinning. "You like those women to think you're a charmer."

"They do think so," said Alden eagerly, although he had heard one of them say something about "big Lord Swanky-heid, wi' his shirt-tails o' velvet", referring apparently to Campbelton.

"We won't have to stay," went on Roy. "We'll talk to them and calm them down. If there's anybody can do that, you're the man."

"Are you so puerile, Edgar, as to imagine that flattery, as crude as dung, can make compassion sprout so monstrously in my breast, as to drive me out of this hotel, into a cold dark night—"

"As a matter of fact, it's coming on to rain," interpolated Alden.

"To pass the night either on my feet like a horse, or like a cow on straw? Amidst hysterical females, with howling young?"

"This is war, Archie."

"I had my war, thank you." He twitched at his trouser leg, but out of pride did not draw it up, to reveal his 1918 scar sustained in a fall over a zinc latrine bucket.

"You're having this one too," said Roy, "whether you like it or not. The man who carried his captain out of no-man's-land under shellfire, and missed the M.M. because of administrative bungling, isn't going to quail before a houseful of distressed mothers and their frightened children."

"Where flattery fails, Edgar, sarcasm need hardly expect to succeed. I did not carry him, as you well know; I dragged him by the feet. It may have been administrative bungling, for that throve then as it does now, but I have always inclined to the opinion that though the captain was grateful enough for having his life saved he nevertheless thought I might, by remaining cooler, have found some other way of retrieving him than by dragging him face downward through some of the most insanitary mud in all France."

"Go and get your coat on, Archie," said Roy, pushing him. "It may be cold tonight in no-man's-land."

"I thought this," murmured Alden shyly, holding up a slim bottle of whisky, "might help. It's full."

It gave Archie the chance to make an impressive exit. As he passed he snatched the bottle from the town clerk's hand. "Drunk as Bacchus," he said, "I might endure it."

As soon as he was gone Roy began to worry out of Alden some method of obtaining food to take with them to Cairnban.

Campbelton's grandiloquent pet, far more than Roy's humanitarian arguments or Alden's diplomatic pleadings, proved useful in overcoming the unwillingness of grocer and ironmonger to leave their houses, in the former's case his bed, go to their shops, and supply the food and utensils immediately necessary. They could not resist the high tone of doom, in which he declared that their disobligingness would not merely mean the death by fright and hunger of a few expendable women and children, but would also open a breach in the country's solidarity: through hundreds of such breaches would sweep disunity, disillusionment, demoralisation, and defeat. They thought he must be drunk, mad, or inspired, just as they thought Roy, who did the ordering, impatient and impertinent; but they hurried, and into the car piled bread, butter, jam, eggs, powdered milk for babies, tea, sausages, bacon, kettles, frying-pans, teapots, dishes, cutlery, and other miscellaneous items which Roy maintained would be needed that night or next morning. Alden's demurs were ignored; he agreed that the town council should pay the bills, as they would receive the government billeting money for every person in Cairnban, but he knew that, whether the expenditure was justified or not, a row would be caused by its recklessness, and he would be blamed for not having curbed it.

The taxi-man, except for one involuntary protest that his cab was not a three-ton lorry, was co-operative. Much more loudly, he said that he himself had a wife and two children, and he would cut the entire German army's throat rather than see them go hungry. Therefore he helped to carry out the goods

131

and stow them on his cushions, and then drove with dimmed lights along the dark roads to Cairnban on the outskirts of the town. There, trees being numerous, darkness was thicker. Rain dripped gently. The avenue up to the house twisted, and its borders were obscured by long grass. The car went by jolts and jerks, like an animal afraid of what lay ahead. Inside, curled up like its palpitating stomach, crouched Campbelton. He kept muttering that only necromancy could have transported him so soon from the comfort of the Curly Lamb to this hideousness. It was a feeling he had often had in 1918; but he was now twenty-one years older.

As the leader, he groped his way up the steps to knock on the door and announce deliverance. Candlelight, seen in some windows as they approached, had now vanished: darkness was complete. One result was that Campbelton cracked his bad knee against what he conjectured to be a stone cupid minus a wing. He cursed and rubbed.

"Have they all gone?" asked Alden, in alarm. He was remembering there was a small loch not far away where a woman had drowned herself because her husband had run away.

Roy banged on the door and shouted.

Silence followed, except for Campbelton's mutterings: with his hand he was still discovering that the thing which had kicked him had a face. It was not the first time in his life he had in darkness put out his hand to feel a face, itself without feeling.

Roy banged again. "Open the door, ladies," he shouted. "It's Mr. Campbelton and Mr. Roy."

There were heard what Alden thought were the cries of women released from terror, but what to Campbelton, stroking that stone face, seemed like the screeches of the witch Cutty Sark and her hellish mates, who had swarmed out of the haunted kirk upon Tam o' Shanter. An iron bar clanked; a key creaked; a bolt squealed back. The door was opened two inches. Candlelight was glimpsed within. By it they were recognised, and within a moment they were, as Campbelton clearly saw, far worse off than Tam, whose beldams had wished to kill

132

him, murder being their nature and duty, for these, shrieking authentically, with clutching talons, streaming hair, and foetid breath, rushed out to hug, fondle, drag in, and even kiss. Campbelton's hat was skited off into the dirt outside, as it ought to be, he reflected, for vine leaves ought to be on his head instead of expensive sophisticated felt. "I am Bacchus," he cried, as he was handled by those tempestuous nymphs; and since he had always had a secret shame of his tame occupation of pedagogue, this new role was momentarily an abandonment, defiance, and joy.

Their shrieks were in the Gowburgh dialect and idiom.

"Sing, women, sing: there's men in the hoose."

"I always said to them wha ca'd Mr. Campbelton a big conceited poultice, they were wrang: he's a gentleman, I always said, a sweet gentleman."

"Oh, Mr. Roy, when we keeked oot at you making eyes at that smasher in Bessie Raeburn's car, we thought you'd forsaken us."

"This hoose was like a morgue for storing folk drooned in the Clyde, but we'll sing hymns in it noo. We'll mak it as merry as the Tent Hall."

Those were samples. There were others. One or two only were bawdy, and these were uttered in the staccato screech identifiable as Meg Aitchison's: they were to the effect that, as their reward, the two teachers could have the pick of the harem; reaching her crescendo, Meg boasted that she had as good a chance of the honour as any, seeing the picking, and whatever else, would have to be done by candlelight.

In the midst of this rout Bacchus beamed, shook hands, patted, laughed, and joined in the dance.

Disenchantment came abruptly. A different voice altogether, though still feminine, was heard subduing the babel. Dry, patient, authoritative, and a little angry, it reminded them all that the house was full of children hungry, babies fretting, and other women paralysed with despair; and it wanted to know what the visitors had brought with them of use and value, apart from their own persons.

It was Mrs. McShelvie's, and it turned Campbelton from

133

wine-god into a rumpled, weary, scandalised, middle-aged teacher with a lump on his knee and a lost hat. He felt he had always distrusted this woman; she represented, in a baleful fashion, the realism of grey-haired, poverty-stricken, harassed maternity.

Roy rhymed off some of the articles they had brought.

"You've been busy," she said.

"So have you," he replied, for glancing into one of the rooms he had seen that beds of a kind had been made up.

"We need light," she said.

"Didn't Jack Houston come to turn it on?" asked Alden.

"Nobody came, except bogles; they came in their thoosands. I was doon in the basement having a look but I'd to come back up to chase awa' a black man wi' a hatchet."

Roy smiled. "I'll take a look," he said. "Archie, will you see to the unloading of the stuff? The women will help you."

Hilariously they claimed him as their leader; they were still his maenads, and he Bacchus; unfortunately by this time he was as sober as John Knox.

"My hat," he said plaintively, "I've lost my hat."

Roy and Mrs. McShelvie set off by candlelight to search the basement.

"Do you think it's going to be a success here?" he asked.

"We'll need chairs to sit on, and tables to eat frae."

"There's to be an appeal tomorrow from the pulpits for furniture. I meant, will these women manage to live here together amicably?"

"As weel as men wad, in the same circumstances."

He chuckled. "You know the circumstances wouldn't be the same with men."

"There wad be nae weans, you mean?"

"That's right. Where there are children there are squabbles."

She said nothing.

"What about your own children, Mrs. McShelvie?"

Her smile there in the flickering light, with the white-washed cobwebbed wall behind, was memorable.

"They're a' right, I suppose," she said.

"None of them here?"

"No. They're weel scattered."

"There's one thing," he said, "you'll be needed here."

"Do you think so?"

"I certainly do. Somebody will be needed as caretaker, umpire, and peacemaker. Nobody could do that better than you. In fact, this is the chance we were hoping for. Do you remember? Look, there's the meter; and there's the handle for turning it on." Slowly they walked across the stone floor.

I could be his mother, she thought, as she shielded the candle with her hand while he seized the handle and wrenched at it; but I'm more like his servant.

"It's stiff," he gasped, pausing to rest. "What is it?" Her look at him had seemed peculiar.

"I thought I heard something, like mice or rats."

"There'll be no rats here, surely."

"No."

He pulled again at the handle and turned it. His hand was thick with dust. He cleaned it with his handkerchief.

"It's peaceful down here anyway," he said, laughing.

They imagined the pandemonium upstairs, with Campbelton in the midst.

"I hope he's found his hat," she murmured.

"I suppose we'd better hurry and warn them," said Roy. "God knows how many taps they'll have turned on."

"They were weel warned about that," she said grimly.

"You know what children are."

They began to go up the stone steps.

"Maybe you'll be interested," she said, "or maybe you'll not; but oor neighbour on one side is the hoose ca'd Lammermuir, where you had Bessie Raeburn billeted."

"Is it, by Jove?"

"We'll need fresh milk in the morning, and there's no telephone in this hoose."

"Somebody will have to go out then and do it."

"Aye."

"But everybody will be in bed at this time!"

"We're no' in bed."

He was thinking that even if Miss Cargill was in bed she

135

wouldn't mind getting up for such a good cause; and surely it was time he was seeing her again?

"I'll go," he said.

Her silence seemed to indicate that in some way she had evened the score.

They were met in the hall by a dejected Campbelton. His hat had been found, and was on his head. It was dirty and dented, but he was too dispirited to care. Women still surged round him; one or two were calling him "Archie".

"Did you find it?" he asked.

"We'll soon see," said Roy. By using a candle he was able to reach the mantles in the chandelier; there were only two unbroken, but the light they gave was cheered. The women rushed off to light the gas in their own rooms.

"What about black-out?" whimpered Campbelton.

"To hell with black-out," said Roy.

"Well," muttered Campbelton, refusing to look at Mrs. McShelvie, "the food's in, and the lights are on. There's really no need for us to stay any longer. We'll have to walk, for Alden's gone with the car; the little beast refused to wait."

"I've to telephone for milk," said Roy anxiously.

"You can do that on the way."

Roy could not say he must telephone from Lammermuir. Archie was not in the mood to tolerate this tiny pathetic green tendril of romance.

"If you two walk oot o' here," said Mrs. McShelvie, "you'll hae a crowd after you like the skailing o' an asylum."

"I suppose that's true," murmured Roy, as if regretfully.

Campbelton could find nothing to say: the inability frightened him as much as the prospect of spending the night there. Had this woman's witchcraft withered his gift of speech?

"We'll make up beds here in the hall," she said.

He could not reply.

"It'll be public," she admitted, "but if they don't see you they'll not believe you're here."

Still he said nothing.

"I'll warn them," she said, "that it's the height of bad manners to spy on folk in the middle of the night. But they'll likely tell me that they'll need to spy to be sure. It's really a compliment to you.

"If you missed your supper at the hotel," she added, "we'll be able to fry you some sausage and egg now that the gas is on. But you'll hae to be like the rest of us, and eat it off the floor."

"Mrs. McShelvie," he said at last, hoarsely, "you have painted a picture of hell such as even Dante could not rival."

She smiled. "I never heard of him."

Next minute they were in the midst of a witches' dance. Meg Aitchison and some friends as skinny and unbraw as herself began to jig to the music of frying-pans and kettles clanged by spoons. Children in pyjamas, nightgowns, and shirt-tails, crowded on the stairs to watch.

"Edgar," whispered Campbelton, in anguish, "what are we to do?"

But Roy was smiling; he even clapped the dancers. Within a quarter of an hour he would be speaking to Elizabeth Cargill.

"When I think of Grahamstone," whimpered Campbelton, "lolling in the manse, I could shed tears. All he has to put up with is an overdose of piety."

The dancers jigged off to the kitchen.

"Now's my chance, Archie," whispered Roy. "Mrs. Mc-Shelvie's got everything under control."

"Don't speak about her. I regard her as the mainspring of this menagerie."

Roy had to appreciate such a fine mixed metaphor.

"I'd better slip across to Lammermuir and make that phone call."

"Lammermuir? Is that where your precious Miss Cargill lives?"

"Yes."

"Then I shall go with you."

"But one of us must stay, Archie."

"Then let that one be you. I can use a telephone, you know."

"It's raining, it's dark, and they'll likely be in bed."

"I am well aware, Edgar, that if I insisted on going I should, on the steps outside, find your dagger between my shoulders.

137

You have been making yourself a disgusting bore with your drivelling inanities about this young woman. In my own interests, as well as in your own, I shall have to allow you to pay this visit, obtain the second, the disillusioning, sight of her, and so return here an intelligent human being once more."

"Thanks, Archie. Tell them not to bother keeping any sausage and egg for me."

"I shall tell you what I propose to do. I shall sit on that bottom stair, and compose an address to Langrigg Town Council. So virulent will it be that any child, or harpy, so much as passing within two feet of me will drop dead. But for God's sake, hurry back!"

Roy gave the promise, but hoped he would not have to keep it.

II

Before he left the gaslight, Roy glanced at his watch: the time was a quarter past twelve; far too late, he could hear his Aunt Mary say, for any respectable young man to go visiting any respectable young lady. Previously her criticisms had been able to be tenderly and truthfully rejected, for on former occasions neither he nor the young females were, in Aunt Mary's sense of the word, respectable: indeed, they would have sickened a little at the word as being synonymous with smug, narrow, joyless, anaemic, and dreary. Now, however, as he stumbled quickly down the drive, he found himself anxious to win Aunt Mary's approbation: respectable now connoted virginal, virtuous, vivid, and vital. Swerving from applying those tests to his own character, he applied them with simple-minded earnestness to Miss Cargill's, and of course she passed with honours. She was the kind of young woman who, if a strange young man woke her up at half-past twelve on a Saturday night or rather on a Sunday morning, would certainly not speak to him in pyjama'd or dressing-gowned person, but would

138

allow her father or a servant to attend to him. She would be as remote as chastity, which was the dawnlit snow on the ultimate peak. (Hitherto it had been the desert at the mountain's foot.) Yet if Miss Cargill was thus chaste, where was the delectable exciting point in his making this journey, upon which he had already twice fallen and bumped against a tree once? He was, he realised, on a whirligig of contradictory wishes; and the effect was to slacken the muscles of his legs, rotate his stomach, and turn his heart into a bag for a set of pipes. The likelihood was, and the tree he had bumped into sneered it in a voice like Archie Campbelton's, that he was falling in love, without his usual parachute of crafty masculine gumption. He did not know therefore whether to be relieved or chagrined when a bush clutched at him, and hissed in that same voice, that Miss Cargill had probably forgotten he was in Langrigg, indeed in existence.

At the gate he discovered he had forgotten to ask whether Lammermuir lay to the right or the left. His method of finding out would formerly have been accompanied by sardonic, even lecherous, chuckles, but now it was carried out like a necessary rite. He lifted up his head into the soft night rain, sampled the air to the right and then to the left, and at once set off in the latter direction confidently. Emanating from her was a magical fragrance, far too subtle for others: it was distinguishable from scent of flowers and trees, and infinitely more evocative of the beauty and richness of the earth. He was much too humble to think that from him emanated a corresponding fragrance, detectable only by her.

When he came to the first gate in the avenue, he was so sure it led into Lammermuir that, as he struck a match to look at the brass plate on the wall, he felt ashamed of his lack of faith. When he saw that the name was not Lammermuir, but Ebenholm where the Rousters lived, he was so astounded and dismayed that he forgot the match, which burnt his fingers. It was at the pain therefore, rather than at his idiotic trust in a method of direction-finding fit to make scouts hoist their poles and spinsters simper, that he swore. The word, not the going out of the match, brought utter darkness. He hated and despised himself; he did not wish Miss Cargill to be courted or even looked at by a man who said —!; he hoped Miss Cargill had never even heard of it; and at the irrepressible mischievous thought that perhaps she used it herself, when ripping her silk stockings or missing a twelve-inch putt, he tried to groan as one should at pernicious folly. Yet he could not altogether banish the suspicion that if this were true love, then the price, this softening of the brain, might be too high for a man with a war to win. Vaguely he understood that behind Archie's rantings in the hotel lounge had been an element of desperate common sense.

By the time he had walked to Lammermuir's gate he had recovered sufficient presence of mind not to regard it as an omen good or bad when he crushed his finger painfully in opening it; nor did he consider his instant and sincere swearing as in any way deleterious to Miss Cargill or unbecoming in himself. Walking up the avenue, he sucked his finger and so remembered the babies on whose behalf he was making this call. He felt encouraged. No windows were lit, of course. Miss Cargill was not pacing her room, tormented by the memory of the tall handsome fair-haired young man she had seen in the school playground. No, she was sensibly asleep, dreaming of golf.

As he put his thumb on the bell-button, he held it there for almost half a minute before pressing: this might after all not be merely an act to set a little bell ringing; it might be setting in motion an intricate and wonderful machinery which no more than the courses of the stars (some of which were now showing in breaks in the clouds) could be arrested, and which would involve his whole future life and Miss Cargill's.

He pressed the bell, and waited. The time, he thought, must be about one. The town hall clock had struck a short time ago, but now that it was amongst the small hours, half-hours and quarters were confusing. He did not look at his watch.

He pressed again.

A window almost directly above opened, in an excellent position for emptying a bucket of water over him, as was done with courting cats and dogs.

"Who's there?"

It was her voice, certainly: the yawn in it, the annoyance and alarm, did not deceive him.

"It's me, Mr. Roy, a teacher from Gowburgh." What a bloody dismal way of declaring himself, he thought. "It is I, Edgar, on a mission of mercy, and of love." That would have been better, if only the galleryite in himself could have been trusted not to guffaw.

"You're not here to visit Mrs. Raeburn, I suppose?" she asked.

That was sarcasm. He felt displeased.

"No," he answered, with dignity. "I must apologise for disturbing you, Miss Cargill, at this very late hour. I have come from the house next door, Cairnban."

"Oh, for goodness' sake," she said, "I'll come down and let you in. We'll be wakening up the whole house." She shut the window.

As he waited, he found his foot tapping: a Scoullarish habit he had got into recently when waiting for an answer from some pupil whom inattention had left unable to answer. To stop it he stood on it with his other foot. At the same time he yawned. Putting up his hand, he felt how bristly his chin was, and cursed himself for not following Archie's example in the Curly Lamb and shaving.

The hall-light went on, a soft dimmed crimson: he contrasted it unfavourably with the harsh gaslight in Cairnban, where Archie squatted on the bottom stair, like a prisoner of female headhunters.

The door opened, and there, asking him in by no means cordially, was Miss Cargill, in a blue dressing-gown and blue satin slippers. She had her hair in curlers, and cream had obviously been wiped off her face in a hurry. She presented a sight years after their honeymoon. Yet somehow, in spite of Archie's prophecy about that second look, he was not disillusioned. On the contrary, he was confirmed.

As he tiptoed in, she had her finger on her lips. Such an imagination as his could hardly fail to be reminded of the improper side of romance. He was grateful, therefore, when a

141

grandfather clock, with Victorian primness, informed him it was twenty to one.

He glanced at his watch.

"I'm afraid it's later than I thought," he muttered. "My watch has stopped."

"It *is* late," she agreed, with a frankness short of lovable.

He spoke formally. "I'd like to use your telephone, if I may."

She thawed instantly. "Is somebody in Cairnban ill?"

How he wished somebody was. There were more than fifty children in the house. Could not one have taken pneumonia for the sake of prospering his courtship? Such a child would not only have recovered; it would have grown up to win first prize in a football pool.

"No," he had to reply. "I was asked to telephone to some farmer or milkman to bring a supply to the house early to-morrow—for the babies, you know."

"Couldn't that have waited till the morning?" she asked.

Of course it could have. But if he had called at seven o'clock would she have been any better prepared? He was convinced her touch of thrawnness, her withdrawal to common sense, were caused by his having caught her with the scaffolding, as it were, upon her beauty.

"Perhaps," he said. "But it's rather a large order, you know. There must be about a hundred people in the house. In any case, everybody there is anxious and excited."

"I can well believe that. We were surprised when we heard the house was being occupied. It hasn't been prepared, has it?"

"No. Nothing has been prepared, Miss Cargill. There were mothers weeping because they were afraid there would be no milk for their babies."

"I'm sorry." She searched for those weeping mothers in his own dry eyes. "The telephone's in here," she said, opening a door and switching on a light. "All the same, I'm afraid whoever you telephone will be in bed. We keep early hours in Langrigg."

The telephone was on a small table in a corner of the sitting-room. As he crossed over to it he was assessing the room with the eye of a prospective suitor, whose bank account was nil, whose salary was smaller than any energetic joiner's working overtime, and whose Aunt Mary, worth about two thousand pounds, was only sixty-three and as tough as teak. The three-piece suite itself was worth half a year of his salary.

"Do you mind if I smoke?" he asked.

She shook her head.

He offered her a cigarette, but she refused.

"I'm in the middle of the night," she murmured.

"Sorry." He grinned, as he lit one for himself. "Whom do you recommend?"

She hesitated, with a smile that implied she really couldn't recommend anybody who'd be very obliging at such an hour.

"I won't mention your name," he offered gallantly.

For some reason she blushed.

"Give my name if you like," she said. "Our milk is supplied by a farmer called McIntyre. He comes round about eight."

"He'll do. Do you know his number?"

"Langrigg 219," she replied, and made for the door. "While you're phoning I'll see if anybody has been wakened." She lingered at the door, with another smile, this time of sweet malice. "Perhaps I ought to warn you, Mr. McIntyre has a nickname; well-earned too."

"Oh. What is it?"

"Girny," she said, and went.

As he picked up the telephone and asked for Langrigg 219, he supposed "girny" meant in Langrigg what it did in Gowburgh: chronically bad-tempered. A girny baby was one which fretted all the time, worst of all about two in the morning. A girny farmer would be one who ploughed up a right-of-way, and resented, with the bucolic rage of a stone-age agriculturist, being roused out of his bed at one in the morning to answer the telephone.

The operator seemed astonished, and aggrieved; it was as if he felt he was being dragged into some mad and criminal prank. Roy had to be imperative.

After a minute or two the operator said no one seemed to answer. Roy asked him to keep on trying, as it was a matter

143

of life and death. Then at last the craven in the exchange told him he was through.

Girny was only normally indignant; perhaps sleep was muffling him.

"Wha in Beelzebub's name is this, in the deid o' nicht?" he screeched. It was a reasonable inquiry.

"You don't know me, Mr. McIntyre," said Roy soothingly. "I'm terribly sorry at having got you out of your bed."

"Leave aff the coo's tail, man, and get to the front. I'm shivering here on the cauld waxcloth in my bare feet. What the deil d'you want?"

"My name's Roy. I'm a Gowburgh teacher. You'll know, of course, we invaded Langrigg today."

"I've got twa here," said McIntyre, "that never saw a pig in their lives afore. What d'you learn them in school these days?"

"Many mothers couldn't be billeted in ordinary houses, because their families are too large. So they were put into a large house called Cairnban."

"I ken it weel."

"These mothers are desperately anxious that fresh milk will be supplied for their babies early tomorrow."

"Early the day, you mean. Are the weans as young as that?"

"Some are weeks old, Mr. McIntyre."

"How much will be needed?"

"I can't really tell. Say three gallons anyway."

"It's coos I hae, man, no' elephants."

"Bring as much as you can spare, then."

"Will this be a steady order?"

"Certainly. And you needn't worry about payment."

"Wha said onything aboot payment?"

"These people are really the guests of the town council." Roy had to pause, because at the other end Mr. McIntyre, perhaps because of his bare feet on the cold linoleum, seemed to be having an attack of bronchitis.

"D'you mean," wheezed the old man, "I've to send the bill to the toon cooncil?"

"That's right. They're entitled to pay."

There was another spasm. "Whit aboot guid fresh butter?"

asked the farmer. "These weans frae the city could be daeing wi' plenty o' that in their wames."

"I'm sure they could, Mr. McIntyre." If this, thought Roy, was what Langrigg called bad temper, God help them once they saw the true Gowburgh fury.

"And eggs?" panted Girny. "They could find a use for twa or three dozen eggs?"

"For twelve dozen."

"The cooncil hasnae authorised you to dae this, has it?" So here at last was the canny peasant emerging.

"Not quite," said Roy.

"They micht be a wee thing unwilling to pairt wi' the money?"

"They might be," admitted Roy. "But they'll pay all right."

"Man, say nae mair. You've said enough. Will you be at the hoose in the morning?"

"I'll be there."

"I'll bring you a special egg for your ain breakfast; a goose's, for a hen's will no' be big enough. You're a voice in the nicht, God bless you, a voice in the nicht. Guidbye."

"Goodbye," said Roy, and put down the telephone.

He turned to find Miss Cargill in the room again. She had covered her curlers carelessly with a blue silk scarf. "Did you manage?" she asked.

"Yes, thanks." He rose. "But why is he called 'Girny'? He sounded more like Santa Claus. He insisted on bringing butter and eggs as well as milk."

She looked at him warily. "He's about eighty," she murmured. "I suppose it's good business for him."

"No, it was more than that. He seemed very interested when I told him the town council would pay the bill."

She laughed, turning away; her fingers raced along the back of the large red sofa.

He sat down on the arm of the sofa and puffed at his cigarette.

"What's the joke?" he asked.

"Joke?" She shook her head. "I just think it's very funny you should have got old Girny up out of his bed. Wait till you see him."

145

"No," he said. "There's something between Girny and the town council. What's he been doing? Ploughing up a right-of-way?"

"There's a feud," she murmured.

"What about?"

She still had her face turned away, but on the sofa her fingers played a light-hearted tune.

"I can't say," she said.

"Why not?"

"It would be indelicate, perhaps," she whispered.

He grinned. "Tell me," he said. "I'm over twenty-one, and I'm from Gowburgh."

"Langrigg is a holiday resort," she said, and paused.

"A good golf course," he remarked.

"It is particularly proud of its main street, which you may have noticed is very wide."

He nodded.

"Girny has a field at the far end of the town," she murmured. "To bring his kye home to be milked he has to drive them along the main street." Again she paused. "He has nearly fifty," she added.

Roy pretended obtuseness. "Well?" he said.

"Visitors complained."

"But I thought in a country town kye were one of the favourite sights."

"In a field, not in the spick-and-span main street."

He murmured a line from Keats: " 'The murmurous haunt of flies on summer eves.' "

"So they asked old Girny to take them by a back road?" he asked.

She nodded.

"And he told them—I mean, he refused?"

"Yes. His kye still come along the main street. Do you know what he did for a while?"

"No."

"You'll not believe it. He used to take a walk into town with a cow on a rope, just like a dog. When he went into a shop he would tie it to a lamp-post outside."

"I take it there's no bye-law against having a cow as a pet?"

"Not so far."

"I think," he said, rising, "I'm going to like Girny very much. In fact, I'm going to like Langrigg after all."

"Weren't you sure, Mr. Roy?"

"I hope I'm going to be here long enough," he said, "for Langrigg to get to like me."

She was very bland. "Is there a chance you may be recalled soon?"

"There is always the summons to join the wild and licentious soldiery."

"I see."

They were now on their slow easily retarded way to the outside door. He pointed to golf clubs in a corner of the hall.

"Yours?" he asked.

She nodded. "Do you play, Mr. Roy?"

"A little."

"We might arrange a game, if you like."

"I like very much." Not thus, he thought, by cow-turds and golf had Romeo and Juliet progressed to passion; crudeness, not poetry, was the language of the twentieth century. It was a pity.

"We'll keep it in mind," she murmured.

They were now at the door. His hand was on the knob.

"You won't be staying in Cairnban all the time you're in Langrigg?" she asked.

"No."

She laughed at his tone. "Just for tonight?"

"Yes."

"Are you the only teacher there?"

"Archie Campbelton's with me. He's a bachelor, who would rather, I believe, be in the lion pit at Edinburgh Zoo, provided the lionesses were excluded."

"Are you married then?" she asked, softly.

"No. But mine is probably a transitory stage; Archie's is permanent."

"I see. Where are you going to live after tonight?"

"We've got a couple of rooms in the Curly Lamb."

"Then it doesn't matter," she said, with a sudden bright smile. "I needn't mention it then."

"Please do," he murmured, in a voice that, he knew, would have turned Archie green with disgust.

"Oh, it was just that my father said we could easily take in a couple of teachers as well as Mrs. Raeburn, if they required accommodation." She did not say her father had meant female teachers. "But it doesn't matter now."

"Perhaps it does," he said, with smooth mendacity. "Our rooms in the inn are temporary."

"Oh."

Then they were interrupted, not by her father's voice demanding with rude common sense what the hell he meant by hanging around there at that time of night, but by Mrs. Raeburn's, so shy, so timid, so apologetic, so self-distrustful, and yet so resolute.

She was on the stairs, with her coat over her nightgown. Her hair hung behind her, tied with a white ribbon; it made her look like a little girl.

"I'm sorry for interrupting," she said. "Mr. Roy, if I could have a word with you before you go, I'd be much obliged."

"It's dreadfully late, Mrs. Raeburn," he said.

"I couldn't sleep," she murmured.

"Speak to her," whispered Miss Cargill, "even if it's just for a minute. She's been miserable all evening. Good night. I hope the milk arrives."

She slipped into the sitting-room, and closed the door.

Roy went forward to the foot of the stairs. He saw she was pale and shivering.

"You're cold," he said.

"It's no' that."

"What is it then? I hope I haven't wakened up the children too?"

"They're sleeping. They ken nae better."

"What's wrong?"

"I think you ken what's wrong, Mr. Roy. I want you to take me oot of here. You couldnae hae wakened me up, for I was never asleep. This is nae place for the likes of me. I've

148

been brought up to pay my ain way, and accept nobody's charity."

He was dumbfounded. Was not Elizabeth Cargill the kindest person in the world?

"I'm sure nobody's forcing charity on you, Mrs. Raeburn."

"What is it then if they gang and buy you a pram for your wean, when you've got as guid a one at hame?"

He found himself unusually reluctant to see her point of view. Even Scoullar would have been more tolerant.

"You're talking nonsense, Mrs. Raeburn," he said sharply. "You know very well your own pram's at home."

"It could hae been sent for."

He made an effort, and smiled. Where was the profit in falling in love if because of it he became churlish towards this other unhappy woman?

"I think you're tired and upset, Mrs. Raeburn," he said. "Let's discuss this some other time, when we're both refreshed and able to see things in a more optimistic light."

"No, Mr. Roy. I want to leave, and naebody has a right to stop me."

"We're your friends, Mrs. Raeburn. We want you to do what's best for you and your two children. You know Langrigg's pretty full up now. It might not be easy for you to find another billet."

"In that case I could go back hame."

"Would your husband like that?"

"Or I could go to this place Cairnban."

Again that Scoullarish annoyance came into his voice. "I'm afraid you don't know what you are talking about, Mrs. Raeburn," he said. "The people there are lying on straw palliasses on the floor. They haven't even got chairs to sit on. They're as overcrowded, too, as any slum in Gowburgh. Likely the sanitary authorities will condemn it."

"I'd raither be there," she whispered passionately, "among my ain kind, and paying my ain way."

He felt like retorting that her husband wouldn't approve of her calling the Aitchisons and the Rosses her own kind.

"You should think of your children, Mrs. Raeburn."

"I am thinking of them. Do you think they'll ever learn independence here?"

It was childish, he knew, but he could not let her go without getting from her an exoneration for Elizabeth.

"You'll never get me to believe that Miss Cargill and her father are any danger to your children's independence."

"They may mean no harm. We're novelties to them."

"Is that not very unfair, Mrs. Raeburn? But it's for you to say. If you insist on being shifted, I'll do my best. All the same, I must say I didn't expect this from you."

"War or no war," she said, as she turned to go upstairs, "we've got our lives to live in the best way we ken. They're gentry, and I'm working-class. I think I'm as guid as they are, but if I was to stay here I wouldnae be able to think that much longer. I'm sorry I've disappointed you, Mr. Roy. You've been kind to me."

"So has Miss Cargill."

"I couldn't deny it. Guid night."

"Good night."

He watched her disappear upstairs. Then he knocked at the sitting-room door. Elizabeth came quickly.

"She wants to go," he said, in amazement.

"Yes."

"God knows why!" he exclaimed, with an incredulity that caused her, despite her concern on Mrs. Raeburn's behalf, to glance away with a smile on her own.

"Didn't she tell you why?" she murmured.

"She told me a lot of silly spiteful rubbish."

"I'm sure she didn't. She's a very conscientious woman. What did you say to her?"

"Oh, I had to promise to get her a shift, if I could."

She put her hand on his arm. "Don't be in a hurry," she said. "Give me a day or two. I believe I can win her over."

"If you can't," he said, with an impulsiveness too naïve to be characteristic, "nobody can."

She hid in flippancy. "How do you know," she asked, "that I'm not really a bully behind closed doors?"

Her hand was still on his arm. He was aware of it as a

small boy of a robin perched on his shoulder; even a shiver of delight might scare it off.

"I might be finding that out pretty soon," he murmured.

"Will you consult Mr. Campbelton?"

"As soon as I see him."

"Good night," she said softly.

"Good night," he replied, and a moment later found himself out on the doorstep, blinking up at the stars and then at the closed door. He did what Scoullar must never know, but what Archie must be told the moment he saw him: he kissed that door.

Intoxication had him jigging and humming all the way back to Cairnban.

Behind him in Lammermuir Elizabeth Cargill, after lingering outside Mrs. Raeburn's room for an unhappy guilty minute, went along to her own and stood in front of the mirror, swinging the tassels of her dressing-gown and challenging her reflection to become soothsayer.

III

That Sunday was historic for all the world: at eleven o'clock the Prime Minister broadcast the declaration of war on Germany. All who heard, old people remembering in tears or youngsters anticipating with thrills, kirk-goers stepping into their Sunday trousers or heathens still abed, would never forget. Every person and every community had their own particular background to that climacteric memory: Langrigg's was the fitting-out of Cairnban.

Roy was in the town council chambers when the broadcast was made. Several Langrigg officials were there with him, some uniformed for kirk: the Provost, Bailie Rouster, Major Orinshaw, Councillor Michaelson, and one or two others; Alden, fitter for pub than kirk, was present too. Roy was the only Gowburgh representative. When the stone of night had been lifted, Campbelton had crawled out of Cairnban to the

Curly Lamb. Grahamstone and Scoullar, in their retreat from the manse, were being sniped at by the minister's apologies and his wife's surprise.

The administrators were congregated, at Alden's request but Roy's instigation, to consider Cairnban: they were in the mood for such sombre meditation. Already they had bowed their heads at the infidelity of that enormous expenditure on food, utensils, and milk: it was sin committed and so irretrievable; expiation was possible, and advised; repetition was piously deprecated. Roy was heretical, unshaven, morose, squeamish with fried sausage eaten at two in the morning, deafened by a pipe-band of babies at six, depressed by a huge household of women and children awakening in a house worse than a reformatory despite the chandeliers, carved cornices, and oak panelling; and above all tantalised by old Girny McIntyre's assertion that Miss Cargill was engaged to a tea-planter in Ceylon.

Therefore he was not appreciative of the councillors' forgiveness of his heterodoxical generosity with their money; nor sympathetic with their suggestions that since the day was Sunday, still God's day in Langrigg, little could be done to relieve Cairnban until tomorrow; nor was he at all grateful for their praises of his personal sacrifice which they took for granted would be repeated again that night. Instead, he was loud, hoarse, and rather abusive.

While the Prime Minister was speaking, and for about three minutes after, there was a hush of truce; then Roy resumed his assault. He was chided, somewhat sadly, by Major Orinshaw, who left the chambers, limping, and was watched by them from the window while he hirpled all the way along the sunlit street to the War Memorial, and stood there at the salute, for quite five minutes, while the church bells began to toll with solemner significance than ever before, and the faithful, with the fear of Christ at last in their hearts, walked from their houses into streets no longer familiar but more deeply beloved.

At the council window the town fathers wished to stand and listen to the discord in the spheres, the cracking of the world's axle, the pity of the dead, and the scourging admonitions of

God the Father, followed mercifully by His promise of favour and victory. They wished in the privacy of their souls to make some admission of personal unworthiness; otherwise they, simple men of Langrigg, might not be granted the meekness, courage, resolution, and faithfulness necessary to overcome the gigantic evil represented by Hitler and his hordes.

Therefore when Roy, with the crass monomania of youth, insisted on returning to the subject of Cairnban, they absolved him with paternal smiles. He and his like would wield the weapons; but he was young, war to him was a game of flying aeroplanes, sailing battleships, driving tanks, of destruction, expropriation, and massive change. To them, white-haired administrators who must serve under the slow stars of home, there could be none of this impetuosity, this fierce excitement, this shouting, this ruthless hunger for action, and this blasting away of cherished and cosy habits. There would be time, they assured him more by looks than by words, for his Cairnban: there would be tomorrow. Then, smothering his protests in the patient good humour that wise experience has for usurping immaturity, all of them with one exception left to go off to kirk.

Before he went Bailie Rouster, with a devout wink, whispered to Alden that he had arranged for the two boys to be transferred to Jimmy Ferrier, a ploughman who lived in a cottage six miles out of town. Would Alden see to the formalities?

Councillor Michaelson was the exception. He had held himself remote from the others the moment he arrived. During the broadcast he had kept stroking his moustache, as a boy might his dead pet mouse. When the rest had crowded to the window to watch the Major, he had sat on in his high-backed chair and consciously had imitated an Egyptian god he had once seen in a museum wearing an expression of weary but satisfied malevolence. That look had symbolised to the small newsagent the verdict of eternity upon the puny antics of mankind; and now, at the beginning of this new holocaust and this debauch of hypocrisy, he achieved it better than he had ever done before.

He left two or three minutes after the others, making a far

more confident exit than they; and yet, though he set off along the street towards his home with that confidence apparently strengthening at every step, he had really no place to go to, no person to confide in, no hope like a hearth to warm himself at, no God to confess to, and no dog or cat or canary or even goldfish to establish kinship with. His wife would have his children and Gordon Aldersyde at church with her; she would be waiting for him by the gate, not in holy love as one should wait by the kirk gate for one's husband, but in despair, for she at long last, after years of his insidious teaching, had learned that in him, as in all humanity, was a dark hell where she and his children suffered for his sins.

Roy and Alden watched him as he went light-footed up the street.

"Who's he?" asked Roy. "What's he got to be so bloody chirpy about?"

Alden was long in answering; he was consulting ancestral voices.

"Nothing," he murmured, "nothing at all."

"Who is he?"

"A stationer. A lonely man."

"Wasn't it him I was speaking to yesterday? He was talking about taking one of our boys. He's married, isn't he?"

"Is to be married to escape loneliness, Mr. Roy?"

Roy then remembered Elizabeth Cargill, and her tea-planter in Ceylon. Did elephants, he wondered, ever trample on tea-planters?

"Is it?" repeated Alden.

"I wouldn't know. I'm not married."

"Is it?" asked Alden again, evidently appealing to some occult authority.

Roy remembered Mrs. Ross. She had remarked to him that morning that sitting on the floor to eat was fun for the children, as it reminded them of Redskins; for her, though a feather stuck in her hair would turn her into a fine squaw, floor-squatting had one disadvantage: once down, she needed at least two neighbours to pull her up again; and none of them seemed as willing the second time as the first.

"It'll be a damned disgrace," he burst out, "if nothing's done to make Cairnban more comfortable before tonight."

"Something will be done."

"But you heard them say we would have to wait till to-morrow."

"Mr. Roy?"

The town clerk was suddenly smiling, as if he'd remembered good news; his fingers tapped at his heart.

"Well?"

"Don't you believe in the human heart?"

So fatuous a question deserved a snort for an answer.

"Didn't you see the Major saluting his dead comrades?"

"And asking them to make room for more."

Alden still wore that smile of revelation; at the same time he found it difficult to think of other local examples of incontrovertible goodness.

"There's Mr. Mair-Wilson," he said, "a millionaire; he's got twenty-four of your boys."

"He's also got his million."

"There's this woman McShelvie you were praising yourself."

"She's earning her pay. She said so."

Alden rattled the coins in his pockets, but his laughter was spiritual.

"Are you sure," he cried, "that by pay she meant money, filthy lucre?"

Roy was silent. He could not, even to squash this sentimentality, denigrate Mrs. McShelvie, who last night could hardly have had two hours' rest, and now, he was sure, still was busy.

"Does not Miss Cargill," cried Alden, with a guile and a gaiety that delighted himself and astonished Roy, "herself redeem the species? Though there is war today, is it not compensation that so lovely and kind-hearted a girl is waiting for a young man with the faith, valour, and eloquence to win her? While that situation exists, in our own town and in hundreds of thousands of other towns, in every country, yes, including Germany, we will not lack an anchor to keep us from drifting on to the rocks of barbarism.

Roy could not help laughing.

"I understood she has a fiancé," he said.

"If she has," replied Alden, squinting, for he was not to know he was Apollo trumpeting truth and beauty from a mountain top, "I never heard of him."

"A tea-planter in Ceylon."

"Tea? Tea? Who told you this?"

"McIntyre the farmer; he said it this morning."

Alden giggled. "How funny!"

"I don't see that it's funny."

"Surely, Mr. Roy. Now outwardly could a dourer more typical Scot be found than old Girny? He has the reputation of a curmudgeon. He dotes on vendettas. Ah, but there's another side to him, a side that's all tea-planters and beautiful heiresses and foundlings who turn out to be the sons of dukes and baronets. He reads the novelettes his servant-girls bring into the house, and either he believes them or else, at seventy-six, wishes to believe them as they make paradise seem all the likelier. At any rate, Mr. Roy, you can be sure Miss Cargill's tea-planter came out of them."

Roy was unconvinced.

"It's true," giggled Alden, "it's wonderfully true. Two or three years ago at Ne'erday he got fou in the Curly Lamb, and he confided in me."

"So there's no tea-planter?"

"None whom Elizabeth Cargill is interested in. Now I propose we adjourn to our hostelry. Nothing will be done till after lunch."

"And after lunch," cried Roy, revived, "we go to Cairnban?"

"Where else? We must stand at the door of the temple to receive the offerings of the faithful."

"If any come."

Alden raised his right hand so grandly he seemed surprised, glancing up, to find no glass with nectar in it.

"Faith, Mr. Roy," he cried, "should come like a charge of cavalry, not howling like wolves."

He led the way, brandishing his arm as if that glass was now a sabre.

Roy, having lost as he feared the battle of Cairnban, was to find when he reached the inn that another stronghold, still more valuable, had been yielded to the enemy through treachery. He had put to Archie Miss Cargill's offer to take them into Lammermuir: Archie, moaning on the bottom stair at half-past two, had muttered that he had no wish to be turned into either chaperon or pander; but he hadn't refused. While Roy was arguing in the council chambers, it seemed Grahamstone and Scoullar, with their luggage, had arrived at the Curly Lamb, plaintive refugees; whereupon Archie had told them about the Lammermuir invitation. A frantic telephone appeal by the headmaster had been answered, tepidly at first, he complained, by the young woman, but warmly afterwards by her father, who had urged them to come immediately. Elizabeth brought the car for them; she seemed curiously withdrawn, so Archie mumbled from under the blankets, and had driven off as if disappointed with her freight. Could there be any explanation?

Roy's reply had been to snatch up the glass of water containing the chuckling traitor's top teeth, and hold it suspended in silence above where the latter's head must appear for breath and survey; when it did he baptised it with the water and bit it with its own fangs. Then he went off to his own room, groaning and cursing as he thought of Scoullar in Lammermuir bungling all the opportunities he would so gallantly have taken. When he got into bed and fell asleep, it was to dream not of Elizabeth Cargill at all, but of Meg Aitchison who, armed with a frying-pan, kept chasing him up and down the big staircase in Cairnban.

That dream was to prove almost prophetic. One of his commonest occupations, during the furnishing of Cairnban that afternoon and evening, was to assist Mrs. McShelvie in sharing out as justly as possible the contributions which, as Alden had foretold, were brought in astonishing quantity. Prominent in that distribution were the clutching claws of Meg. Once, for instance, shamelessly out of turn, she seized a large gilt-framed painting of deer in a Highland forest, shrieked she had as much right to it as anybody since it was not a necessity like bed or table, offered to trade a vaseful of artificial flowers for it, let slip the confession she had all her married life yearned for such a picture, shed tears that some thought false, some brazen, and some pathetic, and finally rushed off into the house, up the stairs, and into her room with her prize clutched to her bosom.

Such scenes thereafter became frequent: one woman fancied a plant with crimson and purple leaves, another a pair of candlesticks similar to those her grannie had, another a cracked mirror with pink roses round it, and still another a brass plaque showing Burns's cottage at Alloway. Where there was no pretender, the decision of the referees was easy; but where, as in the case of the plaque, there were six, decision was hard and disgruntlement stormy. Certain articles, such as a portable gramophone with a boxful of records, a hall clock, and a lavatory brush, were retained by Mrs. McShelvie for the general use: a precaution approved by Roy, but impugned by one excited freebooter of a woman, who accused her of sneaking them off for her own room, which up to that point was by far the most sparsely furnished in the house.

It was altogether a corybantic display, shocking many of the staid Langrigg citizens who, in a spirit of patriotic and holy dedication, drove up with their offerings. One pair of spinster sisters, in particular, were offended: they brought up, among other things, a chamberpot which they had bravely decided was a necessary if unhappily crude gift. Their reward was to see it pulled into view by Meg Aitchison, held aloft in scatological glee, and then clapped on her head like a crown; which seemed to them horribly coarse and irreverent, especially as the king had broadcast to the nation that afternoon.

Twenty beds had been asked for, twenty-five were given. These were of all kinds and sizes: superannuated nuptial couches, cots last slept in twenty years before, divans wrested from lapdogs, iron monsters able to sleep as many as could carry them; beds with castors, beds with none; beds with brass knobs, beds with carvings; beds with straight legs, bow-legged beds. They were carried up, and set up, like leaves borne into an ant-hill; except that the women round them and under them were not silent, nor systematic, nor unresentful of fingers jammed, elbows cracked, or bosoms crushed; and in the ant-hill, of course, the young would have had their ordained places, whereas here children swarmed everywhere in the way out of which they had to be pushed, skelped, kissed, or sometimes kicked. In the commotion it was not always possible for a woman to be diplomatically careful that it was her own child she shoved; but that recklessness, which in other circumstances would start civil war, was here pardonable, indeed sanctioned, if not altogether approved; and only once roused dissension, when the same woman shoved the same child twice, which to its mother proved wilfulness and premeditation.

Roy was soon as rumpled, dusty, cross, and blear-eyed as he had been at dawn that morning. The comedy of the situation soon passed him by. With his tie-knot at half mast, he kept mourning the lost chance to spend his short stay in Langrigg at Lammermuir. It was no consolation either to know that while he was acting here as umpire, peacemaker, porter, and ambassador, Scoullar was pestering Elizabeth Cargill with inanities about war and civilisation and man's inhumanity to man, seated by her side perhaps on that red sofa in the sitting-room. Grahamstone, too, would be pontificating about duty to her father. While in the Curly Lamb Archie Campbelton, arch-traitor and renegade, sniffed and moaned that his teeth no longer fitted.

Two or three of the lady teachers called, but were so embarrassed that they were merely extra encumbrances. One overheard Roy tell a boy of ten he would kick his arse if he did not clear out. However aggravating the child was being—he had whacked Roy's legs with a brush-pole while Roy was staggering under an immense commode—such language used to him by a teacher could only corrupt and deprave him. That the child scuttled out of the way, and stayed out, in no wise altered or mitigated her opinion. When she recounted the incident to her colleagues later in the boarding-house, spelling the offensive word, she was astonished not to win unanimity. Miss Calder, for instance (having the grace to blush) murmured that sometimes she regretted being unable as a lady to use such vocabulary, far more electrifying in its effect than strap or spinsterish scolding.

With his ears quite cool, Roy struggled on at Cairnban. Most of the important people in the town came with offerings. Mr. Mackdoe brought a small gilt wickerwork chair, a fire-guard, and two brass pokers. Major and Mrs. Orinshaw brought the bed their only son had died in. Bailie Rouster brought a car-load of what he modestly called junk; it evoked whistles of awe and shrieks of covetousness from those women in Cairnban, and from that other woman in Ebenholm, his wife, provoked a display of marital invective such as few husbands in Langrigg or elsewhere ever enjoyed. Mr. Sandeman, whose visit was very brief, brought ten Bibles, a gift that produced a kind of paralysis in the recipients, relieved only by the opening of the accompanying envelope and the finding therein of a five pound note.

Miss Hamby-Brewster brought herself. She drove up in a large green car, sat in it for a minute or two eyeing the scene with all the horror and disdain her long thin face could contain, and then summoned Roy over to her as if she had decided that he, despite his youth, was the impresario of this nascent bawdy-house. To Mrs. McShelvie he muttered that he had better not go over, lest he say what he ought to say. Not even when the green car's siren sounded did he budge. She had to come out and go to him. Her name, she explained in a voice so haughty that the women gathering round were ravished with anthropological delight, was Miss Hamby-Brewster. She was a member of the town council. Yesterday she had been out of town, otherwise she would never have allowed this desecration of her friend Captain Wotherspoon's property. She had brought no furniture with her because to do so, especially on the Sabbath, would have been to condone this outrageous proceeding. She was looked up to by many members of the community as the guardian of its morals, and that sacred duty she was determined to discharge, no matter who suffered or what disarrangement might be caused.

One or two of the women were inclined to feel insulted,

and to unsheath their claws; but the majority, led by Meg Aitchison, continued to be ravished. They had never seen Miss Hamby-Brewster's like before. They had seen prudes, killjoys, snobs, vexed virgins, prigs, bitches, and show-offs, but never had they seen all those interesting, if annoying, faults congregated in the one person; and like a kind of garnish was that person's obvious wealth, her gold earrings, her tailored costume, and her magnificent car. They let herself speak herself out, allowing the circumstances of nature to pass comment. For instance, down the steps came toddling Mrs. Jolly's three-year-old son, minus his breeks, and with the instinctive cameraderie of the very young made straight for the lady who was doing all the talking, and began to clutch at her skirt, with hands that even his mother must have washed before kissing. Her grimace of disgust was talked of in Cairnban for months afterwards: it was blamed for all the boils, toothaches, sickness, and accidents that were to afflict the inmates; and everybody agreed it caused the trees in the garden to shed their leaves sooner than trees outside.

Miss Hamby-Brewster ended by demanding to see through the house. Roy consulted the women. They stated they would be pleased to entertain her in a week's time, once they were settled in. During a flitting was not, they suggested, a mannerly time to call. If she came, she would not only be given her tea; she would also have her cup read by Bell McShelvie, who would try her best to see a man in it for her. Thus insulted as councillor, as lady, and as woman, Miss Hamby-Brewster left with the vow they would be hearing from her. On the way down the avenue her car passed Elizabeth Cargill's on its way up.

With Elizabeth were Jess Raeburn and Sammy McShelvie.

Mrs. McShelvie nudged Roy. "Oor families seem to be getting on weel together," she said.

Her smile, shrewd and ironical, was answered by his, glaikit and nervous. He felt like running into the house to hide. It was not fair that she, so assured, should see him thus, dirty, hag-ridden, and glum.

Sammy came tumbling out of the car and raced to greet his mother.

"I've got skates, mither," he cried, "beauties, like silver; and I can go them."

"I hope you havena been practising on the Sabbath?"

He understood and rubbed his hands together in glee. His guilty feet gave little joyful jumps.

"Naebody saw me," he said. "I practised at the back."

She touched his head. "So you've landed lucky?" she asked.

"Sure, mither. It's a great place."

"Whit aboot your sisters and Tom? Do you ken where they are?"

Roy passed them on his way to where Elizabeth sat chatting to Jess, who had Topsy in her arms.

"Hello," he said.

She glanced up, and smiled as one does at a person one has met before, and doesn't really mind meeting again.

"Oh hello, Mr. Roy," she said. "Mr. Grahamstone and Mr. Scoullar send their apologies. They wanted to come and see how you were getting on, but it seems they didn't get very much sleep last night. They're resting."

He saw no pertinent or useful answer which would not include swearing; he just grunted.

"How *are* you getting on?" she asked, sweetly.

"All right."

"Has there been a good response to the appeal?"

"Quite good."

"Quite? I understood it's been miraculous. Everybody's talking about it. We're proud of ourselves in Langrigg."

He grunted again. "Do you know a woman called Hamby-Brewster?"

"Was she here?" Those eloquent eyebrows expressed amusement, wonder, interest, and a little alarm.

Roy scowled. "She was. If they had lynched her, I wouldn't have blamed them. Who is she?"

"She's perhaps the worst golfer in the world," she murmured.

It was a silly answer, of course, but it was the magical means of reviving the joy of last night. Glumness fled; grubbiness was forgotten. Elbow on car, he gazed down at her for a long frank concentrated minute.

162

She blushed. She glanced at the speedometer. So did he. Was her heart racing as fast as his?

"I've brought a couple of carpets," she said, "and a few odds and ends."

"Thanks."

"I must say," she murmured, "you look pretty tired."

He was about to deny it when a yawn betrayed him. "I am," he said.

"Where's your friend Mr. Campbelton?" She looked round for him.

"He's at the Curly Lamb," he said, "but he's not my friend."

"Oh."

He explained.

She was indignant, and made no attempt to conceal it. "That was rather a shabby thing to do."

He was so delighted he forgave Archie there and then. "Wasn't it?" he said. "I was looking forward to being a guest in Lammermuir. Here's Jess will tell me what I've missed."

The little girl smiled at him.

"Is it nice being in Miss Cargill's house?" he asked.

She nodded; as an afterthought she made Topsy nod too.

"Oh, it's my father who's Jess's favourite," said Elizabeth. "I'm little Richard's."

"Lucky little Richard," murmured Roy. Aloud he said: "And how's your mother, Jess?"

"Fine, thanks."

He raised his brows at Elizabeth who firmly nodded.

"Jess's mother is really fine," she said. "Mr. Roy must come and visit us, mustn't he, Jess?"

"If he likes," she murmured.

"Oh, he likes," he said promptly.

Elizabeth smiled.

"It would be better," said Jess, "if my daddy was here."

They looked at each other, and in their sympathy for the sad stoical little girl sped so far forward in their liking that Elizabeth had to brake by murmuring that she was sure Mrs. Raeburn was going to settle down in Lammermuir after all.

"Who wouldn't?" asked Roy, never one for braking.

She stared beyond him at the women and children. "Is that Mrs. McShelvie?" she asked.

He turned and saw Mrs. McShelvie still talking to Sammy. "Yes, that's her."

"I'd like to meet her." As she spoke Elizabeth climbed out of the car. "Jess doesn't want to come out. I was greatly taken with her friend Sammy. He was telling me he's in your class. It seems he's a dunce, but you, Mr. Roy, are wonderful. By the way, I heard that your friends with the paper aeroplane were billeted with the Rousters by mistake."

"Is that so?"

"Yes. I heard too who was to blame. Mr. Grahamstone was annoyed."

She sounded annoyed herself, though she was smiling. Indeed, the versatility and sheer feminine enigmaticness of her smiles reminded him oddly of Mrs. McShelvie who was, surely, in a thousand other respects dissimilar.

"He's always annoyed," he said. "They call him 'Greeting Tam'."

Again she smiled. "Do you know what he said?"

"His utterances may be always crass, but they are seldom predictable."

"He said you'd be safer in an aeroplane travelling at three hundred miles per hour than walking about the streets of Langrigg."

"Did your father hear him?"

"It was no business of mine, of course," she said, "but I couldn't help pointing out how hard you had worked on behalf of all these people."

"Thank you, Miss Cargill."

Then they approached Mrs. McShelvie.

He introduced them. Again he felt rather than saw that astonishing resemblance.

"Sammy was telling me," said Elizabeth, "that he's with Mr. and Mrs. Kilburn. They're friends of mine. I'm sure he and they will get on very well."

"From whit he says," she replied, "he's better off now than he's ever been before: a room to himself, a garden, a wood beside it, a dog and a cat and a budgie to play wi', butter on his bread."

"And silver skates," added Sammy.

"No' forgetting the silver skates," she said, smiling.

She was an intelligent enough woman, Roy knew, to see as tragic irony this lavishing on her son by strangers of the good things of the world, which she had never been able to afford for him. She must have suffered, but she did not show it; bitterness was as far removed from her manner as sycophancy or self-pity.

"Tell them," she said, "I'm grateful."

Miss Cargill shook her head. "They say they're the ones to be grateful. They telephoned me to sing his praises. That was before I met Sammy. Now I know what they meant."

Sammy, standing by, seemed to be practising his skates without having them on.

"You run away now," said his mother, "and find your chums. Bertie Ross and Bob Jolly are in the hoose somewhere playing at draughts."

"Good," he cried, and dashed up the steps.

"At draughts," murmured his mother, "wee Jess there could beat him. How's her mither?"

"She's settling down well."

"I'm glad of that. She deserves it. I doubt if this rough-and-tumble of a place would suit her. But here's that lorry again. If you'll excuse me, I'll see what they've brought this time. If you were thinking of asking Mr. Roy hame for his tea, Miss Cargill, he's got our permission."

"As a matter of fact," said Elizabeth, "I was."

"Good." Mrs. McShelvie walked over to the lorry from the cleansing department leant by Alden.

"I like her," murmured Elizabeth.

"An extraordinary woman," he said. "She's got a sense of humour that makes me feel at times like a silly wee schoolboy in short breeks."

"Yes, I think I see what you mean. Well, are you coming?"

"Och, I need scrubbed and fumigated."

"All right. Go and do it."

"No, I'm sorry, I can't. I have to stay here."

"Mrs. McShelvie said you could be spared."

"Yes, but it would mean all the more for her to do, and she must be nearly dropping. Besides, I have a prior invitation."

"Oh?"

"Yes, we're having a celebration tea here. Some of the women are preparing it now. Can't you smell it?"

She wrinkled her nose. "Bacon?"

"Yes. Well, they asked me and I said I'd be delighted."

"But are you really delighted?"

"Yes. Why not?"

"You'll be the only male present, except for the children."

"What about it?"

"Nothing. Nothing."

They gazed about them.

"I'll have to be going," she murmured. "Perhaps you and Mr. Campbelton would care to come along this evening for supper? You may have business to discuss with Mr. Grahamstone."

He accepted eagerly. "But I've damned little business to discuss with him."

"He thinks so. He's worried that the children are scattered all over Langrigg, some on farms miles out, and he has no idea where. He's talking about having a census taken by the teachers. My father offered the use of the car for visiting the children out of town."

"He'd jump at that, I hope," said Roy, jumping at it himself.

"Yes. Mr. Scoullar is going to accompany me."

"I'm damned—I mean," he added, "he's going to have competition."

She said nothing.

He thought of quiet roads arched with autumnal trees, and upland tracks across the windy moors.

"I'll have to go," she whispered. "Shall I see you about eight?"

"You certainly will."

Three minutes later she was gone.

During the celebrations Roy was much twitted about her. In some cases the badinage was not as refined as he would

166

have wished, but it was always genuine, hearty, and optimistic. There was a clamour to get Mrs. McShelvie to read his cup. She did so, and sure enough found among the tea-leaves a tall young woman with a bonny head that seemed to have its own happy music inside it all the time, a biggish but generous lively mouth, firm delicate hands, a slim enticing figure, and a nature that made up in friendliness what it lacked in snobbery.

Each item of that inventory was cheered and shrieked at. Hands as rough as scrubbing boards banged on the table or on Roy's back. Voices harsh with challenging fate's intentions applauded this one. Roy was their hero, they cried. A hero must have a heroine. Who else but Miss Cargill was worthy? Was not her father a Sir?

In a little speech, during which she smiled and her listeners found their own smiles moistened with tears, Mrs. McShelvie thanked him on behalf of everybody in that house, down to the youngest baby, and assured him that, when he went off to the war which, it seemed, had been declared that morning, they would not forget him in their prayers. In most cases, she added drily, those prayers would start tonight, for though they were now comfortably settled in and though she was sure Cairnban would become a byword for jollity and neighbourliness, still it was in a strange town a long way from home, and from their men. Some of those men, too, would like Mr. Roy find themselves in uniform pretty soon. She herself, she said, amid cries of disagreement, might soon be returning to Gowburgh. She had been hired as a temporary helper; her work was done; but when she went back she would visit as many of their men as she could, and give comforting reports.

When she sat down, she was still smiling; and Roy again felt deeply moved as he tried to guess what she was really thinking. Was this appearance, of natural superiority, of profundity, wisdom, and compassion, of intelligent endurance, and of that humour too deep for tears, genuine? He thought it was, and so did her comrades who, in tears, were congratulating and thanking her, and, in anger, were threatening old Grahamstone with mass assault if he dared to remove her from her position as their guide and protectress.

When Roy returned to the Curly Lamb to get ready for his visit to Lammermuir, Sammy McShelvie accompanied him part of the way. As the boy chattered, Roy felt an exalting sense of human kinship. In that family, he was sure, there was room for Elizabeth Cargill and him.

PART FOUR

I

MRS. Aldersyde had to be escorted home from the station by two neighbours whose pity overcame their dislike. Several times they had to explain by signs and whispers to sympathetic inquirers; and all the way they kept trying to comfort their distracted companion with belligerent asides at the stupidity and callousness of men who caused the wars in which the women suffered most. For a man to lose a limb or his sight was terrible; but for the mother whose son was maimed or blinded there could never again be peace, whatever armistices were proclaimed or treaties signed: only death itself could end her sorrow; and even at the feet of God what would she do but beg Him in His mercy to take care of her son, now that she herself, owing to His decree, was unable. Under the silvery barrage balloons, along the narrow unlovely streets, they walked steadfastly, dowdily dressed, their fat legs gartered under their aprons, their hands clutching their purses, the glamour and mystery of sex apparently as absent in them as in the iron lamp-posts they passed; yet their lament was the same as Hecuba's, Queen of Troy.

They left Mrs. Aldersyde at her close-mouth, with the advice to go straight upstairs, take a couple of aspirins and a glass of hot toddy, and lie down in bed for an hour or two. Their own children were gone to Langrigg; they missed them as sorely as she did hers; but they did not regard her paralytic grief as shaming their own dourer acceptance. She was not that morning Mrs. Aldersyde, the unbraw unlovable puke married to yon wee specky gasping smout of a barber: she was woman

169

stricken by war. When they left her, they did not salute by clashing their heels together, straightening their bodies bent by years of necessary stooping, and whipping their bleached hands to their brows; they just patted her arm, and then shuffled off to buy as thriftily as possible the tatties, the carrots, and the mince for their men's dinners.

Mrs. Aldersyde never knew who brought her home. She was so dazed, indeed, that when she crept into the house and was standing at last before the sideboard on which stood, in their twin silver frames, the portraits of her children, she could not feel the pride, the ecstasy, and the defiance that being their mother inspired in her. Her fingers strayed over the cold cruel glass, and along the names engraved in the silver. Sobbing, she brought her face close until her breath misted the glass. Still they smiled so bonnily, but so strangely. When she swung round, with her face gone crazy, they were not in the room watching her; nor were they in these silver frames, which had cost three pounds each. They were nowhere; they were gone for good; they had been abducted by the government. There was to be no war, it was only a plot to make mothers part from their children, who were to be brought up in institutions, to be clothed in uniforms like convicts, to be fed on bread and butter, and to be made live all together, the clean with the filthy, the honest with thieves, the Sunday school prizewinners with the swearers and gamblers, and the beautiful with the deformed.

That delusion persisted and developed. When her husband came home from work, she told it to him, and screamed him to silence when, shyly, he tried to convince her she was wrong. There was only one way to prevent the government from robbing her of her children, she cried: that was by keeping together and running away. She and the children must take a room in some far-off place, and hide there till the war was over. It was his duty to provide the money. Where was it? It was no use his saying he did not have it. Could he not steal it from the shop? Better her children should have it than his drunken boss. Could he not enlist as a soldier? When he replied that the military authorities would never take him because of his asthma, and that in any case there was no fee for enlisting, she shrieked he was a liar, his asthma was a pretence, and some men were paid as much as fifty pounds for joining the army. He was a confessed coward, she cried; and striking at him wildly knocked off his glasses, so that they hung from his left ear.

As he sat, for a moment, silent, with eyes closed and spectacles dangling, he was not thinking of revenge or even of her faults, but rather of this terrifying love for her children which since the day of their birth had possessed her like a demon.

Fascinated, he had watched that love destroying her. He had not known at first whether he should try to save her from it, and afterwards he had tried when it was too late. Not only had she stolen his share of the children's affections, but ever since they could talk she had encouraged them to despise him as a barber in a slum shop, earning less than three pounds per week. If ever they wished a toy or some treat, which they had to forgo because of the lack of money, fate was not blamed, nor the system of society, nor even his recurrent asthma which prevented him from finding a more highly paid job in a better district; no, she had simply blamed him. His own people had become alienated because he had accepted that public blame without much protest. At first they had refused to agree that the blame even in part was just; later in their bitterness they declared it was, in entirety; and for years they had left him alone to endure his penance. Now he was without resentment towards anyone.

Quietly, setting his spectacles to rights, he suggested she should go down to Langrigg and try to find a room there. She might be lucky enough to get one cheap. He would send her each week as much as he could. But while he was speaking he knew it was not just she who was listening with such cunning attention. Circumstances, impassive as jailers, listened too and did not relent. His small wage was already mortgaged to pay the instalments on her fur coat and clothing for the children. On what remained this house in Gowburgh plus even a single empty room in Langrigg could hardly be maintained. Though their children were now in the charge of others, their own responsibility continued, to clothe them and supply them with many needs.

Nevertheless it was that suggestion which comforted her over that weekend. She petted, nursed, and praised it as a small girl would a doll long ago flung aside and now restored to favour. Since there was to be a war, jobs would be plentiful. Surely he could find one in a munition factory, where high wages would be paid. She herself in Langrigg would soon find work: had she not been the best worker in the carton factory before she was married? With both of them working, the arrangement must be successful: she in Langrigg looking after the children, he in Gowburgh looking after himself. Perhaps, if this war lasted as long as the last one, she and the children would grow so accustomed to Langrigg that they might prefer to spend the rest of their lives there. From what she had heard it was certainly a far cleaner, healthier, and more respectable town to bring up children in. After the war, too, all the evacuees would have returned home. Freed from their envy, Hazel would grow up to be a beautiful lady, and marry a doctor or a banker; while Gordon, deliberately retarded here in Gowburgh by spiteful teachers, would prove he was as brilliant as he was handsome; he would go to college and become famous.

All Sunday her fantasy survived. While the Prime Minister spoke she kept speaking too, faster than he, telling him that though it was true Hitler was wicked there were Hitlers everywhere, all doing their worst to injure people better than themselves. When the Prime Minister committed the country's cause to God, she laughed at him like a triumphant infant, for had she not petitioned God before him, and been promised success? It was as if she took God's bounty to be limited, like a handful of sweets; and when so many had been given to her, how could there be enough for anyone else?

She went to church that evening, and all during the service noticed how, in every way she could think of, Mr. Brownlie the minister was inferior to the man her Gordon would grow to be. He was small, bent, and very thin; whereas her son would be tall, straight, and strong. His face was lined, yellow, and woebegone, his voice anxious and hesitant; but

172

Gordon was admitted even by those who hated him to be very handsome, and Miss Oldswan the infants' teacher had once said that his voice in reciting poetry was loud, clear, and astonishingly confident. Therefore when Mr. Brownlie used the expression, "Christ standing by our sides," she could not see *him*, so soiled and out-of-date, as having such a companion; but Gordon, with his kilt and beauty, looked more likely in that picture than any other male in the church.

Next morning fantasy turned to nightmare. The postcard from Hazel arrived, to say where she was living and that she was well; but there was none from Gordon, nor was he mentioned in his sister's. At first Mrs. Aldersyde thought it was an example of his politeness, in allowing Hazel to write the postcard, and of his modesty, in not making sure he was mentioned. But after reading it many times she began to fear that something was wrong: her children were not billeted together, as she had demanded in writing; Gordon was in the hands of people who were neglecting him; he was shut up in some kind of prison, where he was not allowed to write; or he was missing. Those fears billowed in her mind like smoke. Bewildered by them, she lost sight even of her pride, so that she went from one neighbour's door to another, asking them if they had received postcards from their children. All had: those with more than one child had either received a postcard from each, or one postcard clearly giving all their names: that seemed to be a regulation. She demanded to see those postcards, and even in her tearful perturbation noticed with a pang of envy how in the one sent by little Isa Durward, aged seven, the writing was superior to Hazel's. Of course if Gordon had sent one, his writing would easily have surpassed everybody's: but he had sent none.

Bareheaded and unbreakfasted, she scurried along the streets looking for the postman to ask him to make sure that postcard was not still in his bag: he was not to be seen. Passing the police station she darted in, and after five minutes of being patiently asked to calm down and explain her business intelligibly, was told by the sergeant in charge to go home and stop worrying, for if anything had happened to her boy she

would certainly have heard about it. No, he would not telephone to the police in Langrigg; many things could have
delayed the postcard, including forgetfulness on her son's part.
That last suggestion sent her away more than ever convinced
that all society was conspiring against her and her children;
even the police who were paid to safeguard them were hostile.

In her frenzy she rushed away to her husband's shop. On
the tram-car she could not keep from confiding in a stranger
whose hat, with its clusters of red cherries, seemed expensive
and therefore a token of respectability. The woman listened
willingly and sympathetically, but at the end drily remarked
that all weans were heart-breaks, as soon as you were out of
their sight they forgot you, gratitude was not to be expected
from them, especially if they were boys; and she went on to
relate how her own son, just a year ago, at the age of twenty,
had gone off and got married to a female who was no better
than a "keelie". You brought them into the world, she said,
you suckled them, you reared them, you emptied all the love
in your heart upon them, and they paid you back by preferring
to you a bitch with dyed hair, and to your God-fearing home
a bug-ridden room in a slum-clearance housing scheme full of
thieves, brawlers, razor-slashers, and prostitutes. Mothers were
weeping because of the war, she said, but many a son was
destroyed peacefully at home. In horror and revulsion Mrs.
Aldersyde declared her son would never betray her like that;
whereupon her companion shook the cherried hat and with a
glare withdrew sympathy.

The shop where her husband Robert worked was in a
crumbling defaced tenement in a district said to be the worst
in a city whose slums were reputed to be among the most
squalid in the world. There was no red-and-white striped pole.
In the small window lay bottles of yellowing hair cream that
seemed to have been thrown in years ago as food for flies,
wasps, bluebottles, and even beetles. Only men with dirty heads
and faces would ever go there to have their hair cut or be
shaved. Indeed, as Mrs. Aldersyde walked along the pavement,
trying hard in spite of her anguish to hold her head high in
antiseptic haughtiness, she passed one or two such old men,

174

human rubbish she thought them, like poisoned rats slinking about in the sunshine.

Her husband was the only barber employed in the shop, which was owned by a fat one-armed man called Cramp. The latter was sitting on a chair inside the door, to welcome customers, chat to them, and take their money. He had been a barber himself before he had lost his arm in a bus accident. Part of the compensation he had drunk, with the rest he had bought this shop. There, half-drunk, in that cave smelling of hair, ammonia, and gas, where even the sunshine was polluted, he represented for Mrs. Aldersyde the corruption from which her children must be saved. That he employed her husband and so provided the wages to feed and clothe Gordon and Hazel, merely emphasised how deadly was his disease of dirt, drunkenness, and degradation.

There was no customer present when she entered. Cramp, who had been reading a newspaper, jumped up, called to her husband somewhere in the back of the shop, wiped some grey hair off a chair with a dirty cloth, and asked her to be seated. She took it for granted it was her ladylike appearance in her new coat which made him so nervously attentive; but, of course, as a lady she made no attempt to thank him. For that first minute, in her determination not to degrade herself by showing gratitude, she forgot the terror of her errand. The moment her husband appeared, she remembered.

He was whistling and drying his hands with a grubby towel; he looked more cheerful than she had seen him for years. Immediately she began to weep.

His whistling stopped, and the towel froze in his hands. Cramp, over in a neutral corner, grinned shyly and clenched his one fist.

"This is a private affair," he muttered. "I'll clear out through to the back."

"No, Jim," answered her husband, shaking his head firmly. "Wait. This is your shop."

"But I don't mind, Bob. Of course, if there's anything I can do to help."

"Thanks, Jim."

175

In amazement she noticed the friendship between them: she thought it assumed to mock her own lonely weeping.

"You go through to the back then, with Mrs. Aldersyde," muttered Cramp. "If anybody comes in, I'll hold him off."

"Make your arrangements," she sobbed. "Don't mind me."

"What is it, Peggy?" asked her husband, with an authority he would never have dared to use in the house. She was so astonished she told him quite simply.

"Is that all?" he asked.

She was so shocked she could not speak. She had to glance up to make sure it was really her husband who had asked that curt question. That strange authority was in his face as well as in his voice. At the same time she saw for an instant what so often had infuriated her when people had remarked upon it, the resemblance to him of the children, especially Hazel.

"You can't go on like this, Peggy," he said. "You'll be worrying yourself into a breakdown. You know what Gordon's like. He's not nearly as considerate about other people's feelings as Hazel is. He'll be thinking it makes no difference whether he sends you word today or next week."

"How can you say that about your own son," she whispered, "especially in a place like this?"

"I can say it because he is my own son, Peggy. He's selfish. You've spoiled him."

"I'm not going to sit here and let you say such things."

"No, you can't sit there. Any minute a customer might come in. This is our bread and butter, Peggy." He repeated it, sternly, as he noticed her shiver.

"But what am I to do?" she whimpered.

"Go hame, and stop this worrying. On Saturday, if you like, you can go to Langrigg and visit the children."

"But where am I to get the fare? And you can't get back the same day, either: it wouldn't be worth it, for all the time you'd have. And what if I get no word from Gordon?"

"You'll get word, and you'll get the fare. You don't have to come back the same day. Surely somebody will put you up for a night."

She nodded. It was the sight of her new coat which had

restored her confidence. Seeing it, the Langrigg people would not class her with the ordinary Gowburgh scruff.

As she rose, a customer came in. He was an old man, with a stick; he seemed to be nearly blind, and round his neck was a rag that she would not have used to wipe her children's shoes. His face bristled with white stubble. For shaving him threepence would be earned.

As Mrs. Aldersyde fled, she told herself she would not have touched him with a stick for a hundred pounds. Yet both her husband and Cramp were greeting him by his first name, with laughter, and jokes, and great kindliness. She would, she vowed, reprove Robert furiously for it when he came home, as well as for his sharpness to her in front of a stranger, and for his disloyalty towards Gordon. But somehow that high-minded resolution weakened the minute after it was born, and kept on weakening until it had died long before he did come home. Nor was it altogether through fear he might withdraw his offer to let her go to Langrigg on Saturday. His happy whistling, his friendship with Cramp, his firmness when talking about the children, and above all his kind-hearted welcoming of the decrepit half-blind old man, all those memories were of a different man from her husband, a man whom she shrank from flyting in her usual superior contemptuous way. Secure herself in the love of her children, she had often jeered at him: what had he to live for? Now vaguely and hauntingly she knew.

II

The journey to Langrigg on Saturday was spoiled: not by the coolness of Gordon's postcard, which had come three days late; nor by the information it contained that he was in a different house from Hazel; nor even by the tear-stained dirty smuggled frantically crossed note from the latter, saying she was very unhappy and begging to be brought home. Those anxieties indeed could have been transformed into joys by the knowledge that here she was hurrying in the London express, at sixty miles per hour, to rescue her children. Armoured in her new coat, with her suitcase containing her own nightgown at her feet, she could have sat in her corner, watching the expanses of fields and moors and hills, with occasional farms and once a house turreted like a castle, and felt herself to be the despotic queen of a vaster, richer, and more exciting kingdom: the lives and affections of her beautiful children.

But the journey was spoiled from the very beginning. Into the tram-car which took her to Gowburgh Central Station came two women whom she knew by sight. They were in their Sunday hats and coats, though these were cheaper than hers; one carried a bag, the other a suitcase; both were loud and vulgar with joy. One, the coarser and fatter of the two, handed the conductress a ha'penny, pretending it was a shilling. Her apology was a shriek of gleeful self-reproof: she was, she said, daft with happiness; and she explained she was going to visit her three children who had been evacuated last Saturday to Langrigg. The conductress patted her arm with a Gowburgh familiarity that Mrs. Aldersyde outwardly sneered at but also, deep in her heart, recognised as necessary if life was to be endured.

Perhaps if those two women had been the only profaners of what seemed to her a sacred mission, she could have succeeded in ignoring or forgiving them. As they all came off the tram-car outside the station she made no answer to the sisterly rather timid greeting of the quieter one, but hurried up the iron steps, not altogether haughtily, but merely as if she hadn't heard. At the booking office she met them again, and forestalled any gesture of friendliness by turning away her head, with only enough stiffness to discourage them but not to insult them, unless, of course, in their vulgar stupidity they considered themselves insulted. They did: one laughed regretfully, but the other said something angry. Mrs. Aldersyde was reassured: she had been right after all not to accept them as equals just because they too were mothers parted from their children. Handing over her ticket to be punched she felt that thus, with her sharp pride, had she punctured their commonness and envy.

On the train, however, neither pride, nor maternal love, no

matter how aggressive, nor the most virulent spurts of hatred, could preserve her joyous anticipation. There were at least a dozen persons she knew, all going on the same mission as herself; and three of them especially desecrated it. These were fat, dirty, conceited Aitchison, who lived up the same close as herself, and two of his cronies, Jolly and Ross. Even so early they breathed out the stink of beer, and bottles clinked in their pockets. Aitchison, for all his absurd dignity, was dressed as she had often seen him emptying the ashpan at home, except that he wore a collar which didn't match his shirt, and a tie with a big greasy knot; he had no overcoat or raincoat. Jolly and Ross both had raincoats, the former a fairly new cheap one with a belt, the latter one that had recently been cleaned and now was as white as a baker's overall. They carried parcels and wore cloth caps. They were going to Langrigg, she knew, not for love of their wives and children, but to satisfy their brutal lusts: they would take their wives, as depraved as themselves, into some wood or behind some hedge; nor would they be much embarrassed if their children watched; they were not human beings, but beasts. Had not Meg Aitchison been six months pregnant when she had got married? And wasn't glaikit grinning Ross notorious for his demands upon yon swollen willing slug of a wife? The cheerfulness and fondness of his children with which fools credited him, were merely disguises of lust. As for Jolly, the rumour was he had once been in the hands of the police for shop-breaking.

Those, then, were her fellow-crusaders. No wonder, as she crouched in her corner, she despaired and saw things plain: Gordon would be difficult, Hazel hysterical; neither his nor her landlady would admit to having room; lodgings would be impossible to find, whether for the night or for the duration of the war; and the result of this visit would be either that her children's unhappiness and her own horror at being parted from them would be increased, or else she would be forced to take them back home with her. If they were to be killed in their youth and loveliness, it would be better if she were killed with them; but she would forgive not even Christ Himself if their tomb was to be that dirty hateful tenement in Gowburgh.

Only her husband, she thought, and her enemies would be pleased by her predicament: he would not say it, but he would be sure to be thinking that she ought to have taken his advice and practised patience. Fish in bowls, she had cried to him, were cold-blooded and patient; she was a mother with a warm, torn heart. But now in the train, foreseeing little hope and much disappointment, she remembered the goldfish at home, swimming round and round, and always returning to the same place.

Nor was she left in peace to suffer. While the train was at its fastest, tormenting her with its reckless speed, along the corridor came Aitchison, swaying as much with impudent carefreeness as with the motion of the train. He noticed her, but passed on. Seconds later he returned as if he had rued his rudeness, pulled open the door, and thrusting in his big ill-shaven know-all face began to chat to her in front of those strangers, and what was even worse, to try and console her, as if he, with those eyes accustomed to the filth of his home, had penetrated into her soul's sanctuary and seen the desolation there. She did not answer, she did not look at him.

"Aye, Bob Jolly and Jack Ross and me are luckier than maist," he said, sympathetically amused rather than offended by her snubbing of him. "It seems oor wives hae landed in a hoose as big's a mansion, wi' a wheen o' other women. So there'll be room for us the nicht. It appears they've been haeing high-jinks yonder. War? It seems mair like a female spree. We're going doon to put them back in their places. When women get together in a gang, they're apt to revert to the prehistorical. Man's the civilised partner. That's weel known."

He chuckled, and winked at a man grinning behind a newspaper. At a woman glowering behind hers he directed a long civilising stare. She was dressed like a bourgeoise, but she was buxom, with a backside that took up more than her share of the cushions. For all her disdainful decorated face, and in spite of her obvious opinion that he was fit for shovelling coal or greasing axles, she was biologically in need of him. His Meg, he often thought, was a bit on the skinny side; moreover, she carried her sense of fun into operations where it frustrated

180

rather than exalted. It was no good telling her about old Freud; she only yelled the louder. However, one look at Mrs. Aldersyde and Meg became Juliet or Helen of Troy or even Madame de Pompadour. If union between a man and his wife lacked dignity and finesse, it was a pity; but if it lacked kindliness, then truly it became one of the major punishments of hell.

Having indulged in these philosophical reflections, he wished Mrs. Aldersyde good luck, and returned to his own compartment to find Jack Ross showing photographs of his tribe to people whom only politeness kept interested. Not only were the Ross kids so damnably like kids, but the background was the common midden on a sunny day. Jack, though, saw them as cherubs in paradise. He was, ruminated Roger Aitchison, one of the millions of simpletons who provided machine-minders and cannon fodder for capitalism, and was proud of it.

The express dropped them at a wayside station, from where a small train took them along a branch line to Langrigg. Mrs. Aldersyde could not find a compartment with no Gowburgh people in it; but though they were all uncritically and forgetfully affable in the delight of soon seeing their children and wives, she did not demean herself by returning their smiles and words of comradeship. Whatever happened, she would never come creeping to the likes of these for support. They might give it, but only after they had enjoyed her abasement. That was a pleasure they would never get.

At the station dozens of evacuees were waiting. As soon as the train appeared, with familiar heads sticking out of the windows, the cheers and jeers of welcome began. Children jumped and shrieked to see their mothers or fathers; women wept and brandished babies on catching sight of husbands who, after all, had managed to come. Everybody wanted to know all the private and public news in that first minute. Were the rumours true that Gowburgh had been bombed?

It was like a scene, thought Mrs. Aldersyde, at the gate of a prison; she felt so ashamed she could scarcely bring herself to seek amongst those howling cheering waving jailbirds for her own two children. She saw Meg Aitchison rush towards her husband and, imitating a film heroine, fling her skinny arms round his neck and kiss him with a passion and a length also typical of the screen, but with a comicality of twittering fingers and jumping heels typical only of herself. Ross, hopping on his haunches like a big white frog, went round his family one by one, with the result that his wife at the end had to help him up, so cramped were his legs. While Jolly lifted up his youngest son and held him high above his head, which demonstrated nothing except that at three years of age the child still used napkins.

Mrs. Aldersyde so far had not been able to see her children. She did not blame them for not mingling with these scruff: had she not trained them to keep apart? Yet she felt so anxious that she had to ask a woman there, whose own husband had not come, but who was finding compensation in watching these other reunions. Yes, she said, very amiably; she had seen Hazel, but not Gordon. Mrs. Aldersyde at once snapped she must have been mistaken for, of course, her children would be inseparable, especially here to meet her. The other woman then had the insolence to show pity, and to shake her head sorrowfully, repeating she was sure Hazel had been alone, and had been weeping. From that pity Mrs. Aldersyde rushed away, as from something loathsome and infectious.

Minutes later she was still seeking. Hazel and Gordon were not on the platform. Someone volunteered the information that Hazel had been at the station a good half-hour before the train came. A girl, in Hazel's class at school, said she had noticed Gordon outside the station; maybe Hazel had gone off with him.

Soon Mrs. Aldersyde was in the centre of a crowd, all feasting upon her dismay, and offering suggestions as cruel as knives. One woman, a tall dark-faced creature called Meikle, even remarked that if there was a more callous self-sufficient boy on God's earth than Gordon Aldersyde then God had little reason to be proud of such handiwork.

Thus provoked, Mrs. Aldersyde was on the point of giving way to desperation, but just in time a girl shouted that yonder Hazel was coming back.

Mrs. Aldersyde pushed past them and ran out of the station to meet her daughter under a tall tree. Knowing they were being watched, she first remedied little faults in Hazel's dress; only then did she kiss her; and during that kiss whispered to her not to weep, whatever had happened to Gordon, whether he was ill or injured or even dead, not to weep, for such tears were like wine to those watchers.

Arm in arm they set off from the station. To Hazel's bewilderment her mother kept looking about with great interest, and asking questions about the town that the girl could not answer. She did not ask where Gordon was.

They entered the little public park, and sat down amidst flowers, as if their purpose was to feed the ducks and swans in the pond.

"It's bonny here," said Mrs. Aldersyde.

Hazel nodded; it was beautiful, but she was afraid of it.

"Where is he?" asked her mother then, in a sudden harsh misery. "Didn't he get my letter? Didn't he know I was coming today?"

Hazel sobbed.

"He knew fine," she said.

"What kind of word is that to use? Fine's Scotch and vulgar, all right for those hooligans that laughed at us in the station."

Mrs. Aldersyde gazed over the flowers and the swans, past the red church with its high steeple, past the high green trees, to where her persecutors still plotted their laughing mischief against her and her children. Though she gazed defiantly, she knew there was a breach in her defences, which must be repaired.

"If he knew," she said, "why isn't he here? Is he ill?"

"No, he's not."

"Please don't snivel. We're in public, remember. How can you tell he's not ill?"

"He was near the station."

"But he could still be ill for all that."

"He looked all right."

"You're not a doctor, Hazel. Gordon might be one some day, and you'll be proud of him then. You'll be sorry you said he wasn't ill the day he couldn't come to meet his mother off the train."

Hazel didn't quite understand. "He was at the station," she insisted. "When he saw the train coming he ran away."

For a whole minute Mrs. Aldersyde sat gazing at that bitter incredibility.

Hazel went on: "He said he was never going back to Gowburgh. He said he was going to get the people he lives with to adopt him."

"They can't do that," murmured her mother, shaking her head.

"He said they could if he wanted to."

"They hae bewitched him wi' their wealth."

Hazel agreed. "They're not nearly as well-off as Mrs. Merrick, the lady I'm with," she said.

"But Gordon's an exceptionally sensitive boy," said Mrs. Aldersyde. "You and me know that, don't we, Hazel?"

Hazel nodded; she saw she must accept everything her mother said; otherwise she would feel terrified and insecure. At the same time she remembered how cool, deliberate, and confident Gordon had been; he had been chewing sweets.

"Girls are different," said her mother. "Their minds are not so delicately balanced. I think," she added, in a bleak irrelevancy that revealed the depth of her despair, "more men are in asylums than women."

"But I want to go home, mummy," said Hazel, "and he doesn't."

"That's it," said her mother eagerly. "Can't you see, Hazel, that's just it?"

"What?"

"He can't think of yon horrible place in Gowburgh as home. Neither can I. He and I hae always seen things alike."

"But where can we go?" asked Hazel, whimpering.

"Surely in this beautiful town we can find ourselves a new home?"

Hazel was dubious. "What about daddy?" she asked.

"Let him look after himself."

"People say there's no room in Langrigg," said Hazel.

Her mother was not listening. With tears in her eyes, she was dreaming.

She dreamt that in spite of her entreaties Gordon had chosen to live with these people called Michaelson. Her husband, the McShelvies, and all the rest tried to pity her by blaming him; but she repudiated both pity and blame. Better than any of them she knew that her son had faults. Suppose then he deserted her in favour of these Michaelsons, it was her duty to pretend to understand. She would say, for instance, that since it was obvious she could not with three pounds per week give so brilliant a boy the chance in life he deserved, she had decided, out of her love for him, to let him stay with the Michaelsons in the meantime. He would not be lost to her for good. When he became a man, successful and rich, he would seek her out and make amends. On his knees he would thank her for the magnificent sacrifice she had made on his behalf. He would take her away to his mansion, where she would live in luxury for the rest of her life.

When she stood up, and saw the flowers, the white and crimson asters, she hated them with a hatred that was to linger for the rest of her life. They were then the representatives of reality; theirs was the duty of telling her her dreams were false.

"Do you know where these Michaelsons live?" she asked.

"Yes. They've got a shop in the main street."

"What kind of shop?"

"It sells newspapers and things."

"Is it a big shop?"

"Quite big, mummy."

"It'll bring in more than three pounds a week."

"I don't know, mummy."

They walked out of the public park.

"This woman you're with, this Mrs. Merrick, is she rich?"

"I think so, mummy. It's a huge house, with beautiful furniture."

Mrs. Aldersyde smiled. "Is there room for me in it?" she asked.

Hazel looked away, not knowing what to answer. Her mother's smile frightened her.

"Do you think I wouldn't be good enough for such a house?" asked Mrs. Aldersyde, still smiling.

"You know I don't think that, mummy."

"You do think it, Hazel."

"It's both of us, mummy," whispered the girl, in anguish. "It's too grand."

"You blame your brother, but you're worse than he is."

A car passed them in the main street. It was driven by Roy the teacher; beside him sat a young woman Mrs. Aldersyde had never seen before. It was a big glossy car. They were laughing together. The young woman was lovely.

Mrs. Aldersyde turned and gazed after them.

"Was that Roy?" she asked.

Hazel was smiling. "Yes," she said.

"Who's that he's with?"

"Her name's Miss Cargill," whispered Hazel. Like the rest of the Gowburgh schoolgirls she was impressed by the romance between the teacher and the smiling young lady whose father was a Sir. "Her father's called Sir Robert."

"Sir!"

Hazel nodded, entranced. "Do you know who lives in her house?"

"How could I know that, Hazel? This is my first time in this town, and as you said it's too good for me."

The pleasure and hope roused in the girl by the fairytale felicity of Roy and Miss Cargill was crushed. "I didn't say it was too good for you, mummy," she whispered.

"Yes, you did. But who does live in her house?"

"Mr. Grahamstone and Mr. Scoullar."

"Trust them to make themselves safe and comfortable. What about Roy? Doesn't he live there too?"

"No. But there is somebody else." Hazel had not meant to mention the Raeburns, lest it should provoke her mother more; but somehow she could not resist. "Not a teacher."

"McShelvie?"

"No. Mrs. Raeburn."

Mrs. Aldersyde laughed sarcastically. "They'll hae put her in the basement," she said.

"Miss Cargill takes them about in the car," murmured Hazel.

They were walking on again, away from the main street, down one of the quiet avenues of large houses.

"I always thought that one Roy was a snob at heart," said Mrs. Aldersyde. "Why isn't he off to the war, such a hero as he thinks he is?"

Hazel was silent: she had overheard two of the lady teachers discussing Mr. Roy's future: it seemed he was expecting his call-up to the Air Force any day. She did not mention this to her mother for fear the latter said something mocking. To Hazel, as to the two spinsters, Roy would not be protected from death by his romance with Miss Cargill: handsomeness, courage, gaiety, and happy young love were death's favourite harvest in war. Hazel had seen some women from Cairnban, right in the centre of the main street, cheer the car as it had gone past. They had been, she felt, not only thanking him for all he had done for them, but also trying to throw a charm over him to save him from the disruption and annihilation that might lurk ahead.

They had now reached the avenue of bungalows where the Michaelsons lived. Rattling down it towards them on his skates was Sammy McShelvie. He was not yet skilful in his use of them, and every four or five yards clung to lamp-posts or railings. He was thus clinging when they came up to him.

He was a little sheepish because for all his boasts he was still a clumsy skater, and also because Hazel Aldersyde, with her long black ringlets, was the prettiest girl he had ever seen. He showed his embarrassment by hugging the lamp-post and grinning, so Mrs. Aldersyde said, like a specky imbecile. Hazel smiled, for she always found Sam McShelvie funny: she never, however, despised him for it.

"Hello," he said cheerfully.

"Hello," replied Hazel, in spite of her mother's tugging.

"We're pestered with that sort enough in Gowburgh," said Mrs. Aldersyde, "without having to suffer them here. An imbecile."

They heard a clatter. Sammy had fallen. He seemed to have hurt his elbow, for he was rubbing it.

187

"An imbecile," repeated Mrs. Aldersyde, pleased. "What fool gave him skates? He'll slide under a bus on them."

Those were dreadful words, but Hazel knew none to annul them; inwardly she prayed Sammy would not slide under a bus.

"He'll be going to visit his mother in Cairnban," she whispered.

"Where's that?"

Hazel was trying to describe the big white mansion with its complement of Gowburgh women and children, as they approached the gate of the Michaelson bungalow.

"This Cairnban," snapped Mrs. Aldersyde, who was examining the neat little house in front of her, "sounds like a menagerie to me. I'm surprised they let a good house to such a crowd of sluts and vagabonds." She dropped her voice and nodded towards the bungalow. "This can't be as big as your Bona Vista?"

"Oh no."

Mrs. Aldersyde was pleased. "This Mrs. Merrick must be real upper class," she said. "Really well-off, I mean."

"I think so, mummy."

Mrs. Aldersyde nodded. "I can respect that," she said. "But this, this is nothing."

She marched up the short paved path and pressed the bell-button. In a struggle for Gordon's affection she felt confident she could defeat these people: their house was far from being a mansion, if they had a car it would be a small one, they were not gentry since their money came from a shop, and the curtains in their windows were no better than her own at home.

Her confidence was increased by the sight of Mrs. Michaelson who opened the door, proving there was no maid. She was as small as Mrs. Aldersyde herself, and much less assertive; indeed, she seemed a sad-faced dull-witted creature with not enough liking for herself, far less for other people. When she heard who they were, she welcomed them in with a cordiality that, bright at first, quickly faded. She began to stare at her visitor's suitcase: it was as if she saw in it an intention or desire to stay the night, and lacked both the decency to say yes

188

and the ingenuity to find a plausible no. She seemed to Mrs. Aldersyde an easy enemy.

"Gordon's not in," she murmured, as she showed them into a sitting-room that, though well enough furnished, was small and ordinary, with nothing massive or rich to compel respect or awe.

"He forgot the time of my train," said Mrs. Aldersyde.

Hazel did not pass judgment upon that defiant lie; it was one of a multitude told on her brother's behalf.

"Did he know you were coming?" asked Mrs. Michaelson.

"Certainly. I wrote to him."

"Yes, he got your letter all right; but he didn't mention there was anything in it about you paying us a visit."

"Correspondence is private, I suppose."

Mrs. Michaelson turned pale. "Oh, I didn't mean we had a right to know," she said hastily. "But if he'd let us know I could have been prepared."

Mrs. Aldersyde rose. "If I'm not wanted——" she said.

The other woman was shocked. "Oh, please sit down," she cried. "Of course you're welcome."

Mrs. Aldersyde sat down firmly, as if she had won a round. Beside her on the sofa Hazel looked miserable.

"I considered I had a right to come and satisfy myself that my son was in respectable hands," said Mrs. Aldersyde.

"Of course. We like having Gordon here." Mrs. Michaelson's voice shook, as always when she was not telling the truth. A week of Gordon had been enough for her. He was always too sweet, too obliging, too self-effacing, too obviously playing a part. What had puzzled, and also alarmed her, was the way her husband, usually so sharp in detecting deceit that he saw it where none existed, had been taken in, or, what was worse, pretended to be.

"You've got quite a nice little house here," admitted Mrs. Aldersyde.

Was this rudeness, wondered Mrs. Michaelson, or just stupidity, aggravated by natural concern for her son? Certainly it seemed usual, judging by the poor girl's resigned shame.

"Thank you," she murmured.

"Before I decide I would hae to see where my boy sleeps."

"Of course."

"You've not to think that because he's from Gowburgh, it's a hovel he has for a home."

"I never thought that," said Mrs. Michaelson, although from Gordon's pathetic description hovel seemed understatement. But she had to change the subject before she became angry with this silly unhappy woman. "So this is Hazel," she went on, smiling at the shy pretty girl, and much preferring her to her brother.

"She's his twin."

"Yes. They're very much alike."

"They're considered the bonniest pair of twins in the whole of Gowburgh."

"Mother!" gasped Hazel.

Modest herself, and sensitive to ridicule, Mrs. Michaelson was amazed by such boasting; she was also, paradoxically, moved to pity. Before she could find a reply, there was a quiet knock on the door, and in came her husband, really amused as she could see, but smiling in apparent sorrow.

"So you've come to take Gordon home, Mrs. Aldersyde," he murmured, without waiting to be introduced.

"Nobody said that, John," protested his wife.

Mrs. Aldersyde was silent; she was suddenly afraid to speak. This small bald man with the moustache as black as a beetle, and the psychiatrist's smile, seemed with his first careless glance to see beyond her arrogant confidence to the timidity, despair, and even, in the darkest depths of her soul, to the imprisoned appeal.

He spoke soothingly. "There's no need to, you know. He's happy here, and we're happy to have him. He's a fine boy."

"There's none finer," she said.

"You're entitled to think so, Mrs. Aldersyde," he murmured. "We've only known him a week, but already we think very highly of him. Don't we, May?"

His wife, clumsy at lies, nodded; but she could not smile.

"The pity is," he went on, "ours is a small house. Otherwise we'd be pleased to have his sister here too."

"We've got two girls of our own," explained Mrs. Michaelson. "They're next door, playing with their chums."

"That was why I wanted a boy," murmured her husband, who then, as if he had cured Mrs. Aldersyde, turned with his healer's smile to Hazel.

"Gordon was telling us you want to go home," he said.

She nodded, and pressed closer to her mother. She did not trust him.

"To dirty old Gowburgh?" he asked, playfully.

Again she nodded, without a smile; yet it was that very smilelessness he was angling for.

"To the nasty bombs?" he said.

"John, please," protested his wife.

He gazed at her in innocent surprise, and then appealed to Mrs. Aldersyde.

She shook her head angrily. "There might never be any bombs," she said. "I don't believe everything the papers say." And she looked at him in contempt, for he earned his living through selling those papers that lied.

"You think not?" He cocked his head to the side, like a bird on a lawn, and seemed to be listening not for bombs, but for the dread of them in their hearts.

"There have been none so far," she said, triumphantly.

He kept listening. Then he began to nod. "There will be," he announced. "Europe will be a shambles before this war is ended."

"Let Europe look after itself," she cried.

"Did you not hear Mr. Chamberlain last week?" he asked. "What he said made us a part of Europe. We will get our share of destruction. Not here in Langrigg, perhaps, but in Gowburgh certainly."

He grinned at Hazel. "Why do you want to go back, Hazel?" he asked. "I would have thought Bona Vista a splendid house in which to pass the war. Or do you find Mrs. Merrick too overpowering? Most people do."

"I'm sure she just wants to be with her mother," said his wife.

"And with her father too, of course," he added.

191

Mrs. Aldersyde sniffed, Hazel sighed, and Mrs. Michaelson shivered. Gordon had let them know, with deliberate ingenuousness, how insignificant his father was.

"Was it Mrs. Merrick who asked you to take her home?" inquired Mr. Michaelson.

"No. Why should she?" snapped Mrs. Aldersyde.

"Why indeed? Hazel would adorn any home. She is a lovely girl, almost a young lady." As he spoke he leered at the girl, so that his wife over by the window knew he was hinting at what Gordon had told them, oh so discreetly and with such heartsore loyalty, about his sister: at Bona Vista she wet the bed every night.

Then Mrs. Michaelson, glancing out, saw Gordon at the gate. It was almost as if he was giving a performance of a boy in no hurry to look for his mother whose train he had not tried to meet at the station. He lounged against the wall, with his hands in his pockets. What he was expressing was, she suddenly realised, the same malignant selfishness she had so often seen in her husband. Anyone else not so practised would have taken him for an ordinary boy loitering in the sunshine, unaware his mother had arrived to visit him. She noticed, too, with pity as well as revulsion, how solitary he always was.

"It's Gordon," she said. "He's at the gate. I'll tell him you're here."

As she left, Mrs. Aldersyde rushed to the window to rap on it and wave. It was a risk to test him thus, in the very first second, in public, before these despised strangers; but she just could not wait.

He turned and saw her. His jaws, busily chewing, did not falter; but the caramel sweetness they contained seemed for a moment to grow venomously sour. Next moment that sweetness was restored, ten-fold.

Mr. Michaelson was at the window beside her.

"Usually," she said, "I keep his kilt for Sundays, and special days."

"Is this not a special day, Mrs. Aldersyde?"

In the little hallway Mrs. Michaelson was whispering to Gordon: "Your mother and sister are here. Your mother's come all the way from Gowburgh to see you. You must have missed her at the station. Be nice to her now."

Chewing, he nodded: not to agree that he ought to be nice to his mother, but to signify he understood well enough all the implications, and could be trusted to deal with them in his own interests.

Mrs. Michaelson almost struck him. The impulse staggered her, for she had suffered for years from similar persecution by her husband, without ever wishing such revenge: this blow, however, would have been struck on behalf of someone else.

He entered the sitting-room, demure and gravely glad. His cap was in his hand; his toffee was swallowed; his affection was properly adjusted, so that when his mother rushed and embraced him, wailing in her sincerity, he withstood it well.

"You weren't at the station, dear," she cried.

He hung his head.

"I was afraid," he whispered.

"Afraid? Afraid of your own mother, dear? You know I love you, you know that if the world was mine to gie, I'd gie it all to you."

"I was afraid," he said, "you were coming to take me back to Gowburgh."

"No, no. I'm here to stay beside you."

He glanced past her at Mr. Michaelson, as if inviting *him* to tell her there was no room for her in that house.

Mr. Michaelson obliged. "Our house is small, as you can see," he said. "I doubt if it's a quarter the size of Bona Vista."

"There are other places," she said. "I'm not penniless. I can find somewhere."

"Don't count too much on that, Mrs. Aldersyde. This is a small town, and it's crammed."

"There are hotels," she said grandly.

"True. They're full too, I understand. Besides, they're expensive. The Royal, I know for a fact, is charging ten guineas for an attic room. But as I said, they're full."

"I shall find a place."

"It has happened before, Mrs. Aldersyde, that there was no room at the inn."

She did not see his blasphemy; his wife did.

Gordon interrupted. "But if you were to stay in Langrigg, mummy," he asked, "what would daddy do?"

"Fend for himself, for a change."

"Why not," put in Michaelson, the peacemaker, "try Bona Vista? Mrs. Merrick undoubtedly has room. Of course she does not take in boarders; the idea's preposterous, as you'll agree once you've seen her wealth. But some arrangement might be reached."

"I really don't think," said his wife, "it's fair to build up Mrs. Aldersyde's hopes. It's very unlikely Mrs. Merrick will take her in."

"Am I not good enough?" cried Mrs. Aldersyde.

"Of course. But she is a very strange lady. She's something of a hermit."

Mrs. Aldersyde rose, pretending a decision that seemed to Mrs. Michaelson brave but piteous.

"I'm not here to beg from anyone, rich or poor," she cried. "I intend to visit this Mrs. Merrick, but it's to let her know I'm taking my child away from her."

"Won't you stay for some tea?"

"No, thank you. Come, Hazel; and you too, Gordon."

He looked genuinely astonished. "Me?"

"Yes, dear. I need you."

"But what's the good of it?" he demanded. "I don't want to go to Bona Vista. Hazel told me Mrs. Merrick doesn't like boys. Maybe she wouldn't let me in. And I don't want to go back to Gowburgh. I want to stay here with Mr. and Mrs. Michaelson."

"Go with your mother, Gordon," murmured Michaelson. "It is your duty, in the absence of your father, to help and support her. Nobody wishes you to go back to Gowburgh. When you have seen your mother and sister fixed up some-where, of course you will return here."

"Is that right?" he demanded of his mother.

She could not trust herself there to praise his rudeness, and appear to be overjoyed with his selfishness. Had she spoken, she would have wept; and those tears might have washed away

194

the illusionment of years. It was inexplicable that, in that moment of agony, she should remember her husband's shop.

"Is that right?" Gordon repeated. "You're not going to take me back, if I don't want to?"

"No, dear," she murmured, and wept. She blundered to the door, almost as if she no longer cared whether he followed or not. Hazel, sobbing too, hurried after her.

Gordon remained. He smiled at Michaelson: it was to indicate his shrewd humorous indulgence of this weepy perversity of females. He got a wink in reply that satisfied him.

"Go with your poor mother, Gordon," said Michaelson. "Do what you can to comfort her."

"And then I come back here?"

"By all means. Is that right, May?"

His wife nodded, not eagerly, as Gordon noticed; but he had already learned to discount her.

"All right," he said, and swaggered off.

"God forgive me," muttered Mrs. Michaelson, covering her eyes with her hand, "I don't like him. I'm getting to feel sick when he's in the room with me."

"He is as God made him."

"He's as his mother, poor creature, has made him."

Michaelson was now over at the window.

"Are not our mothers the chief instruments of God?" he asked, with a chuckle. "All of us are selfish monsters. Hence this war. And who shaped us thus, if not our mothers? I would dearly like," he added, "to be present at the interview between her and Mrs. Merrick."

"Have you no pity?" whispered his wife.

"Pity? To have pity is to be implicated, to be implicated is to be responsible. Much better to be detached and curious; then the antics of such as Mrs. Aldersyde and her precious Gordon are not only intelligible, but also amusing."

"If you have no pity, John, you can expect none."

Smiling, he watched the Aldersydes till they were out of sight.

"Heil Hitler," he murmured.

III

Had Mr. Michaelson been present at the interview in Bona Vista's drawing-room, he would have been disappointed. Its conclusion was certainly as he had anticipated, the departure of the Aldersydes humbly from the large house; but the way in which it was conducted, both by Mrs. Merrick the grand lady, and by Mrs. Aldersyde the barber's wife, would have disconcerted him and sent him home with little for his malevolence to feed on. The reason was that the two women accepted each other's station in life without contempt or envy, and so avoided personal complications.

Mrs. Merrick, for instance, boldly heeded all the persevering hints about some kind of domestic employment, and dismissed them in a bunch as out of the question. She was no less frank in declaring that though she had at first enjoyed having Hazel's company, the girl's daily nostalgic weepings had become monotonous and depressing. As for the bed-wetting, she mentioned it not censoriously as a landlady seeking indemnity for spoiled sheets, but compassionately, as one who understood well what stresses the mind could inflict upon a flowering body. She hinted that her own lameness was the outcome of a majestic grief. At the door she laid her hand on Hazel's shoulder, and asked God to bless her. Mrs. Aldersyde's hand she shook. Gordon she ignored, as she had done all the time: he was male, and so in her house a ghost.

Mrs. Aldersyde went away, humble and unembittered. Indeed, she had found the display of that wealth and breeding a reassurance after the impertinences of the shopkeeping Michaelsons. Mrs. Merrick was a true lady, and had spoken to her, not as an equal naturally, but as an inferior entitled to respect. She would never have spoken to McShelvie, say, or Aitchison in that way. These she would have received in some other room, not in that magnificent drawing-room; and they would have been shown to the back door by a servant. Never, in the constitution of the world, war or no war, bombs or no bombs, would she have shaken hands with them at parting or blessed their children.

Therefore when Mrs. Aldersyde had muttered that she was much obliged, she had been nervous but sincere, although any spectator might have thought she had been shown no kindness that merited gratitude. Mrs. Merrick was such a spectator: for hours afterwards she felt uneasy and contrite at having sent away the big-nosed little woman in the tawdry coat and with the atrocious Gowburgh accent which her attempts at refinement had made even more intolerable.

They walked slowly back to the main street. Hazel carried her own case, and Mrs. Aldersyde hers; Gordon, empty-handed, urged them to hurry so that they would be in time for the last train back to Gowburgh. His mother would not. What had seemed to her children a humiliation, comic in Gordon's opinion, terrifying in Hazel's, had been to her the kind of vindication she had been waiting for for years. Solemnly she explained it to them. It was one thing, she said, to be humble in the presence of one's betters—that was an instruction in the Bible itself—but it was a different thing altogether to be humble in the presence of vulgar upstarts like the Michaelsons or Gowburgh scum like the McShelvies or Rosses or Aitchisons. Towards these it was necessary to be as rude and contemptuous as possible, otherwise they would take advantage. A lady like Mrs. Merrick, on the other hand, would never abuse proper humbleness.

Gordon contradicted her: he thought Mrs. Merrick was a mean pig, she hadn't given Hazel so much as a penny as a gift.

"I should hope not," said his mother proudly. "Had she done so she would not have been a lady. We would have been insulted."

He began to whistle as if, after all, his interest in the matter was altruistic: *he* had a home to go to in Langrigg, *he* was in no quandary about a last train, *he* had no reason to feel spite against Mrs. Merrick. Nevertheless he paused in his whistling to repeat that she was a mean pig.

"She could have given Hazel a pound," he said.

His mother did not want to exasperate him. "You don't understand, dear," she said. "You will when you are grown up. You will learn that it is better to be given respect than money."

She noticed that Hazel was sulky and snivelling. Crossly she demanded why.

"I'm tired, mummy," whimpered the girl, "and I'm frightened."

"Frightened of what? But first of all, please, wipe your tears away and stop crying. As you well know, this place is full of scruff who know us, and who would be only too pleased to see that we are meeting with a little difficulty."

"And I'm hungry."

"So am I, and I'm not crying. When we get to the main street we'll go into a restaurant and have a meal. Then we will look for a place to stay tonight."

The town hall clock struck as she spoke.

"You've still got time for the train," said Gordon.

"We're not going to be driven out, like vagabonds," she replied. "Your father would have the last laugh if we let that happen."

"I think you should catch it," he said. "So does Hazel."

Hazel nodded.

"You can eat on the train," he added.

"We shall eat," said his mother proudly, "in the best restaurant in Langrigg."

"There are only two," he said.

"In the best," she repeated.

Outside that restaurant they met Mrs. McShelvie, or rather were accosted by her, because although they turned their backs on her she spoke to them.

They had seen her come strolling along the main street, with Jean clinging to one arm and Effie to the other. All three were happier than the Aldersydes had ever seen them before; they seemed to be singing there in public. Mrs. McShelvie, especially, looked so much younger, fresher, and lighter in heart, that Mrs. Aldersyde, knowing her to have deserted her jigging keelie of a daughter and her anaemic bauchle of a husband, was not only disgusted, but affronted too. What right had this typical Gowburgh close-dweller, this gossiper at middens, this grey-haired slum trollop, to walk so gaily and to look so calmly at home here in this town of not one, but a hundred Bona Vistas? Seeing her caused Mrs. Aldersyde to become aware, for the first time that day, of the tremendous wealth of blue in the sky, and of the illimitable richness of the sunshine. The leaves on the pavement under Mrs. McShelvie's small debonair feet became like guineas, expendable not in places of business like shops, but in places of joy and freedom, like gardens and sunny woods and hills.

Jean and Effie whispered to their mother not to stop. They were afraid that Mrs. Aldersyde would try to spoil their happiness. For years she had squealed at them not to chalk the pavements for peever, not to play with a ball in the back-court, not to light squibs, not to come guising to her door on Hallowe'en, not to sing coming up the stairs in the fearful dark, and not to play with her children. It was better, they whispered, to pass on with smiles; and in any case she didn't want to talk to them, for she had turned her back.

But they knew their mother, and were resigned to stop. Just as they associated Mrs. Aldersyde with the stifling of happiness, so they saw their mother as its encourager, reviver, and creator. More than once they had seen a neighbour come weeping to their house to ask her help in some trouble about husband, children, or debt. She, who was as poor in money as any of them, sent none away unsustained. Now, in Langrigg, on this sunny late afternoon, she seemed so happy herself they were sure not even Mrs. Aldersyde could resist her. At the same time, with the blow-for-blow kiss-for-kiss ethics of children, they thought that Mrs. Aldersyde, so rude in turning her back, did not deserve their mother's kindness.

"Guid afternoon, Mrs. Aldersyde," said Mrs. McShelvie warmly.

Mrs. Aldersyde did not turn round. She saw the other woman's reflection in the shop window, and was able to sneer at the age and shabbiness of her coat; but the friendliness, composure, and above all the strange authority impressed her against her will.

"Hello, Hazel," said Mrs. McShelvie, smiling at the girl. "How are you liking Langrigg?"

199

Hazel half-turned and tried to repay the smile.

"I'm not liking it very much, Mrs. McShelvie," she whispered.

"I'm sorry to hear that." She had heard it several times from inhabitants of Cairnban, some of whom she had rebuked for seeming to enjoy the poor girl's homesickness.

"Whether you are sorry or no'," said Mrs. Aldersyde, turning round, with this excuse of pride, "it is none of your business, and I would be obliged if you would kindly refrain from interfering. I can look after my ain children without your assistance, thank you. I am not one of those who believe that because you can read teacups gives you any right to force your advice on people who haven't asked for it and never will."

Mrs. McShelvie smiled. "There's twa of us in that society," she said, "for I don't believe it myself. I'm sorry you think I'm interfering. It just occurred to me when I saw you that maybe you wanted to stay the night here so that you could be longer wi' your weans. I ken a' the hotels are packed: some of the teachers couldn't get into them. So I thought I wad offer you a spare bed I've got in my room at Cairnban. It's for Jean and Effie if I get the job there as caretaker. The council's meeting next week to decide. But the bed's empty the night, and you're welcome to it."

Hazel's relief and gratitude were in contrast to her mother's indignation and resentment.

"Are you suggesting," asked Mrs. Aldersyde, "that I should go yonder amongst those sluts and filthy swearing brats?"

Mrs. McShelvie continued to smile.

Mrs. Aldersyde came close to her. "Those whores," she hissed. "I saw Aitchison and Ross on the train. Will they be there?"

"With their wives? I expect so."

"Wives!" Mrs. Aldersyde sent up to the blue sky a puff of scorn and incredulity: it indicated that those marriages had never been made in heaven, even if there were bits of paper to prove they had been made on earth.

"I'm sorry," said Mrs. McShelvie. "I just wanted to be friendly."

"I choose my ain friends, thank you."

200

Mrs. McShelvie recalled what Meg Aitchison had once said: Mrs. Aldersyde's friends could be counted on the left hand of a drunken sawyer, five times unlucky. But she merely nodded, as if to her it was axiomatic that Mrs. Aldersyde, being a human being, must have friends.

"Well, guid luck anyway," she said. "As far as I'm concerned the offer's always open. But I'm sorry there's a condition attached to it now: you'd hae to respect the other folk there. Goodbye, Hazel," and with a last smile at the girl she walked away. Within a moment her own two girls had greedily and joyously claimed her arms again.

Hazel gazed after them in longing; they represented what she yearned for most: friendly companionship.

She was quite roughly shaken by her mother.

"Would you shame me," said Mrs. Aldersyde, "by wanting to go and sleep in the same room with the likes of that? I've not seen it, but I know it'll be a pigsty. Last week you had a taste of what it was like to live with a real lady. That woman's a witch; I saw her trying to win you away from your ain mother."

"I like Mrs. McShelvie," said Hazel, with unexpected candour and courage.

Before their mother could challenge such treachery, Gordon turned from contemplating the display of cream cakes in the restaurant window. He had the air of one who has borne adult irrelevance long enough.

"Aren't we going in for tea?" he asked.

"I want to go for the train," sobbed Hazel.

"You could still catch it," he agreed.

Their mother hesitated. If she took the train, there would be a place for her and Hazel to sleep that night; but it would be in a house more detestable than ever after the grandeur of Bona Vista. If she waited in Langrigg, and was not able to find a lodging cheap enough and good enough, that bed in Cairnban might begin to shine in the darkness with a witch's enticement.

As she hesitated, the two women she had snubbed on the Gowburgh tram-car passed, hurrying with their children to the station. They were all laughing together, and their visit evidently

201

had been a happy one; likely it would be repeated next week, and so on, week after week. For a hateful moment she envied them; and the only antidote to that envy was to make this visit of hers last longer than theirs.

"We'll go in for our tea," she said. "We're not going to run away just to make a joke for a crowd of sluts and wastrels."

The tea did not please Gordon. His mother was too economical, allowing him only two cakes and two chocolate biscuits. She herself, as Hazel noticed, ate little; she said she wasn't hungry. Every penny was needed for their lodging, she explained; they knew as well as she did how miserably small their father's wage was. To appease her forebodings, she described her visit to his shop, and poured forth all her bitterness and perplexity in maligning the old half-blind man in the greasy jacket who had come in for a shave and had been welcomed as if he was a millionaire.

They listened in silence, Hazel because she was depressed, Gordon because he was bored. When his mother paused he reminded her that she had promised to buy him a new fountain pen weeks ago. How could he do well at school and beat the others if, like them, he had to use a school pen with a rusty nib?

Hazel scowled at him. "You don't need a pen at all," she muttered.

He smiled, and left the contradicting of her to their mother.

"Of course he needs a pen," said Mrs. Aldersyde, "and I'll see he gets one as soon as I can afford it."

"If you'd gone by the train," he murmured, "you could have afforded it. There's a good one with a real gold nib in Mr. Michaelson's shop; it's only seven and six, which is cheap for a real gold nib."

The way he pronounced his host's name frightened her. He had always been a too-affectionate child. Even as a baby in his pram he had been too generous with his smile for outsiders; these had only to offer him sweets or biscuits, and he would turn from her to them. It was, perhaps, a weakness in his character. Now this man Michaelson, whom she distrusted so much, was alienating him. It seemed to her that forces more than human were against her: Mrs. McShelvie was a witch, and Michaelson a demon.

"I'll get you a pen," she said.

"When? At Christmas?"

"Sooner than that, dear."

"Today?"

"You know I've to pay for a place for me and Hazel. You wouldn't want your mother and sister to sleep in the street, would you, dear?"

"You could sleep at Cairnban. That would cost nothing."

"Nothing but our pride, Gordon, which is more valuable than all the money in the world."

His disgust at that sentiment was seen by her as appreciation.

"If we stick together, we three," she said, "we'll win in the end. This is our own war."

"I heard the Prime Minister last week," he remarked. "The Michaelsons have a radiogram; it's as high as this table, and it's got six valves. It gets American stations."

"He talked a lot of rubbish," she said sharply. "What right has he telling us we're at war with the Germans? I've got no spite against them. They never did me any harm. But there are folk in Gowburgh I hae a spite against. My war's against them. But we'd better go if we've to look for a place."

"What about my pen?" he asked, as they went out.

She did not answer. Hazel's nudge he repaid with a vicious jab.

"Am I to get it?" he persisted.

"But I thought I explained," whispered his mother.

"Am I to get it?"

"I just couldn't afford seven and six at this moment, dear."

He seemed to consider, pouted, nodded, shrugged, and walked away.

She ran after him. "Where are you going?"

"Home."

The word was like a blow.

"Yon place is not your home, dear," she said. "Your home is with me and Hazel."

"Here?" he asked, indicating the pavement.

Hazel, standing by, noticed people staring; but her embarrassment was not so great as her anger against her brother. She did not speak, knowing that if she were to accuse him his mother would seize it as an excuse to give way to him.

"Aye, here if need be," replied Mrs. Aldersyde, hoarsely.

He looked insulted by the flippancy of such an answer. "I've got a place to go to," he said, and again set off towards it.

She could not run or call after him; love itself seemed paralysed in her, so that she stood there open-mouthed, like a dead woman.

"Let him go," sobbed Hazel.

By this time he was dawdling, waiting to be called back. At Michaelson's window he halted and stood gazing in at the kind of pen he wanted. He tried to appear like a brilliant and hard-working scholar prevented from winning the prizes he deserved just because of his lack of such a pen.

Moaning, his mother re-awakened and hurried along to him. After her trudged Hazel, sighing and resigned; she knew he would get the pen, he would not be grateful, and soon he would be asking for something else. He might even sell the pen for a shilling for sweets as he had once done with a new knife.

He did not give his mother a chance for any more pleading. "That's the kind," he said, pointing. "See, it says the nib's real gold."

She stared into the window as eagerly as if the guarantee promised with the pen was not that it would be repaired free of charge, but rather that it would make its recipient grateful, loving, and merciful.

By the time Hazel reached the shop they had gone in. She stood outside, with her back to the window: that pen represented to her a wickedness which she could not have named, but which she knew might destroy her mother.

When they came out, Gordon had the pen clipped in his breast pocket. It had been sold to them by Michaelson himself, who had enjoyed himself evading Mrs. Aldersyde's desperate insinuations that he ought to sell it to them at wholesale price, seeing Gordon was living with him.

Hazel refused to admire it. When her brother thrust it under her nose, she shrank back in aversion and shut her eyes, as if it was a wriggling snake. He taunted her with jealousy, and her mother peevishly reprimanded her. She gazed away from both of them, her eyes blind with tears of shame.

IV

The search for a lodging was long and fruitless. Most places were full, and their landladies too busy to advise someone obviously more particular than her means justified. Of the very few places with vacancies, all were too expensive, except one, an attic in a dingy boarding-house, with a single bed and holes in the one small strip of carpet. There was no couch or armchair on which Mrs. Aldersyde could have slept to allow Hazel comfortable use of the bed. On hearing of their need for thrift, the proprietrix stiffened rather than yielded. Now that the war was on she evidently expected the room to be taken any day by a long-term boarder. She said it was against her principle to charge half-rate for a child over twelve. The Aldersydes had to leave.

Not long after that repulse Gordon deserted. He said he was tired; there was no sense in his staying with them any longer; now that it was dark the Michaelsons would be wondering where he was; as their guest it was his duty to cause them no inconvenience. While he was talking, Hazel without warning struck him on the mouth, as hard as she could, her fist tight with the whole day's exacerbation. He was genuinely indignant, for his fear of displeasing the Michaelsons was no pretence. Ignoring his mother's shrill solaces, and her even shriller scoldings of Hazel, he ran off into the darkness.

This happened in the street just opposite the ancient abbey. Seats were there for holidaymakers to rest and ponder over the enigma of a past so inspired as to achieve such a beautiful monument to faith, and yet so savage and wanton as to desecrate it and murder its guardians. Mrs. Aldersyde sank down on one of those seats and wept: for her the present was savage, and faithless too. When she saw those shattered walls against the night sky, it seemed God Himself was mocking her, to show her His own house in ruins, in this very place where hers had collapsed.

Beside her Hazel was terrified: broken buildings for her were always haunted, especially at night; and her mind then could supply spectres that without taking any recognisable shape froze her blood. She waited for her mother to blame Gordon: that would not have brought relief, but by sanctioning her blow would have made her terror more comprehensible.

Her mother did not blame him. She blamed everybody but him; particularly did she blame Mrs. McShelvie, whose witch's spell had prevented them from finding a place to sleep, and also Mr. Grahamstone the headmaster, who was sitting at his ease in the Cargills' house while people, who should have been under his protection, were left to roam the street like tramps.

She jumped up and said they would go to Lammermuir. If he would not help them, they would report him to the police.

Hazel was pleased. In Lammermuir were Mr. Roy and Miss Cargill, as well as Mrs. Raeburn and wee Jess; these were people she liked and trusted, who would not turn them away, no matter what her mother said to them. At Cairnban, too, were others, rougher perhaps, but just as kind and obliging. Therefore as Hazel trudged wearily along to Lammermuir those spectres vanished out of her mind and were replaced by people with known smiling faces and friendly hands. She did not heed her mother's bitter prophecies: these were too familiar, and too often disproved.

Nevertheless, as they crunched up the path to the door of the house she pleaded with her mother not to be angry.

"I shall be angry if I find cause to be angry," replied her mother.

Hazel sighed: she knew now her mother would blame and find fault and be sorry for herself, evoking from those in the house the usual annoyed pity.

Her mother stopped. "Don't sigh at me," she said. Her voice, though, was different: the grief in it seemed strangely purged.

206

"My son, whom I've nourished wi' my hert's bluid, has deserted me."

In Hazel, listening to cheerful music from the house, hope died: she understood then not just what her mother was suffering now, but had been suffering for years; and she knew that kindness from other people could never avail.

"You should not have struck him," went on her mother, in that same voice. "But I'm not blaming you. They hae told me, who hate me and mine, and wish us destroyed, that I should hae chastised him; but were I to die in the gutter here, destitute and hameless, I would not wish to lift my hand against him."

"No, mummy," said Hazel. She could think of nothing better.

"He has deserted me," said her mother, "and I am the one to suffer. Am I no' then the one to forgie?"

"Yes, mummy."

"Then I forgie him. You hear me saying it: I forgie him."

She was silent for a minute or two, and then walked on towards the house.

A servant opened the door. It was an ordinary act, and she performed it with the ordinary patience of one brought from other tasks; but to the two on the doorstep it revealed wonders. Light and warmth streamed out; and singing was heard, by a voice they knew, deep, humorous, and somehow comforting. Roy was the singer, and the song one he taught to his classes: "O gin I were a baron's heir".

Sharply Mrs. Aldersyde explained she wished to see Mr. Grahamstone on urgent business. Hazel listened in tears to the singing. She was sure Miss Cargill was playing the piano, and that the song was for her.

"I'll see if he'll speak to you," said Jessie the maid.

"He'll see me."

"I wadnae be so sure o' that. Ye wadnae be the first he's chased awa'. He says a' business has to be done at the school. But I'll tell him. Ye'd better step in so that I can get the door shut. It's a jailing offence noo to let the licht be seen."

Mrs. Aldersyde entered with dignity, and stood beside two bags of golf-clubs that seemed to have been dumped there

207

recently. To her they were symbols of callousness; but she did not say so, and appeared to be listening, with pleasure, to the foolish and lying song.

"For I hae nocht to offer ye
Nae gowd frae mine, nae pearl frae sea,
Nor am I come o high degree,
But, lassie, how I lo'e thee!"

Then out of the room where the singing was came Graham-stone, clad in a long-sleeved cardigan, and smoking his pipe. He wore a smile so smug and self-contented it was able to sustain the involuntary scowl at seeing who his disturber was.

"What is it?" he demanded. "Can't I be given some time off? Didn't I issue instructions I was to be interviewed in the school between ten and twelve?"

"I know nothing of your instructions, Mr. Grahamstone."

"Well, you ought to. Have you been squabbling with the folk you're billeted on?"

"I am billeted on no one. I came from Gowburgh today to take my daughter home; she was not happy here. We have missed the train, and we have tried to find a lodging for tonight, without success. I have come here, because I consider it your duty to assist us."

"Oh you do, do you?"

Then the drawing-room door opened again, and out ran Mrs. Raeburn.

"I thought I recognised your voice, Mrs. Aldersyde," she cried, in delight.

Mrs. Aldersyde gazed coldly at this interloper. "I am here on private business," she said.

Mrs. Raeburn refused to be snubbed. She even seized her neighbour's hand.

"I heard you were in Langrigg," she said. "I met Mrs. McShelvie down in the town, and she told me."

"I was not aware I gave her permission to discuss my affairs; or you either."

"But we're all neighbours here in a strange place. We've

got to be interested in one another; that's not interfering, surely?"

"To me it is."

Campbelton had come out into the hall in time to hear those last exchanges. At Mrs. Raeburn's eager neighbourliness he had smiled and nodded; at Mrs. Aldersyde's churlish repudiation he pouted and swelled. He was about either to retreat into the drawing-room where his host, Sir Robert, was waiting to checkmate him in two moves, or else to rebuke Mrs. Aldersyde for her false, barren, and nasty pride. Instead, he smiled again, a great compassionate beam, and hurried forward to give the sour-faced tight-lipped little woman a bow and chivalrous salutation. To do so it was necessary to push his puffing chief out of his way; this he did, without harm to his own graciousness.

"We cannot expect Mrs. Aldersyde to tell us what her troubles are," he said, "here in this publicity. Let us adjourn to the dining-room."

"Dammit, Archie," muttered Grahamstone into his ear, "we can't use the house as if it was our own."

Campbelton ignored that boorish tactfulness, and taking Mrs. Aldersyde by the arm led her past the drawing-room. Resolutely she resisted the ill-mannered desire to look in; but Hazel succumbed, and saw Mr. Roy standing by the piano, with Miss Cargill seated at it; they were laughing together over some pages of music. She also saw Mr. Scoullar, who was seated on a sofa reading a book.

In the dining-room Campbelton switched on the electric fire, drew a chair up to it, and invited Mrs. Aldersyde to sit. She did so, with a mannerliness that outdid his; so much so that he, whose performance was partly satirical, was suddenly smitten with remorse.

"You'll be comfortable and private here, Mrs. Aldersyde," he said. "I'm sure Mr. Grahamstone will give you all the assistance you need. As for myself, my host Sir Robert is waiting for me; he and I are in the middle of a game of chess."

She let him go, as indifferent as a queen.

Grahamstone was surprised and not too pleased at being

left in command. "Well," he asked, "what d'you want me to do?"

Mrs. Aldersyde would not speak; her silence, however, was positive.

Mrs. Raeburn understood. "I ken I've nae right to be here," she said, "and so I'll go. But I wanted to tell you that when I was speaking to Bell McShelvie this afternoon she said that if I saw you I was to let you ken that the bed in Cairnban is still yours if you want it. I think you should take it, Mrs. Aldersyde. Bell will make you very welcome. But I'll go now. I promised Jessie I'd help her wi' the supper things. Goodbye, Mrs. Aldersyde, and good luck. Goodbye, Hazel."

"Goodbye, Mrs. Raeburn," whispered the girl. "Is Jess here?"

"She's up in her bed. Will I tell her you were asking for her?"

Hazel nodded, in tears. "And wee Richard too."

Her mother sat neutral during that display of goodwill; but as soon as Mrs. Raeburn had gone she turned to her daughter.

"You greet too easy," she said. "You'll learn to prize your tears; or else the day will come when they'll let you droon in them."

Grahamstone too had been listening to Mrs. Raeburn.

"What's this about a bed in Cairnban?" he asked.

"Nothing."

"Did Mrs. McShelvie offer you one?"

"She had the impertinence."

"Impertinence! I can't see any impertinence in that. Do you mean to tell me you're here to ask me to find you a lodging for the night?"

"In my opinion, it is your duty."

"Who's being impertinent now?" he cried. "I'll be the judge of what's my duty. Every Tom, Dick, or Harry seems to think he's got a right to order me about. I'm not having it any more. Mrs. Aldersyde, I'm going to talk to you bluntly; I can see it's the only language you'll heed. If you wish to take your girl back to Gowburgh and run the risk of having her killed or crippled in a bombing raid, that's your prerogative. Personally,

I wouldn't allow it; but higher authorities have washed their hands of it, and so I'm not taking it upon my shoulders."

"I hae two children," she said.

The remark, and her tragic tone, nonplussed him. He gaped.

"There'll be an exodus," he muttered, "but I'll not be Moses. Now, Mrs. Aldersyde, I want you to understand that I'm just a guest in this house. You can see my position. The folk here are decent, but I can't presume on their good nature."

"Are you telling me I ought to go and not trouble you any longer?"

"I'm not telling you anything of the kind. Well, yes, in a way I am. You have a place to go to. You're not really homeless. Cairnban's all right, for one night."

She rose. "I hae an innocent child here," she said.

He looked, startled and dubious, at Hazel: after nearly forty years as a teacher he still granted innocence in children, in theory; in practice he found it safer to deny its existence altogether.

"Have you any idea of what's going on in this Cairnban?" she whispered.

"Certainly. I am in touch with every household where one of my people is billeted. Mr. Roy, as my representative, calls at Cairnban every day."

"Some men came down in the same train as myself," she said. "They are spending the night in Cairnban."

"Husbands, I take it?" he asked anxiously.

"They pass as husbands."

He was alarmed. "What do you mean? Are you making out I'm tolerating rascality under my aegis? In any case, I don't think there's any regulation forbidding visits of husbands. In fact, the regulations governing Cairnban have still to be drawn up; that'll be the town council's job, not mine. But it seems to me that visits of bona-fide husbands will have to be permitted, provided they're not too frequent or prolonged. You can't regulate nature out of existence after all, even if it does have its unpleasant side."

She walked to the door. "If I am asked," she said, "I shall certainly say you turned my daughter and I into the night. It will be the truth."

He kept following her out of the dining-room into the hall. "Who's going to ask you?" he demanded. "I'm not turning you away. I'm sending you to Cairnban, where there's accommodation promised."

She paused, as if to admire for a few moments the piano playing.

"I would rather lie under a hedge," she said, "than be beholden to such scum. They say, Mr. Grahamstone, that pride and independence are deid in Scotland; they are not deid in me."

"Nor in me," he said peevishly, for her every sneer was an accusation of servility.

"Come, Hazel," she said, and in another moment they were gone.

Disconsolate as a baby with its bottle empty, he stood sucking at his cold pipe. What officials armed with what thunderbolts could she complain to? Lofty authority, he knew, often consolidated itself at the expense of humbler authority by such a wilful and illogical championing of some perverse unimportant individual. Had he not himself more than once found favour in the eyes of parents by taking their part against some young inexperienced teacher?

As he stood there, mumbling and sucking in wind, Mrs. Raeburn appeared. When she saw him alone, eagerness fled from her mild maternal face.

"Are they gone?" she asked.

He nodded.

"But I was going to ask them into the kitchen for some tea."

"She wouldn't have accepted," he muttered. "Only the dining-room and the best silver would have satisfied her."

"Have they gone to Cairnban?"

"I don't know. She said she'd lie under a hedge first. You know," he added, as he shambled at a weary sexagenarian's pace towards the drawing-room, "it all lands on me. Some sing, some read, some play chess, some knit: I'm left to carry the burden of all these people's woes."

Shaking his head, he entered the room, to find Scoullar callously turning a page, Roy gazing down in oblivious and

212

selfish dalliance at Elizabeth who was playing quiet romantic music, and Campbelton giggling at the imminent loss, in the third game, of his too dashing Queen. Even Sir Robert, snowy-haired ailing ex-bureaucrat, was more engrossed in the useless subtleties of chess than in schemes to frustrate young Roy's far more obvious and sinister moves.

As he sat down by the fire, and picked up the newspaper he had been reading, he felt himself almost wishing he was back in the manse: there neglect had been shocking and unforgivable, but it had also been assailable; here, disguised as luxury and kindness, it could not be opposed.

"What happened?" asked Campbelton, waiting for his host to tighten the garotte.

"Happened? I packed her off to Cairnban. It seems Mrs. McShelvie there offered to give her a bed. She didn't want to go; thought it wasn't good enough for her. She's a trouble-maker, that one; thinks her children were specially created."

"Weren't they?" murmured Campbelton, with a cynical smile towards the budding courtship.

"Your Queen is doomed, I'm afraid," said Sir Robert, with relish.

"My Queen," said Campbelton, mockingly sad. "My Mary of Scots. My Cleopatra. My Boadicea. My daughter of Jephthah. My Bell McShelvie."

"And she's such an uncouth sort of woman," grumbled Grahamstone. "Why can't she see she just makes herself ridiculous by putting on such airs and graces?"

Over at the piano Elizabeth whispered: "Who are they talking about?"

But Roy shook his head, smiling: such sad lovely music, so nourishing to a warrior's love, must not be stultified by chatter about Mrs. Aldersyde. In two weeks he was to report to an Air Force station in the south of England: unthinkable therefore to squander even a minute of that time on any subject which did not bring in Elizabeth. Cairnban brought her in, for, more enthusiastically than himself, she had adopted that rumbustious place; but Mrs. Aldersyde's wretched little snobberies brought in only exasperation and blight.

V

They were out of the house, down the drive, through the gate, and walking along the dark avenue, before Hazel found courage and energy to ask where they were going.

"To Cairnban," replied her mother, in a low, hoarse, restrained voice.

Hazel was cunning enough to hide her own gladness.

"This is the wrong direction," she said.

Her mother stopped, shivered, and slowly turned.

"A' my life," she muttered, so indistinctly Hazel could not make it out, "I hae been going in the wrong direction."

Hazel did not ask her to repeat it. As they walked on, she wondered if she should help her mother to find excuses for this surrender: she could say, for instance, that she was very tired, which was the truth; she could point out that it would now be impossible to find any other place; she could put the blame on Mr. Grahamstone, who had ordered them to go to Cairnban; she could argue that, since Cairnban did not belong to any of the women in it, not even Mrs. McShelvie, none of them had any right to object. Each of these excuses seemed to her sufficient in itself: together they made their going to Cairnban not a surrender at all but a kind of triumph. Some instinct, however, kept her from uttering them: better to let her mother find her own reasons; and better not to know what those were.

In sympathy and love she took her mother's arm. Whatever happened in Cairnban, whatever was said, she would support her mother and not feel ashamed. At the same time she prayed that they would get into Mrs. McShelvie's room without meeting any of the other inhabitants.

Her prayer was dismissed, at the very gate of Cairnban. There two persons were standing close together, a man and a woman; they seemed to be indulging in an amorous quarrel, and drew apart as the Aldersydes approached. It was not too dark for Mrs. Aldersyde to see who they were: a Mrs. Fairlie, deserted by her husband, and her co-habiter called Williamson, reputed to be the father of her latest child. Neither was drunk,

214

but he seemed so distracted he would have persisted in his angry endearments had his paramour not harshly silenced him.

She herself spoke. "Guid evening, Mrs. Aldersyde," she said, in a fierce experimental friendliness.

Mrs. Aldersyde did not reply. As she walked past she pulled her daughter away, as if from contamination.

"You wee upstart," cried Mrs. Fairlie after her. "I've a guid mind to come after you and knock some manners into you."

"Quiet, Maggie," whispered Williamson. "She's nothing to us."

"Is she no'? Are you sure o' that? I'll tell you what she is to us: she's the kind that'll christen oor wean a bastard, and see that the name sticks a' his life."

Mrs. Aldersyde let Hazel go: it seemed a symbolical act, an admission that the evil in the world was so encompassing no one could be saved from it. Yet she murmured: "I hae no spite against their child."

Hazel said nothing, although she had more than once been led to believe by her mother that wee Charlie Fairlie, blue-eyed and curly-haired in his pram, was some kind of monstrosity.

The door was unlocked, and they entered upon a hall where three little girls were sitting on the bottom stairs playing with dolls. From some room upstairs shrieks of maudlin song were heard.

Hazel smiled at the little girls.

"Ask them," said her mother, "where the room is."

Hazel went over to the biggest, Charlotte Cockburn, aged seven.

"Can you tell us, Charlotte, where Mrs. McShelvie's room is?"

Charlotte was slow of understanding; many, including Mrs. Aldersyde, had long ago condemned her as mentally defective. She gawked at Hazel.

Her sister, Cissie, four years younger, answered for her, slowly but calmly.

"It's up there," she said, pointing. "It's got a white handle."

"Will you show us where it is, Cissie?"

Cissie nodded, clasped her doll with one hand and pulled

herself up the stairs with the other. The Aldersydes crept behind her.

She stopped in front of a door on the first floor; it had a white handle.

"That's Bell's," she said.

"Thanks, Cissie," said Hazel, and knocked on the door, so that her mother would not have to do it. Cissie stood by, watching.

Before the knock was answered, another door, behind which the revelry was going on, opened, and out shot Meg Aitchison, shrieking, as if being chased by Germans.

She saw Mrs. Aldersyde. "Suffering Jesus!" she cried, and then yelled into the room, "Come and get a dekko at this, for Christ's sake."

As Mrs. Jolly, Mrs. Ross, and one or two other women, with Mr. Jolly amongst them, crowded in the doorway to stare, she herself came slinking along, with all her skinniness, of arms, of legs, of neck, of body, expressing cannibalistic and comic menace.

"So it's wee Lady Muck frae Glabber Castle," she cried. "Weel, meet the Duchess o' Dunghill." And she curtseyed, in a way to emphasise the bareness, pallor, dirt, and varicose veins of her legs; she overdid it, purposely, and crashed down on her behind. There she sat laughing like a madwoman.

Cissie Cockburn, hugging her doll, watched in an amusement apparently detached, ironical, and civilised.

Then Mrs. McShelvie opened her door. She showed no surprise at seeing who her callers were, nor at seeing Meg on the floor.

"So you've managed to come," she said to the former. "I'm glad. Come awa' in." She held the door wide for them to slip quickly past. "Meg," she said then, "if you hae any respect for me, hae some for onybody I invite to my room."

Meg rose up, and made a gesture of disgust too overwhelming for speech; nevertheless, she tried. "That one," she said, "wad gie respect itself a pain in the belly." Then, overcome by her own wit, she burst again into fanged amiable mirth.

Cissie Cockburn stepped forward. "Bell," she said.

Mrs. McShelvie gazed down at the solemn three-year-old. "Are you no' in bed yet, Cissie?" she asked.

"It was me that showed the wumman your hoose, Bell."

"Guid for you, Cissie. Just you come in then, and get a biscuit."

Cissie strode in, like one accustomed; but she was baulked by the Aldersydes who stood silently at the fireside. The biscuit tin was on the mantelpiece.

"Excuse me," said Mrs. McShelvie to her guests, as she stretched up for the tin. "Cissie's a good lass. She's always helping folk. She helped me yesterday to scrub oot this room."

Cissie took the biscuit and praise with equanimity. "Ta," she said. "I'll go back doon, Bell." And off she went.

Mrs. McShelvie showed her out. "You tell your mither I said she was to put you straight to bed."

"Aye, Bell."

Mrs. McShelvie lingered at the door, perhaps delighting in the sight of that tiny innocent self-assurance, perhaps reluctant to go in and face her visitors.

"Cissie's a favourite of mine," she said, when she did go in. "But come on, sit you doon by the fire. I'll tak' your coats. I was just going to mak' myself a cup o' tea. I'm glad you're here in time to keep me company. Tea's nae hermit's drink; it's sweeter if there are freen's to talk to."

Mrs. Aldersyde so far had not spoken a word, nor had she cast one glance of criticism round the room. She stood as quiet and reserved as a well-trained child: a bearing in contrast with her twitching lips and desperate eyes.

Hazel, shy too, kept smiling. She understood, intuitively, that the episode with Cissie Cockburn, purposely prolonged by Mrs. McShelvie, represented the sanity, security, and simplicity of home; her confidence in Mrs. McShelvie was therefore strengthened. To humour her mother that night, she knew, was a task few people would undertake, far less manage successfully; but Mrs. McShelvie would do it.

"I'd better show you your quarters," said their hostess. "Hae you ever seen one room turned into twa at the toss of a curtain? Just watch."

The room was large, and already had a string across it diagonally. Over the string she threw a large yellow curtain that had a few rents in it fixed by small gilt safety-pins. It did not completely divide the room, but it gave privacy to the corner where the Aldersydes were to sleep.

"I thocht I'd better hae some arrangement like this," said Mrs. McShelvie, "if I'm to hae my twa lassies to bide wi' me. They'd hardly get sleeping wi' the licht on, and I'm no' just auld enough yet to gang to bed at half-past eight."

"You'd think," said Mrs. Aldersyde, "a big house like this would hae electricity."

"Wouldn't you?" agreed Mrs. McShelvie, now busy preparing the tea. "A' the same, the gas has come in handy. Maist of us hae gas-rings like this fitted up."

"Is that all you've got to cook on?"

"No. There's a fine big kitchen doonstairs, wi' twa cookers. We've got some kind of system working noo; but there's still a guid cheery chew-the-fat at every meal."

"Have you been appointed the caretaker?"

"No' yet. I micht no' be. If no', it's back to Gowburgh. I'm nominated. But it seems the toon cooncil's got to be satisfied I'm a fit person. They're meeting next week. I've to be there. Mr. Roy tells me I'll be fairly put through my catechism."

"Will you be paid?"

"Seemingly. That's to be discussed as weel."

"If you get your two girls here with you, it should be a good arrangement."

"Aye, it'll suit us fine."

There was a pause.

"I hope you do," said Mrs. Aldersyde.

"Thanks. Now Hazel lass, you'll sit here, nearest to the fire; you, Mrs. Aldersyde, here. Did you ever see such an assortment of chairs? But the china makes up for them. Braw, isn't it? It caused a great rumpus in the cooncil. Mr. Roy bought it for us withoot consulting them. Being the sort of young fellow he is, he made it the best. Foolish, of course; for I believe half's smashed already."

"I wouldn't call it foolish. Surely you're entitled to the best? Wasn't it them who dragged you from your ain homes?"

"There's that way to look at it. Now I'm sorry there's naething grand: there's plenty of bread and butter, and jam, and cheese."

"It will do fine, thank you."

Mrs. McShelvie smiled. "I don't say a grace myself," she said, "but if you do, go ahead. It'll not do a sinner like me ony harm for once."

"Grace?" repeated Mrs. Aldersyde, with a groan that many people would have found laughable. Mrs. McShelvie gravely nodded.

Hazel waited, in terror. Would her mother, who had already blamed God that night, blame Him again; and would that blame turn into an hysterical attack on Mrs. McShelvie?

"Yes," said Mrs. Aldersyde at last, "it's our custom at home." She bowed her head and shut her eyes. "For what we are about to receive, may we be truly thankful. For Jesus' sake. Amen."

"Fine," murmured Mrs. McShelvie. "Now eat up. Help yourself, Hazel. You're terribly quiet. I think you're wanting your bed."

Hazel nodded and smiled.

Mrs. Aldersyde began to shiver and even let the knife fall out of her hand. Mrs. McShelvie pretended not to notice.

"She washes herself and brushes her teeth every night," said Mrs. Aldersyde.

"I can see that. She's got as bonny a complexion and as fine a set of teeth as any lass I ever saw. My Sammy thinks there's naebody as braw as Hazel. The bathroom's just a step or twa alang the landing. I should hae shown it to you right away. That's the trouble, I'm too fond of making folk listen to my blethers."

That was the time, thought Hazel, to thank Mrs. McShelvie. She looked at her mother with the hint bright but timid on her face. Her mother saw it but did not speak.

The silence that fell was broken by a knock on the door.

Mrs. McShelvie rose in a hurry. "I'd better see wha it is," she said. "There are some in this hoose nae respecters of privacy."

But at the door her voice softened. "Oh, it's you, Nan," they heard her say. "Weel, that's gey thoughtful of you. I'm sure they'll appreciate it. Come in yourself and do it."

It was Mrs. Ross she brought in, so swollen in her apron that the work which that garment suggested, such as the scrubbing of floors, seemed in her case ludicrously impossible: once on her knees, she could never get up unaided. Yet as she waddled across the floor with her toes visible through holes in her stockings and slippers, she had her massive arms bare to the shoulders, as if about to start off on that very scrubbing. Instead of scrubber, however, in her hand were two chocolate biscuits in blue and silver wrappings. These she held out as an offering to Mrs. Aldersyde.

"For your tea," she said.

It was, Hazel saw, a crisis: her mother had always professed an especially virulent contempt for this fat placid woman with the large family. Therefore the girl expected, with a dread that swiftly chilled her from waist to feet, that her mother would either shrilly spurn the biscuits, or else madly throw them back. What Mrs. McShelvie could do then, to mend what was broken, she did not know.

Nothing was broken. Her mother, with a smile that for all its difficulty made her look younger, took the biscuits.

"Thank you," she whispered.

"You're welcome," said Mrs. Ross.

"You'll join us, Nan?" said Mrs. McShelvie.

"Oh no, no," cried Mrs. Ross, laughing and waddling back to the door. "I've got a roomful of weans to hush. Don't mind Meg, Mrs. Aldersyde," she added, as she was about to leave. "It's just her way. She means naething by it. Where you or me or Bell here wad think a wee laugh sufficient, she's got to screech like yon. My man says if I had a voice like hers he'd put a muzzle on me. Guid night. Enjoy your tea. You too, lassie."

Then she was gone, closing the door behind her not too softly, as if to suggest something fragile was left in that room, and not too loudly, to suggest anything startling or annoying or puzzling. Seldom was a door shut so well.

Mrs. Aldersyde unwrapped her biscuit.

"I hae often wondered," she said, "how she manages to keep so happy."

"I don't think she could tell you that. It's a gift. She's got nae bed of roses either. I've seen her break her heart."

"She lost two children." As she spoke Mrs. Aldersyde was eating the biscuit, watched by her daughter and her hostess as if it was some sacramental wafer.

"Aye," said Mrs. McShelvie.

"That must be the greatest sorrow a woman has to bear."

Mrs. McShelvie nodded.

There was a silence.

"I wonder," said Mrs. Aldersyde, "if you would mind reading my cup?"

Mrs. McShelvie was astonished. "Och, that's just a game for daft wives," she said. "A sensible body like yourself cannae believe in such nonsense."

"I would be obliged."

Mrs. McShelvie hesitated. "I tell you what," she said. "Let's get this young lady to bed first."

Mrs. Aldersyde, looking into her cup, thought she saw a school-cap shaped by the leaves; it was a symbol of hope.

"It's naething but superstition," whispered her hostess.

But to Mrs. Aldersyde, who had said grace despite God's unfairness to her, it seemed that those leaves had been arranged so hopefully by His command. She set the cup down on the table gently, and covered it with a saucer.

Within half an hour Hazel was washed, in bed, and asleep. She had found an opportunity to thank Mrs. McShelvie, and so slept with a smile.

On the other side of the yellow curtain, with the gas turned down, her mother and Mrs. McShelvie sat by the fireside, the latter with the cup in her hands, the former whimpering in her impatience to be told that her prayer was to be answered.

Mrs. McShelvie for a long time did not speak. She had not been able to dissuade her guest, who did not wish, like Meg Aitchison for instance, to be amused by the impishness of fate around the corner, but rather demanded to be comforted, reassured, and restored to her former arrogance. Gordon, about whom her brags used to be so incontinent and aggressive, had not once been mentioned. It was obvious he had, in some profound revolutionary way, offended her; and it was still more obvious that she looked to the magic in the tea-leaves to propitiate him, to win his forgiveness for her being offended, and to release her from this agonising confinement of silence about him. If there was to be no such release, might she not, soon, perhaps in this very room, be driven to antics in horrible earnest, even more grotesque than those Meg had performed in fun out in the lobby?

Fondling the cup in her hands, Mrs. McShelvie felt she had a human soul in her keeping, which might shatter as easily as the cup would if dropped on the hearth. Yet she did not know what to say.

She had to say something; perhaps the usual silly fibs would be enough.

"I can see you're going on a journey," she said.

"Likely enough. Amn't I to go back tomorrow?"

"Not as soon as that; this journey in the cup I mean. There's something new for wearing here, something for the hands, gloves maybe, or it could be a ring."

"I hae only this ring," said Mrs. Aldersyde, twisting her wedding-ring round her finger cruelly.

God help me, thought Mrs. McShelvie, she's going to break, and there's nothing I can say to prevent it, nothing that I know to be truth; and deliberate lies about the future, for whatever purpose, are not only sinful but dangerous.

"Is that all?" cried Mrs. Aldersyde.

"Wheehst!" Mrs. McShelvie glanced towards the curtain behind which Hazel lay sleeping. As she did so, something trickled down her brow into her eye; it was sweat.

She put the cup on the table.

"Mrs. Aldersyde," she said, "if I can help you, I will, to the very limit of my power. But no' that way."

Mrs. Aldersyde began shaking her head, faster and faster.

"You can't help me," she shouted. "Nobody can."

"Wheehst! Wheehst! You'll waken your lassie."

Mrs. Aldersyde kept shaking her head and screeching.

As Mrs. McShelvie rose she remembered having read once, or seen in a film, that the way to stop hysterics was by a hard slap on the face; afterwards the victim was grateful and forgave the blow: here it might not only fail, but also end forever Mrs. Aldersyde's effort to become a member of the community.

She took her by the shoulders, firmly but gently.

"You just cannae go on like this," she said, "for your ain sake as weel as for the lassie's; aye, and for the laddie's too. I ken he's the cause o' it. If you want to tell me I'll be glad to listen and to help if I can; but if you'd raither not, if you'd prefer to keep it to yourself, though it should break your hert, you must thole it quietly."

Mrs. Aldersyde was suddenly quiet.

"I hae tholed it for years," she said, "withoot telling a living soul."

Mrs. McShelvie took away her hands. As an excuse for movement, and for a respite, she walked softly across to the curtain and glanced behind it at Hazel. The girl still slept, looking so innocent, and yet so like her brother, that after all there was no respite.

She returned to the fireside.

"Don't mak' too much of it, whatever it was," she said. "What a wean does, he's got a lifetime to rue and mak' amends." She did not add that many never made use of their lifetimes; and that Gordon Aldersyde was likely enough amongst these.

"A mither's no' blind, Mrs. McShelvie," said Mrs. Aldersyde. "She sees her children's faults better than any."

"She should do."

"I hae seen his for years."

"I suppose you hae."

"But I never showed I knew. Why should I, surrounded by folk only too pleased to see my heart was breaking?"

"We surely hae the right to keep such things to ourselves." But as she spoke Mrs. McShelvie was wondering whether she too, in this game of truth-telling, was a player or only a listener. Ought she to keep quiet when neighbours like Nan Ross and

Bessie Raeburn were being reviled? Now that the wound was discharging, would it not be kindness to scrape it clean?

"I never had any support frae my husband," said Mrs. Aldersyde.

"He's worked hard, has he no', whiles when he wasn't fit for it?"

"He had no right to marry and bring children into the world when he wasn't fit for it."

There was then, Mrs. McShelvie knew, to be no complete redemption, no cleansing and healing of the wound. A little humility had been learned, and might as soon as tomorrow be forgotten.

"What faults the boy has," said Mrs. Aldersyde, "he got from him."

"They say a' our faults come frae the same heritage in the long run."

After a pause, during which Mrs. Aldersyde kept staring down at her hands on her lap, almost as if at last willing to be reconciled, she began to weep. They were not tears of animosity or vengefulness towards her husband, nor even tears of sorrow for her son's unkindness: they were tears that flowed from the vaster universal sorrow of humanity thwarted in its love by its own limitations.

As Mrs. McShelvie listened, she laid her hand on her neighbour's head and hushed her, as one would an infant that did not yet know language, but knew already fear and pain and the overpowering need of love.

PART FIVE

I

ON the evening of the council meeting to discuss the reducing of Cairnban and the installing of a commandant or head jailer, there was much hilarity, excitement, and comradeship in that threatened fortress. Bell McShelvie was well supplied with arguments, not only on her own behalf: Meg Aitchison, for instance, wanted her to petition the council to deprive of his licence every shopkeeper in the town who, in a country at war, spurned the trust and amity of tick; while Mrs. Lawson urged with fervour that another W.C. must be demanded, for though rotas could be drawn up for baths or use of cookers and gramophone, there was no known means of enforcing fair share of the lavatory.

Besides all that advice, articles of wear were pressed on Bell: a pink hat with a veil, kid gloves, a fox fur with a face not unlike Meg's (though nobody said so), silk stockings, and a ponyskin coat in which the few mangy places could easily be hidden by careful brushing. She was their ambassadress, they declared, and it was their duty to see that she was equipped to represent them worthily. When she remarked that they must surely regard her in her own clothes as a scarecrow, they denied it vociferously, with their hands on their hearts, and pointed out that not one of them could hope to equal the united resources of them all: her own gold brooch, for example, a wedding gift from Isaac, was the most beautiful in the house. Nevertheless she declined, and it was Meg who dressed up in that concentration of finery, despite the protests of its various owners, and went prancing and ogling about as the Duchess

225

of Cairnban, with gestures more appropriate, so some said, for an apprentice street-walker.

Roy had promised to come for Bell in the Cargills' car. Ten minutes before the time she was ready, wearing her own old coat, and her faded blue dress, specially laundered. Isaac's brooch too had been polished, and she had yielded in her independence in the matter of Mrs. Fairlie's scented talcum powder, presented to her at the door of the bathroom. Hence she smelled, so Meg shrieked, like a bride; and of course within a second Meg was off on another frolic, impersonating Bell's knock-kneed squinting money-bagged Langrigg groom, spouting refined gibberish, and also the minister, big Sandeman, who stood in a dwam of holy annoyance as if he had forgotten what God had just told him personally and exclusively. Everybody laughed, but at the end, when Meg had collapsed on the bed, Bell said she felt more like a criminal going to trial.

In the car that feeling was reinforced by Grahamstone who, with Campbelton, sat at the back. As soon as she entered, he had peered forward to see if she was respectably enough dressed: a snort indicated modified dissatisfaction. Then he proceeded, like a lawyer, to make sure she could be trusted not to commit some folly, part of which might ricochet on to him.

"Remember this," he said, "they're the people with the say: impudence will get nowhere with them."

She felt Roy nudge her, and knew it meant: don't let the old fat-head's havers upset you. But as the envoy of Cairnban, she was not allowed such magnanimity.

"Were they the town's paupers," she replied, "I wouldn't be impudent."

"And sarcasm won't do either," he said sharply. "Most of these folk are well-to-do."

"I think we can trust Mrs. McShelvie to handle them tactfully," said Roy.

"In any case," remarked Campbelton to his chief, "I would have thought you would enjoy the spectacle of Sandeman, say, being roasted in the hell-fire of Gowburgh truthfulness."

Somehow Roy's chuckle, sympathetic though it was meant to be, irked Bell. Her foolish unpardonable envy of the young teacher had never been allayed, for all his active kindnesses; now, indeed, it was stronger than ever because of his romance with the bonny Cargill girl. They stood hand-in-hand, ready to run together into life, which lay before them like a great scented meadow with sunlit hills beyond and a blue sky above; whereas she and Isaac had walked up the narrow smelly close to the room-and-kitchen in Wallace Street.

"I hope, gentlemen," she said, "you've no' brought me alang as a tame bear, to scart the faces of folk wha hae offended you?"

Roy again chuckled, this time repentantly. As she glanced at him driving the car along the dark wet street, she imagined him similarly piloting an aeroplane through far-off night skies. Remembering her reputation as spae-wife, she looked in him for signs of disaster. Such looking, and especially such finding, were of course even more wicked than her envy.

"And what wages do you expect to get?" asked Grahamstone.

That had been debated by the Cairnban sisterhood. Meg had proposed five pounds per week, on the principle they would give only half of what was asked; but two pounds had been agreed on by the majority. Bell had disconcerted and huffed some of them by reminding them it was really her business, and that though she was grateful for their interest and advice she would decide for herself. It was their figure she now mentioned.

"Two pounds a week!" shouted Grahamstone. "My God, they'll laugh at us if you ask for that."

"Is it no' enough?" she asked. "Do you think I'd be cheapening the name o' Gowburgh?"

Again Roy nudged her; again he laughed. But his happiness had little to do with her or with Cairnban.

"Not enough!" cried Grahamstone. "It's exorbitant."

"To gie ony less wad surely shame them," she said.

He laughed. "It never shames well-off people," he said, "to pay small wages."

He said it so wisely, as if to a thick-skulled piteous ignoramus, that for a moment she was almost provoked into letting him know that, as far as the ways of the world with money were concerned, *he* was the infant, and she the headmistress: her university having been a life of hardship and deprivation, not spent as one of a community of peasants on a barren land, but within a penny tram-ride of opulence and plenty in the celebrated Gowburgh shops. But she refrained proudly, and he was still philosophising about the financial obduracy of the rich when the car stopped.

"Here we are," said Roy.

"Is this the jail then?" she asked.

He understood at once, as did Campbelton; but Grahamstone didn't, and wanted to know what she meant.

The first person they saw when they entered the building was a policeman.

Grahamstone reassured her. "They'll always have one on duty," he said, "when the council's meeting: in case some ratepayer with a grudge causes a commotion."

"In Gowburgh," said Campbelton, "it is of course the councillors who cause the commotions."

Grahamstone chuckled. "Don't let them hear you say that, Archie," he whispered, "if you want to be a heidie."

The policeman showed them where to go; there they were received by Miss Cheam, Alden's secretary, with her forefinger glued to her lips. It seemed the council was in session next door. They listened, and heard self-important voices; one soon predominated, shrill, hard, and feminine, like a shrew's with a dozen husbands.

It was soon evident Miss Cheam wished she had five fore-fingers, one for each of them. She would allow them to speak only if they were inaudible to each other. The result was that Campbelton, still nettled by his chief's gibe, began to whistle "Bonny Dundee". Grahamstone scowled like a buccaneer captain not sure whether this was off-duty or on. Roy too whistled: his tune was familiar but at first Bell couldn't name it, until, remembering it was a favourite of Isaac's, she knew it was: "My luve is like a red red rose".

Bell herself sat like a fifty-year-old version of Jess Raeburn: all she lacked was the equivalent of black-faced Topsy. She

228

had recognised the woman councillor's voice as Miss Hamby-Brewster's; at times it sounded like Meg Aitchison's, without the coarseness and fun, and with the conceit undiluted by self-derision.

Then a babble as of schoolchildren broke out in the council chamber, and soon Alden appeared. He was delighted to see them, and closing the door came over on his tiptoes, with a curious stoop, like a traitor about to divulge his side's secret strategy.

"Well, gentlemen," he whispered, winking, "as you may guess, Cairnban's been under heavy fire. Miss Hamby-Brewster is for having the place shut up, abandoned, and abolished; she has supporters. Major Orinshaw's our man; he's standing up to her, but"—here his voice dropped still lower—"he's always liable to give in. Sometimes his capitulation's quite sensational. They say he becomes haunted by some German prisoners inadvertently killed while in his custody. Mind you, he was himself wounded."

"And he is our chief ally?" asked Campbelton in scorn, for he too had been wounded.

Alden nodded. "The provost's neutral; but he has a shrewd respect for a *fait accompli*. Henderson's with us, I believe; but he's a waverer; he never has a thought without another to cancel it out; he calls the process intelligence; incidentally, he lectures on temperance. Michaelson hasn't yet opened his mouth; he's a rare hand at waiting. With whom is Rouster? With history. At least so he has said. I don't think anybody understood."

"What about Sandeman?" asked Grahamstone. "What's he saying?"

"Nothing so far."

"He's another one good at waiting; and by God he makes sure everybody else waits too."

"Quite so. Well, gentlemen, your testimony is to be heard first. They wish to interview Mrs. McShelvie alone. I am inclined to think they will judge Cairnban by her."

"Fair enough," said Roy. "A better representative couldn't be got."

229

The little town clerk bowed towards her.

Campbelton spoke to some nymphs' heads carved on the ceiling. "If our testimony is to be ignored," he said, "why should we bother to give it?"

Grahamstone bent over her. "Just remember what I told you about their attitude to money," he whispered. "That's the secret of handling these people. Don't run away with the idea that because they live in villas and mansions they're careless with it. The sure way to please them is to ask for as little as you can."

"I hae no doubt that wad please them," she agreed, and he rose up, satisfied with his teaching.

Then Alden, brisk as impresario, collected his male chorus, Roy, Campbelton, and Grahamstone, lined them up in single file, resisted just in time the temptation to pull the headmaster's tie-knot up into his collar and to tickle the superciliousness out of Campbelton's smile, and, after calling on Miss Cheam to look after Mrs. McShelvie (which surveillance, according to his doorward wink, was to include the prevention of eavesdropping), ushered them into the council chamber, closing the door after them twice just to make sure. It appeared that the town clerk, though aware of the shortcomings of the council as individual human beings, accorded them a mystical respect in the aggregate.

Miss Cheam, frowning like a wardress, sat by a desk and manicured her nails. Mrs. McShelvie glanced at her own and decided that her toes needed such attentions more. She could not help smiling as she pictured the prim sulky young woman's astonishment and revulsion if she were to remove shoes and stockings, and begin paring her toenails. Yet were not toes as decent as fingers? Somehow that inconsistency of society gave her confidence, not because it made her feel superior, but because it made her feel more at home.

She tried to listen to the voices behind the door. Roy's advocacy, she thought, would be helpful and sincere enough; Grahamstone's would be in the proportion of one word for Cairnban to a dozen for himself: he had no intention, he had grumbled, of returning to Gowburgh with that albatross round

230

his neck. She had known what he had meant, but not what the bird had to do with it.

Mr. Campbelton she could not hear at all, but she did not think he would be altogether mute. He was too proud of his cleverness with words not to exhibit it, especially to those amateur orators; but he was also too astute to vulgarise what he had to say with loudness, emphasis, or passion. He would wait till some councillor made an unwary remark, more tactless than callous, and then he would quietly flay its perpetrator, with that noble-browed high-minded air he was so expert at. He did not care whether he helped her cause or Cairnban's. When she went in she might find half the councillors with their skins off, so that every innocent word she said would sting them like an insult. The one consolation was that Miss Hamby-Brewster, being so vulnerable, might not be so offensive; although from her behaviour at Cairnban she appeared to have at least six skins, as well as two thick armours, one of coin, and the other of childlessness.

Miss Cheam became fidgety when she noticed how intently Mrs. McShelvie seemed to be listening. She came over and interposed a screen of inane and perfunctory chatter about Cairnban, and also about Mrs. McShelvie's opinion of Langrigg. Bell answered politely, and with sly ingenuousness switched the conversation upon Alden, the wee town clerk: how he had mismanaged the billeting, how he had sent women and children to a dark empty house, how he was reputed to drink more than was good for his health, wits, or position, and how, like many another drunkard, he could be redeemed only by some good woman making the sacrifice of marrying him. All that was conveyed in her most earnest simple-minded plebeian manner, as if what wisdom and mischief were in it were by accident.

Miss Cheam was shocked but fascinated: such knowledge of her William could have been acquired in so short a time only by one with some kind of second sight, such as she had heard this shabby bare-headed working-class woman to possess. She wondered, in excited anguish, if she should invite her home some evening to read her cup. Discretion cried no; but desire, with its longer echoes, cried yes; for if William was to be won it must be soon, before age, that patient but inexorable witch, turned lipsticked mouth, crimsoned nails, and nightly oiled bust, into ludicrous toys no one could ever play with.

When Alden returned, with Roy, Campbelton, and Grahamstone, and beckoned her to come, Bell rose with the feeling that once again she had put her own strength of mind, her own conquest of ambition, and her own discovery of where the limits of life lay, to ignoble use. She had, indeed, revenged herself upon this unhappy young woman: not for pestering her with insincerities, but rather for making her doubt whether the boundaries of hope and joy were really as restricted as she had ascertained them to be. If there were territories beyond, much strength and faith would be needed to explore them, and she knew she had none to spare.

As she went into the council chamber, therefore, she did not acknowledge Roy's pat of encouragement or his whisper: "Just remember Sammy". She was too perturbed by this latest revelation of the evil so quietly and snugly at work in her: she had betrayed Isaac, abandoned Flora, disregarded her other children, envied Roy and Elizabeth Cargill, turned a war to her advantage, and now had amused herself with a woman barrenly in love with an amiable feckless drunkard. She had said, in Cairnban, that she had felt more like a criminal than a bride; and so she had deserved to feel.

The councillors were seated round a large rectangular table, with the Provost at the top, furthest from the door. Miss Hamby-Brewster sat upright on his left, while Bailie Rouster lolled on his right. As Bell entered, they were all smoking, talking, and laughing. Some gave her quick glances and then returned to their private laughter, as if to be the first to notice her presence publicly would be to incur some kind of shame. None rose, not even the Provost; and she sat down on the chair to which Alden directed her, opposite the middle of the table, but so far from it no flea in one night could hop that far.

As she waited, seeing them as jury, as prosecutors, and as representatives of their superior class appointed to subdue and castigate her as the representative of hers, one of them suddenly jumped up, unsteadily, knocked back his heavy chair with a clatter that silenced them all, and limped across to her with his hand outstretched, shaking. He did not smile because he could not.

"Good evening, Mrs. McShelvie," he said. "My name is Major Orinshaw. You must not be nervous. We are your friends."

As she thanked him, it seemed to her he must have some disease from which he was visibly dying. His hand was cold, and his thin throat was convulsed every few seconds as if he was swallowing blood or some bitter misery. That he was a Major, was well-dressed, spoke so properly, and yet was thus incurably troubled, did not amaze her as it would have Meg Aitchison; who believed, or under the influence of her husband pretended to believe, that only the poor had a right to be miserable: with the rich, it was a pastime, like slumming.

The Provost at last was hammering on the table. Small, dapper, white-bearded, meek, and beneficent, he looked like Christ in old age. Beside him Miss Hamby-Brewster, with her large nose high, waited like a vulture; while on the other side Bailie Rouster leered like a bear with honey on its paws.

The Bailie, though he had got rid of the two Baxter brothers, was not unpopular in Cairnban, where his excuse of a bitch of a wife was generously accepted. He had paid one visit to the house. Everything he had seen had amused him, so that he had gone from room to room with undaunted inquisitiveness, hawhawing in a tranced male stupidity that no Gowburgh wife could ever fail to recognise and appreciate.

"You will understand why we have asked you here, Mrs. McShelvie," said the Provost. "We have now discussed the matter of Cairnban thoroughly, and it has been decided that there is no alternative: that is to say, the house must continue to be used for its present purpose of harbouring all those families."

She nodded: if they were evicted from Cairnban, they might have to be taken into villa, manse, or mansion.

Miss Hamby-Brewster fluttered her arms so that her bangles rattled like bones.

"Frankly, it was a reluctant decision," went on the Provost.

"Cairnban is a very handsome house, and we of the town council are responsible to its owner Captain Wotherspoon."

"Does the Captain ken we're in his hoose?" she asked, again the simpleton.

The Provost was not so much embarrassed himself; but he had loyally to share in Miss Hamby-Brewster's embarrassment. He did not, however, go so far as dilate his nostrils, rattle his earrings, claw the table-top, and reveal false teeth worth fifty pounds. He merely stroked his beard as if it was the petal of a rose.

"The Captain has been informed," he replied, at last.

She said no more.

"The Captain's far too good-hearted," cried Miss Hamby-Brewster. "He's got a soldier's outlook, and we all know that in many respects soldiers have got to be protected from their own reckless gallantry. I mean, has he considered that the house will be turned into a slum? Does he realise that it's people who make slums, not bricks and stones?"

Mrs. McShelvie kept steadily attending to the Provost, like an obedient studious girl who despite the distractions of fellow pupils intends not to miss a single precious word of what the teacher has to say.

"We have decided that a caretaker will be absolutely necessary," said the Provost. "She will be responsible not only for the orderly conduct of the inhabitants but also for ensuring that the house itself is kept in good repair." He glanced at his notes. "Her duties will include the supervision of the washing, by turns, of all public places, such as stairs, inside and out, lobbies, bathrooms, kitchens, cellars, lavatories; the drawing-up of just rota systems for use of wash-house, cookers, and other services; the disciplining of children; the inspection of every private room to see that all these are being kept clean, and that there is no wilful defacing or damaging of walls, floor, doors, ceilings, or any parts of the fabric whatsoever. In short, she will be expected to prevent the house from becoming an eyesore, a nuisance, and an expense."

Here, having run dry, the Provost appealed to Miss Hamby-Brewster for refreshment.

234

"It's all very well to stress physical dirt," she cried. "There are other kinds, if you follow me."

She waited to see if Mrs. McShelvie and all the council were following her to that hinted Sodom.

"Last Saturday night," she said, "singing was heard from the house, drunken singing, and the playing of a concertina. And when I took a walk through the grounds myself on Sunday afternoon, on my way home from church, do you know what I found lying hidden in a bush? This." With a flourish she snatched out of a bag at her feet an empty beer bottle, held it before her as if it was a bone with rotted flesh sticking, and then dropped it with dramatic disgust, so that it rolled along the floor and came to rest by Mr. Sandeman's feet. He gave it a gentle kick, as one might a dog more friendly than fragrant.

"Explain that!" cried Miss Hamby-Brewster.

"It's a beer bottle," replied Bell, "empty."

"Good heavens, woman, I know that." Here the councillor tossed up her hands in a jewelled despair at such proletarian obtuseness. "What I want you to explain is how it got there."

"Maybe somebody tossed it ower the wall."

"Do you mean, some Langrigg person?"

Bell nodded. "I don't ken if beer is drunk in Langrigg," she said.

One or two councillors laughed. Bailie Rouster guffawed; but his fellow bailie, Henderson, frowned.

Alden smirked like a man who had been told on the best authority that beer was drunk in paradise by ordinary immortals, but whisky was the drink of the elite even there.

The best authority in sight was Sandeman, and certainly he looked very knowing, in a mysterious way, although he did not speak.

There seemed a smell of beer in the air. It was an awkward cul-de-sac in which to turn a debating team and drive them out.

"Please, please," cried the Provost, smiling, as if he was enjoying the joke but thought it in dubious taste.

Then the Major beat rather fretfully on the table.

"This is foolishness," he said. "I'm sure Mrs. McShelvie

knows very well what she'll have to do; in fact she knows better than we do."

It was the Provost's chance. "Ah, Major," he cried, "you are hurrying us on too fast. No appointment has been made yet. Mrs. McShelvie understands that, I am sure."

He asked for, and got, her nod.

"Thank you," he said, in his relief. "Now if anyone has any questions to put to Mrs. McShelvie, I'm sure she'll be only too pleased to answer them."

"I'll do my best," she said, not impudently, not sullenly either, and certainly not obtusely.

Two or three of them, hitherto bored by the Provost's soft prolixity, Miss Hamby-Brewster's beer-bottle obsession, and by the Major's usual turning into a deed of heroism the showing of a little pity, were interested by her tone. They had thought, listening to the Provost's list of duties, no woman alive could ever accomplish them, and only a saint would try for the wage that the Provost had up his sleeve. They waited to hear, not what questions would be put, for these they could guess, but what replies she would make.

"What's your age?" asked Miss Hamby-Brewster.

Smiling at her, Bell waited for a few moments; during them she saw again Nan Ross, Meg Aitchison, Maggie Fairlie, and the other women in Cairnban, come hurrying into her room, each with her own prized article of dress to lend. That whole accumulation of grandeur, in terms of money, was not worth a twentieth of the rings that glittered on Miss Hamby-Brewster's fingers; but in terms of human kindness it out-valued those, or any diamonds, a thousand times.

"Fifty," she said at last, and made it sound to those astonished councillors that that half-century, spent in what they would call a Gowburgh slum, was not only cherished by her, but rightly so. One of them sheepishly said she didn't look it.

"The weans ca' me auld Bell," she said, and so introduced an atmosphere of exotic Gowburgh homeliness that made most of them uncomfortable but somehow pleased.

"How many children have you?" asked Miss Hamby-Brewster.

"Five."

"Are they all here, in Langrigg?"

Again Bell paused. These questions were hostile; they were meant to hurt her and dishonour her children.

"No," she said quietly. "The eldest is at hame. The other four are here."

"But they're not with you in Cairnban?"

"No."

"Do you intend to have them to stay with you in Cairnban? Is that your ruse?"

There were some murmurs of deprecation round the table. Sandeman visibly jotted them down in a mental notebook.

"I hae twa lassies," said Bell. "If I get permission, I wad hae them to keep me company. The twa boys are happy where they are."

"A sensible idea," murmured a small man whom up to that time she'd thought looked glaikit.

Another chipped in; he was fat, bald, with a plump mottled nose and a red bow-tie as if to match. "I think we ought to keep in mind the fact that Mrs. McShelvie is obliging us more than we're obliging her."

More astute colleagues, even those sympathetic to her, tut-tutted, raised brows, or showed teeth, at such a legislative gaffe; but he did not care, and seemed to inflate his nose in contempt at such small-minded orthodoxy. It seemed ungrateful of Bell to see his tie as a gorgeous butterfly that had landed on the wrong flower.

"Mrs. McShelvie." It was Sandeman who spoke, in the tone of one broaching at last the vital subject. "What attempt would you make to encourage those people to attend church, or at least their children to attend Sunday school?"

"Nane."

"None?" He smiled, but it was not clear whether to dissemble personal pique or professional horror.

"My ain lassies gang to Sunday school in Gowburgh," she said, "and so they will here; but I can be answerable for nobody else's weans."

"Do you attend church, Mrs. McShelvie?"

"No."

"I can't see that this is any of our business," said the bald-headed bow-tie. "We've no right to pry into Mrs. McShelvie's religious beliefs."

"I agree." It was Michaelson who spoke. "There is one question I should like to ask. It is by no means irrelevant. Mrs. McShelvie, are you a personal friend of these women in Cairnban?"

She had already studied him: as far as she knew, this was the man who had joined with Gordon Aldersyde to send the boy's mother home with a heart a little larger perhaps, but infinitely sorer.

"Some are my friends," she said. "But I ken them all. They are my neighbours."

At the word Sandeman looked up.

"Yes," said Michaelson, "they are your friends. Now what I wonder is, will you have any authority over them? It seems to me friendship and authority cannot exist together. Advantage is taken, rebuke is half-hearted, licence prevails, authority flees."

"That's my point entirely," cried Miss Hamby-Brewster. "A Langrigg woman ought to be put in charge."

"That has already been discussed," said the Provost. "You know the difficulty."

Bell knew it too: no Langrigg woman had been found willing to live in the jungle of Cairnban for the small pay the council was prepared to offer.

She thought it was now time for her to speak.

"I admit I would be pleased to get the job," she said. "If I don't get it, I'll hae to return to Gowburgh, for my weans are all of school age, and so I would hae nae right under the evacuation scheme to stay. And I want to stay."

"Why?" asked Bailie Rouster, laughing.

"Because I like Langrigg. It's in the country, and I like the country."

"Not all your townswomen share your liking," said the Provost. "Some of those billeted in the houses down the glen are complaining that the silence is driving them mad. It has driven some of them home, back to the tram-cars and buses."

"I've heard of them," she said.

"So you like the country?" asked Bailie Rouster.

She nodded.

"Well, nobody can say we haven't got grand country here," he cried. "There's Brack Fell too; you'll be for climbing it?"

"I might be."

"Damned good!" he cried, and then felt, as always, that phenomenon which impressed him most about Sandeman: from the latter poured disapproval as cold as a draught from an open window. Yet if any man looked like a shut window it was Sandeman.

"But I would hardly hae the cheek," said Bell, "to take the job just because it suited me. If the other women objected, that would be the finish as far as I was concerned. But they hae asked me to apply; they think I can help them. This gentleman said there would be nae obedience among friends; there can be co-operation surely, which is better. I ken their ways, and I speak their language; but if I was appointed caretaker, I would take care nae matter what they thought or said. There would be nae destruction. I like the idea of living in a braw hoose too weel to let it be ill-used; and there wouldn't be a tree or a flower harmed if it was given to me to protect them. But the place has to be run as a household, no' as an institution. There has to be singing; there has to be the noise of weans playing; there has to be laughter; and nae doubt there will be greeting. But there will be naething bad or shameful. The neighbours will hae nae just cause for complaint."

"I understand," said Alden, "that you are already on good terms with one of your neighbours; I mean, Miss Elizabeth Cargill."

"She has visited us once or twice."

There was a pause.

"There is one last point," said the Provost. "If you were given this position, for a trial period, what wage would you expect?"

There was this time a keenness in their waiting.

"It's hard to say," replied Bell, laughing. "It's an odd kind of job. There's hardly ever been one like it before." Then she

239

caught sight of Alden flicking at his whiskers with three fingers. "But I'll say three pounds a week."

They did not, as she expected, denounce her for greed.

"We thought two pounds ten," said the Provost, rather timidly.

"I would agree to that," said Bell.

"Very good. Well, Mrs. McShelvie, all that remains is for me to thank you for attending. We shall consider the matter further, and let you know our decision in a day or two. Good evening."

Most of them wished her good evening.

Alden escorted her out.

In the other room, before Grahamstone bore down on them like a child about to demand its share of the secrets, Alden said: "You've got the job all right, but why didn't you hold out for three pounds?"

"Who's the bald man wi' the big red nose?" she asked.

"That's Mr. Selkirk; he owns the Royal Hotel; that's the biggest one: royalty has stayed there."

She was surprised to find how pleased she was that her champion was a man of substance: it seemed not only the headmaster, now demanding with voice and fingers, was still a child. As a little girl she had always identified herself with the damsel about to be devoured by the dragon, and rescued by the glittering knight just in time. Now she was a woman, with childish things put away, she saw that as a dragon the town council, even with Miss Hamby-Brewster as its head and the minister as its long slippery tail, was hardly awe-inspiring; but as a deliverer Mr. Selkirk, with his baldness, bow-tie, and strawberry neb, was as genuine as any in the story-books.

She began, with firm-minded charity, to dole out Mr. Grahamstone his share; he gulped it down with impatience, and soon was making noises like mental belches.

Campbelton and Roy took their share like gentlemen, murmuring polite congratulations. She preferred the old man's greed: somehow he was at the same trough as herself. These other two were more fastidious, and would go hungry rather than feast on such common scraps.

240

As she sat in the car going back she knew she was being unfair to Roy at least; and what was worse, was determined to foster that unfairness until, at the chosen time, it might contribute to the spoiling of his happiness. When that time would be, and who would choose it, she did not know; but it seemed she had willingly placed herself under evil orders, and was now waiting, like an inspired hypocrite, to repay his help and kindness with treachery. She might try to pretend that his finding enjoyment and escape in the war, as well as an opportunity for winning medals, made his punishment inevitable, under Christ's own hand; but she could scarcely believe that now, for when he went off to the war he would leave behind him a love so fresh and sweet and new that no other glory on earth was better. No, there was no explanation: she, who had acknowledged Selkirk the wealthy hotel owner's goodness, and had seen it not as a single act but as the fruit of a tree that had been growing since the infancy of the race, was without cause or reason thrawn in this perverse and shameful spite.

The women were waiting for the car at Cairnban, and rushed out to drag her in and question her. Though they rumpled her hair and pulled her about, reverting to the bridal theme, she was grateful to them for giving her an excuse to say nothing to him except a quick good-night.

Later, alone in her room, preparing for bed, she discovered that she had lost the wedding brooch from her coat. She put on her coat over her nightgown, and slipped downstairs with a torch to look for it. Though rain dripped down, she searched for almost ten minutes without finding it; and in the end, believing the loss symbolical, she returned to her room, soaked, shivering, and showing in the mirror a face that appalled her, so ghastly was it with some unappeasable nameless hunger. "I, wha spake so proud," she whispered, "am not fit to look after even my ain weans."

Next day the brooch was found, broken. When Meg proposed that it be mended at the communal expense, everybody was willing; but Bell refused the offer, with a sharpness that only Meg found amusing. To Meg it was the first sign, so she cried, of Bell the gaffer; and she jumped up on to a chair, and in a parody of her man Roger made a speech, prophesying the tyranny to come. To those who knew Roger as an unwashed work-shy gasbag, and knew too that his wife truly loved him in spite of it, this vigorous and effective guying of him was not only entertaining, but also very touching. They were reminded of their own husbands, who often many a time had reshaped the world at the family hearth; so they laughed and shed tears of pride and love and fondest contempt.

Afterwards Bell threw the brooch into the back of a drawer.

II

In spite of her guiltiness towards Roy, which could often be forgotten if it could never be removed, those weeks after her appointment at Cairnban were the happiest Bell had ever spent. In bearing and appearance she bloomed, so that Gowburgh women meeting her in those still alien streets would be sincere and baffled in their congratulations. Those who had known her in the early days of her marriage remembered her as a brave smiler in her own and—what was harder—in other folks' misfortunes; but now in her smiles were also zest, hope, and even gaiety, which were more infectious and more inspiring than her former example of intelligent endurance.

So amazed were her compatriots, they discussed her florescence in her absence, seeking the true reason, for after all the long winter of war was beginning. Some found the reason in the little affluence she and her family now enjoyed; others in the presence of her children; others again in her post at Cairnban, where she was able to make use of the qualities of leadership and service she had always possessed; and there were even one or two who believed her own story that she was in training to climb the great hill Brack Fell, to whose summit, as inaccessible as Everest's to their own domestic pavement-plodding feet, she would point with a steady hand that somehow could be imagined placing a stone upon the cairn which was said to lie like a nipple upon that gigantic pap.

These few, who divined the true source of Bell's revivification, were nevertheless more mystified than all the rest whose guesses were more humdrum. To them, burdened with babies, it seemed impossible that any life-giving milk could ever be sucked from that tremendous lump of rock covered with grass, heather, and bracken. They were not surprised when they were told that on its slopes was a monument to a Covenanter who had been shot there by soldiers, three hundred years ago, because he had defied the government in the matter of religion. It seemed to them an appropriate place for such a heroic sacrifice, which the subsequent indifference to religion, as exemplified by themselves, had proved to be useless.

For Bell, however, there were private moments of terror and revelation. They came upon her as she walked along the roads under bronze and golden trees, or as she lay in bed listening to the contented sighs of her two girls asleep on the other side of the yellow curtain. Then it was made clear to her that all this good fortune was not accidental, nor was it, as Isaac avowed, a recompense for her patient goodness. If it was a reward, it must be given not for what she had done in the past but for what she had still to do; and only the powers of darkness rewarded in advance.

These intimations, or premonitions rather, lasted only for seconds, and soon, in the grandeur and sunlight of trees, or in the calmness and shade of sleep, were forgotten.

Isaac began to visit every Saturday and stay till Sunday. He declared that anticipation of those weekends made the rest of the time spent in the house in Gowburgh pass not just quickly but also happily. He looked well, seemed fatter, and had a little colour in his cheeks. His job in the ropeworks, he said, was light, pleasant, and interesting. It seemed to Bell, therefore, that she was justified in deciding that his cheerfulness and optimism were genuine. He brought down from Gowburgh the *McShelvie Queen*, the model yacht he had made himself. With Sammy and Tom he sailed it in the pond in the Langrigg public park, and certainly his enthusiasm and devotion outlasted his sons'. During the week the yacht stood on the sideboard in the room in Cairnban.

Flora too paid visits. If she came with her father, there were always plenty of neighbours in Cairnban willing to give her a bed for the night. They offered at first for her mother's sake, and not her own: she had been unpopular among them because of her reckless uncompromising sixteen-year-old contempt of their acceptance of the thraldom of marriage, children, and poverty. She had been equally frank in letting them know that a life of cynical pleasure and selfishness was to her far more preferable than their kind of kitchen respectability. Some of them, provoked, had wished upon her a retributive and apocalyptic pregnancy; others, not so severe, hoped maturity would sadden her into admitting that life in a single-end or a room-and-kitchen, though drabber than life in a ten-roomed mansion, or a hundred-roomed palace, must nevertheless be defended and cherished, for the excellent reason that it was the only one available. Now, it appeared, a fate far less prophesiable than pregnancy or submission had befallen her, in the shape of a young apprentice engineer who was serving his time in a foundry making shells, and also in a gospel hall preaching the fear of God. He visited Cairnban once, which was enough to let them see, as Meg Aitchison put it, that he had not been God's favourite in the handing out of the good looks: he was tall, long-chinned, huge-nosed, and splay-footed, with big hands that held a Bible as purposefully as they would a spanner. During that visit to Cairnban he successfully communicated the fear and the fun of God: only the former was intentional. What Flora saw in him the Cairnban wives could not see; but obscure freakishness on the part of a woman choosing a mate never surprised them: each had her own example to study, and, more fruitfully, that of her every neighbour. Nevertheless it did seem extravagant that a girl whose lips had used up more lipsticks than they had recited psalms should have chosen a man who disapproved of all make-up, considered smoking sinful, permitted not a single dram even on a snowy Ne'erday, and summed up picture-going as a lure of Satan. If Flora's intention had been to save the young chap from that peculiar kind of intoxication, she would, of course, have been following in an honourable and by no means outworn feminine tradition:

but, just as it was wrong tactics to accompany a husband into a pub just to make sure he didn't drink too much, so it was a mistake surely for young Flo to join his gospel sect, and go round with him slipping propaganda leaflets through letter-boxes.

Meg Aitchison and company did not altogether hide their amusement from Bell: they thought that if she was true to her character she must herself be amused, although as Flo's mother she would be allowed some anxiety too.

Bell was amused. At first she thought the astounding friendship was a joke on Flo's part. If the embodiment of her dreams could not be found, handsome, rich, and wonderful in his lovemaking, then might not the disappointment be turned into some kind of perverse triumph by leading on, in a spirit of fashionable mockery, this earnest, gawky, old-fashioned youth, who frequently and familiarly used names like Jeremiah and Isaiah and Job, as if all those were his uncles. But she soon found, on questioning Flora, that she was attributing to the girl her own subtlety and lack of faith. Flora liked him for reasons which, despite her inability to express them, were nevertheless sincere and profound. His religious oddities she defended as fervently as she would have his splayed feet had these been criticised; and Bell had to conclude that the joke after all was not her daughter's.

One Saturday with Isaac she visited Tom at the Mair-Wilsons'; with other parents they had been invited to inspect the boys' quarters. As they walked up the long avenue they saw their son playing football with some friends in a park in front of the magnificent house. He seemed so much at home there on that splendid estate that Bell, for a minute of ironic indulgence, pretended she was its mistress and it had been in her family for hundreds of years. The delight and awe of that fantasy were real; nor were they stultified by her calm full consideration of the reality, represented by Isaac at her side so indelibly plebeian in his new hat. She remembered how once, watching a parade of pipers, he had surprised her by claiming that his family long ago in the Highlands had been important people, related to the chief of the clan. She had gently laughed at him for that boast, which every breekless Hielandman out of the heather made when drunk with whisky or the pipes. Here on this avenue, in sight of this great mansion, seeing it in some way as ancestral, she laughed at herself; but again it was not bitter or contemptuous laughter.

As they walked on again, she reflected dispassionately on her true lineage. Dukes and prize dogs could have their pedigrees traced back many generations; she, in common with most of her class, could not go beyond her grandparents. If there ever had been a family Bible, with the names of bygone Maitlands in ink faded to pink, she had never seen it; likely there had been none, for she could not remember her parents ever having been at church. All the men in her family had been manual workers: none had risen to become teacher, lawyer, minister, or even clerk: that first ascension, sacrificed and striven for in so many Scots families, was still to be made in hers. She could have achieved it herself: at school she had always topped her class; but when her father had brought her and Grace and their mother into the city where his forbears had come from, it had been to send them to work as weavers, so that he could sit at home and pity his legs crippled and tortured by rheumatism. Her mother had died when Bell was twenty-five; Grace had married and emigrated to Canada, where she was as good as dead, buried in that cessation of correspondence so common among exiles grown acclimatised; while their father, sustained by his failure to forgive these desertions, had taken eight long years to die himself. By that time Isaac had come along, humble, kind, considerate, weak in body, but stubborn in his wooing of her. A month after her father's funeral she had married him out of fondness and weariness, and gone to live in the room-and-kitchen in Wallace Street. Flora was born a year later, after a birth so difficult and painful it was almost fatal. Five years later came Sammy. Then, as if in some kind of capitulation where hostages were demanded, Effie, Tom, and Jean were conceived and born. The last had turned out to be the brightest as far as lessons were concerned; with a little luck, which was possible, and with much determination, which was unlikely, she might become a schoolteacher, say, and so raise the first banner of respectability. Poor timid affectionate Jean, menaced on all sides by her brothers and sisters, and their unregenerate progeny; she would never have the ruthlessness to look down and back at them, and so keep them at bay.

It had been a tale of crudeness, ignorance, paganism, violence, hardship, selfishness, and greed: unfolded in hovels in the country and grimy tenements in the city; without the alleviation of what was called culture; purposeless, unless eating, sleeping, working, and reproducing were purposes; and unredeemed even by any sense of suffering, of crucifixion, of being kept out in the wilderness with paradise shut off by a wall as high as a mountain, over which nevertheless the tormenting fragrances were wafted.

As in sight of the castle she recalled that tale she resolutely and without self-pity saw the compensations: the quiet waitings on Hogmanays for the bells to ring out the old year and ring in the new; the gossiping cups of tea with neighbours while the children were at school; the illusion, produced always by the sight of a happy child, that happiness was endorsed and eternal; and similar oases which accentuated the vastness and menace of the surrounding desert. She knew that many would accuse her of being a traitress, not merely to Isaac by her side, but to every friend and neighbour, and to her class; but she did not feel ashamed or remorseful. At least she was not betraying the truth, as Roger Aitchison did, for instance, with his assumption that every person not of the working-class was a Miss Hamby-Brewster, whereas no member of that class was lazy like himself, or spiteful and snobbish like Mrs. Aldersyde, or stuck in indolent good-nature like a fly in jam as Nan Ross was, or greedy and vulgar like his own wife, or depraved like the members of the Gowburgh gangs who slashed at each other with knives and razors in streets adjacent to her own. Let him use what refutations and extenuations he could: she would never find fault with this gracious wide park with its quietness and trees, and with this house, which seemed to her a promise that Gowburgh and the many other cities with their dense warrens would not always mutilate, degrade, and mock the dignity of human beings.

When she entered the house and was received by Mr. and Mrs. Mair-Wilson she did not shrink from acknowledging that their kindness, though not so spontaneous, or even as sincere as Nan Ross's, was expressed with a graciousness of speech and manner that suited the house. Accordingly, her own bearing towards them was free from Isaac's obvious discomfort and involuntary sycophancy. Her dignity, however, was not a retaliation on behalf of, or on account of, the houses where she had been born, brought up, married, and would die. It was rather in spite of those, and drew its strength from this beautiful house, and the great park outside, and the hills beyond. She would probably never enter this house again, yet in a fertile sense it would be hers for the rest of her life: just as, if she was ever to climb Brack Fell, it would become hers. Such possessions, held in the mind, always enriched, even if the hands were empty or if the body, ill-nurtured, lived in a dirty stone box in a maze of dirty stone boxes.

Walking back home to their room at Cairnban, Isaac commented with admiration and a little distrust on her lack of diffidence in speaking to those wealthy people in the midst of so much evidence of their wealth. Listening to Bell and Mrs. Mair-Wilson, he said, a stranger would not have known who was the rich woman and who the poor. Maybe not, she replied, if that stranger was blind. He had to nod, miserably, as if the shabbiness of his wife's clothing was his fault. And also, she added, if the stranger was deaf. This time he did not understand, and when she contrasted the roughness of her voice and speech with the polish of Mrs. Mair-Wilson's, he looked still more penitent and miserable, for though in his meek obstinate way he was again willing to shoulder this responsibility, he knew he was not able. With grim affection and pity, she absolved him: as long as he did not defend the squalor and harshness produced by centuries of poverty, she would not blame him. He nodded, but still looked unhappy and bewildered; and though she was aware that he was shocked to find her saying what she had often condemned Mrs. Aldersyde for saying, she did not try to show him how her own attitude differed, and how it really sprang from loyalty to her friends and neighbours, not as members of any class or nation or sect, but simply as human beings deprived, by tragic omissions, of so much beauty, nobility, and refinement.

When he had gone home to Gowburgh on the Sunday afternoon, Nan Ross came into Bell's room in Cairnban that night after the children were in bed, and sat down by the fire.

"You've got Isaac worried, Bell," she said straight away.

Bell smiled. "Is that so, Nan?"

"Aye, it is. I ken I can speak plain to you, Bell."

"You can."

"He's got a feeling that hobnobbing wi' a' these posh folk here has gi'en you a scunner against your ain kind."

"To ca' it hobnobbing's daft, of course, as I hope you told him. But did he say what kind mine was?"

Solid in her chair, and in her friendship, Nan laughed.

"Was there ony need for him to say that, Bell?" she asked.

"I think there was. Is my ain kind women of fifty wi' humps on their backs and five weans?"

Nan still laughed. "I ken fine you think we're no' as guid as we might be."

"I'll admit that, Nan, but you'll hae to count me in too."

Nan shook her head: not only the thickness of her neck restricted the gesture: denial was so obviously contrary to her nature.

"You're superior to the rest of us in this hoose, Bell," she said, "aye, and in this toon. You should be here as the mistress, wi' jewelled rings on your fingers, and silken dresses to your toes, and gold-framed pictures on the wa's, and carpets on every floor, and bookcases packed to the ceiling wi' books. You would be fit then to receive the best in the land, withoot a blush."

"I'm blushing noo, Nan."

"I'm serious, Bell. You hae always been superior, even in Wallace Street yonder, standing at your close-mooth; but you never showed it in a way to mak' other folk feel sma'."

"I must hae been a wonder, surely."

Nan smiled to sweeten that burst of bitterness.

"You were aye that to me, Bell, a wonder."

"But I'm showing it noo? Is that it? Am I making you a' feel sma'?"

"Not me, Bell." Then for a few moments Nan was silent. "I hae nae right to come into your hoose and sit here at your fireside and say what micht hurt you, even if my wish is to help you because I like you and your man and your weans."

"I'm no tawpie to be hurt by plain words, Nan. Say what you came to say."

"It's just this, Bell: don't get to like this place Langrigg too weel. Some day you'll hae to go back."

"Surely I'm aware o' that?"

"Aye, Bell. But are you aware that while the rest of us are pining to go back, and dozens are going back every week, you yourself are enjoying yourself here so much it's made you look ten, aye, twenty years younger? Nae wonder Meg says you're like a bride."

"Meg says mair than her prayers. Since when was it an offence, Nan, for a body to enjoy herself?"

Nan rose up. "I've made you angry, Bell."

"You have not."

Nan waddled rather sadly across to the door.

"I hae, Bell," she said, softly so as not to disturb the sleeping girls, "and I'm sorry. Tak care: the deeper the sea, Bell, the fiercer the storm." As she spoke she opened the door a little and listened: there was the sound of a child's painful fretting. "I thocht it was one of mine," she said, "but it's wee John Lawson; he's no' weel, and he's bothered wi' his teeth into the bargain. Do you ken this, Bell, the brawest sight ever I saw was in Gowburgh, no' far frae oor street? It was the Clyde at Dalmarnock Bridge yonder. I counted nineteen swans, a' red, like the water itself, for the sun was sinking ahint the lums o' the power station. And the sky was a' smoky and red. And in the red water these red swans were swimming. It was so braw I felt sad. Just listen to that: she's yelling at him again, as if the wean's to blame for the pain in his gums. There was something else I meant to speak to you aboot, Bell, but it's slipped my mind."

"Come back to the fire here and sit doon till you remember."

"I mind noo. It was aboot Sammy."

"What's he been doing?"

"He's got a new pal, I see."

"Do you mean Gordon Aldersyde?"

"That's him. He's a bad influence, Bell. Didn't he drive his mither hame in tears?"

"I asked Sammy to befriend him; he was lonely."

Nan was about to say something, but changed her mind. Bell guessed it had to do with the reason for Gordon's loneliness.

"It ill becomes any grown person," said Nan instead, "to speak ill against a child, especially when that person has as mony weans herself as I hae."

"Few folk wad hae the decency to see that and say it."

"But I'd better say no more, Bell. Guid night."

"Guid night, Nan."

When she was gone Bell was afflicted by a mood that had her moving round the room, holding on to the yellow curtain, standing over her girls, stroking the sails of the model yacht, opening the drawer and looking at the broken brooch, pokering the fire, and shifting the kettle's position on the hearth. It seemed to her that this was the kind of malaise that only prayer, or religious communion, could cure. In that prayer she might ask forgiveness for having underrated the goodness in such people as Nan Ross, and might also give thanks for it; but she did not know whom to ask or to thank, nor would she pretend that she knew; and that ignorance seemed in her mind to increase gigantically until, as she stood gazing down at the fire, she felt she knew nothing at all, except her own unworthiness. It was a terrifying visitation that left her shaken and isolated, with fragments of terror still glittering in her mind, never perhaps to be dimmed or dissolved.

Nevertheless, in spite of those revelatory moments, she was as happy then as Nan had described. With a map of the district given her by Elizabeth Cargill she set out every afternoon when the children were at school, and walked to all the places of interest marked on it; to the remains of the Roman fort, for instance, where she sat on a stone, secretive as a druidess; to the old mossy keep about which Sir Walter Scott had written

251

a poem of tragic love; to the moorland site of the skirmish between the dragoons of bluidy Clavers and some Covenanters, where she picked up the bone of a sheep; to the waterfall called the White Mare's Tail, approached by a steep narrow path, that turned her giddy; and even, though it was five miles away, to the lovely St. Margaret's Loch, where for the first time in her life she saw a heron.

She became inured to the slow astonished stares of shepherds, roadmen, sheep, and cattle; even a weasel once watched her from the top of a dyke. Eating her bread there, in the midst of those vast high lonelinesses, she seemed to be casting off her old grey skin of dreary custom, and growing in its place one fresh, sensitive, and delicate; which was, in truth, her bridal mantle.

III

The altercation which brought Bell hurrying downstairs that bright cold Tuesday at the end of November, had had many predecessors.

Those evacuees who still remained in that outpost of duty among the frosted hills were no longer bound in comradeship by the two-fold danger, from Hitler the outside enemy, and from the native Langrigg snobs. Gowburgh, and other cities in Britain had not after all been bombed, and, it now seemed, never would be. More than half therefore had fled back home, so that in the school in the cul-de-sac of Gordon Street, commanded again by Mr. Grahamstone, there were more pupils than in the morning session at Langrigg Academy, when the Gowburgh contingent attended. Those who remained consisted of children whose parents heeded the government's warning that danger was not yet over, children whose parents found their absence convenient, and children who, having grown to like Langrigg, pleaded with their parents every weekend not to take them home.

In addition, there were some women with babies and infants,

who had been lucky in being billeted in houses much superior to their own in Gowburgh, and also in having landladies who had become friends. The best example of these was Mrs. Raeburn, who was now so much at home in Lammermuir that she had to keep reproving herself for putting on airs when visiting neighbours in Cairnban. One or two of those neighbours appreciated Bessie's efforts not to look down upon them; they acknowledged that the improvement in her speech, and in her manners when taking a cup of tea, for instance, was not only inevitable but even necessary: when you lived with a Sir you had to behave like a Sir; and they had no difficulty in keeping malice and anger out of their chuckles afterwards. Others of course, headed by Meg Aitchison, were not so fair-minded or charitable: they saw in her a working-class woman corrupted by the flattery and friendship of the rich, and liking that corruption. It was no surprise to them, and no amusement either, when Dick Raeburn spent a leave in Lammermuir and marched in his khaki about the streets of Langrigg as if, so Meg said, every lamp-post was an inspecting general.

Meg, alas, was not always now so characteristically humorous in her prejudices. Things were not prospering with her or her family. She was even growing thinner, so much so that, as she said herself, if she stood in a corner of the lobby at Cairnban long enough somebody would take her for the communal mop and have the lavatory swabbed out before the mistake was discovered. Her hair, too, despite a home-made perm in which a dozen hands co-operated, was lanker and less lustrous than ever. Her celebrated tolerance of children, which had previously allowed her to read her horoscope in the newspaper or write a letter to Roger with a cushion fight waging or a chamber being banged as a drum or a pistol firing caps or all these combined, was now like herself reduced to brittle bone, with the fat of good-nature shrivelled off. She took to beseeching them, for Christ's sake, to give her peace; or else she tried to enforce such peace by kicking or dragging them out of her room, with screamed instructions to go and raise hell for somebody else. The only other legitimate someone else was, of course, Roger, her partner in their creation. It was whispered indeed that her rapid deterioration was caused by suspicion that in Gowburgh he was being unfaithful to her. Certainly every time she mentioned returning home he discouraged her. One or two realists, who suggested to him that her trouble might be consumption, found that he agreed.

Thus that frosty Tuesday, as Bell rushed downstairs to separate Meg and Maggie Fairlie playing tug-o'-war in the hall with what looked like a child's teddy-bear, the atmosphere in the house had for weeks past been growing sullen and dismal, with the old devil-may-care hilarious camaraderie withered to sad stalks and leaves, like the flowers in the garden.

Other women were present, more inclined to take sides rather than act as peacemakers. Gary Aitchison and Charlie Fairlie sat on the floor howling, in danger of being trampled on by their wrestling mothers. Neither child was washed or combed or dressed in clean clothes.

It was the kind of scene that nowadays roused Bell's angry contempt, and no relieving compassion.

She broke between them and pushed them apart.

"If you behave like scruff," she cried, "why are you so annoyed when folk ca' you scruff?"

The word, deliberately repeated, hurt them like blows. Meg stood panting; spittle misaimed at her adversary gleamed on her own chin; her fists kept clutching at the air as if, rather than a dismembered teddy-bear, she strove to grasp self-respect, tattered but still desirable. Oaths of quite poignant obscenity gushed from her lips.

Maggie Fairlie, on the other hand, seemed to have yielded to some greater authority than Bell. She stood looking down at the floor in shame. Soon she was weeping quietly.

The two children still howled. Other children looked on from a distance. The other women, still partisan, shrilly explained to Bell who was to blame. One or two she noticed slipping away, taking their children with them. For their sake, she thought, she should moderate her scorn.

She did not, however; and her voice was bitter and contemptuous.

"Shut your mouths, all of you," she cried, "As for you, Meg, will you stop that filth?"

Meg suddenly let out a yell like a madwoman. Her arms gesticulated above her head. In her voice was a wild fierce pathos.

"Whit did I tell you?" she shrieked. "Didn't I tell you she would turn oot to be a worse snob than Bessie Raeburn? Didn't I warn you she'd come to use the rest of us to wipe the mud off her feet when she came back frae her walks to look at the coos and the hills? Maybe the rest o' you were taken in; but not me. Nobody's going to get me to believe that she walks a' thae distances juist to look at coos. Go on, Bell, tell us the truth. Whit shepherd is it you get behint the dykes wi'? Everybody kens you've got a man that's never been able to satisfy you. Everybody kens that you and your lass Flo hae a heat in ye worse than cats."

With the teddy-bear in her hand Bell listened, smiling. It seemed to her that most of the women, though pretending to be scandalised, really approved: they were enjoying her revilement, as if it was a kind of revenge. She tried to remember that not so long ago they had been her friends and comrades, eager to lend her their most precious possessions. She had not uttered a word to alienate them, except for this present word scruff; but it was obvious that she must for some time have been acting towards them as if she thought them scruff. Perhaps, if she was to tell the truth, she had not altogether been unconscious of her attitude. What Nan Ross had forewarned her about, had come to pass; and Nan herself, goodhearted and honest, was no longer there to help her further, if she was willing to be helped. Nan was now back in Gowburgh, where one of her children was in hospital with pneumonia.

"Don't heed her, Bell," said Mrs. Fairlie. "We ken it's lies."

Meg pretended to make another assault. It was easily held off by Bell, who said: "I think, Meg, the best thing you can do is to tak your wean upstairs and gie him a guid wash."

Meg pointed to Charlie Fairlie. "Are you going to tell me he's clean?" she howled.

"I am not. He could do with a wash too."

Meg was willing to side with her opponent against this common foe; but Mrs. Fairlie rejected the alliance.

Bell held up the teddy-bear, part of whose stuffing hung out.

"For this," she said, "fit for the midden, you would throw away your dignity as human beings, and behave worse than beasts."

It was not what she had intended or wished to say. She had thought words of reconciliation had been gathering in her mind.

Mrs. Fairlie, still weeping, nodded. But Meg, and most of the others, were infuriated.

"Beasts!" they yelled. "So it's beasts we are now? Scruff's not bad enough, we've got to be beasts as weel."

"Worse than beasts, I said," she cried scornfully, "for they ken no better."

"If we're beasts, Bell," said one, "then you get paid for looking after beasts, mind that."

"I mind it."

"What do you ca' yourself, Bell, if we're beasts?" asked another.

She seemed to think there could be no answer to her question.

"A human being," said Bell.

At that reply Meg became hoarse and serious.

"Was I no' fighting for my rights?" she asked. "Are human beings no' expected to fight for their rights? Whit's the war for, I'd like to ken? That bear belongs to my Gary. That wee bastard stole it; his mither helped him. There are women here will tell whether I'm speaking the truth or not."

Her supporters said it was the truth; Mrs. Fairlie's said it was a lie.

Bell looked from the torn bear in her hand to the two crying children, and found herself, with a vivid and excruciating sense of wrong, thinking them of no more account than it: dirty now in body, they would grow up dirty in mind and soul; and throughout the world were many millions like them.

It was at that moment that they all heard with astonishment and alarm the car come racing up the avenue and stop outside the door. She alone had an intimation that it brought instant retribution.

Accordingly when she opened the door and saw Elizabeth Cargill, bareheaded, wearing a black fur coat, and very pale, she was the calmest woman there; so much so that, ignoring Elizabeth for those first few terrible moments, she called out to the children gathering round the car to keep back from it. Seated in it was Mr. Kilburn, in whose house Sammy was so happily billeted.

"Come in, Miss Cargill," she said. "We don't see very much of you these days."

It was evident the fur coat had been snatched down from the peg and flung on. Even now, despite the admiring and envious glances of these other women, one of whom could not resist the urge to stroke it, its wearer disregarded it utterly. At other times perhaps she took pride in its beauty and expensiveness; but not now. She had never been, so Cairnban had long ago decided, a beauty herself: her mouth was too big and somehow too prominent; but she was always so pleasant, so intelligent, so genuinely interested, and, of course, so well dressed, that Roy's choice had been commended and his good fortune proclaimed, even to his face. Now, however, as she stood there in the hall amidst them, with Gary Aitchison still bawling, and the women gazing at her like tribeswomen with almost alien expectancy, she looked more ravaged than any of them. She still held her head high, as she would always do; but there was no lilt to it, and she did not smile.

She could not bring herself to say what she had come to say.

"What is it?" asked Bell.

She glanced upstairs to where she knew Bell's room was: she had drunk tea with Roy in that room.

"Shut your gub!" This was Meg whispering to her Gary, who still complained of the world's injustice. Her whisper did not silence him.

"Is it for me alone," asked Bell, "whatever it is?"

Elizabeth nodded. Tears were in her eyes. Some of those watching gasped, and found tears in their own.

Bell now stood alone amongst them, marked out by the pointing finger that every one of them knew and dreaded. They remembered her haughtiness, but they did not look on themselves as revenged; rather did they feel persecuted in her.

"Shall we go up to your room?" asked Elizabeth.

Bell shook her head.

"Whatever it is, tell me here," she said. "These," and she cast round at them a glance that because of its intimidating ambiguity caused them to shiver, "are my friends."

"Aye, that's right, Bell," cried Meg. "We're your friends." They all nodded, eager not to be left out.

"You'll need your friends, Mrs. McShelvie," said Elizabeth. "It's Sammy. He's had an accident; I'm afraid, a serious one."

Bell's restraint seemed all the more unnatural contrasted with the fur-coated young woman's frank weeping. They remembered what had sometimes been thought, and even whispered, that Bell lacked the common touch, and lacked it deliberately.

Meg Aitchison clutched Elizabeth's sleeve.

"Christ, miss," she said, "don't say he's deid?"

"I don't know that. He was unconscious."

"God Almighty," muttered Meg, and looked at Gary as if he had become transfigured; she crouched down and kissed him, not minding at all that he resented the endearment and thought it some kind of treachery.

"Was it his skates?" asked Bell.

"Yes," said Elizabeth. "Apparently he fell and struck his head against a wall." She did not add that perhaps he had not fallen; according to Mr. Michaelson, outside whose window it had happened, he had been pushed by Gordon Aldersyde. The latter, pale but tearless, had denied it.

"Where is he?" asked Bell.

"In the cottage hospital. We came here as quickly as we could."

"I'm sure you did. I'm grateful. If you'll excuse me for a minute or twa, I'll gang up and get my coat."

They watched her go up the stairs as unhurriedly as though to soothe a child unreasonably fretful.

"If it was me," whispered one, "I'd be paralysed wi' fricht."

"If you were, Aggie," said a friend, "I'd understand you. It would be natural."

Mrs. Fairlie now was holding up her head, as if her tears were as honourable as Miss Cargill's.

"I understand Bell," she said.

Meg glared at her. "Bell's been my neighbour," she said, "for eight years. She and I are cronies."

At the landing, Bell turned. "My twa lassies are at the shops," she said. "If they come back don't tell them onything. I'd raither do it myself, whatever there is to tell."

Sadly they promised, and then they waited for her to return.

"Sammy," whispered one woman, who had been transferred to Cairnban only a fortnight ago, "is that the one wi' the specs, that's always smiling?"

Others nodded, and made comments that were really epitaphs.

"They say he was a dunce at school, but what does cleverness at sums maitter in the long run?"

"If he'd met a beetle on its back, he'd hae turned it ower."

"Isn't there a saying, that it's the guid that die young?"

"Bell once said to me," said Meg, "that everybody has something special to gie to the world: Sammy was hers." She giggled desolately. "Christ kens what's mine."

One of them took pity on Miss Cargill.

"How's Mr. Roy getting on?" she asked.

"Quite well, I believe."

"Mind and tell him that when he comes hame on leave he's got to pay us a visit."

"I don't think he needs any reminding to do that."

"He was a great help to us," conceded Meg, "though I've got to admit that whiles I thought the whole affair was one big joke to him."

"I don't agree," said Mrs. Fairlie. "The first night we landed here, withoot food or anything, and he came to help us, he was far frae thinking it a joke."

"It was Bell herself," said Meg peaceably, "wha first suggested it to me, and I think you'll admit she sees deeper into folk than the maist of us. But to be fair to her, she also said he was

259

entitled to his laughs, seeing he was doomed to be ca'd away to drap bombs, which is nae laughing maitter."

Two or three of them kept nudging or winking at Meg as she spoke. She was aware they were counselling her to be more tactful, but she did not heed. Untactful truth, her Roger had instructed her, was the most powerful weapon of the proletariat when talking to capitalists. He had generously allowed that in talking to the proletariat itself, in pubs or washing-houses, it might not be so effective.

Miss Cargill, though friendly, was a capitalist. Were not the fur coat, the gold bracelet, the delicate pink fingers, the smooth neck, even the tears so fragrantly and fastidiously wiped away, all trademarks as unmistakable as cigars or gold chains across fat bellies or wallets bloated with fivers? As a capitalist therefore she must be provoked by the truth, as bulls in Spain were by the darts with ribbons on them. Mercy might be felt but never shown: otherwise the revolution would be retarded.

Miss Cargill was not provoked, at any rate into a defence of her sweetheart. Others thought that she suffered Meg's rudeness with marvellous courtesy, but Meg herself, trained to look closer, saw that behind the sleek and elegant armour the wound bled. Again, pity might be felt but not shown.

Then Bell came down the stairs. She had been longer than they all thought seemly. Certainly if a woman was going to a hospital where her son lay dying or dead, she must first wash her face, brush her hair, polish her shoes, and take off her apron; but need she, as Bell now announced, have wasted time in pinning a broken brooch on to her coat, even if it was golden, bought for her by her husband as a wedding present? Sammy, after all, was not even the first-born.

"We micht pass my lassies on the road," she said, as she went out after Miss Cargill. "If we don't, just tell them I've gone oot for half an hour."

"But, Bell, it might be hours before you're back," said one.

"Don't worry aboot your lassies," said another. "We'll take care of them."

"I'll be back soon," she said, and then was gone.

It was clear to them she had no hope; she was sure the boy was dead.

They watched her being assisted into the car by Mr. Kilburn who, as the giver of the skates, was in a white-haired dither of guilt and contrition. It was evident that she had to reassure him, as one would a weeping child that had dropped a valuable plate.

Then the car driven by Miss Cargill sped away. Bell did not once wave back at them, so that, in spite of their sorrow, pity, and premonitions, they remembered her calling of them scruff and beasts. It occurred to them that Bell therefore stood in the shadow of some divine punishment, from which neither their forgiveness nor her own courage could save her. Inevitably then they realised they all stood in such a shadow, even there on the steps of the house in the bright wintry sunshine. Were not they banished from their beloved homes, and was not all Europe for the second time in their lives at war, with years of exile, slaughter, mutilation, hunger, and increasing hatred, in store for every nation?

"God forgie me," murmured one of them, shuddering, "but there are whiles when I think it's no' worth it."

Meg shuddered too; but at the same time she shook her head to deny such pessimism. Roger had said that when the working-class were really scunnered by the guff off the rotting corpse of capitalism they would revolt, and thereafter peace and plenty would prevail on earth. Perhaps she did not shake her head as vigorously as in the past. It was not easy to go on believing in an oracle whom you suspected of philandering with a woman plumper than yourself.

"Cheer up," she muttered. "Better times are coming, if you live to see them. Come on up to my room, and we'll hae a cup o' tea."

Most accepted.

"You coming, Maggie?" asked Meg, with leering shyness, of Mrs. Fairlie.

"Surely, Meg."

The teddy-bear, which had caused the quarrel, lay where Bell had dropped it. Meg kicked it out of her path as she led the way upstairs. Similarly she kicked aside the scruples that had occurred to her about the untidiness of her room. In a world where men were training to kill other men in millions, and where an innocent boy cracked his skull fatally on a wall where cats usually slept in the sun, only a puny mind could object to such trifles as beds unmade, dishes unwashed, chamber unemptied, and fire unlit.

"We women hae flags to keep flying," she said cryptically, "though they cannae be seen."

Cryptic though it was, they understood and approved.

IV

On the way to the hospital Mr. Kilburn could not be quietened. He was a conscientious man who sought but never found relief and assurance in talking; what he said was repetitious and foolishly irrelevant. He kept describing the skates, and how he had seen to it himself that they were in good order, with no screw loose; he even mentioned how much he had paid for them, as if in dearness safety ought to dwell. Elizabeth twice gently suggested to him that it was better in the meantime to say nothing. But Bell remembered how Sammy had often praised this timid little man who could charm chaffinches and bluetits on to his outstretched hands.

"If there's one body I'd never blame, Mr. Kilburn," she said, "it's you."

"But I blame myself, Mrs. McShelvie," he cried, and on he went blaming himself.

They saw Effie and Jean dawdling along the road, swinging the basket between them.

"You wouldn't think," said Bell, "there was half a dozen eggs in it."

"Shall I stop?" asked Elizabeth.

"If you please."

The girls were surprised when the car halted beside them, but when they saw their mother in it they were delighted, and began to giggle.

She could not get the window down to talk to them; she did not, however, become angry with the jammed mechanism. When Elizabeth leant over and opened the door she thanked her before addressing the girls in a voice that in no way pretended unconcern but also betrayed no panic.

"Sammy's had an accident," she said. "I'm going to the hospital to see him. You get back to the hoose and wait for me. I'll no' be long."

Shyness in presence of Elizabeth prevented them from showing their full alarm; indeed, they still giggled a little.

"Whit kind of accident, mither?" asked Effie.

"He fell and hit his heid."

"Will he be a' right, mither?" whispered Jean.

"We a' hope so, pet."

Jean, the tender-hearted, began to weep. Effie, not seeing in her mother the cue for tears, was displeased with her sister.

"If you're no' back by school-time, mither," she asked, "will we just go to school?"

Bell hesitated. "No. Wait for me."

Effie became suspicious. "Is Sammy serious, mither?"

"He might be."

"But what will you do if he is, mither?"

"I'll need to wait and see. Mind and look after your sister."

Effie was not yet weeping when the car left her. She was stoically gathering all the tragic implications of her brother's accident; when that was done, she would weep more bitterly and inconsolably than Jean, whose tears had their source in softness and fear. Effie's, like her mother's, never flowed easily.

As the car moved on Elizabeth Cargill found herself resenting this dry-eyed stoicism of Mrs. McShelvie. To have taught oneself to control and subdue hope, joy, faith, and even love, was surely wrong. Was it not in a way to throw the burden of suffering on to others? Or what was worse, was it not to cheapen that suffering, and therefore the humanity that endured it? Stoicism could become frozen bitterness. Elizabeth could not forget that this woman, refusing to weep for her son in pain or perhaps in death, had so wickedly misrepresented Edgar Roy's cheerfulness.

As they got out of the car at the hospital gate, they were approached by a boy who had been leaning against the wall there. He was Gordon Aldersyde. His cap was set carelessly on his head, and he steadfastly chewed a caramel. These might have been appearances assumed to hide an anxiety that a hostile world would have taken as an admission of guilt. As a consequence the innocence which he proceeded to plead, by word and look, seemed calculated.

Elizabeth Cargill thought him loathsome. Here was another mean with tears, which in normal childhood were so prodigal.

"It was an accident, Mrs. McShelvie," he said. "I wasn't to blame."

"Leave Mrs. McShelvie alone," said Elizabeth. "Haven't you caused enough trouble already?"

He shifted the caramel in swift indignation from one cheek to the other. Yet she was too well-dressed not to be immediately forgiven.

"That's not fair, Miss Cargill," he said. "It was an accident."

"I don't believe you, and nobody else will," she said, and walked away, ashamed of herself but without pity for him.

He looked after her, with the very sweetness arrested in his mouth. He knew that Michaelson was in the hospital, spreading the story that it had been a treacherous push which had caused Sammy to overbalance and strike his head against the wall. But it was not true, and he did not think anybody would believe it. Mrs. Michaelson had said she did not believe it; she knew what a liar her husband was. It meant, of course, that Gordon would have to leave the bungalow, but he had been planning to leave for weeks, owing to Mr. Michaelson's vendetta against him under the cloak of kindness. A change would not only be simple, it would also be advantageous: there were many houses in Langrigg far bigger and more comfortable than the Michaelsons'. But here was Miss Cargill, whom everybody said was kind and fair-minded, turned against him because of that lie. If others did the same, he might not be able to find another place; and they would send him back to Gowburgh.

He clutched Mrs. McShelvie's coat.

"You believe me, don't you?" he cried.

264

"Why should I?"

He was astonished and aggrieved. "Because it's the truth."

"It's also the truth you broke your mither's hert."

That change of subject maddened him. "Never mind her," he cried.

She stared at him, trying to see him as a child, only months older than Sammy, and hardly any brighter at sums. She could not see him as such. Now he was an agent of destiny or of God or Satan. Guilt of some kind attached to those chosen for such purposes: it was inconceivable they were altogether blameless.

"It's the truth," he insisted. "I was playing with Sammy. I never pushed him. He'll tell you that himself when he gets better."

"Is he going to get better then?"

"I don't know."

"I thought you would. Hae you been in to see him?"

"They wouldn't let me."

"Do you want to?"

He nodded. "I'd like to ask him to tell you all whether I pushed him or not."

"All right. You can come wi' me."

Shyly, yet with a smile at this unanticipated turn, he followed her into the hospital.

The first person they saw was the little newsagent, standing by a window in the corridor, with one hand across his breast in a Napoleonic gesture of sorrow. Though he seemed to be gazing prophetically at the sunny field outside, he was at once aware of their entry, and came forward as if, she irrepressibly thought, she was a wealthy customer in to buy a twopenny newspaper. Gordon he ignored.

"Ah, Mrs. McShelvie," he said, holding out his hand, "I am most deeply sorry. I saw the whole unhappy affair."

Now he looked at Gordon, and slowly gave one shake of his head as if, by that gesture, he was denying what had been his lodestar in life, his staunchest faith, his perennial consolation: belief in the purity of childhood.

"I am myself to blame," he said. "I encouraged the friendship."

She remembered his hint at the council meeting, that friendship, being inevitably false, must produce evil.

Then the matron appeared, accompanied by Elizabeth Cargill. Both carried the same news in their dissimilar faces; Elizabeth's tormented and despairing, the matron's firm with professional pride.

"You are Mrs. McShelvie, his mother?" asked the matron.

Bell nodded.

The matron paused.

"So he's deid?"

The matron frowned.

"I'm sorry. The doctor did all he could. It seems the boy's skull was very thin."

"He was gey thin all over."

Mr. Kilburn was crumpling his hat in his hand, and moaning. Elizabeth Cargill had instinctively taken hold of Bell's arm to sustain her, but had almost at once let go. She herself wept. Michaelson dabbed now at one side of his moustache and now at the other, with his knuckle: he was imitating the swing of the gravedigger's spade.

Gordon Aldersyde, with his cap sticking out of his pocket, lounged against the wall. He gazed down at his toes which played at coming together and then separating, as if to music.

"Would you care to see him, Mrs. McShelvie?" asked the matron.

"If it's convenient."

The word struck the matron as peculiar, but in her experience of leading people to the fresh corpses of their loved ones she had heard many expressions no less odd.

"This way, please," she said.

"What about you, Miss Cargill?" asked Bell.

Elizabeth hesitated and then nodded: she seemed to imply that the ordeal would be harder for her to bear than for Bell, even though the latter was the boy's mother.

Bell turned to Gordon Aldersyde. "What about you?" she asked.

The matron had halted a few yards along, outside the circle of privacy; now she resolutely entered it.

266

"Children are not allowed," she said. "I'm sorry. There will be other opportunities." Her voice dropped at that last word.

"I'll wait here," said Gordon.

His voice was so matter-of-fact that the matron looked sharply at him. Grief, she knew, took strange forms. Casualness like this could well be followed by shrieking hysteria.

"Is he his brother?" she whispered.

"No," said Bell. "A friend. He was playing with my boy when it happened."

Gordon nodded; he put on sadness; but he was wondering what had happened to the skates, and who would get them. Likely it would be Tom McShelvie.

"I see," said the matron, frowning. "Please come, then."

At the door of the room where Sammy lay in bed they met the doctor. He was a big man whose face, always obtuse through its fatness, was more so then because of a mixture of exasperation and regret. That a tumble on skates should so quickly kill a reasonably healthy lad of thirteen, despite the skill and contrivances of twentieth-century medical science, seemed to him discouraging and ominous. There would be battlefields soon where death would not be so modest.

He was more brusque than he meant.

"Are you his mother?" he asked.

"I am."

"There was nothing anybody could do. I give you my word for that. He went out like a light. I'm very sorry."

She nodded: he too was merely an agent; what skill he had, whether great or little, was immaterial. Yet when, in going out of the room, he laid his hand upon her shoulder in an unrehearsed gesture of sympathy, she was almost shocked out of her trance of fatalistic acceptance. Before the sheet was lifted off Sammy's face by the matron, she had managed again by an effort of will that exhausted her, to draw that other sheet of outward indifference over her own face. She saw, from the matron's unguardedly human glance of surprise from the one face to the other, that the resemblance so often remarked on must now be at its greatest. Well, if Sammy was calm so must she be. If there in that room where the walls were the colour of sunlit grass she had looked upon her dead son and howled, as Meg Aitchison would have done, and begged for comfort from Miss Cargill and Mr. Kilburn, and even from Michaelson who had stolen in, hat in hand, she would never again have been able to remember him without feeling that she had dishonoured him irretrievably.

She looked upon him, therefore, and touched his brow, with the resignation of one who understands why the sacrifice of death had to be made. Thus a mother might receive the courageous death of her son in war. Only Bell's war was the private one she had been fighting all her life. Sammy, at whom strangers laughed, had been one of her victories.

Without his spectacles and his grin, he seemed to her strange. Even his unresentfulness and cheery adaptability were missing. This final trick which had been played on him, this last push in the back, severing him from his brother, sisters, and parents, without a goodbye, had defeated him. As he lay there under her hand, so far away, he looked lonely, unprotected, and incomplete.

Beside her Elizabeth Cargill still wept. Glancing aside at the young woman, whose braceleted hand was covering her face, Bell thought what an extraordinary expensive grief for so ordinary a child of Gowburgh back streets. But expensive though it might be, it was also genuine.

Michaelson tenderly guided the sobbing Mr. Kilburn out into the corridor.

"Don't you think," he murmured, "that the council, on behalf of the whole town, might do something special about the funeral?"

Mr. Kilburn did not understand.

"Something really special," repeated Michaelson.

"As a symbol of unity," he added, "in defiance of our foes."

"Even our budgerigar," sobbed Kilburn, "which is old now, and so a little cross, took to him at once."

Michaelson strolled away, holding his hat. Until he reached the open air and covered his baldness he had an itch of expectation that Kilburn's fabulous superannuated crotchety bird might swoop down on him like some gigantic falcon. It was the kind of fantastic thought that solaced him: obliquely it expressed not only his contempt, but also his incomprehension, of all life, feathered or on skates, old or young, laughing or weeping, pious or godforsaken.

To his disappointment Gordon was gone; but that interview could wait.

Bell declined all Elizabeth's offers of help. She preferred to return to the sympathetic but inquisitive clamour of Cairnban rather than to the hushed tactfulness of Lammermuir. Her girls would be waiting for her, she said, and it was better they should be told what had happened against a background with which they were familiar. No, it was not necessary for Isaac to be fetched from Gowburgh that very day by car; he could come next morning by train. As for money, which Elizabeth offered in an anguish of embarrassment, it was not needed: the boy was insured.

She asked only to be put down at the Post Office so that she could send a telegram to Isaac.

V

Michaelson's idea of something special for the funeral, though conceived in mockery, was adopted throughout the town with enthusiastic sadness. Not only would the tedium of the reluctant war be relieved, but the fiasco of the evacuation itself might be safely redeemed. It was hardly desired that those evacuees who had returned in hundreds to Gowburgh should surge back to Langrigg: that would have been a cross few foster-parents of compulsory children would gladly carry again. But it was thought that by using the funeral as a kind of rallying cry, sorrowful but bravely defiant, the valiant remnant might be prevailed upon to stay till Christmas at any rate, by which time it was possible that the war, so slow to blossom forth, might wither away altogether. What had begun at the railway station in patriotic and humanitarian chaos amidst the September roses might with propriety and universal

269

self-congratulation end at the festival of the Prince of Peace's birthday. This funeral would represent the climax.

It was ideal for such a purpose. The burial would take place in a free lair in Langrigg cemetery, on the edge of the moors, with the eternal hills presiding: it would be like a conventicle of old. A Langrigg minister would conduct the service, preferably Mr. Sandeman if his wife could be persuaded to let him accept the honour: it would be an opportunity any minister of godly ambition might smack his lips at, combining as it would simple human grief, triumphant national defiance, and humble homage to Almighty God. The council would be represented by two or three councillors led by the Provost, if the day was warm enough, and by Bailie Rouster if it was very cold. Wreaths could be expected from dozens of Langrigg sympathisers, and a few might be contributed by Gowburgh folk: the graveyard would be turned into a radiant garden in this first winter of the war. The school would be closed for the day. Children, Langrigg and Gowburgh mingled, would line the road leading to the cemetery: there might be a few truants who would sneak off to play at football or to roam the hills, but these could be spared. Perhaps a bugler from the Boy Scouts would sound the Last Post; that the dead boy had never been a member could scarcely be held against him now. Reporters from the national press would be invited, with photographers; and they would not come flocking like vultures, as Mr. Campbelton was supposed to have said with typical cynicism, but rather like pigeons to carry back the inspiring message to the whole country. Descriptions of the dead boy's amiable disposition would be given with those sad embroideries always pardonable on such occasions. Perhaps it would not be advisable to include a portrait of him alive, if any existed, because, as far as Langrigg recollected, he had looked more glaikit than tragic; of course it was inconceivable to show him dead. If the day of the funeral was as clement as the day of the death, so far as weather went, then it might be more spectacular to revert to the antiquated custom of making it public, with hundreds of mourners pacing behind the hearse, rather than having an invited few travelling in cushioned limousines. On the other hand, if it snowed, as was likely enough with so snell a wind, there would be no need to devise spectacle, though fortitude might be required in those attending.

Thus coiled and recoiled Langrigg fancies on the subject. The Gowburgh agreement, cautious at first, was thereafter generous. Everybody was pleased there was no internecine jealousy. Those two or three Gowburghers who objected to what they considered a Langrigg usurpation found no supporters. Indeed, it was noticed that these objectors were always dry-eyed, whereas those who gave the Langrigg promoters credit for sincerity sniffled much and wept often. Meg Aitchison was one such: her tears in fact were so frequent and excessive that some suspected they sprang from some personal affliction, with the boy's death an excuse. However, she had always been known to be a sentimentalist behind her mask of aggressive humour. What surprised most, and disgusted some, was her praise of Langrigg's promised munificence. When she heard that Mr. Mair-Wilson had offered to provide a tombstone, instead of analysing his motive and finding capitalist cunning at its heart, as she should have if faithful to Roger's teaching, she upset all her friends and foes too by going about in a hand-wringing morbid awe, wondering what shape the stone ought to be, whether a plain slab or a simple cross or an urn with flowers or even a squad of angels. It was not a time, she feebly explained, for keeping up old spites and bitterness. After the funeral, after the soiling and the stealing of the wreaths, they would find her back at her old post at the gates of heaven, daring the rich to enter. Those closest to her, her Cairnban cronies, thought they understood. Meg, they had previously thought, would never scart a grey head; now they saw in this fascination with Sammy McShelvie's funeral a sign that her own might not be far distant. A reading of her cup, they were convinced, would reveal what a reading of her gaunt cheeks, sunken chest, and peevish coughing had been hinting for weeks. But of course there could be no asking Bell McShelvie these days to read any cup, however urgent. Indeed, there could be no asking Bell to do anything that required human contact. Though a scandal, it was no surprise, when it was discovered

271

that all those dreams of a splendid and cathartic funeral were to be cruelly denied by her.

It appeared all she would agree to was to have the boy buried in Langrigg; she gave economy as the reason. The funeral was to be private: she herself would invite the mourners, who would be few. There were to be no flowers, no wreaths; even some sprigs of holly with red berries stolen from an estate by the Baxter brothers and delivered to Cairnban by their own scratched chapped hands were refused for the coffin, but accepted for the mantelpiece. Above all, there was to be no religious service either in the house or at the graveside, not a word from the Bible: the boy was to be abandoned to the mercy of Christ Jesus with only the worms of decay to intercede for him. It was known that Isaac, weeping like his long-bearded namesake in Genesis, begged her to relent; that her girls, both collectors of Sunday school tracts, wept in terror; that Flora's evangelical boyfriend was shocked to jilting point; that Messrs. Sandeman and Mackdoe, as solemn as two John Knoxes, visited her at Cairnban and on their knees (though this was questioned) strove to untie the bitter atheistical knots in her mind; that Elizabeth Cargill and all the Kilburns, including the budgerigar, pleaded in vain; that Mr. Campbelton, instigated by a letter from his chief, pointed out to her in his suavest tones that she would be letting down not only her own family but also the whole community of Gowburgh, renowned the world over for its austere observation of the Sabbath; and that Mr. Roy was trying to wangle a couple of days' leave to be present at the funeral, although it was reported he was not included amongst the chosen tassel-holders.

All those things were known and whispered; but the commonest topic was Bell's own failure to shed one tear.

There were several suggested explanations. One was simply anger against God, or whatever power it was that said come or go; another was ignorant thrawnness; but the most popular, as far as her Gowburgh friends were concerned, was pride. It was recalled that Bell had always considered herself superior to the folk fate had forced her to live beside. Had she not shown her true opinion that very morning of the accident, when she had called women as good as herself scruff and beasts? Had she not pretended to be fond of hills and lochs and woods just to be different from her fellows from Gowburgh who detested and feared those sinister silent alien presences? While her Sammy was alive, with his specs and freckles and not very wise grins, she had been forced to admit she was one of the crowd, most of whom had sons and daughters akin to poor Sam. Now that he was gone she felt freed from that society, forgetting that in young Tom she had the makings of as good a delinquent as any, or in Flora either a religious maniac or a dance-hall trollop, not to mention in Isaac her man as true a Gowburgh ashpan-emptier as ever wound a grubby muffler round a scraggy neck. No, Bell was in no way freed; which made this queen-like arrogance of hers as ridiculous as it was insupportable.

In one respect she seemed to yield to convention: she put death notices in the *Gowburgh Evening Times* and the *Langrigg Herald*; but even these had that twist of difference which perturbs rather than consoles. Decent ordinary people at a time of grief shunned originality: they were humbly content with some well-used phrase like "Dearly missed" or familiar poetry such as:

> "Though it is God's will we part,
> Forgive a mother's sorrowing heart."

Bell, however, though everybody knew she was no scholar, walked to the school and saw Mr. Campbelton in his room there, surprising him, it appeared, in the working out of a crossword puzzle. In the room stood a large bookcase filled with books, many of them containing poetry. She asked him if he could recommend two lines appropriate for the death of her son. Mr. Campbelton, as everybody could well appreciate, was thunderstruck: scholar though he was, he would not see any connection between her in her old drab coat, and poetry. It was easy and reassuring to picture him with graceful furtiveness slipping the puzzle into a drawer, and then turning to deal with her as urbanely as he did with any parent whose

273

mission was to complain about some teacher too fond of using the tawse. But easier still to imagine, and more reassuring than ever, was his consternation when she pointed to the bookcase and made her request.

How many books he consulted, how many lines of poetry he recommended, or what were her reasons for rejecting them in turn, could never be known. Since he was proud of his knowledge of poetry, it was certain that he would make many recommendations. These she had, it seemed, cracked open, examined, and flung aside, so that all round her like nutshells lay these discarded scraps of wisdom. It was as if the greatest poets, as well as the Bible, were not good enough for her.

But the greatest mystery was why she chose the two lines she did, which were not only incomprehensible and wholly inappropriate, but also seemed to contain an insult to everybody who read them, and of course she was bound to know everybody in Langrigg did, and many in Gowburgh. Some wondered why the editors of the newspapers published such an intimation, but others were not quite so naïve as that. It was established that Shakespeare was the author. As Meg Aitchison said, he was English and so did not understand Scottish feelings nearly as well as Rabbie Burns. But Bell was evidently out to betray the whole human race, not just the Scottish nation.

Her championing of Gordon Aldersyde was part of that betrayal. Nobody wished the boy to be tried for murder or even manslaughter; nobody was so exalted as to imagine that punishing him would resurrect Sammy; but everybody was sure that he did deserve some punishment more severe than simply being returned in disgrace to Gowburgh. Bell was again the stumbling-block. She said she did not believe Councillor Michaelson's story that the push had been deliberate; even if it had been, she added, such pushes were common enough amongst boys at play. When she was reminded what a selfish black-hearted envious greedy callous brute young Aldersyde was, she wanted to know what right they had to throw so many stones. It was particularly aggravating to have the words of Christ quoted against them by one who had, as it were, muzzled Him by her son's graveside. As considerately as possible her inconsistency was pointed out to her; whereupon she had replied that so far as she knew Christ Himself had not always been consistent.

Altogether, during those three days between Sammy's death and his burial, Bell sat in Cairnban like a queen making decisions and giving orders which all her court, and all her advisers, thought disastrous, but which they nevertheless had to obey.

VI

The day of the funeral turned out to be so raw, wild, cold, and with such vicious gusts of sleet, that most people were glad after all it was not a public occasion, at which honour might have obliged them to be present. At the same time few felt sorry for Bell, who surely had done her best to provoke these cold blasts from heaven.

Mrs. Lawson, a thin woman whom wintry winds rattled like a dry bush, met Bell on the stairs in the morning, and felt compelled to pass some remark upon the weather. She had been out shopping in it, and its white spits were still melting on her face.

"Sleet, Bell," she reported, in a whine that she thought suitable for addressing a bereaved mother on the funeral day, "wi' bursts o' wind like slaps in the face."

"Maybe, Jean," was Bell's reply, "but on the hill-taps it'll be snaw." And then she passed on, with what looked almost like joy on her face.

That shock was even icier to Mrs. Lawson than those of the wind. She had to creep into Mrs. Jolly's room and beg a cup of tea. Once revived, she tried over and over again to describe that look on Bell's face: joy was in it, she was sure of that, and something else; to name that something else Mrs. Lawson found very difficult.

The coffin lay in an attic room in the empty top flat. The

275

undertaker had demurred at such a choice, which gave his men so many extra stairs and turnings to descend with burdened dignity. Her reason astonished him: from that window the best view in the house could be had. He insinuated that surely the most beautiful view on earth held no attraction for a risen soul. Later he discovered that she herself spent hours in the attic alone. No one knew why.

She had invited six to accompany the coffin to the graveyard and see it interred. These were Isaac, Tom, Benny or Ebenezer, Isaac's brother, Mr. Kilburn, Mr. Aldersyde, whose invitation had offended many, and herself, although it was contrary to Scots custom for a woman to hold a cord.

It turned out there was a seventh at the graveside: this was Roy.

He arrived in Langrigg that very forenoon in his officer's uniform, and after a quick visit to Lammermuir appeared at Cairnban. Those aborigines there who met him on his way to the McShelvies' room thought it a pity they could not tease him about his new position, or reminisce with him about those early days. It was not only the atmosphere of grieving in the house that prevented them. He seemed in himself aloof from them. Though he still gave the impression of recklessness, it was of another kind: he could scarcely be expected now to carry a crying baby, or order in the name of the town council sets of the best dishes in the shop; but he would obviously do other things, far more audacious, but not nearly so amusing, no matter how flippant and witty the slang in which they were described. He had, in short, put on in so brief a time that remote air of dedication, not unlike a young priest's, which men trained to lead others to kill or die must acquire if they are to be successful. Those women, indeed, who formerly in their romantic gratitude had dreamed of him or his like as their lover, now discovered they preferred their own husbands, on account of that very frowsty familiarity with such humdrum things as prams and napkins and hearth-rugs, which had before been the cause of their discontent. Miss Cargill, they now decided, was welcome to him; in her black fur coat she could walk beside his uniform without shaming it; and if he was blown to pieces without enough of him being recovered to make a funeral even as limited as this afternoon's, why then, she had the education, the accent, and the financial resilience to show the requisite grief.

As the women nodded and smiled shyly at him, therefore, and as the children gawked, they were acknowledging that he no longer belonged to them or to Cairnban. The snapshot of him which Meg Aitchison had somehow obtained, and which stood on her sideboard amidst jammy dummy-teats, empty milk bottles, and pellets of chewed gum, was no longer a merry compliment, characteristically impish, but irresistibly heart-warming. No, it seemed now only an impudence. Even Meg herself saw that, after she had had a long keek at him as he stood talking to Bell at the latter's door.

He did not get beyond that door. From Elizabeth he had heard how perversely Mrs. McShelvie had been behaving, and also how she had all along harboured animosity against him. Her first glance at him seemed to confirm what Elizabeth had said, although he had rather sharply refused to believe her.

"Hello, Mrs. McShelvie," he said.

"Hello." She did not invite him in. "Is it still trying to snow?"

His coat glistened with melted sleet.

"Yes. I arrived this morning, just about an hour ago. I don't have to tell you how I feel about Sammy."

She closed her eyes for a moment, as if he had brought up a subject fresh perhaps to him, but for her long since exhausted.

"He was your worst dunce, I ken that," she said.

He was shocked. "He was not, but what does that matter now?"

"If he'd been spared, it would hae maittered. I would never hae had the pleasure, for one thing, of seeing him in a uniform like that."

This was the old irony turned savage.

"Would that have been a pleasure?" he asked.

"Doesn't every mither like to see her son a hero?"

"I hope not. Not, anyway, if a war's to last seven or eight years to give her the chance."

"Aye, he was thirteen. I see you remember that."

"I remember a lot more."

"I'm sure your ain mither's a proud woman these days, Mr. Roy."

He was sure she had known previously his mother was long since dead. Had she really forgotten, or was she quite unscrupulous in her revenge?

"I hardly think so, Mrs. McShelvie," he said. "Where she is, I hope these things," and he moved his hat in his hand, "aren't appreciated."

She understood, but did not apologise. "If there exists," she said.

"If it does."

She smiled. "They tell me, Mr. Roy, you've rushed all the way frae the south of England just to see my Sammy buried. But I told them you had other attractions to bring you back here. Was I right?"

"Yes. But this time it was Sammy."

"I can scarcely credit it, Mr. Roy, that they'd let you, an officer, interrupt your training to come all this way to attend the funeral of a boy whose only connection wi' you was that for a few months you tried to teach him sums, withoot much success."

"Do you honestly think that was the only connection I had with Sammy?"

She kept her smile, but did not answer.

"Do you think so, Mrs. McShelvie?"

Still she did not answer.

"Whatever you may think of me," he said, "don't deny the goodness of your own boy."

"Goodness?"

"Yes. Would you believe me if I was to tell you Sammy's always been a comfort to me? This sort of thing," again he moved his hat, "is I believe necessary, but it needs some kind of faith. I haven't enough of the usual kind. Sammy helped to make up for it."

"You can hardly expect me to believe that, Mr. Roy."

"Why not? You knew him better than any of us. He was a load off anybody's mind."

"Not off Mr. Grahamstone's. He put cleverness at sums first."

"You know what I mean."

She nodded.

"There must be his like in Germany," she said. "I'm sure of it."

Again she paused.

"Do you want to see him?" she asked suddenly. "Or do you think you'll be haeing your fill of daith before very long?"

"I would like to see him."

"All right."

She set off along the landing and up the stairs. As he followed, aware of being peeped at through doors ajar, he was even more conscious of her continuing scrutiny, although as she calmly went up the stairs she seemed indifferent as to whether he came or not. She had said all she needed by her remark that there were boys in Germany like Sammy. It was of course not news to him or to his mess-mates. Bombs would have facetious names chalked on them, as if the death they would deal out would be facetious too. Those who dropped them would blow kisses after them, or perhaps say a bawdy and scurrilous grace before dropping them. He would join in. Atonement would have to wait. Probably it would wait too long.

She lifted off the lid like a saleswoman with goods to display in the profits from which, however, she would not share. That peculiar pride, which asked for no return, moved him far more than if she had fumbled and wept. He had never believed her son's death meant little to her; now he had a glimpse of how much it did mean.

Looking at the dead boy, he felt a great desire to smile; and he did not try to resist it. Peace and confirmation were here. If ever a soul lay safe in Abraham's bosom, here it was. Suddenly, he felt exultant within him: whatever happened to him, whatever happened to others through him, in this memory would be solace and absolution.

"His specs were smashed," said his mother, as if to suggest that otherwise he would have them on.

He helped to replace the lid.

"You'd hear how it happened?" she asked.

"Gordon Aldersyde pushed him, I believe."

"So they say."

"I hear he's been sent home."

"Aye. Some thought he should be birched." She had gone over to the window. "They tell me he was on his knees, begging them. If he'd been given the option of being birched or staying, there's nae doubt which he'd hae chosen. Poor lad."

Though he was well aware of Gordon Aldersyde's fondness for Langrigg, or rather of his aversion for Gowburgh, nevertheless he was surprised by the force and complexity of passion she managed to express in those two quiet words.

"I hear many have gone back," he said.

"Mair than half, and they're still going. A friend of yours went back just last week: Mr. Scoullar."

He smiled. "Cairnban still seems pretty full."

"Aye. There's always somebody anxious to come in if a room's been emptied. There's mair freedom here."

"And more fun."

They were going back down the stairs.

"Not so much of that now," she said. "The novelty's worn off."

"What about yourself, Mrs. McShelvie? Will you stay to the end?"

"The end comes automatically for me if this hoose shuts doon. My family want to go back, I think: except Tom, wha's one of the lucky ones wi' Mr. Mair-Wilson."

"But you would like to stay?"

They were now outside her door. She did not answer his question; instead she asked him if he wanted to go to the funeral.

"Yes, I would."

"You'll be welcome. It leaves here at two o'clock. Maybe I should warn you there's to be no service."

He shook his head.

"I believe I hae offended the entire toon," she said.

"I'm afraid my religion's not nearly strong enough for me to claim to be offended."

"You're honester than maist, then. But you'll be getting married by the minister?"

"Maybe."

"I heard, frae a guid source, there's talk of it happening soon."

He knew her source was Mrs. Raeburn. He nodded. But she did not, as he hoped, offer congratulations.

"Well, I'll be going now," he said. "I'll be back just before two. Will that be all right? By the way, do you want me to change?"

She shook her head. "No. He would hae been—" and then, unable to finish, afraid it seemed of weeping, she turned away. "Like maist boys," she went on, still turned away, "he had a pride in sodgers and airmen." Then quickly she turned towards him again. "You've not to think that because I would hae nae service I hae nae faith."

"I don't think that at all, Mrs. McShelvie."

"Then you're the only one." Instead of weeping, as he expected, she smiled.

Greatly moved, he hurried out of the house. He was a good way down the avenue before he remembered to put on his hat, although sleet was still falling. Turning, he looked up at the window of the attic, and before he realised what he was doing touched the peak of his hat in a salute that no martinet, and perhaps not Sammy himself, would have approved.

VII

Less than a week after the funeral, following upon wind, sleet, and rain, came a day of calm clear winter sunshine, in which the whole landscape sparkled, but especially the snow on the highest hills. It was the day Bell had been waiting for.

As soon as she had seen the girls off to school, wearing the black armbands that they had sewn on themselves, she put on her coat, wrapped her scarf round her neck, slipped into her pocket the sandwiches she had ready, and left the room. Going downstairs she met Meg Aitchison peching up, with little Gary bawling after, clutching her skirt.

"I used to be able to carry him," said Meg, gasping. "Now I just cannae." She sank down on a stair. "Like a piper at his last blaw, that's me a' the time now. Whit's the tune, Bell? I'll tell ye: fareweel to Cairnban."

"I'm sorry I've no time to chat, Meg."

"Fareweel to the whole jing-bang, mair likely," added Meg, trying to turn a cough into laughter.

"I'll need to go, Meg. There's nae daylight to spare."

"It's me that kens that, Bell. But whit's wrang wi' gaslight? A bob in the meter, and you can cheat the dark for a while longer."

Bell was now past her and the sobbing child.

"Where to, Bell, in sich a hurry?" she cried. "I ken it's braw ootside, for them wi' fat on their banes."

Bell turned at the foot of the stairs.

"Meg," she said, "maybe I should tell you."

"Tell me whit, Bell? Make it guid news."

"I'm away to try and do what I've wanted to do from the first day I arrived in this toon."

"And whit's that, Bell?"

"Climb this mountain Brack Fell."

Meg at first gaped. Then she cried, with a curious desolation: "Oh Jesus Christ!" Clutching at the banister she hauled herself up like a drunk woman. "Don't torment me, Bell. You're kidding. No, no, no," she yelled, as Bell slipped quietly out of the door, "you're not kidding." She began to howl and weep and beat on the banister, so that neighbours bustled out to see what was wrong. "I cannae climb these stairs," she cried, "and there's Bell away to climb the mountain. And she's double my age."

They could not be sure whether she was in earnest. What she was yelling about Bell McShelvie and the mountain seemed, even for Meg, too outrageous; and the tears she was shedding were so vehement that surely they were coming from the wild jocular side of her nature. Last week's tears for Sammy McShelvie had been as mild as a kitten's.

With her face pressed against the banister and hidden by her arms, she ignored all their shouts and chaffing. Some quicker than others grew convinced she was giving a display, not of leg-pulling or of madcap high spirits, but of unprecedented despair: they were watching the breaking of a brave heart. They carried Gary off, and led her into her own room.

There, after a sip of medicinal whisky, and after several embraces and one good therapeutic shake, she began to notice them again. Ruefully she giggled, so that most of them had to giggle back, so comical was her dishevelled gap-toothed bony self-derision.

"I should be spitting basins o' bluid," she said, leering round at all their faces as if each one, though familiar and well-liked, was bloodthirsty.

"Don't talk like that, for God's sake, Meg," they said. "It's time you saw a doctor, lass. That man of yours had better stir himself off his fat backside or he'll be left wi' a handful o' weans to rear."

Meg drew herself up and squinted, giving her impression of a duchess; only this time they weren't sure that she was joking.

"You'd oblige me, ladies," she said, in a voice to suit, "by keeping your long nebs oot o' my private business."

"You're our business, Meg," said one, who had been with her in Cairnban from the beginning.

"I'm my ain business," retorted Meg. "Let everybody mind that. One thing I'll ease your minds aboot: there'll be nae objections to flowers at this funeral. My favourites are roses, cream roses."

One thought it judicious to take the talk back to Bell Mc-Shelvie.

"Whit was it you were saying aboot Bell?" she asked.

Meg clapped her hands to her cheeks, and spoke out of her squeezed mouth.

"Oh my God!" she cried. "That was it. I've been wondering what it was ca'd me dizzy. Bell's awa' to climb the mountain."

They frowned at one another, wondering if this was a real mountain, or one towering up in some premonitory nightmare.

"Whit mountain, Meg?" asked one quietly.

283

"I forget its name. She said it was the highest around here. So the snaw on it will be the whitest. If ever she comes back, it'll be wi' a lump of it in her fist, melting and dropping like bluid."

Again they noticed the obsession with blood.

They spoke in coaxing voices.

"Did Bell actually say she was going to climb it?" asked one.

"She did, Molly; she did, as calm as if it was yourself saying you were going up to the picture-hoose balcony for a change."

"But, Meg, I never gang to the balcony," said Molly.

Meg laughed in good-natured pity at her comrade who, though fat and blessed with a pair of sound lungs, never made a joke, seldom saw one, and often asked for elucidation.

"It's no' worth the extra money," insisted Molly. "Forby, the balcony's for snobs."

"Good for you, Molly. Maybe so's the highest mountain for snobs."

"Aboot Bell, though," said another. "Whit's her idea? We ken she stravaigs, but climbing a mountain is dangerous."

"She always had a hankering to do it," said Meg. "So she's awa' to do it." She began to laugh. "Sounds sensible enough said like that. When she told me a minute or twa ago, I thought it was the daftest thing ever I heard. You ken how it set me off. But now, it's as sensible as going in to buy a fish supper if you feel like a fish supper."

"Fish suppers aren't sold on the taps of mountains, Meg."

Another pointed to the window. "It gets dark suddenly. Even if she got to the tap, she'd never get back doon."

"Weel then," said Meg, as if offering a solution anybody could accept, "they'll find her frozen to daith in the snaw."

One coughed with solemnity.

"Do you ken what I've been thinking?" she asked.

She was not very popular; therefore no one cried out to her to share her wisdom.

"Maybe this," she said, "is Bell's true funeral."

"That's an odd thing to say, Isa," they muttered. "What d'you mean? It's no use trying to be clever. That's Bell's ain failing, so don't you start, Isa."

One who had had a quarrel with her about three weeks ago challenged her directly.

"Are you making oot Bell's heid's been turned?" she asked. "So that she thinks the boy's buried at the tap of this mountain?"

"No, Betty," said Isa peaceably, "I'm not making that oot at a'."

"Then whit made you say sich a foolish thing?"

Isa could not explain; she peered within, but saw no light.

"Foolish it may be, Betty," she admitted. "It was an idea I had. We a' ken Bell's heart was never in yon apology for a funeral that we saw leave this hoose. After a', Betty," she pressed on, having at last seen a glimmer, "we ken that poor Sammy, wherever he is, isnae lying in yon glaury hole. His soul I mean, or whatever you like to ca' it."

"I ca' it nothing," snapped Betty.

"Maybe not," said Isa. "But it's my opinion that if Bell thinks she's mair likely to find her boy again on the tap of that mountain, then she's entitled to think it."

Betty mumbled that Bell, and somebody else, were also entitled to a ride in a blue van: a Gowburgh euphemism for being packed off to a mental asylum.

Isa heard, but carried her huff with dignity.

"If whit I've got to say isnae appreciated," she said, "I'll say no more."

Then Mrs. Lawson, as the senior woman there, took command.

"There's no sense in squabbling," she said. "Whit we've got to decide is: whit are we going to do aboot Bell?"

"One thing we'll no' do," said Meg, chuckling, "is to run after her. Nane of us is able; nane of us; not one."

Some breathed deeply as if to refute that, and patted their thighs. None of them spoke.

"Should we tell the police?" asked Mrs. Lawson.

"What for?" they demanded. "Climbing a mountain may be daft, but it's no' criminal."

"I ken that as weel as onybody," she replied sharply. "I also ken it's dangerous. Men properly equipped for it hae perished

285

on the hills. We a' ken Bell hasn't been normal for the past week or twa."

"If my wean was deid, I wouldn't be normal," said Meg.

"That's true, Meg," said Mrs. Lawson. "We're a' mithers here, and it could happen to ony one of us, though God forbid it should. What I was going to say was that there's sich a thing—" here she paused to search cautiously for the best word in her meagre vocabulary—"as normal grief."

"I've never seen it," said Meg. "Every woman greets and laughs in her ain fashion."

Too many of them agreed with her. Mrs. Lawson was peeved.

"I was just trying to help," she said, "but I've noticed before this that it's far frae easy to get a thing discussed sensibly in this hoose o' women. I've heard them say that if women were gi'en the job of running the world, there'd be nae wars. I cannae believe it. Gie Bell her due, she's nae ordinary woman to hae kept things going here the way she has."

Instantly they were upon her, yapping, yelping, and worrying. Whatever else was gained, at any rate it took their minds off Bell, now more than a mile along the road towards the path up the mountain.

She was walking to that tune of Meg's: Fareweel to Cairnban; and in it was the gallant humorous pathos with which Meg had christened it. The stonechats that skipped so swiftly and daintily along the top of the drystane dyke, as if to mock her own heavy slowness, kept chirping it. Immaculate blackbirds hopped to it under holly bushes. Rabbits in a field lolloped to it. Amidst glistening stubble rooks strutted; and strung up on the wire of a fence the decaying corpses of two or three hundred moles seemed to owe their very immobility to that irresistible music of retreat.

Every night since Sammy's death Effie and Jean had pleaded with her by the fireside to take them back to Gowburgh. When without committing herself she had patted and hugged them into bed, she had listened from behind the curtain to their prayers, which were louder than was necessary surely, since

God, according to one of their tracts, could hear the growing of a flower: they asked Him to use His omnipotence against her. Isaac too, without ever saying or writing a word on the subject, was always urging the same request: his boasts of self-sufficiency were really admissions of loneliness. As for Flora, her grumbles took the unexpected form that with so much to do in the house, cleaning, washing, and cooking, she hadn't enough time to devote to helping her evangelist, who, defying the commandment, had after all not punished her for her mother's sin of impiety.

They all wanted her to go home: even Tom did, although he himself had no intention of going with her. Her presence in Langrigg rather spoiled for him the adventure of Mr. Mair-Wilson's castle, which his imagination pictured as being in a wild land hundreds of miles from home. It was too disillusioning, therefore, when with a few followers, he ventured into the main street, as intrepid and expectant as Cortes entering Montezuma's capital, to be confronted by his mother and ordered to wipe his nose, pull up his stockings, and explain his intentions. If she took the girls home, he promised, he would write her a letter every week.

She did not want to go home; indeed, as she sat by the fireside calmly putting curlers in her daughters' hair, and listening to their catalogues of all their friends now happily restored to Wallace Street, she had felt within her a revulsion so strong that it might, under less control, have had her striking those small selfish beloved heads with their paper curlers. Afterwards, when they were in bed, with tears for home and for their dead brother still wet on their cheeks, she sat on by the fire, seeing in the black flecks of soot, not signs of a stranger coming to visit, as the superstition said, but rather that little black terrier, which, so long ago, she had watched limp down Wallace Street, sniffing for food and fleeing from stones. She remembered how she had praised it for not whining for mercy, and pitied it for being lost in that labyrinth where at every corner it found hostility or treacherous friendship. Likely it was still wandering there, thinner, lamer, hungrier, and wearier, but still showing as much dexterity as it could in avoiding lorries or stones or kicks or even the kind clutches of someone willing to take the trouble to carry it to the shop where it would be painlessly killed. It had nothing but life to live for, and yet it lived on so tenaciously.

Thus, if she returned, might she live: shamefully, because in the welfare of her husband and children she would have a purpose as honourable as any that human existence at any level could offer. Often before a child was born its parents, anxious to propitiate whatever power controlled creation, humbly asked that it be like its fellows, in appearance, character, and intelligence. Greed and conceit in demanding beauty, goodness, wisdom, and wealth, might be savagely punished with deformity, wickedness, or imbecility. Afterwards, of course, when normality was assured, the greed and conceit might revive: but now they were simply and adequately punished by having their demands ignored, so that ultimately most parents had to be content with the mediocrity that had been given. Some might persist with desperate boasts, so patently unjustified as to win derision and even hatred; Mrs. Aldersyde was one of these. In the end they too were forced to see the truth. That sight could be beneficial and even redemptive; on the other hand it could destroy.

Bell all along had been guilty of that conceit: hence perhaps her sympathy for Mrs. Aldersyde. If she had had amongst her children only one with exceptional ability, through whom she could make contact with that ampler, brighter, more lovely life which went on in the world outside the back streets of Gowburgh, she would have been content. But all of her children were ordinary, no more gifted than her neighbours': each one therefore was to her a door slammed, a window bricked up, a skylight opaque with soot. Sammy sometimes had been able to scrape away some of that soot, and let in a little light. Now he was gone, and the prospect back in Wallace Street seemed to her unbroken darkness, whether bombs fell or not.

For those around her, for Mrs. Lawson, say, or Mrs. Jolly, or Nan Ross, and for thousands of the like, that darkness was tolerable. Indeed, most of them would refuse to admit it, applying the spartan philosophy by which they had to live:

What you never have you never miss. What yearnings they did have could be satisfied by the vicarious triumphs of the pictures. Their tears and laughter were given an outlet there in the dark, with a caramel to chew. Afterwards with a bill to pay, or shoes to supply, they did not recall those tears or that laughter to curse them as false and insidious. They were not fools or saints enough to renounce that relief. She who had renounced it was no doubt a fool; but she had always been aware, while watching those fables on the screen, how untrue they were to her experience, and also, in some way she could scarcely describe, how insulting they were to her own aspirations. Yet were those aspirations any more realistic or noble? With what secret passionate tears had she agreed with Nan Ross when the latter had said she ought not to be the caretaker of Cairnban, but its mistress rather! How often in the past few weeks had she dreamed of herself as such, watching from behind velvet curtains snow on the hills or the likes of Meg and Nan go by on the road, pushing their prams and discussing their typical daily trivialities.

Her ambitions had not been so innocent as those of her neighbours; thwarted, they had turned bitterer than she herself had known, and driven her to exact revenge from people who liked, respected, and trusted her. She had let her jealousy of Roy and Elizabeth Cargill grow; worse, she had deliberately insinuated into that girl's generous mind a foreboding that the war would make her not only a quick bride but a widow too. She had been contemptuous of poor Meg already struggling with an antagonist whom neither heroism nor prayer could defeat. And had she not forbidden religion at Sammy's funeral out of some obscure squalid desire for revenge? And had she not from the beginning been grateful for the war, although when it began everybody, she included, thought it would mean the quick destruction of many cities and the deaths of millions of innocent people?

She was a worse traitress than Mrs. Aldersyde, because all along she had been aware of her treason. Before it was too late, she must make amends to the folk she had betrayed. Returning to Gowburgh would do, but only if she returned cleansed and unresentful, prepared to create as much light there as she could, not only for herself and her family, but for her neighbours. This then was the reason the women at Cairnban were at that moment trying to discover; this was why she was attempting to climb Brack Fell. By its cairn she would make her vow.

Even before she had left the road, all these inward anxieties, self-accusations, scruples, and forebodings, had begun as usual to be made appear less sinister and formidable simply by contact with such ordinary outward things as rocks, trees, dykes, and even the wobbling gate she had to climb over to reach the path which, her map indicated, would lead her to the shoulder of the mountain. All these inanimate things, when she laid her hand upon them, appeared to have some quality of endurance and confidence which they drew like sap from the earth, and which they were able in some way to communicate to her. She had observed a similar miracle in human beings: in solitary broodings seen as self-seeking, malicious, lazy-minded, and envious, every one of them in actual bodily presence was always somehow never so bad. It was as if they too by their very separate existence on the earth were granted this virtue of diminishing the accumulated evil that was in the world. Some called it, she knew, the grace of God; and many were never aware they had it. In Wallace Street it existed as well as anywhere else.

Soon, breathing heavily, sweating, and aching, she had climbed so high above the road that birds flew between it and her. The top of the hill could not of course be seen: she knew there would be several tantalising ridges before the final one. These southern hills were as alike as the backs of cattle lying close together. Indeed, she had had to study the map for minutes at the wobbling gate before deciding that this particular green flank would lead to the summit of Brack Fell. From the road it had looked like one long unbroken ascent, but in reality it became many ascents, some steeper than others, with here and there a descent to cross a burn.

She had known beforehand how foolishly ill-equipped she was for climbing hills. Soon her shoes were sodden from walking across stretches of marsh. Her coat hampered her at every step, especially in scaling dykes or fences, and in scrambling up slopes too steep for walking. Her legs and back ached, and she began to pech as loudly as Meg on Cairnban's stairs, so that she too felt like "a piper at his last blaw".

It became colder, as the wind on the heights strengthened; it seemed also to become darker, though the sun still shone. The top of the hill, for all her strivings, remained hours away. At one point, afraid she would not have enough daylight to reach the top and come back again, she began to hurry. Within two or three minutes she had to give that up, because she was staggering about as if drunk, and once fell on her hands and knees. You can't at fifty, she told herself as she knelt there, run up a mountain, even to make a vow at the top.

An hour or so later, walking very slowly, too exhausted to find any pleasure or triumph in the height she had reached, she was beginning to admit that she would never gain the summit with time and energy left to descend again safely. For nearly half an hour after that admission she still climbed, until at last a wide deep gully, whose presence she had not suspected, forced her to halt. With her face uplifted to where she thought the summit lay, she stood for a minute, acknowledging defeat and waiting for the disappointment to gather in her heart.

Across that gully, about two or three hundred feet up from the burn roaring at its foot, gleamed the first patch of snow. She had been sure in setting out that she would at least touch the snow which from the streets of the town shone so brightly, like a signal. Now it lay ahead of her. If she tried to reach it, she might do so just as darkness fell, and bright though the snow was two handfuls of it would not light her down the hill. She would die up there in the cold. The snow's call therefore must be resisted, even though it said that beyond it was the top and the cairn, upon which she had meant to lay the stone she had picked up from the earth at Sammy's grave.

Taking the stone from her pocket, she let it fall where she stood, to mark the highest point she had reached. Then for the first time she turned and faced in the direction of the town, towards the inhabited country.

As she gazed down, that disappointment gathering in her heart began to fade. In its nest of dark green trees the town, silvery-grey with smoke, suggested peace, innocence, and above all faith: it was the most poignant sight she had ever seen. She felt amazed, for in that brilliancy of light she could make out places which ought to have suggested other things altogether; the steeple of Sandeman's kirk, for instance, where the most expensive religion in the town was purveyed; the white stones of the graveyard; the golf course where Roy and Elizabeth Cargill had so often played; the main street where Michaelson's shop was; the council buildings where Alden and Miss Cheam avoided love; and the school where the Cairnban adventure had begun. These she saw, all contained within those silvery-grey eggs in the nest of dark green trees. She could not rouse any rancour towards them. The whole town, under the mountain, had a faith as simple and courageous as any bird's. She remembered its motto, inscribed on the lamp-posts outside the Provost's house, and on the badges of the schoolchildren: Gang wi' God's Grace.

Lifting her eyes, she gazed beyond the town to the north where, nearly a hundred miles away, lay Gowburgh back to which she must soon go. With its huger, blacker smoke, its many emptier kirks, its thousands of tall chimneys, and its million people, it could not be in her vision as peaceful, innocent, or full of faith; but for that reason, because somehow of its vulnerability, it seemed to her even more dear. She did not forget how in its mixture of wealth and squalor it represented mankind's greed and brutal indifference to what was beautiful; and how it contained so many streets like her own, where human beings had to live their only lives in a sordid confinement. There on that hill, with space so vast and radiant around her, she withdrew nothing of her condemnation of Nan Ross's city; but over it nevertheless she wished most profoundly to cast whatever protection her blessing offered.

If it was bombed, if places she had seen daily for forty years were shattered and burnt, she would weep, even if no one she knew lay dead beneath them. The very stones whose age and grime she had so often condemned would, if she were to touch them with her hand, prove to have more sustenance for her spirit than these rocks on the unblemished hill. The city was not just Nan Ross's; it was hers too; and Meg Aitchison's; and Mrs. Aldersyde's; and Isaac's; and Sammy's; and Mr. Grahamstone's; and her children's. Its faults might not be forgiven, otherwise they would never be remedied; but it must not be hated or ill-used.

So as she set off down the hill, with the sky reddening and the light fading at her feet, she felt more and more grateful that she was hurrying home to Gowburgh women who would be anxious on her behalf, would scold her humorously for her mad whim, and would urge on her hot tea that had been stewing faithfully on the hob for the past two hours.

When in dusk by the wobbling gate she turned and gazed up at the darkened hill she no longer saw defeat or disappointment, but only a necessary resolution.

As she plodded along the road her feet stung and her whole body ached; but she was smiling, with the tears running down her cheeks.

THE AWAKENING OF
GEORGE DARROCH

Those who took part in the Great Disruption of 1843—a bitter conflict which split the Church of Scotland down the middle—were to find themselves faced with a stark choice, either abandon their principles, or defy the church and risk losing everything. George Darroch is one minister who seems prepared to throw away his career for the sake of his principles—but he is a complex, ambiguous character, driven as much by lust and ambition as by his religious beliefs. *The Awakening of George Darroch* is a powerful and compelling story of personal and political upheaval, based on a momentous event in Scottish history.

*'A novel of ideas and emotions, set in
a country obsessed by sin and lust,
rank and rebellion'*
THE TIMES

---

*Available from all good bookshops,
or direct from the publishers:*

*B&W Publishing,
233 Cowgate, Edinburgh,
EH1 1NQ.*

VISA

Tel: 0131 220 5551